ALTADENA LIBRARY DISTRICT

D0060076

DATE DUE

FEB 2 1 2004	APR 1 9 2007
MAR 1 2 2004	SEP 0 4 2007
APR - 1 2004	OCT - 6 2007
APR 1 5 2004	OCT - 6 2007
MAY - 1 2004	NOV 2 9 2007
JUL 3 - 2004	JAN 3 2008
	FEB 2 6 2008
JUL 1 9 2004	MAY 1 0 2008
AUG 2 2 2004	OCT 2 8 2008
APR 2 0 2005	MAY 2 1 2010
MAY 2 1 2005	6-11-10
JUL - 9 2005	6-30-10
JUL - 9 2005	SEP 1 3 2010
SEP 2 2 2005	JUL 1 5 2011
FEB 1 1 2007	JAN 2 8 2013

DEMCO, INC. 38-2931

EMPRESS ORCHID

BOOKS BY ANCHEE MIN

RED AZALEA

KATHERINE

BECOMING MADAME MAO

WILD GINGER

EMPRESS ORCHID

FIC
MIN

EMPRESS ORCHID

Anchee Min

HOUGHTON MIFFLIN COMPANY

BOSTON · NEW YORK

2004

Copyright © 2004 by Anchee Min

All rights reserved

For information about permission to reproduce selections from
this book, write to Permissions, Houghton Mifflin Company,
215 Park Avenue South, New York, New York 10003.

Visit our Web site: www.houghtonmifflinbooks.com.

Library of Congress Cataloging-in-Publication Data is available.
ISBN 0-618-06887-2

Book design by Melissa Lotfy

Frontispiece illustration by Jacques Chazaud

Printed in the United States of America

MP 10 9 8 7 6 5 4 3 2 1

AUTHOR'S NOTE

All of the characters in this book are based on real people. I tried
my best to keep the events the way they were in history. I translated
the decrees, edicts and poems from the original documents. Whenever there were differences in interpretation, I based my judgment
on my research and overall perspective.

ACKNOWLEDGMENTS

My thanks go to my husband, Lloyd Lofthouse, to Sandra Dijkstra
and the team at the Sandra Dijkstra Literary Agency, to Anton
Mueller and the team at Houghton Mifflin, and to the Museum of
Chinese History, the China National Library, the Shanghai Museum and the Forbidden City Museum in Peking.

For my daughter, Lauryann,
and all the adopted daughters from China

My intercourse with Tzu Hsi started in 1902 and continued until her death. I had kept an unusually close record of my secret association with the Empress and others, possessing notes and messages written to me by Her Majesty, but had the misfortune to lose all these manuscripts and papers.

> —Sir Edmund Backhouse,
> coauthor of *China Under the Empress
> Dowager* (1910) and *Annals and Memoirs
> of the Court of Peking* (1914)

In 1974, somewhat to Oxford's embarrassment and to the private dismay of China scholars everywhere, Backhouse was revealed to be a counterfeiter . . . The con man had been exposed, but his counterfeit material was still bedrock scholarship.

> —Sterling Seagrave,
> *Dragon Lady: The Life and Legend of
> the Last Empress of China* (1992)

One of the ancient sages of China foretold that "China will be destroyed by a woman." The prophecy is approaching fulfillment.

> —Dr. George Ernest Morrison,
> London *Times* China correspondent,
> 1892–1912

[Tzu Hsi] has shown herself to be benevolent and economical. Her private character has been spotless.

> —Charles Denby,
> American envoy to China, 1898

She was a mastermind of pure evil and intrigue.

> —Chinese textbook (in print 1949–1991)

1. Orchid's palace
2. Imperial Gardens
3. Nuharoo's palace
4. Lady Soo's palace
5. Grand Empress's palace
6. Lady Mei's palace
7. Lady Hui's palace
8. Lady Yun's palace

9. Lady Li's palace
10. Palace of Celestial Purity
11. Emperor's palace
12. Senior concubines' palace and temple
13. Hall of Preserving Harmony
14. Hall of Perfect Harmony
15. Hall of Supreme Harmony
16. Gate of Supreme Harmony

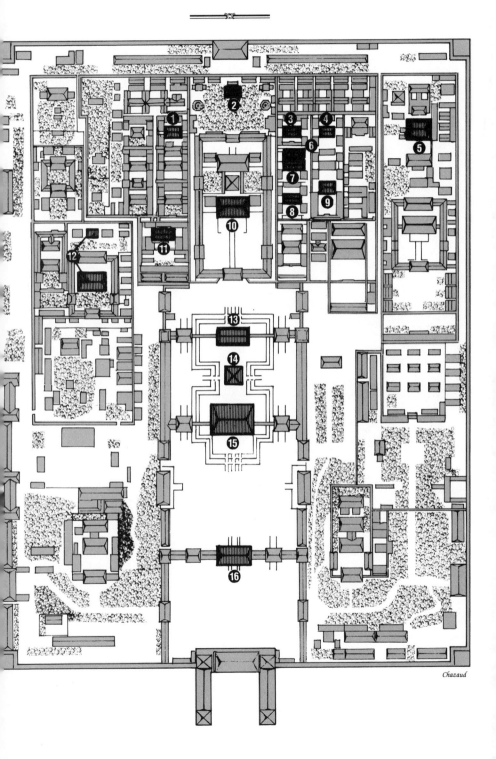

Chazaud

Prelude

THE TRUTH IS that I have never been the mastermind of anything. I laugh when I hear people say that it was my desire to
rule China from an early age. My life was shaped by forces at
work before I was born. The dynasty's conspiracies were old, and men
and women were caught up in cutthroat rivalries long before I entered
the Forbidden City and became a concubine. My dynasty, the Ch'ing,
has been beyond saving ever since we lost the Opium Wars to Great
Britain and its allies. My world has been an exasperating place of ritual
where the only privacy has been inside my head. Not a day has gone
by when I haven't felt like a mouse escaping one more trap. For half a
century, I participated in the elaborate etiquette of the court in all its
meticulous detail. I am like a painting from the Imperial portrait
gallery. When I sit on the throne my appearance is gracious, pleasant
and placid.

In front of me is a gauze curtain—a translucent screen symbolically
separating the female from the male. Guarding myself from criticism, I
listen but speak little. Thoroughly schooled in the sensitivity of men, I
understand that a simple look of cunning would disturb the councilors
and ministers. To them the idea of a woman as the monarch is frightening. Jealous princes prey on ancient fears of women meddling in politics. When my husband died and I became the acting regent for our
five-year-old son, Tung Chih, I satisfied the court by emphasizing in my
decree that it was Tung Chih, the young Emperor, who would remain
the ruler, not his mother.

While the men at court sought to impress each other with their intelligence, I hid mine. My business of running the court has been a constant fight with ambitious advisors, devious ministers, and generals who commanded armies that never saw battle. It has been more than forty-six years. Last summer I realized that I had become a candle burnt to its end in a windowless hall — my health was leaving me, and I understood that my days were numbered.

Recently I have been forcing myself to rise at dawn and attend the audience before breakfast. My condition I have kept a secret. Today I was too weak to rise. My eunuch came to hurry me. The mandarins and autocrats are waiting for me in the audience hall on sore knees. They are not here to discuss matters of state after my death, but to press me into naming one of their sons as heir.

It pains me to admit that our dynasty has exhausted its essence. In times like this I can do nothing right. I have been forced to witness the collapse not only of my son, at the age of nineteen, but of China itself. Could anything be crueler? Fully aware of the reasons that contributed to my situation, I feel stifled and on the verge of suffocation. China has become a world poisoned in its own waste. My spirits are so withered that the priests from the finest temples are unable to revive them.

This is not the worst part. The worst part is that my fellow countrymen continue to show their faith in me, and that I, at the call of my conscience, must destroy their faith. I have been tearing hearts for the past few months. I tear them with my farewell decrees; I tear them by telling my countrymen the truth that their lives would be better off without me. I told my ministers that I am ready to enter eternity in peace regardless of the world's opinions. In other words, I am a dead bird no longer afraid of boiling water.

I had been blind when my sight was perfect. This morning I had trouble seeing what I was writing, but my mind's eye was clear. The French dye does an excellent job of making my hair look the way it used to — black as velvet night. And it does not stain my scalp like the Chinese dye I applied for years. Don't talk to me about how smart we are compared to the barbarians! It is true that our ancestors invented paper, the printing press, the compass and explosives, but our ancestors also refused, dynasty after dynasty, to build proper defenses for the country. They believed that China was too civilized for anyone to even think about challenging. Look at where we are now: the dynasty is like a fallen elephant taking its time to finish its last breath.

Confucianism has been shown to be flawed. China has been defeated. I have received no respect, no fairness, no support from the rest of the world. Our neighboring allies watch us falling apart with apathy and helplessness. What is freedom when there has been no honor? The insult for me is not about this unbearable way of dying, but about the absence of honor and our inability to see the truth.

It surprises me that no one realizes that our attitude toward the end is comical in its absurdity. During the last audience I couldn't help but yell, "I am the only one who knows that my hair is white and thin!"

The court refused to hear me. My ministers saw the French dye and my finely arranged hairstyle as real. Knocking their heads on the ground, they sang, "Heaven's grace! Ten thousand years of health! Long live Your Majesty!"

—

EMPRESS ORCHID

One

MY IMPERIAL LIFE began with a smell. A rotten smell that came from my father's coffin—he had been dead for two months and we were still carrying him, trying to reach Peking, his birthplace, for burial. My mother was frustrated. "My husband was the governor of Wuhu," she said to the footmen whom we had hired to bear the coffin. "Yes, madam," the head footman answered humbly, "and we sincerely wish the governor a good journey home."

In my memory, my father was not a happy man. He had been repeatedly demoted because of his poor performance in the suppression of the Taiping peasant uprisings. Not until later did I learn that my father was not totally to blame. For years China had been dogged by famine and foreign aggression. Anyone who tried on my father's shoes would understand that carrying out the Emperor's order to restore peace in the countryside was impossible—peasants saw their lives as no better than death.

I witnessed my father's struggles and sufferings at a young age. I was born and raised in Anhwei, the poorest province in China. We didn't live in poverty, but I was aware that my neighbors had eaten earthworms for dinner and had sold their children to pay off debts. My father's slow journey to hell and my mother's effort to fight it occupied my childhood. Like a long-armed cricket my mother tried to block a carriage from running over her family.

The summer heat baked the path. The coffin was carried in a tilted position because the footmen were of different heights. Mother imagined how uncomfortable my father must be lying inside. We walked in silence and listened to the sound of our broken shoes tapping the dirt. Swarms of flies chased the coffin. Each time the footmen paused for a break the flies covered the lid like a blanket. Mother asked my sister Rong, my brother Kuei Hsiang and me to keep the flies away. But we were too exhausted to lift our arms. We had been traveling north along the Grand Canal on foot because we had no money to hire a boat. My feet were covered with blisters. The landscape on both sides of the path was bleak. The water in the canal was low and dirt-brown. Beyond it were barren hills, which extended mile after mile. There were fewer inns to be seen. The ones that we did come upon were infested with lice.

"You'd better pay us," the head footman said to Mother when he heard her complaint that her wallet was near empty, "or you will have to carry the coffin yourselves, madam." Mother began to sob again and said that her husband didn't deserve this. She gained no sympathy. The next dawn the footmen abandoned the coffin.

Mother sat down on a rock by the road. She had a ring of sores sprouting around her mouth. Rong and Kuei Hsiang discussed burying our father where he was. I didn't have the heart to leave him in a place without a tree in sight. Although I was not my father's favorite at first — he was disappointed that I, his firstborn, was not a son — he did his best in raising me. It was he who insisted that I learn to read. I had no formal schooling, but I developed enough of a vocabulary to figure out the stories of the Ming and Ch'ing classics.

At the age of five I thought that being born in the Year of the Sheep was bad luck. I told my father that my friends in the village said that my birth sign was an inauspicious one. It meant that I would be slaughtered.

Father disagreed. "The sheep is a most adorable creature," he said. "It is a symbol of modesty, harmony and devotion." He explained that my birth sign was in fact strong. "You have a double ten in the numbers. You were born on the tenth day of the tenth moon, which fell on the twenty-ninth of November 1835. You can't be luckier!"

Also having doubts regarding my being a sheep, Mother brought in a local astrologer to consult. The astrologer believed that double ten was too strong. "Too full," the old hag said, which meant "too easily spilled." "Your daughter will grow up to be a stubborn sheep, which means a miserable end!" The astrologer talked excitedly as white spittle gathered at the corners of her mouth. "Even an emperor would avoid ten, in fear of its fullness!"

Finally, at the suggestion of the astrologer, my parents gave me a name that promised I would "bend."

This was how I was called Orchid.

Mother told me later that orchids had also been the favorite subject of my father's ink paintings. He liked the fact that the plant stood green in all seasons and its flower was elegant in color, graceful in form and sweet in scent.

My father's name was Hui Cheng Yehonala. When I close my eyes, I can see my old man standing in a gray cotton gown. He was slender with Confucian features. It is hard to imagine from his gentle look that his Yehonala ancestors were Manchu Bannermen who lived on horseback. Father told me that they were originally from the Nu Cheng people in the state of Manchuria, in northern China between Mongolia and Korea. The name Yehonala meant that our roots could be traced to the Yeho tribe of the Nala clan in the sixteenth century. My ancestors fought shoulder to shoulder with the Bannerman leader Nurhachi, who conquered China in 1644 and became the first Emperor of the Ch'ing Dynasty. The Ch'ing had now entered its seventh generation. My father inherited the title of Manchu Bannerman of the Blue Rank, although the title gave him little but honor.

When I was ten years old my father became the *taotai,* or governor, of a small town called Wuhu, in Anhwei province. I have fond memories of that time, although many consider Wuhu a terrible place. During the summer months the temperature stayed above one hundred degrees, day and night. Other governors hired coolies to fan their children, but my parents couldn't afford one. Each morning my sheet would be soaked with sweat. "You wet the bed!" my brother would tease.

Nevertheless, I loved Wuhu as a child. The lake there was part of the great Yangtze River, which drove through China carving out gorges, shaggy crags, and valleys thick with ferns and grasses. It descended into a bright, broad, richly watered plain where vegetables, rice and mosquitoes all thrived. It flowed on until it met the East China Sea at Shanghai. *Wuhu* meant "the lake of a luxuriant growth of weeds."

Our house, the governor's mansion, had a gray ceramic-tile roof with the figures of gods standing at the four corners of the tilted eaves. Every morning I would walk to the lake to wash my face and brush my hair. My reflection in the water was mirror-clear. We drank from and bathed in the river. I played with my siblings and neighbors on the slick backs of buffalo. We did fish-and-frog jumps. The long bushy weeds were our favorite hiding places. We snacked on the hearts of sweet water plants called *chiao-pai*.

In the afternoon, when the heat became unbearable, I would organize the children to help cool the house. My sister and brother would fill buckets, and I would pull them up to the roof where I poured the water over the tiles. We would go back to the water afterward. *P'ieh*, bamboo rafts, floated by. They came down the river like a giant loose necklace. My friends and I would hop onto the rafts for rides. We joined the raft men singing songs. My favorite tune was "Wuhu Is a Wonderful Place." At sunset Mother would call us home. Dinner was set on a table in the yard under a trellis covered with purple wisteria.

My mother was raised the Chinese way, although she was a Manchu by blood. According to Mother, after the Manchus conquered China they discovered that the Chinese system of ruling was more benevolent and efficient, and they adopted it fully. The Manchu emperors learned to speak Mandarin. Emperor Tao Kuang ate with chopsticks. He was an admirer of Peking opera and he hired Chinese tutors to teach his children. The Manchus also adopted the Chinese way of dressing. The only thing that stayed Manchu was the hairstyle. The Emperor had a shaved forehead and a rope-like braid of black hair down his back called a queue. The Empress wore her hair with a thin black board fastened on top of her head displaying ornaments.

My grandparents on my mother's side were brought up in the Ch'an, or Zen, religion, a combination of Buddhism and Taoism. My mother was taught the Ch'an concept of happiness, which was to find satisfaction in small things. I was taught to appreciate the fresh air in the morning, the color of leaves turning red in autumn and the water's smoothness when I soaked my hands in the basin.

My mother didn't consider herself educated, but she adored Li Po, a Tang Dynasty poet. Each time she read his poems she would discover new meanings. She would put down her book and gaze out the window. Her goose-egg-shaped face was stunningly beautiful.

Mandarin Chinese was the language I spoke as a child. Once a month we had a tutor who came to teach us Manchu. I remember nothing about the classes but being bored. I wouldn't have sat through the lessons if it hadn't been to please my parents. Deep down I knew that my parents were not serious about having us master the Manchu language. It was only for the appearance, so my mother could say to her guests, "Oh, my children are taking Manchu." The truth was

4

that Manchu was not useful. It was like a dead river that nobody drank from.

I was crazy about Peking operas. Again, it was my mother's influence. She was such an enthusiast that she saved for the entire year so she could hire a local troupe for an in-house performance during the Chinese New Year. Each year the troupe presented a different opera. My mother invited all the neighbors and their children to join us. When I turned twelve the troupe performed *Hua Mulan*.

I fell in love with the woman warrior, Hua Mulan. After the show I went to the back of our makeshift stage and emptied my wallet to tip the actress, who let me try on her costume. She even taught me the aria "Goodbye, My Dress." For the rest of the month people as far as a mile from the lake could hear me singing "Goodbye, My Dress."

My father took pleasure in telling the background to the operas. He loved to show off his knowledge. He reminded us that we were Manchus, the ruling class of China. "It is the Manchus who appreciate and promote Chinese art and culture." When liquor took hold of my father's spirit, he would become more animated. He would line up the children and quiz us on the details of the ancient Bannerman system. He wouldn't quit until every child knew how each Bannerman was identified by his rank, such as Bordered, Plain, White, Yellow, Red and Blue.

One day my father brought out a scroll map of China. China was like the crown of a hat ringed by countries eager and accustomed to pledging their fealty to the Son of Heaven, the Emperor. Among the countries were Laos, Siam and Burma to the south; Nepal to the west; Korea, the Ryukyu Islands and Sulu to the east and southeast; Mongolia and Turkestan to the north and northwest.

Years later, when I recalled the scene, I understood why my father showed us the map. The shape of China was soon to change. By the time my father met his fate, during the last few years of Emperor Tao Kuang, the peasant revolts had worsened. In the midst of a summer drought, my father didn't come home for months. My mother worried about his safety, for she had heard news from a neighboring province about angry peasants setting their governor's mansion on fire. My father had been living in his office and trying to control the rebels. One day an edict arrived. To everyone's shock the Emperor dismissed him.

Father came home deeply shamed. He shut himself in the study and refused visitors. Within a year his health broke down. It didn't take him long to die. Our doctor bills piled up even after his death. My mother sold all of the family possessions, but we still couldn't clear the debts. Yesterday Mother sold her last item: her wedding souvenir from my father, a butterfly hairpin made of green jade.

Before leaving us, the footmen carried the coffin to the bank of the Grand Canal so we could see the passing boats, where we might get help. The heat worsened and the air grew still. The smell of decay from the coffin grew stronger. We spent the night under the open sky, tormented by the heat and mosquitoes. My siblings and I could hear one another's stomachs rumbling.

I woke at dawn and heard the clattering of a horse's hooves in the distance. I thought I was dreaming. In no time a rider appeared in front of me. I felt dizzy with fatigue and hunger. The man dismounted and walked straight toward me. Without saying a word he presented me with a package tied with ribbon. He said it was from the *taotai* of the local town. Startled, I ran to my mother, who opened the package. Inside were three hundred taels of silver.

"The *taotai* must be a friend of your father's!" Mother cried. With the help of the rider we hired back our footmen. But our good luck didn't last. A few miles down the canal we were stopped by a group of men on horses led by the *taotai* himself. "A mistake has been made," he said. "My rider delivered the taels to the wrong family."

Hearing this, Mother fell to her knees.

The *taotai*'s men took back the taels.

Exhaustion suddenly overwhelmed me and I fell on my father's coffin.

The *taotai* walked to the coffin and squatted as if studying the grains of the wood. He was a stocky man with rough features. A moment later he turned to me. I expected him to speak but he didn't.

"You are not a Chinese, are you?" he finally asked. His eyes were on my unbound feet.

"No, sir," I replied. "I am Manchu."

"How old are you? Fifteen?"

"Seventeen."

He nodded. His eyes continued to travel up and down, examining me.

"The road is filled with bandits," he said. "A pretty girl like you should not be walking."

"But my father needs to go home." My tears ran.

The *taotai* took my hand and placed the silver taels in my palm. "My respects to your father."

I never forgot about the *taotai*. After I became the Empress of China I sought him out. I made an exception to promote him. I made him a provincial governor, and he was given a handsome pension for the rest of his life.

Two

W E ENTERED Peking through the south gate. I was amazed at the massive rose-colored walls. They were everywhere, one behind another, winding around the entire city. The walls were about forty feet high and fifty feet thick. At the hidden heart of the sprawling, low-lying capital sat the Forbidden City, the home of the Emperor.

I had never seen so many people in one place. The smell of roasting meat fluttered in the air. The street before us was more than sixty feet wide, and for a mile went straight to the Gate of Zenith. Along each side were rows of deep huddled mat-constructed booths and shops festooned with flags announcing their wares. There was so much to see: rope dancers twirling and spinning, fortunetellers throwing interpretations of the *I Ching*, acrobats and jugglers performing tricks with bears and monkeys, folksingers telling old tales in fanciful masks, wigs and costumes. Furniture craftsmen were busy with their hands. The scenes were right out of classic Chinese opera. Herbalists displayed large black dry fungi. An acupuncturist applied needles to a patient's head, making him look like a porcupine. Repairers mended porcelain with small rivets, their work as fine as embroidery. Barbers hummed their favorite songs while shaving their customers. Children screamed happily while sly-eyed camels with heavy loads strutted elegantly by.

My eyes were drawn to sugar-coated berries on sticks. I would have felt miserable if I hadn't seen a group of coolies carrying heavy buckets on bamboo poles across their bare shoulders. The men were collecting

8

feces for the night-soil merchants. They moved slowly toward waiting boats by the canal.

A distant relative whom we called Eleventh Uncle received us. He was a tiny-framed, sour man from my father's side. He wasn't pleased with our arrival. He complained about his troubles running a dry-food shop. "There hasn't been much food to dry in recent years," he said. "All eaten. Nothing left to sell." Mother apologized for the inconvenience and said that we would leave as soon as we got back on our feet. He nodded and then warned Mother about his door: "It falls out of its frame."

Finally we buried our father. There was no ceremony, because we couldn't afford one. We settled down in our uncle's three-room house, in a kinsman's compound in Pewter Lane. In the local dialect, the compound was called a *hootong*. Like a spider web, the city of Peking was woven with *hootongs*. The Forbidden City was at the center, and thousands of *hootongs* made up the web. My uncle's lane was on the east side of a street near the canal of the Imperial city. The canal ran parallel to the high walls and served as the Emperor's private waterway. I saw boats with yellow flags travel down the canal. Tall trees were thick behind the walls like floating green clouds. The neighbors warned us not to look in the direction of the Forbidden City. "There are dragons, the guardian spirits sent by the gods, living inside."

I went to the neighbors and peddlers at the vegetable market hoping to find work. I carried loads of yams and cabbages, and cleaned the stalls after the market closed. I made a few copper pennies each day. Some days no one hired me and I would come home empty-handed. One day, through my uncle, I landed a job in a shop specializing in shoes for wealthy Manchu ladies. My boss was a middle-aged woman called Big Sister Fann. Fann was a heavyset lady who liked to apply her face paint as thick as an opera singer's. Her makeup flaked off in bits as she talked. Her oily hair was combed back tightly against her skull. She was known to have a scorpion mouth but a tofu heart.

Big Sister Fann was proud that she used to serve the Grand Empress of Emperor Tao Kuang. She had been in charge of Her Majesty's dressing room, and she considered herself expert in court etiquette. She dressed magnificently but had no money to clean her clothes. During lice season, she would ask me to pinch off the lice around her neck. She would scratch herself raw under her armpits. When she caught the creatures, she crushed them between her teeth.

In her shop I worked with needles, waxed thread, twisters, pliers and hammers. First I decorated a shoe with strings of pearls, encrusting it with stones, then raised the sole on a central wedge, like a streamlined clog, which added extra height to the lady who would wear the shoe. By the time I got off work, my hair would be coated with dust and my neck painfully sore.

Nevertheless I liked to go to work. It was not only for the money, but also to enjoy Big Sister Fann's wisdom about life. "The sun doesn't just hang on one family's tree," she would say. She believed that everybody had a chance. I also loved her gossip about the royal families. She complained that her life had been ruined by the Grand Empress, who "awarded" her to a eunuch as a figurehead wife, dooming her to childlessness.

"Do you know how many dragons are carved around the Hall of Heavenly Harmony in the Forbidden City?" Above her misery she bragged about the glory of her time in the palace. "Thirteen thousand eight hundred and forty-four dragons!" As always, she answered her own question. "It was the work of the finest craftsmen over generations!"

It was from Big Sister Fann that I learned about the place where I would soon live for the rest of my life. She told me that the hall's ceiling alone housed 2,604 dragons, and each had a different meaning and significance.

It took her a month to finish describing the Hall of Heavenly Harmony. I failed to follow Big Sister Fann and to keep count of the number of dragons, but she made me understand the power they symbolized. Years later, when I sat on the throne and *was* the dragon, I was very much afraid that people would find out that there was nothing to the images. Like all my predecessors, I hid my face behind the gorgeous carvings of dragons and prayed that my costumes and props would help me play the part right.

"Four thousand three hundred and seven dragons inside the Hall of Heavenly Harmony alone!" Gasping, Big Sister Fann turned to me and asked, "Orchid, can you imagine the rest of the Imperial glory? Mark my words: a glimpse of such beauty makes one feel that one's life has been worthy. One glimpse, Orchid, and you will never be an ordinary person again."

One evening I went to Big Sister Fann's place for dinner. I lit a fire in the hearth and washed her clothes while she cooked. We ate dumplings stuffed with greens and soybeans. Afterward I served her tea and prepared her pipe. Pleased, she said that she was ready to tell me more stories.

We sat into the night. Big Sister Fann recalled her time with her first Majesty, Empress Chu An. I noticed that when she mentioned Her Majesty's name, her voice had a worshipful tone. "Chu An was scented with rose petals, herbs and precious essences since she was a child. And she was half woman and half goddess. She exhaled heavenly aromas as she moved. Do you know why there was no announcement and ceremony when she died?"

I shook my head.

"It had to do with Her Majesty's son Hsien Feng and his half-brother Prince Kung." Big Sister Fann inhaled deeply and continued. "It took place about ten years ago. Hsien Feng was eleven and Kung was nine. I was part of the servant group who helped raise the boys. Among the nine sons Emperor Tao Kuang had, Hsien Feng was the fourth and Kung the sixth. The first three princes died of illness, which left the Emperor six healthy heirs. Hsien Feng and Kung showed the most promise. Hsien Feng's mother was my mistress, Chu An, and Kung's mother was the concubine Lady Jin, who was the Emperor's favorite."

Big Sister Fann lowered her voice to a whisper. "Although Chu An was the Empress, and as such enjoyed the greater power, she was extremely insecure about her son Hsien Feng's chances for succession."

According to tradition, the elder son would be considered the heir. But Empress Chu An indeed had reason to worry. As the greater physical and intellectual talents of Prince Kung began to declare themselves, it gradually became obvious to the court that if Emperor Tao Kuang had good sense, he would select Prince Kung over Hsien Feng.

"The Empress arranged a plot to get rid of Prince Kung," Big Sister Fann continued. "My mistress invited the two brothers for lunch one day. The main meal was steamed fish. The Empress had her maid Apricot put poison on Kung's plate. Now I would say that Heaven must have meant to stop this act. Right before Prince Kung lifted his chopsticks, the Empress's cat jumped onto the table. Before the servants were able to do anything, that cat ate Prince Kung's fish. Immediately the animal showed signs of poisoning. It wobbled, and in minutes it fell flat on the floor."

Much later I would learn the details of the investigation conducted by the Imperial household. The first suspects were the people who worked in the kitchen. The chef, especially, was questioned. Knowing that he had little chance to live, he committed suicide. The next to be interrogated were the eunuchs. One eunuch confessed that he saw Apricot speak secretively with the chef on the morning of the incident. At that point Empress Chu An's involvement was exposed. The matter was brought to the Grand Empress.

"'Fetch me the Emperor!'" Big Sister Fann mimicked the Grand Empress. "Her voice echoed through the hall. I was attending my mistress and thus witnessed Her Majesty's face turn from red to white."

Empress Chu An was found guilty. At first Emperor Tao Kuang didn't have the strength to order her execution. He blamed the servant girl Apricot. But the Grand Empress stood firm and said that Apricot wouldn't act alone "even if she borrowed a lion's guts." Eventually the Emperor gave in.

"When Emperor Tao Kuang entered our palace, the Palace of Pure Essence, Her Majesty sensed that she had reached the end of her life. She greeted her husband on her knees and was unable to rise afterward. His Majesty helped her up. His swollen eyes showed that he had been crying. Then he spoke, expressing his regret that he could no longer protect her, and that she must die."

Big Sister Fann sucked on her pipe, unaware that it had gone out. "As if accepting her fate, Empress Chu An stopped weeping. She told His Majesty that she knew her shame and would accept the punishment. Then she begged for a last favor. Tao Kuang promised to grant anything she wished. She wanted to keep the true reason for her death a secret. When the wish was granted, the Empress bade her husband farewell. She then sent me to fetch her son for the final time."

Tears began to well up in Big Sister Fann's eyes. "Hsien Feng was a fragile-looking boy. From his mother's face he sensed tragedy. Of course he wouldn't have guessed that in the next few minutes his mother would be gone from the face of the earth. The boy brought his pet, a parrot. He wanted to cheer his mother up by making the bird talk. Hsien Feng recited his new lesson, one he had been having trouble with. She was pleased and hugged him.

"His laughter brought more sadness to the mother. The boy took out his handkerchief and wiped her tears. He wanted to know what was bothering her. She wouldn't answer. Then he stopped playing and became scared. At that moment the sound of drums came from the courtyard. It was the signal to hurry Empress Chu An on her way. She held her son again. The drumbeat got louder. Hsien Feng looked terrified. His mother buried her face in his little vest and whispered, 'I shall bless you, my son.'

"The voice of the minister of the Imperial household echoed in the hallway. 'Your Majesty the Empress, on your way, please!' To protect her son from seeing the horror, Empress Chu An ordered me to take Hsien Feng away. It was the hardest thing I ever did. I stood like a dead tree trunk. Her Majesty came and shook me by the shoulders. From her wrist she took off a jade bracelet and tucked it in my pocket. 'Please, Fann!' She looked at me pleadingly. I woke to my senses and dragged the screaming Hsien Feng away from his mother. Outside the gate stood the minister. He was holding a piece of folded white silk—the hanging rope. Behind him were several guards."

I wept for the young boy Hsien Feng. Years later he would become my husband, and I kept a tender spot for him in my heart even after he abandoned me.

"A tragedy foreshadows good luck. Let me tell you, Orchid." Big Sister Fann took the pipe from her lips and knocked the ashes out on the table. "And this applies exactly to what happened next."

In the shadows of the candlelight, the story of my future husband continued. It was autumn, and the aging Emperor Tao Kuang was ready to choose a successor. He invited his sons to Jehol, the Imperial hunting ground in the north, beyond the Great Wall. He wanted to test their abilities. Six princes joined the journey.

The father told the sons that Manchus were known as great hunters. When he was their age he had killed more than a dozen wild animals in half a day—wolves, deer and boar of all sorts. Once he took home fifteen bears and eighteen tigers. He told the sons that his great-grandfather Emperor Kang Hsi was even better. Every day he rode six horses to exhaustion. The father then ordered the sons to show him what they could do.

"Knowing his own weakness, Hsien Feng was depressed." Big Sister Fann paused for a beat. "He knew that he wouldn't survive the competition. He decided to withdraw but was stopped by his tutor, the brilliant scholar Tu Shou-tien. The tutor offered his student a way to turn defeat into victory. 'When you lose,' Tu said, 'report to your father that it was not that you couldn't shoot. Say that it was your choice not to shoot. It was for a virtuous reason such as benevolence that you refused to perform your hunting skills to their fullest.'"

In Big Sister Fann's words, the autumn hunting scene was grand.

The bushes and weeds were waist high. Torches were lit to flush the wild animals. Rabbits, leopards, wolves and deer ran for their lives. Seventy thousand men on horseback formed a circle. The hunting ground thundered and quaked. The men slowly closed in. Imperial guardsmen followed each prince.

On top of the highest hill stood the father. He was on a black horse. His eyes followed his two favorite sons. Hsien Feng was dressed in a purple silk robe and Prince Kung in white. Kung charged back and forth. The animals fell one after another before his arrows. The guards cheered.

The sound of a trumpet called the hunters back at noon. The princes took turns presenting their father the animals they had shot. Prince Kung had twenty-eight. His handsome face was marked by the scratch of a tiger claw. The wound was seeping blood. His white robe was stained. He smiled with elation knowing that he had performed well. The other sons came. They showed their father the animals tied under the bellies of their horses.

"Where is Hsien Feng, my fourth son?" the father asked. Hsien Feng was summoned. He carried nothing under the belly of his horse. His robe was clean. "You didn't hunt." The father was disappointed. The son replied as the tutor had instructed: "Your humblest son had trouble killing the animals. It was not because I refused Your Majesty's order or lacked skill. It was because I was moved by the beauty of nature. Your Majesty taught me that autumn is the time when the universe is pregnant with spring. When I thought about all the animals that would be caring for their young, my heart felt for them."

The father was stunned. Instantly, he made a decision on his heir.

The candle had gone out. I sat quietly. The moon was bright outside the window. The clouds were thick and white, like giant fish swimming across the sky.

"It is my view that Empress Chu An's death played a big part in the selection of the heir too," Big Sister Fann said. "Father Emperor Tao Kuang felt guilty that he took the mother away from her child. The fact that he never granted Lady Jin the wish to be titled Empress after Chu An was the proof. My mistress got what she wanted after all."

"Isn't Lady Jin the Grand Empress today?" I asked.

"Yes, but she didn't get that title from Tao Kuang. Hsien Feng gave it to her when he became the Emperor. Again it was Tu's advice. The act helped to add greatness to Hsien Feng's name. Hsien Feng understood that the public knew that Lady Jin was Chu An's enemy. He wanted people to believe in his benevolence. It was also to squelch the doubts of the nation, because Prince Kung was still on everyone's mind. The father didn't play fair. He didn't keep his promise."

"What about Prince Kung?" I asked. "After all, he scored the highest during the hunt. How did he feel about his father honoring a loser?"

"Orchid, you must learn never to judge the Son of Heaven." Big Sister Fann lit another candle. She stuck her hand in the air and drew a line under her neck. "Whatever he does is Heaven's will. It was Heaven's will that Hsien Feng was made Emperor. Prince Kung believes this too. And that is why he assists his brother with such devotion."

"But . . . was Prince Kung even a little bit jealous?"

"There has been no sign of it. However, Lady Jin was. She was bitter about Prince Kung's submission. But she managed to hide her feelings."

It was a terrible winter. Frozen bodies were found in the streets of Peking after an ice storm. I gave all that I earned to Mother, but it was not enough to pay the bills. The lenders lined up at our door. The door had repeatedly fallen out of its frame. Eleventh Uncle was uneasy and his thoughts were written all over his face. I knew he wanted us to move out. Mother took a cleaning job but was fired the next day, for she became ill. She had to lean against the bed to stand up, and her breath was labored. My sister Rong brewed herb medicine for her. Along with the bitter leaves the doctor prescribed cocoons of silkworms. The foul smell was in my clothes and hair. My brother Kuei Hsiang had been sent to borrow money from neighbors. After a while nobody would open the door for him. Mother bought cheap burial clothes, a black gown, and wore it all day long. "You won't have to change me if you find me dead in bed," she said.

One afternoon Uncle came with his son, to whom I had never been introduced. His name was Ping, meaning "bottle." I knew that Uncle had had a son by a local prostitute and that he hid him because he was embarrassed. I didn't know that Bottle was retarded.

"Orchid will make a good wife for Bottle," Uncle said to my mother, pushing Bottle toward me. "How about I give you enough taels to help pay off your debts?"

Cousin Bottle was a slope-shouldered fellow. The shape of his face matched his name. He looked sixty years old, although he was only twenty-two. Besides being "slow," he was an opium addict. He stood in the middle of the room smiling at me from ear to ear. His hands went constantly to pull up his pants, which fell right back to where they were, below his hips.

"Orchid needs decent clothes," Uncle said, ignoring Mother's reaction, which was to shut her eyes and bang her head on the bed frame. Uncle picked up his dirty cotton sack and took out a pink jacket patterned with blue orchids.

I ran from the house into the snow. Soon both of my shoes were soaked and I could no longer feel that I had toes.

A week later Mother told me that I was engaged to Bottle.

"What do I do with him?" I cried to her.

"It's not fair for Orchid," Rong said in a small voice.

"Uncle wants his rooms back," Kuei Hsiang said. "Someone offered him more rent. Marry Bottle, Orchid, so Uncle won't kick us out."

I wished that I had the courage to say no to Mother. I did not have any choice. Rong and Kuei Hsiang were too young to help support the family. Rong had been suffering from severe nightmares. To watch her sleep was to watch her going through a torture chamber. She tore up the sheet as if possessed by demons. She was constantly afraid, nervous and suspicious. She walked like a frightened bird—wide-eyed, freezing in the middle of her movements. She made rattling sounds when she sat down. During meals she would continually knock her fingers on the table. My brother went the other way. He was disoriented, careless and lazy. He gave up his books and would do nothing to help.

All day long at work I listened to Big Sister Fann's stories of men of charm and intelligence, men who spent their lives on horseback, conquered their foes and became emperors. I went home only to face the reality that I would be married to Bottle before spring.

Mother called from her bed, and I sat down beside her. I couldn't bear looking at her face. She was bone-thin. "Your father used to say, 'A sick tiger that loses its way on a plain is weaker than a lamb. It can't fight wild dogs who come to feast.' Unfortunately that is our fate, Orchid."

One morning I heard a beggar singing in the street while I was brushing my hair:

> To give it up is to accept your fate.
> To give it up is to create peace.
> To give it up is to gain the upper hand, and
> To give it up is to have it all.

I stared at the beggar as he passed my window. He raised his empty bowl toward me. His fingers were as dry as dead branches. "Porridge," he said.

"We are out of rice," I said. "I have been digging up white clay from my yard and mixing it with wheat flour to make buns. Would you like one?"

"Don't you know that white clay clogs the intestines?"

"I know, but there is nothing else to eat."

He took the bun I gave him and disappeared at the end of the lane.

Sad and depressed, I walked to Big Sister Fann's in the snow. When I arrived I picked up my tools and sat down on the bench and started to work. Fann came in with breakfast still in her mouth. She was excited and said she saw a decree posted on the city wall. "His Majesty Emperor Hsien Feng is looking for future mates. I wonder who the lucky girls will be!" She described the event, which was called the Selection of Imperial Consorts.

After work I decided to go and take a look at the decree. The direct route was blocked, so I weaved through the lanes and alleys and got there by sunset. The poster was written in black ink. The characters were blurred from the wash of wet snow. As I read it, my thoughts began to race. The candidates had to be Manchu, to keep the purity of the Imperial bloodline. I remembered Father once told me that among four hundred million people in China, five million were Manchu. The poster also said that the girls' fathers had to be at least the rank of Blue Bannerman. That was to ensure the girls' genetic intelligence. The poster further declared that all Manchu girls between the ages of thirteen and seventeen must register with their state for the selection. None of the young Manchu women were allowed to marry until the Emperor had passed them up.

"Don't you think I have a chance?" I cried to Big Sister Fann. "I am a Manchu and seventeen. My father was a Blue Bannerman."

Fann shook her head. "Orchid, you are an ugly mouse compared to the concubines and court ladies I have seen."

I drank from a bucket of water and sat down to think. Big Sister Fann's words discouraged me, but my desire was not diminished. I learned from Fann that the Imperial court would review the candidates in October. Governors all over the nation would send out scouts to gather beautiful girls. The scouts were ordered to make lists of names.

"They missed me!" I said to Big Sister Fann. I found out that the Imperial household was in charge of this year's selection, and the beauties from each state were being sent to Peking for the household committee to review. The chief eunuch, who represented the Emperor, was expected to inspect more than five thousand girls and select about two hundred from among them. Those girls would be presented to Grand Empress Lady Jin and Emperor Hsien Feng for viewing.

Big Sister Fann told me that Hsien Feng would select seven official wives, and that he would be free to "reward happiness" to any court ladies or maids in the Forbidden City. After the official wives were chosen, the rest of the finalists would be kept and would live in the Forbidden City. They might never get a chance to mate with His Majesty, but they were guaranteed a lifetime of annual taels. The amount given was based on title and rank. All told, the Emperor would have three thousand concubines.

I also learned from Big Sister Fann that besides the consort selection, the Selection of Imperial Maids was also held this year. Unlike the consorts, who were given magnificent palaces to live in, the maids lived in barracks behind the palaces. Many such quarters had been left to decay and were barely fit to live in.

I asked Big Sister Fann about the eunuchs, two thousand of whom lived in the Forbidden City. She told me that most of them came from poverty. Their families were utterly beyond hope. While only castrated boys were qualified to apply for the positions, not every castrated boy was guaranteed a place.

"Besides being quick-witted, the boys had to be above average in looks," Big Sister Fann said. "The smartest and handsomest would have a chance to survive or even become favorites."

I asked why the court wouldn't hire normal boys.

"It is to guarantee the Emperor as the sole seed planter," she explained. The system was inherited from the Ming Dynasty. The Ming Emperor owned ninety thousand eunuchs. They were his in-house police force. It was a necessity, because cases of murder are not infrequent in a place where thousands of females compete for one male's attention.

"The eunuchs are creatures capable of extreme hatred and cruelty and also loyalty and devotion. Privately they suffer a great deal. Most wear thick underwear because they constantly leak urine. Have you ever heard the expression 'You stink like a eunuch'?"

"How do you know?" I asked.

"I married one, for heaven's sake! The leaking puts a lot of shame on the man. My husband had a profound understanding of mistreatment and suffering, but that did not stop him from being vicious and jealous. He wished everyone tragedy."

I didn't tell my family about what I intended to do, because I was aware that my chance of success was one in a million. The next morning I went to the local courthouse before work. I was nervous but determined. I announced my purpose to the guard and was guided to an office in the back. The room was large. Its columns, tables and chairs were wrapped with red cloth. A bearded man dressed in a red robe sat behind a large redwood desk. On the desk was a rectangular piece of yellow silk. It was a copy of the Imperial decree. I went up to the man and got down on my knees. I stated my name and age. I said that my father was from the Yehonala clan and was the late *taotai* of Wuhu.

The bearded man measured me with his eyes. "Do you have better clothes?" he asked after a hard stare.

"No, sir," I replied.

"I am not allowed to let anyone enter the palace looking like a beggar."

"Well, may I have your permission to ask whether I am qualified for the entrance? If I can get a yes from you, sir, I shall find a way to prepare my appearance."

"Do you think I'd bother to waste my breath if I didn't find you qualified?"

"Well," Mother said, a bit relieved, "I will just have to tell your uncle that Bottle has to wait until the Emperor passes you up."

"Maybe by then Uncle will get hit by a cart or Bottle will die of an opium overdose," Kuei Hsiang said.

"Kuei Hsiang," Rong stopped him, "you don't curse people like that. After all, they sheltered us."

I always found that Rong had better sense than Kuei Hsiang. That was not to say that Rong was not afraid. She continued to be delicate and fearful throughout her life. She would spend days working on an embroidery and then suddenly abandon it, saying that she saw its color turning. She would conclude that there must be a ghost at work. She would panic and cut up the piece.

"Why don't you study, Kuei Hsiang?" I said to my brother. "You have a better chance than Rong and I. The Imperial civil service examination comes up every year. Why don't you give it a try?"

"I don't have what it takes" was Kuei Hsiang's reply.

· · ·

19

Big Sister Fann was surprised that I passed the entrance exam at the office of the Imperial household. Grabbing a candle, she studied my features.

"How did I miss it?" She turned my head right and left. "Bright almond-shaped single-lid eyes, smooth skin, a straight nose, a lovely mouth and a slender body. It must be the clothes that diminished your looks."

Putting down the candle, Fann folded her arms. She paced around the room like a cricket in a jar before a fight. "You are not going to look like this when you enter the Forbidden City, Orchid." She placed her hands on my shoulders and said, "Come, let me transform you."

It was in Big Sister Fann's dressing room that I was turned into a princess.

Big Sister Fann proved to me her reputation — she who was once in charge of dressing the Empress wrapped me in a light green satin tunic embroidered with lifelike white pheasants. Embroidered borders in a darker shade decorated the neck, cuffs and edges.

"This tunic was Her Majesty's. She gave it to me as a wedding present," Big Sister Fann explained. "I hardly wore it because I was afraid of stains. And now I am too old and heavy. I loan it to you, the matching headdress too."

"Won't Her Majesty recognize it?"

"Don't worry." Fann shook her head. "She has hundreds of similar dresses."

"What will the dress make her think?"

"That you have her taste."

I was thrilled and told Big Sister Fann that I couldn't thank her enough.

"Remember, beauty is not the only measurement at the selection, Orchid," Big Sister Fann said as she dressed me. "You can lose because you are too poor to bribe the eunuchs, who will in turn find a way to point out your shortcomings to His and Her Majesties. I have personally attended this kind of occasion. It was so exhausting that every girl looked the same by the end. His and Her Majesties' eyes wouldn't register beauty anymore, and that's why most of the Imperial wives and concubines are ugly."

Over the endless months of waiting, I could scarcely contain my agitation. I slept fitfully and awoke from dreams full of dread. Then the waiting ended: tomorrow I would enter the Forbidden City to compete for the selection.

Clouds hung high in the sky and the breeze was warm as my sister and I strode through the streets of Peking. "I have a feeling that you will be one of the two hundred concubines, if not one of the seven wives," Rong said. "Your beauty is unmatchable, Orchid."

"My desperation is unmatchable," I corrected her.

We continued walking and I held her hand tightly. She was dressed in a light blue cotton gown with stitch pads neatly sewed on her shoulders. She and I looked alike in terms of features, except sometimes her expression gave away her fear.

"What if you never get to spend a night with His Majesty?" Rong asked. Her raised eyebrows formed a line on her forehead.

"It is better than marrying Bottle, isn't it?"

Rong nodded.

"I'll send you the most fashionable clothes patterns from the palace," I said, trying to be cheerful. "You'll be the best-dressed girl in the city. Fine fabrics, fabulous lace, peacock feathers."

"Don't you go out of your way, Orchid. Everyone knows that the Forbidden City has strict rules. One wrong move and your head could be chopped."

For the rest of the walk we were quiet. The Imperial wall seemed taller and thicker. It was the wall that would separate us.

Three

I WAS WALKING among the thousands of girls selected from all over the country. After the first round of inspections the number dwindled to two hundred. I had been among the lucky ones and was now competing to become one of Emperor Hsien Feng's seven wives.

A month before, the household committee had sent me for a physical examination. The process would have shocked me if I hadn't been preparing myself. It took place on the south side of Peking, in a palace surrounded by a large formal garden. The house and grounds had once been used as a vacation palace for the emperors. There was a small pond in the middle of the courtyard.

I met many girls whose beauty I didn't have words to even begin to describe. Each maiden was one of a kind. The girls from the southern provinces were slender, had swan-like necks, long limbs and small breasts. The girls from the north were like ripe fruit. They had breasts like gourds and pumpkin-sized buttocks.

The eunuchs checked our birth signs, star charts, height, weight, the shape of our hands and feet, our hair. They counted our teeth. Everything had to match the Emperor's own charts.

We were instructed to undress and line up. One by one we were examined by a head eunuch, who had an assistant recording his words in a book.

"Uneven eyebrows," the head eunuch pronounced as he walked past us, "crooked shoulders, a laborer's hands, earlobes too small, jaw too narrow, lips too thin, puffy eyelids, square toes, legs too short, thighs too fat." Those girls were instantly dismissed.

Hours later we were guided to a hall with peach-flower-patterned curtains. A group of eunuchs came holding tapes. My body was measured by three eunuchs. I was pinched and squeezed.

There was no place to hide. "Shrink or stick out your head—either way you won't escape the dropping ax." The head eunuch pushed my shoulders and yelled, "Straighten up!"

I closed my eyes and tried to convince myself that the eunuchs were not men. When I opened my eyes again I found this to be true. In the countryside men drooled at the sight of an attractive girl even when she was fully clothed. Here the eunuchs acted as if my nakedness made no difference. I wondered if they were truly unfeeling or simply pretending to be.

After being measured we were taken to a bigger hall and ordered to walk. The girls who were marked down as lacking grace were dismissed. Those who passed waited for the next test. By evening there were still girls waiting outside to be examined.

Finally I was instructed to put my clothes back on and I was sent home.

Early the next morning, I was brought back to the mansion. Most of the girls I had met the day before were gone. The survivors were regrouped. We were instructed to recite our name, age and place of birth and our father's name in a clear voice. The girls who sounded too loud or too soft were dismissed.

Before breakfast we were guided to the back of the palace where several tents were set up in the open garden area. Inside each tent were tables made of bamboo. When I entered, the eunuchs told me to lie down on one of the tables. Four senior court ladies appeared. Their painted faces were expressionless. They stuck out their noses and began to smell me all over. They went from my hair to my ears, from my nose to my mouth, from my armpits to my private parts. They checked between my fingers and toes. One lady dipped her middle finger in an oil jar and stuck it inside my rear end. It hurt but I tried not to make any noise. When the lady pulled her finger out, all the other ladies jumped up to smell it.

The last month went by in an eyeblink. "Tomorrow His Majesty shall decide my fate," I told Mother.

Without saying a word, she went to light incense sticks and knelt down before a picture of Buddha on the wall.

"What's on your mind, Orchid?" Rong asked.

"My dream of visiting the Forbidden City will come true," I replied, thinking of Big Sister Fann's words: *A glimpse of such beauty makes one feel that one's life has been worthy.* "I will never be an ordinary person again."

My mother stayed up all night. Before I went to bed, she explained the meaning of *yuan* in Taoism. It was about how I should follow my destiny and alter it like a river moving through rocks.

I listened quietly and promised that I would remember the importance of being obedient and of learning how to "swallow the spit of others when necessary."

I had been ordered to be at the Gate of Zenith before dawn. Mother had spent her last borrowed taels and hired a sedan chair to carry me. It was draped with fancy blue silk cloth. Mother had also hired three plain-looking sedan chairs for Kuei Hsiang, Rong and herself. They were to accompany me to the gate. The footmen would be at the door before the rooster's first cry. I didn't fuss about the way Mother spent the money. I understood that she wanted to send me off in an honorable manner.

At three in the morning Mother woke me. My being chosen as an Imperial consort had filled her with hope and energy. She tried to hold back her tears as she did my face. I kept my eyes tightly closed. If I opened them I knew that my tears would flow and ruin the carefully applied makeup.

When my sister and brother woke up I was in Big Sister Fann's beautiful dress. Mother tied up the laces. After all was set, we ate porridge for breakfast. Rong gave me two walnuts that she had saved from last year. She insisted that I eat them both for good luck, and I did as she wished.

The footmen arrived. Rong helped me to keep the dress off the ground until the footmen lifted me into the sedan chair. Kuei Hsiang was in our father's clothes. I told him he looked like a Bannerman, except that he must learn to do the buttons properly.

The girls and their families gathered at the Gate of Zenith. I sat inside the sedan chair. It was cold. My fingers and toes grew stiff. The gate looked imposing against the dark purple sky. There were ninety-nine copper-colored cups embedded in the gate, like turtles parked on a giant panel. These covered the huge bolts that held the wood together. A footman told my mother that the wall-thick gate had been built in 1420. It was made of the hardest wood. Above the gate, on top of the wall, was a stone turret.

Dawn broke. A company of Imperial Guards poured out of the gate.

They were followed by a group of eunuchs dressed in robes. One of the eunuchs took out a book and began to call out names in a high-pitched voice. He was a tall middle-aged man with the features of a monkey, a pair of round eyes, a flat nose, an ear-to-ear thin-lipped mouth and a wide space between his nose and upper lip. His forehead sloped. He sang the syllables as he made the calls. The tune lingered on the last note for at least three beats. The footman told us that he was the chief eunuch. His name was Shim.

The eunuchs dispensed silver coins in a yellow box to each family after a name was called. "Five hundred taels from His Majesty the Emperor!" Chief Eunuch Shim's voice rang again.

Mother broke down when my name was called. "Time to part, Orchid. Watch your step."

I got out of the sedan chair carefully.

Mother almost dropped the box given to her. She was escorted back into her sedan chair by the guards and was told to go home.

"Consider yourself boarding a ship of mercy on the sea of suffering," Mother cried, waving at me. "Your father's spirit will be with you!"

I bit my lip and nodded. I told myself to be happy, because with the five hundred taels my family would be able to survive.

"Take care of Mother!" I said to Rong and Kuei Hsiang.

Rong waved and raised a handkerchief to her mouth.

Kuei Hsiang stood like a wooden post. "Wait, Orchid. Wait awhile."

I took a deep breath and turned toward the rose-colored gate.

The sun popped out of the clouds as I made my way to the Forbidden City.

"The Imperial ladies walking!" Chief Eunuch Shim sang.

The guards at the entrance lined up on either side, creating an aisle through which we passed.

I looked back for the last time. The crowd was bathed in the light of the sun. Rong was swinging her arms with the handkerchief, and Kuei Hsiang held the box of taels over his head. Mother was nowhere to be seen. She must have been hiding inside her sedan chair, crying.

"Goodbye!" My tears fell freely as the Gate of Zenith slammed shut.

If it hadn't been for Chief Eunuch Shim's voice, which kept giving orders, making us turn left or right, I would have believed that I was in a fantasy world.

As I walked, a group of palatial buildings presented themselves. They were solemn in atmosphere and gigantic in size. Glazed yellow roofs glistened in the sunshine. Slabs of carved marble lay under my feet. Not until I saw the Hall of Supreme Harmony did I realize that what I was seeing was just the beginning.

For the next two candle-times, we passed ornate gates, spacious courtyards and hallways with carvings on every beam and sculptures in every corner.

"You are taking the side ways, which are the paths for servants and court officials," Chief Eunuch Shim pointed out. "No one except His Majesty uses the center entrance."

We walked through empty space after empty space. No one was there to see our elaborate dresses. I recalled Big Sister Fann's advice: "The Imperial walls have eyes and ears. You'll never know which wall conceals the eyes of His Majesty Emperor Hsien Feng or Grand Empress Lady Jin."

The air felt heavy in my lungs. I glanced around and compared myself to the other girls. We all had painted faces in the same Manchu style. On the lower lip was a rouge dot, and the hair was coiled around the head in two parts. Some girls wound their tails all the way up to the top of the head and draped them with glistening jewels and jade flowers, birds or insects. Some used silk to create an artificial plate, pinned with ivory clips. Mine was a swallowtail wig, which took Big Sister Fann hours to fasten onto a thin black board. A large purple silk rose was pinned to the center of the board, with two pink ones on each side. Also in my hair were fresh white jasmines and orchids.

The girl who walked next to me wore a heavily laced headpiece. It was in the shape of a flying goose and was draped with pearls and diamonds. Yellow and vermilion threads were braided in patterns. The headpiece reminded me of those worn in Chinese operas.

As a shoemaker I naturally paid attention to what the girls wore on their feet. I used to think that if I knew nothing else, I knew shoes. But what I saw put my knowledge to shame. Every pair of shoes the girls wore was encrusted with pearls, jade, diamonds and embroidered patterns of lotus, plum, magnolia, Buddha's hand and peach flower. The sides of the shoes were crowded with the symbols of fortune and longevity, fish and butterflies. As Manchu ladies, we didn't bind our feet as Chinese ladies did, but we didn't want to miss the opportunity to be fashionable, which was why we wore extra-high platform shoes. The intent was to make our feet look smaller, like Chinese feet.

My feet began to feel sore. We passed through glades of bamboo and larger trees. The path became narrower and the staircases steeper with each turn. Chief Eunuch Shim hurried us along, and all of the girls grew short of breath. Just when I thought we had reached a dead end, a grand view unexpectedly revealed itself. I held my breath as a sea of golden roofs suddenly spread out before me. I could see the massive gatehouses of the Forbidden City in the distance.

"Where you are standing is called Prospect Hill." Chief Eunuch Shim rested his hands on his waist and drew in big breaths. "It is the highest spot in all of Peking. Ancient *feng shui* experts believed that this area possessed the most vital energy and spirits of wind and water. Girls, take a moment to remember this, because most of you will never get a chance to see this again. We are lucky to have a clear day. The sandstorms from the Gobi Desert are resting."

Following Chief Eunuch Shim's finger, I saw a white pagoda. "That Tibetan-style temple houses the spirits of the gods who have protected the Ch'ing Dynasty for generations. Be careful what you do, girls. Make sure you never distract or offend the spirits."

On our way down the hill Shim took us along another path, which led to the Garden of Peace and Longevity. It was the first time I had seen real pippala trees. They were gigantic and their leaves were as green as fresh grass. I had seen pictures of them in Buddhist manuscripts and temple frescoes. They were considered the symbol of Buddha and were rare. Here such trees, hundreds of years old, were everywhere. Their leaves draped the ground like green curtains. In the garden, large, beautiful stones had been arranged in a pattern pleasing to the eye. When I raised my eyes, I saw magnificent pavilions hidden in the cypresses.

After many turns I lost my sense of direction. We must have passed about twenty pavilions before we were finally led to a bluish one carved with plum flowers. It had a snail-shaped roof inlaid with blue tiles.

"The Pavilion of Winter Blossom," Chief Eunuch Shim pointed out. "Here lives the Grand Empress Lady Jin. You are going to meet both Majesties soon."

We were told to sit on stone benches while Shim gave us a quick lesson in the expected etiquette. Each of us was to speak a simple line, wishing His and Her Majesties health and longevity. "After expressing the wish, remain silent and answer only when you are spoken to."

Nervousness spread among us. One girl started to cry uncontrollably. She was immediately taken away by eunuchs. Another girl began mumbling to herself. She too was taken out.

I became aware of the constant presence of eunuchs. Most of the time they stood against the walls, silent and expressionless. Big Sister

Fann had warned me that the experienced eunuchs were dreadful and that they fed on others' misfortune. "The young ones are better," she had said, "especially the newcomers, who are still innocent. The eunuchs' nastiness doesn't show until they reach adulthood, when they realize the significance of their loss."

According to Big Sister Fann, the powerful eunuchs ran the Forbidden City. They were masters of intrigue. Because they had suffered a great deal, they had amazing endurance for pain and torture. The newcomers were beaten with whips daily. Before taking their boys to the palace, the parents of eunuchs purchased three pieces of cowhide. The new eunuchs would wrap the hide around their back and thighs to cover where the whip would land. The cowhide was nicknamed "the Real Buddha."

Later on I would learn that the penalty for the most serious transgressions by the eunuchs was death by stifling. The punishment would be carried out in front of all the eunuchs. The convicted eunuch would be tied to a bench with his face covered with a piece of wet silk. The process was similar to mask-making. With everyone watching, the executioners would add wet cloths, layer after layer, while the victim struggled to breathe. The eunuch's limbs would be held down until he ceased struggling.

During my early life in the Forbidden City, I cursed such punishments. I was appalled by their cruelty. Over the years my view gradually changed. I found the discipline a necessity. The eunuchs were capable of grand crimes and equal cruelty. The anger they harbored was so uncontrollable that only death could contain it. In ancient times eunuchs had incited riots and worse. During the Chou Dynasty the eunuchs had burned down an entire palace.

According to Big Sister Fann, when a clever eunuch worked his way up and became the Imperial favorite, as Shim had, he would live his life under one person but above the nation. It was this possibility not only of survival but also of becoming a legend that yearly led more than fifty thousand poor families in China to send their boys to the capital.

From Big Sister Fann I had learned to identify the eunuchs' status by the way they dressed, and it was now time to apply my knowledge. Those who held high positions wore velvet robes draped with fine jewelry and were served by apprentices. They had their own tea makers, dressers, messengers, accountants, and figurehead wives and concubines. They adopted children to carry on the family name and purchased property outside the Forbidden City. They became rich and ruled their households like emperors. When one famous eunuch found out that his wife was having an affair with a servant boy, he hacked her to pieces and fed her to his dog.

By now I was starving. The two hundred of us had been divided into groups of ten and then scattered to different corners of the garden. We sat or stood on wooden or stone platforms or large river-smooth rocks. Spread before us were man-made ponds dotted with floating lotus and rippled by rising koi. Between us were carved wood panels and stands of bamboo.

The eunuch who was responsible for my group had a bronze decoration on his hat and a quail on his chest. He reminded me of my brother Kuei Hsiang. The eunuch had a naturally rosy mouth and girlish features. He was skinny and seemed shy. He kept his distance from us, and his eyes constantly traveled between the girls and his superior, a eunuch who wore a white decoration on his hat and had an oriole on his chest.

"My name is Orchid." Whispering, I went up to the skinny eunuch and introduced myself. "I am very thirsty, and I was wondering—"

"Shush!" He pressed his index finger to his lips nervously.

"What's your name? How should I address you?" I continued.

"An-te-hai."

"Well, An-te-hai, could I please have some water?"

He shook his head. "I can't talk. Please don't ask me questions."

"I would stop if—"

"I am sorry." He spun on his heels and quickly disappeared behind bamboo bushes.

How long could I stand like this? I looked around and heard the other girls' stomachs grumbling.

The sound of water from a nearby stream made me feel thirstier. The girls were slowly becoming frozen into an ancient tableau. It was a picture composed of elegant trees, dangling vines, swaying bamboo and young maidens.

I stared at this tableau until I saw a figure moving like a snake through the bamboo.

It was An-te-hai. He returned with a cup in his hand. His steps were swift and soundless. I realized that the eunuchs were trained to walk like ghosts. An-te-hai's soft soles touched the ground while his feet rocked like boats.

Stopping in front of me, he passed me the cup.

I smiled and bowed.

An-te-hai turned and walked away before I finished my bow.

I sensed eyes shooting at me from all directions as I raised the water to my lips. Knowing how they felt, I took a sip and then passed the cup around.

"Oh, thank you so much." The girl who stood next to me took the cup. She was slender and had an oval face. Her double-lidded deep eyes were bright. From her accent and graceful movements, I guessed that she was from a wealthy family. Her silk dress was embroidered with the most sophisticated patterns, and diamonds hung from her head to her toes. Her headpiece was made of golden flowers. She had a long neck, and her poise seemed effortless.

The cup traveled from hand to hand until there was not a drop left. All the girls seemed to relax a little. The beautiful oval-faced girl with exotic eyes waved at me from her bench. As I approached her, she moved to one side.

"I am Nuharoo." She smiled.

"Yehonala." I sat down beside her.

It was in this fashion that Nuharoo and I introduced ourselves. Neither of us could then foretell that we had just made a connection that would last a lifetime. We were called by our last names in the court, indicating the clan to which we belonged. Without further explanation we understood that we were from the two most powerful clans of the Manchu race: the Yehonala and the Nuharoo. The two clans used to be rivals and had fought countless wars over the centuries. It was not until the king of the Nuharoo clan married the daughter of the king of the Yehonala clan that the two families united and eventually took over China, creating the Celestial Purity, or Ch'ing, Dynasty.

I smelled the scent of lilies from Nuharoo's hair. She sat still and gazed at the stands of bamboo as if drawing them with her eyes. She radiated contentment. For a long time she didn't move. It was as if she were studying the details of each leaf. Her concentration was undisturbed by the passing eunuchs. I wondered what she was thinking, if she shared my longing for my family, my anxiety about the future. I wanted to know what drove her to try for the selection. I was sure that it was neither hunger nor money. Had she dreamt of becoming an empress? How was she raised? Who were her parents? There was not the slightest nervousness in her expression. It was as if she simply knew that she would be selected. As if she had come only to receive this news.

After a long while Nuharoo turned toward me and smiled again. She had an almost childlike smile, innocent and free of worry. I was sure she had never suffered. She must have had servants in her house to fan her to sleep on hot summer nights. Her gestures suggested that she was trained in manners. Had she attended schools for the rich? What did she read? Did she like opera? If she did, she must have a hero or heroine that she admired. Suppose we loved the same operas, and suppose we were both lucky enough to be chosen . . .

"What do you think about your chance of being chosen?" I asked Nuharoo after she revealed to me that her father was Emperor Hsien Feng's distant uncle.

"I don't think about it much," she said quietly. Her lips opened like the petals of a flower. "I do whatever my family asks of me."

"So your parents know how to read wood grains."

"Pardon me?"

"One's future."

Nuharoo turned away from me and smiled gently into the distance. "Yehonala, how do you see our chances?"

"You are born of an Imperial relative and you are beautiful," I said. "I am not sure about my chance. My father was a *taotai* before he died. If my family hadn't been heavily in debt, and if I had not been forced to marry my retarded cousin Ping, I wouldn't have . . ." I had to stop, because my tears were welling up.

Nuharoo put a hand into her pocket and took out a lace handkerchief. "I am sorry." She passed the handkerchief to me. "Your story sounds terrible."

I didn't want to ruin her handkerchief, so I wiped my tears with the back of my hands.

"Tell me more," she said.

I shook my head. "My story of misery would be bad for your health."

"I don't mind. I want to hear it. This is the first time I have stepped out of my house. I have never traveled like you."

"Travel? It was not at all a pleasant experience." As I continued speaking, my mind flooded with memories of my father. The decaying smell of the coffin and the flies that followed it. To remove myself from the sadness I switched subjects.

"Did you go to school when you grew up, Nuharoo?"

"I had private tutors," she answered. "Three of them. Each taught me a different subject."

"What was your favorite subject?"

"History."

"History! I thought that was only for boys." I remembered hiding a book from my father, *The Record of the Three Kingdoms.*

"It was not general history as you are imagining." Nuharoo smiled as she explained. "It was the history of the Imperial household. It was about the lives of empresses and concubines. My classes focused on those of the greatest virtue." After a pause, she added, "I was expected to model myself after Empress Hsiao Ch'in. My parents have told me since I was a young girl that I would one day join the ladies whose portraits are hung in the Imperial gallery."

No wonder she looked like she belonged to this place. "I am sure you will impress," I said. "I am afraid that I am the least educated in this aspect of life. I don't even know how the ranks work for the Imperial ladies, although I know plenty about the eunuchs."

"It will be my pleasure to share my knowledge with you." Her eyes glowed.

Someone yelled, "On your knees!"

A group of eunuchs rushed in and lined up in front of us. We dropped to our knees.

Chief Eunuch Shim appeared through the arched door. He struck a pose, lifting the side of his robe with his right hand. He made a single step and came into full view.

From my knees I saw Chief Eunuch Shim's blue boat-shaped boots. He held the silence. I felt his power and authority. Strangely, I admired his manner.

"His Majesty Emperor Hsien Feng and Her Majesty the Grand Empress Lady Jin summon . . ." Pitching his voice, Chief Eunuch Shim sang out several names. ". . . and Nuharoo and Yehonala!"

Four

I HEARD THE SOUND of my dangling headwear and earrings. The girls in front of me swayed gracefully in their magnificent silk robes and high platform shoes. The eunuchs walked back and forth around the seven of us, constantly responding to the hand signals of Chief Eunuch Shim.

We passed through countless courtyards and arched doors. Finally we arrived in the entry hall of the Palace of Peace and Longevity. My inner shirt was soaked with sweat. I was afraid I would humiliate myself. I glanced at Nuharoo. She was as calm as a moon in a pond. A lovely smile hung between her cheeks. Her makeup was still immaculate.

We were led to a side room and given a few moments to freshen our appearance. Inside the hall His Majesty and Her Majesty were said to be sitting. When Shim went in and announced our arrival, the air around the girls intensified. Our small movements made our jewelry clatter like poorly made wind chimes. I felt a slight dizziness.

I heard Chief Eunuch Shim's voice, but was too nervous to figure out what he was announcing. His syllables sounded distorted, like those of an opera singer playing a ghost, speaking in a stylized tone.

A girl next to me suddenly dropped. Her knees had given in. Before I was able to assist her, the eunuchs came and removed her.

Buzzing noises filled my ears. I took several deep breaths so I wouldn't lose control like the other girl. My limbs were stiff and I didn't know where to place my hands. The more I thought about calming myself, the worse my composure became. My body began to tremble. To distract myself, I stared at the art works around the doorframe. Calligraphy written in gold on a black wooden board featured four giant characters: *cloud, absorption, star* and *glory.*

The girl who had collapsed returned. She looked as pale as a cut-paper doll.

"His Majesty and Her Majesty!" Chief Eunuch Shim announced as he entered. "Good luck, girls!"

With Nuharoo leading and me as the tail, the seven of us were guided through a wall formed by the eunuchs.

Emperor Hsien Feng and the Grand Empress Lady Jin sat on a *kang,* a bed-sized chair covered with bright yellow silk. Her Majesty was on the right side and His Majesty on the left. The rectangular room was spacious with a high ceiling. There were two potted orange coral trees on each side of the room against the walls. The trees looked too perfect to be real. The court ladies and the eunuchs stood against the walls with their hands folded before them. Four eunuchs, each holding a long-handled peacock-feather fan, stood behind the chair. Behind them was a huge tapestry with a rainbow-colored Chinese character — *shou,* longevity. Looking closer, I noticed that the character was made up of hundreds of embroidered butterflies. Next to the tapestry was an ancient fungus, as tall as a man, in a golden pan. Opposite the fungus was a painting entitled *The Immortal Land of the Queen Mother of the Middle Kingdom.* It had a Taoist goddess riding a crane in the sky, looking down at a magical landscape of pavilions, streams, animals and trees, under which children played. In front of the painting was a carved red sandalwood container. It had a riotous mass of double gourds, blossoms and leaves carved in high relief. Years later I would learn that the container was used to hold tribute gifts to the Emperor.

The seven of us performed the kowtow ceremony and stayed on our knees. It seemed as if I had just stepped onto a stage. Although I kept my head down, I could see the beautiful vases, the magnificently carved legs of water basins, the floor lanterns with tail lace touching the ground and large good-luck locks draped with silk around the corners of the walls.

I ventured a glance at the Son of Heaven.

Emperor Hsien Feng looked younger than I had imagined. He seemed to be in his early twenties and had a fine complexion. His large eyes tilted upward at the corners. His expression was gentle and concerned, but without curiosity. He had a typical Manchu nose, straight and long, and firm lips. His cheeks were feverishly red. He did not smile when he saw us enter.

It felt like I was dreaming. The Son of Heaven was dressed in a full-length golden robe. Sewn into the fabric were dragons, clouds, waves, the sun, the moon and numerous stars. A yellow silk belt rounded his waist. Hanging from this belt were green jade, pearls, precious stones and a little embroidered bag. His sleeves were the shape of a horse's hoof.

The boots His Majesty wore were the most magnificent I had ever seen. Made of tiger skin and dyed tea-leaf green, they were inlaid with tiny gold good-luck animals: bats, four-legged dragons and *chee-lin*—a mixed lion and deer, the symbol of magic.

Emperor Hsien Feng did not appear to be interested in meeting us. He shifted in his seat as if bored. He leaned to the left and then to the right. He glanced repeatedly at two plates placed between him and his mother. One was made of silver and the other gold. On the silver plate were bamboo chips that bore our names.

The Grand Empress Lady Jin was a plump woman with a face like a dried-up squash. Although she was only in her early fifties, wrinkles hung from her forehead to her neck. As Big Sister Fann had told me, she was the favorite concubine of Tao Kuang, the Emperor before His Majesty. Lady Jin was said to have been the most beautiful woman in China. Where had her beauty gone? Her eyelids drooped and her crooked mouth was pulled toward the right side of her face. The rouge dot on her lip was painted so large that it looked like a giant red button.

The robe Her Majesty wore was made of radiant yellow satin deco-rated with a cornucopia of natural and mythological symbols. Sewn onto the dress were egg-sized diamonds, jade and precious stones. Flowers, rubies and jewels dangled from her head and covered half her face. Her gold and silver necklaces must have been heavy, for Her Maj-esty seemed to lean forward under their weight. Bracelets were stacked from her wrists to her elbows, locking both of her forearms in place.

The Grand Empress spoke after a long and silent observation. Her wrinkles danced and her shoulders went back as if she was tied to a post. "Nuharoo," she said, "you have come highly recommended. I un-derstand that you have completed your study in the history of the Im-perial household. Is it true?"

"Yes, Your Majesty," Nuharoo answered humbly. "I studied for sev-eral years under tutors introduced by my granduncle Duke Chai."

"I know Duke Chai, a very accomplished man." The Grand Empress nodded. "He is an expert on Buddhism and poetry."

"Yes, Your Majesty."

"Who are your favorite poets, Nuharoo?"

"They are Li Po, Tu Fu and Po Chuyi."

"Of the late Tang and early Sung dynasties?"

"Yes, Your Majesty."

"They are my favorites too. Do you know the name of the poet who wrote 'Awaiting Husband Stone'?"

"It is Wang Chien, Your Majesty."

"Would you recite the poem for me?"

Nuharoo rose and began:

> *Where she awaits her husband,*
> *On and on the river flows.*
> *Never looking back,*
> *Transformed into a stone.*
> *Day by day upon the peak,*
> *Wind and rain revolve.*
> *Should the journeyer return,*
> *This stone would utter speech.*

The Grand Empress raised her right arm and wiped her eyes with her sleeve. She turned toward Emperor Hsien Feng. "What do you think, my child?" she asked. "Isn't that a moving piece?"

Emperor Hsien Feng nodded obediently. He reached out and his fingers played with the bamboo chips in the silver plate.

"Tell me, my son, do I have to wear out this seat to get you to make up your mind?" the mother asked.

Without answering, Emperor Hsien Feng picked up the chip with Nuharoo's name on it and dropped it in the gold plate.

At that sound, the eunuchs and the court ladies drew in their breath in unison. They threw themselves at the feet of His Majesty and cheered, "Congratulations!"

"The first wife of His Majesty is selected!" Chief Eunuch Shim hailed toward the outer wall.

"Thank you." Nuharoo kowtowed with her forehead lightly touching the ground. She took time to complete her bows. After the third, she rose and then threw herself down on her knees again. The rest of us went down on our knees with her. In a perfectly trained voice, Nuharoo said, "I wish Your Majesties ten thousand years of life. Your luck shall be as full as the East China Sea and your health shall be as green as the Southern Mountains!"

The eunuchs bowed to Nuharoo and then escorted her out of the hall.

The room returned to its former quietness.

We stayed on our knees and I kept my chin low. Nobody spoke or moved.

Unable to tell what was going on, I decided to peek again.

My breath stopped the moment my eyes met the Grand Empress's. My knees jerked and I hit the ground with my forehead.

"Somebody is trying to hurry up." Emperor Hsien Feng spoke with a hint of amusement in his voice.

The Grand Empress made no response.

"Mother, I heard thunder," His Majesty said. "The cotton plants in the countryside will soon be drowned in rain. What can I do with all the bad news?"

"First things first, my son."

The Emperor sighed.

I had an urge to look at His Majesty again. But I remembered Big Sister Fann's warning that the Grand Empress disdained girls who were too eager to catch the Emperor's attention. Once the Grand Empress had ordered one of the Imperial concubines beaten to death because she seemed to be flirting with the Emperor.

"Come closer, girls. All of you," the old lady said. "Take a good look, my son."

"No fried cicadas for dinner," Emperor Hsien Feng uttered, as if he were the only one in the room.

"I said *closer!*" the Grand Empress yelled at us.

I stepped forward together with the other five.

"Introduce yourselves," Her Majesty ordered.

One after another we pronounced our names, followed by the phrase "I wish Your Majesties ten thousand years of life."

My intuition told me that Emperor Hsien Feng was looking in my direction. I was excited and hoped that I could sustain his attention, but knew I could not afford to displease the Grand Empress. I kept my eyes on my toes. I sensed some movement from the Emperor and stole a glance while the Grand Empress was asking Chief Eunuch Shim why all the girls appeared slow and had no spirit. "Have you scraped them off the streets?"

Shim tried to explain, but the Grand Empress stopped him. "I don't care how you produce. I judge only by the goods you deliver, and I am not pleased. I'll die drowning in the spit of the Imperial ancestors!"

"Your Majesty." The eunuch got down on his knees. "Did I not say that a good chime also needs a heavy beater to make it sound right? It all depends on how you tune the girls, a task at which we all know you excel."

"Death to your tongue, Shim!" The old lady burst into laughter.

The Emperor flipped the chips back and forth on the silver plate as if annoyed.

"You look exhausted, my son," the Grand Empress said.

"I am, Mother. Don't count on me to come tomorrow, because I won't."

"Then you must decide today. Concentrate and look harder."

"But I have been, haven't I?"

"Then why can't you make up your mind? Perform your duty, my son. Before you are the best maidens the kingdom can bestow on her Emperor!"

"I know."

"It is your big day, Hsien Feng."

"Every day is a big day. Every day a long metal stick is driven into my skull."

The Grand Empress sighed. Her anger was about to spill over. She breathed deeply to control herself. "You liked Nuharoo, didn't you?" she asked.

"How would I know?" The Son of Heaven rolled his eyes toward the ceiling. "My head is full of holes."

The mother bit her lips.

His Majesty ran his fingers through the remaining bamboo chips, making a loud noise.

"My bones are screaming to have me lay them down." The Grand Empress stretched in her seat. "I have been up since two o'clock this morning, and it is for nothing!"

Shim shuffled up to her on his knees. His arms were up in the air, holding a tray with a wet towel, a powder box, a brush and a green bottle.

The Grand Empress took the towel and wiped her hands and then picked up the brush to touch up her face with the powder. After that she picked up the green bottle and sprayed a mist onto her caked face.

A heavy scent filled the room.

I took the opportunity and raised my eyes. His Majesty was looking at me. He squashed his nose and mouth together as if trying to get me to laugh. I didn't know how to react.

The mocking continued. He seemed to be more interested in getting me to break the rules.

My father's teaching came to my mind: "Young people see an opportunity where older people might consider it a danger."

The Son of Heaven smiled at me. I smiled back.

"This summer is going to be nice and breezy." Emperor Hsien Feng played with the chips.

The Grand Empress turned her head toward us and frowned.

My thoughts went to the girl who had been beaten to death, and my back was instantly wet with sweat.

The Emperor raised his right hand and pointed a finger at me. "This one," he said.

"Yehonala?" Chief Eunuch Shim asked.

I felt the heat of the Grand Empress's stare.

I lowered my eyes and endured a long, unbearable silence.

"I have done what is required, Mother," the Emperor spoke.

The Grand Empress offered no comment.

"Shim, did you hear me?" Emperor Hsien Feng turned to the eunuch.

"Yes, I did, Your Majesty, I heard you perfectly." Eunuch Chief Shim smiled humbly, but his intention was to give the Grand Empress the opportunity to say the final word.

The "yes" finally came.

I sensed His Majesty's elation and Her Majesty's disappointment.

"I . . . I wish Your Majesties ten thousand years of life," I said, struggling to gain control over my trembling knees. "Your luck will be as full as the East China Sea and your health as green as the Southern—"

"Wonderful! My longevity has just been shortened," the Grand Empress interrupted me.

My knees gave in and my forehead was on the ground.

"I am afraid I just saw the shadow of a ghost." The Grand Empress rose from her chair.

"Which one, my lady?" Chief Eunuch Shim asked. "I'll catch it for you."

"Yes, Shim. Let's call everything off."

Suddenly there came the loud clang of a bamboo chip being thrown into the golden plate. "Time to sing, Shim!" ordered the Emperor.

"Yehonala stays!" Shim sang.

I couldn't remember much after that, only that my life had changed.

I was startled when Chief Eunuch Shim got down on his knees in front of me and called me his mistress and himself my slave. He helped me back onto my heels. I didn't even notice what became of the other girls or when they had been escorted out.

My mind was in a strange state. I recalled an amateur opera back in Wuhu. It was after the New Year's feast and everyone was drunk, including myself, because my father let me sip the rice wine so I could see how it tasted. The musicians were tuning their instruments. The sound was oddly mournful at first. Then it turned into the sound of a horse being beaten. Then, broken and strained, the notes sounded like wind whistling through the Mongolian grasslands. The opera began. The actors entered, dressed in women's gowns with blue and white floral prints. The musicians hit their bamboo tubes with sticks as the actors sang and beat their thighs.

Crack! Crack! Crack! I remembered the sound. It was unpleasant and I couldn't understand why people liked it. My mother told me that it was a traditional Manchu performance mixed with elements of Chinese opera, originally a form of entertainment for commoners. Once in a while rich people would request it performed, "to taste the local delicacy."

I remembered sitting in the first row. My ears grew numb from the loud drums. The sounds of the sticks beating the bamboo tubes felt like a hammer coming down on my skull. *Crack! Crack! Crack!* My thoughts were beaten out.

Chief Eunuch Shim had changed his costume. The fabric featured hand-painted red clouds floating over a hill of pine trees. On both of his cheeks, two red tomato-like circles had been drawn. The eunuch must have painted them in a hurry, for the color had smeared. Half of his nose was red too. A narrow white line ran from his forehead down the bridge of his nose. He had a goat's face, and his eyes looked like they had grown out of his ears. He smiled, revealing a set of gold teeth.

The old lady was cheered. "Shim, what are you going to say?"

"Congratulations on your gaining seven daughters-in-law, my lady. Remember the first line the mother-in-law said to her new daughter-in-law in the opera *The Wild Rose*?"

"How can anyone forget?" The old lady laughed again as she recited the line: "'Get your water bucket, daughter-in-law, and go to the well!'"

Chief Eunuch Shim cheerfully called in the six other girls, among them Nuharoo. The girls entered like goddesses descending from Heaven. They lined up next to me.

Shim lifted one side of his robe and took two steps, placing himself at the center of the hall facing Emperor Hsien Feng and the Grand Empress. He turned his face to the east and then back to the center. Crisply, he bowed and cheered, "May your grandchildren be counted in the hundreds and may you live forever!"

We repeated the line after Shim as we got down on our knees.

Outside the hall came the sound of drums and music.

A group of eunuchs, each holding a silk-wrapped box, entered.

"Rise." The Grand Empress smiled.

Chief Eunuch Shim announced, "His Majesty summons the ministers of the Imperial court!"

The sound of hundreds of knees hitting the ground came from outside the hall. "At your service, Your Majesties!" the ministers sang.

Chief Eunuch Shim announced, "In the presence of the spirit of the Imperial ancestors, and in the presence of Heaven and the universe, His Majesty Emperor Hsien Feng is ready to pronounce the names of his wives!"

"*Zah!*" the crowd responded in Manchu.

Boxes were opened one by one, revealing pieces of *ruyi*. Each *ruyi* was a scepter that had three large mushroom- or flower-shaped heads interconnected with a stem. The heads were made of gold, emeralds, rubies and sapphires, and the stem was carved jade or lacquered wood. Each *ruyi* represented a title and a rank. *Ru* meant "as" and *yi* meant "you wish"; *ruyi* meant "everything you wish."

Emperor Hsien Feng took one *ruyi* from the tray and walked toward us. This *ruyi* was of carved golden lacquer with three entwined peonies.

I continued to hold my breath, but I was no longer afraid. No matter what kind of *ruyi* I would receive, my mother would be proud tomorrow. She would be a mother-in-law to the Son of Heaven, and my siblings Imperial relatives! I regretted only that my father hadn't lived to see this.

Emperor Hsien Feng's fingers played with the *ruyi*. The flirtatious expression on his face had disappeared. He now looked unsure. He hesitated, frowning with his eyebrows. He shifted the *ruyi* from one hand to the other, and then, with flushed cheeks, he turned to his mother.

She gave him an encouraging nod. The Emperor began to circle us like a bee dancing around flowers.

Suddenly the youngest girl in our line broke out with a muted cry. She looked to be no more than thirteen years old.

Emperor Hsien Feng walked up to her.

The girl choked and then began to weep.

Like an adult giving a crying child a piece of candy, Emperor Hsien Feng put the *ruyi* in her hand.

Gripping it, the girl dropped to her knees and said, "Thank you."

Chief Eunuch Shim pronounced, "Soo Woozawa, daughter of Yee-mee-chi Woozawa, is selected as the Imperial consort of the fifth rank. Her title is Lady of Absolute Purity!"

From that moment, things began to flow. The Emperor took little time to bestow the rest of the *ruyi*.

When it was my turn, Emperor Hsien Feng walked up to me and placed a *ruyi* in my palm.

Like a rooster Shim sang, "Yehonala, daughter of Hui Cheng Yehonala, is selected as the Imperial consort of the fourth rank. Her title is Lady of the Greatest Virtue."

I looked at my *ruyi*. It was made of white jade. Instead of looking like mushrooms, the heads were carved floating clouds interconnected with a divining rod. I remembered my father once telling me that in Imperial symbolism the floating clouds and the rod represented the constellation of the dragon.

The next *ruyi* went to the girls named Yun and Li. They were pronounced Imperial consorts of the second and third rank and both titled Lady of Superiority. Their *ruyi* had the shape of a *lingzhi* mushroom, the fungus known for its healing power. The heads were decorated with bats, symbols of blessing and prosperity.

After Yun and Li were Mei and Hui. They ranked sixth and seventh, Ladies of Grand Harmony. I had difficulty remembering who was who, because Mei and Hui looked alike and dressed like twins. The heads of their *ruyi* carried a stone chime, the symbol of celebration.

Nuharoo was last. She was pronounced Empress and was given the finest *ruyi*. The scepter was made of gold inlaid with chunks of jewels and jade. The ornamented stem was carved with symbols of the harvest: grains and fruit-bearing branches, peaches, apples and grapes. The three heads were gold pomegranates, signifying numerous offspring and immortality. Nuharoo's eyes glowed and she bowed deeply.

Led by Nuharoo, the seven of us got up and then went down on our knees, over and over. We kowtowed to Emperor Hsien Feng and the Grand Empress. We sang our drill in one voice: "I wish Your Majesties ten thousand years of life. May your luck be as full as the East China Sea and your health as green as the Southern Mountains!"

Five

A FTER SUNSET I was brought back to my family on a palanquin escorted by a group of eunuchs. I was wrapped in a golden dress like an expensive gift. The head eunuch told my mother that until the day of the Imperial wedding ceremony I was to stay home.

Also coming home with me were gifts from the Emperor to my father, mother, sister and brother. My father was given a set of eight feather fasteners for a mandarin's court hat. Each hollow porcelain cylinder was used to fasten a peacock feather, with a ring on top of the tube to connect it to the hat. The gift would pass to my brother.

My mother was given a special lacquered *ruyi* carved with auspicious designs. The top showed the three star gods, who granted blessings, wealth and longevity. The center showed a bat carrying a stone chime and double fish, signifying abundance. On the bottom were roses and chrysanthemums representing prosperity.

Rong received a gorgeously carved sandalwood good-luck box, which held a set of green jade carvings. Kuei Hsiang was granted a set of enameled belt hooks with dragon heads ornamenting the tops. On the hooks he could hang his mirror, pouch, seal, a weapon or a money purse.

According to the court astrologer, I was to enter the Forbidden City on a particular day and hour—the Imperial Guards would fetch me when the proper moment arrived. The head eunuch gave my family a set of instructions to follow regarding court ritual and etiquette. He patiently went over the details with us. Kuei Hsiang would stand in my father's place. And Rong would be given a dress for the day. My mother was granted ten thousand taels to furnish the house. Her mouth fell open when she saw the taels being carried into the room in cases. She quickly became afraid of robbery. She asked Kuei Hsiang to keep the windows and door locked at all times. The head eunuch told my mother not to worry, since the house was already heavily guarded. "Not a fly will get in, mistress."

I asked the head eunuch if I was allowed to visit friends. I wished to say goodbye to Big Sister Fann.

"No," he told me.

I was disappointed. I asked Rong to return the dress I had borrowed from Big Sister Fann, and to take her three hundred taels as a farewell gift. Rong went immediately and came back with Big Sister Fann's blessing.

For many days Mother and Rong shopped while Kuei Hsiang and I cleaned and decorated the house. We hired laborers to do the heavy work. We put on a new roof, repaired the old walls, installed new windows and fixed the broken gate. My uncle took the opportunity to order a brand-new redwood door, elaborately carved with the image of the god of money. We replaced the old furniture and painted the walls. We hired the best carpenters and artists in town. Everyone took his job as a great honor. Fancy patterns were created on window frames and doorsills, mimicking the Imperial style. The craftsmen made incense holders, altar tables and staircases. Sometimes they had to work with toothpick-sized knives in order to fashion the desired details.

The head eunuch came to inspect the house after the work was completed. He made no comment and his expression revealed little. He showed up again the next day, however, and brought with him a group of people. They tore apart the whole place and said that they had to start from scratch. The roof, the walls, the windows, even Uncle's new door—all of it had to go.

"The decree will not be delivered if your door faces the wrong direction!" the head eunuch said to Mother and Uncle.

Nervous, Mother and Uncle begged for advice.

"Which direction do you think you should kneel to thank His Majesty?" the eunuch asked, and then answered his own question. "North! Because the Emperor always sits facing the south."

My family followed the head eunuch as he walked around the house, pointing his finger at everything.

"The shade of paint is wrong." His hand drew circles in the room. "It should be a warm beige instead of a cold beige. His Majesty expects cheerfulness!"

"But Orchid told us that His Majesty would not be present in our house," Mother said. "Did Orchid misunderstand?"

The eunuch shook his head. "You must learn to see that you are no longer your old self. You have become part of His Majesty, and you represent the Imperial aesthetics and principles. What you did with your house could ruin the appearance of the Son of Heaven! My head wouldn't be where it sits if I allowed you to do whatever you like. Look at your curtains! They are made of cotton! Didn't I tell you that cotton is for ordinary people and silk is for the Imperial family? Did my words go through your ears like the wind? It'll bring your daughter bad luck if you try to be cheap!"

At my repeated pleading the head eunuch agreed to let us get out of the house while his men conducted the renovation. Mother took us to Peking's most prestigious teahouses, in an expensive shopping district called Wangfooching. For the first time Mother spent like a rich lady. She tipped the busboy, the kitchen hands, even the stove man. The owners themselves brought the finest wines to our table. I was glad to see Mother happy. My being chosen had changed the condition of her health overnight. She looked well and was in exuberant spirits. We drank and celebrated. I had no real reason to be proud, because my good looks had nothing to do with me. But I thanked myself for having had the courage. I would have missed the opportunity if I had hesitated or carried myself poorly.

Mother wanted to know if the newly selected Imperial concubines would get along living together in the Forbidden City. I didn't want her to worry, so I told her that I had already made friends. I described Nuharoo's beauty, her admirable manners and knowledge. I also described Lady Yun. I didn't know much about her character or family background, so I concentrated on her beauty. I mentioned Lady Li as well. I described the difference in their characters. While Yun was daring and cared little about the opinions of others, Li wondered if she was the reason that people coughed.

Rong was a bit jealous when I mentioned Lady Soo, the youngest, who wept in front of the Majesties. Soo's sensitivity needed tenderness and care. She was an orphan, adopted by her uncle at the age of five, and she was obviously both sad and scared. The Grand Empress sent doctors to examine her; they concluded that she had a disturbed mind. Soo's weeping didn't stop after she was officially chosen. The eunuchs called her the Weeping Willow. The Grand Empress became concerned about the quality of the "eggs" that Soo would produce. "No quality eggs, no ladyship," she had said to all of us. If Soo continued to be who she was, Her Majesty would give her away.

"Poor child." My mother sighed.

I went on to speak of Lady Mei and Lady Hui, the two who looked like twins. They had less beauty but strong bodies. They were the Grand Empress's favorites. Their breasts were as big as melons and their buttocks were the size of washbasins. They were gifted in flattery and hovered around Nuharoo like pets. Cheerful and animated in front of the Grand Empress, they were wooden and silent by themselves. They didn't like to read, paint or do embroidery. Their only hobby was to dress alike.

"Did the Grand Empress Lady Jin look like the paintings we have seen, beautiful and elegant?"

"She must have been a beauty when young," I replied. "Today I would say that the pattern on her dress is more interesting than her looks."

"What was she like?" both Mother and Rong asked. "What does she expect from you?"

"That is a hard question. On the one hand, we are expected to follow the rules. 'As royal members,'" I mimicked Her Majesty, "'you are the models for our nation's morality. Your purity reflects our ancestors' teachings. If I catch you passing around books of a salacious nature, you will be hanged like those before you.' On the other hand, the Grand Empress expects us to mate with Emperor Hsien Feng as often as we can. She told us that her achievement will rest in the number of heirs we produce. The Emperor is expected to outperform his father and grandfather. Emperor Kang Hsi, Hsien Feng's great-great-grandfather, sired fifty-five children, and Emperor Chien Lung, Hsien Feng's grandfather, twenty-seven."

"That shouldn't be a problem." Kuei Hsiang smiled slyly as he threw a fistful of roasted nuts into his mouth. "His Majesty has more than three thousand ladies all to himself. I bet he can hardly make the rounds."

"But there are obstacles," I told Mother. Hsien Feng's performance in the Record Book of Imperial Fertility, a diary kept by Chief Eunuch Shim that traced His Majesty's bedchamber activity, was poor. The

Grand Empress had accused the Emperor of "deliberately wasting the dragon seeds." Too often, His Majesty was said to favor a single concubine, forgetting his duty to spread his seeds by sleeping with different ladies each night. The Grand Empress spoke angrily of past concubines who had been possessive of His Majesty. She saw them as "wicked-minded" and didn't hesitate to punish them severely.

I told Mother that the Grand Empress had taken us to the Hall of Punishment, where I saw for the first time the famous beauty Lady Fei. She used to be the favorite concubine of Emperor Tao Kuang, but now she lived in a jar. When I saw that Lady Fei had no limbs I almost fainted. "Lady Fei was caught having the Emperor all to herself, and she fooled nobody but herself," the Grand Empress said coldly. The only reason Lady Fei was kept alive was to serve as a warning.

I would never forget my horror that afternoon at the sight of Lady Fei. Her head rested on the rim of the jar, her face was filthy, and green mucus dripped from her chin.

Mother grabbed my shoulders. "Promise me, Orchid, that you will be careful and wise."

I nodded.

"What about the thousands of beauties selected?" Kuei Hsiang asked. "Is His Majesty encouraged to take ladies at a moment's interest? Can he take a maid who is a courtyard sweeper?"

"He can do anything he wants, although his mother doesn't encourage him to take courtyard sweepers," I answered.

Rong turned to Mother. "Why would His Majesty want a maid when he has beautiful wives and concubines?"

"I can only say that the Emperor might resent the fact that he doesn't get the chance to sleep every night with the woman he loves."

We went quiet for a while. "His Majesty probably hates the ladies forced on him by his mother and the eunuchs," Mother continued. "He must feel like a hog led by the nose."

"Orchid, what are you going to do?" Rong asked. "If you obey the rules, you will attract no attention from the Emperor; but if you try to be alluring, and His Majesty desires you, the Grand Empress may remove your limbs!"

"Let's go to the Temple of Mercy and consult your father's spirit," Mother said.

We had to climb hundreds of steps to reach the temple, on the top of Goose Mountain. We lit incense and paid the most expensive contribution. But I didn't receive any advice from my father's spirit. My mind was troubled, and I was very aware that I was on my own.

Father's grave was on the side of the mountain facing the northwest part of Peking. His coffin lay under knee-high grass. The graveyard keeper was an old man who smoked a clay pipe. He told us not to worry about robbers. "The dead are known for their debts in this area," he said, and advised that the best way to pay our father respect was to purchase a lot higher up on the hillside, in the sunnier area.

I gave fifty taels to the man and asked him to guard my father from wild dogs, who dug up the bodies for food. The man was so shocked by my generosity that he dropped his pipe.

Gifts in huge boxes from the Imperial palace arrived. Every inch of our house was filled. The boxes were piled on the tables and beds. There was no place to sit or sleep. Still the gifts kept pouring in. One morning, six Mongolian horses were delivered. There were paintings, antiques, bolts of silk and embroidery from Soochow. Besides magnificent jewelry, splendid garments and headwear and shoes were given to me. My mother was given gold tea sets, silver pots and copper basins.

The neighbors were ordered to lend us their homes for storage. Large pits were dug in the ground around the neighborhood to serve as coolers, to stock meat and vegetables for the coming celebration banquet. Hundreds of jars of century-old wine were ordered, plus eighty lambs, sixty pigs and two hundred chickens and ducks.

On the eighth of the month the banquet was held. The head eunuch, who was in charge, invited a thousand people, among them nobles, ministers, court officials and Imperial relatives. Each guest was served twenty courses, and the meal lasted three days.

My time, though, was unbearable. I could hear the singing, laughing and shouting of drunkards through the walls, but I was not allowed to join the banquet. I was no longer permitted even to expose myself to light. I was shut in a room decorated with red and gold ribbons. Dry squashes painted with children's faces were hung around the room, and I was told to stare at the faces to boost my fertility.

My mother brought me food and water, and my sister came to keep me company. My brother was being trained by the head eunuch to perform my father's duty—to see me off when the day came. Every six hours, a messenger sent by the Emperor updated my family on what was going on in the Forbidden City.

I didn't learn until later that Nuharoo had been the choice not only of the Grand Empress but of the clan elders as well. The decision that she would be the Empress had actually been made a year before. It had taken the court eight months of debate to reach the conclusion. The honorary treatment given Nuharoo's family was five times what mine received. She was going to enter the Forbidden City through the center gate while the rest of us would go through a side gate.

Many years later people would say that I was jealous of Nuharoo, but I wasn't at the time. I was overwhelmed by my own good fortune. I couldn't forget the flies covering my father's coffin and my mother's having to sell her hairpin. I couldn't forget the fact that I had been engaged to cousin Ping. I couldn't thank Heaven enough for what was happening to me.

In the small red room I wondered what my future would hold. I had so many questions regarding how to live my life as Emperor Hsien Feng's fourth concubine. But my biggest question was, who is Emperor Hsien Feng? As a bride and groom we hadn't even spoken.

I dreamed about becoming His Majesty's favorite. I was sure that all the concubines dreamed the same dream. Would there be harmony? Would it be possible for His Majesty to distribute his essence equally among us?

My experience growing up in the Yehonala household offered no help in preparing my way. My father had had no concubines. "He couldn't afford one," Mother once joked. In fact my father didn't need one—he couldn't get enough of my mother. I used to think that this was the way it should be, a man and a woman entirely devoted to each other. No matter how much they might suffer, having each other was happiness itself. This was the theme of my favorite operas. Characters survived to enjoy the rewards of a happy ending. My hopes had been high until Cousin Ping was pushed into my face. Now my life seemed to be gliding on a piece of watermelon skin—I had no idea where it would lead me. Trying to keep a balance was all I could do.

Big Sister Fann used to say that in real life, marriage was a market in which women competed for the highest bidder. And like any business, no one should confuse a rabbit with a squirrel—your worth says who you are.

The day my father died, I learned to separate wishful thinking from reality when his former friends turned up to reclaim a debt. I also learned something from my uncle by the way he treated us. Mother once told me that one had to lower one's head when passing under low eaves in order to avoid injury. "Wishful thinking does not give me dignity," Big Sister Fann used to say. "There is not one mother in the world who is happy to sell her child, but she sells her."

My uncle and Cousin Ping came to see me, and they had to get down on their knees. When Uncle bowed and called me Your Majesty, Ping laughed. "Father, that's Orchid!" The head eunuch slapped his face before Ping finished the phrase.

It was too late for Uncle to mend our relationship. He was nice only because he wanted to benefit from my status. He forgot too quickly what he had done. It was unfortunate, because I would have loved to help him.

Rong came to me as soon as Uncle and Ping stepped out. After rambling for a long time, she came to the point. "If you see any possibility, Orchid, I would like to marry a prince or a minister of the court." I promised that I would keep my eyes open for her. She held me and wept. My parting was harder on her than on me.

June 26, 1852, had been announced as the wedding day of His Majesty Emperor Hsien Feng. The night before, Kuei Hsiang had taken a walk through the streets of Peking and was excited by what he saw.

"There are celebrations everywhere," my brother reported. "Every family has hung a large ceremonial lantern in front of its door. Fireworks are being shot from the rooftops. People are dressed in bright red and green. The main boulevards are decorated with lanterns for miles and miles. All the couplets hanging in the air read, 'We wish the Imperial union to be an everlasting one!'"

The Forbidden City started its celebration at dawn. Gate-to-gate red carpets were laid for receiving the brides and guests. From the Gate of Zenith to the Palace of Supreme Harmony, from the Palace of Heavenly Purity to the Palace of Universal Plenty, there were hundreds of thousands of red silk lanterns. The lanterns were decorated with the images of stars and battle axes. Also hung were umbrellas made of apricot-colored satin embroidered with lotus flowers. Columns and beams were draped with red silk embroidered with the character *shee,* happiness.

This morning tables were set in the cavernous Hall of Celestial Purity, where the Record Book of Imperial Marriages was placed. Two Imperial orchestras set up outside the hall—one to the east and the other to the west. Ceremonial flags filled the hall. From the Gate of Eternal Harmony to the Gate of Zenith, about a three-mile distance, twenty-eight palanquins waited, ready to fetch the brides from their homes.

The palanquin that was to carry me was the largest I'd ever seen. There were windows on three sides, covered with red cloth embroidered with a *shee*. The roof over the chair was laced with golden threads. On top of the roof were two small stage-like platforms. On one stood two golden peacocks, each holding in its beak a red brush—the symbol of the highest authority, intelligence and virtue. On the second stood four gold phoenixes—symbols of beauty and femininity. In the center of the roof was the Ball of Harmony—the symbol of unity and infinity. I was to be accompanied by one hundred eunuchs, eighty court ladies and two thousand guards of honor.

I woke before dawn and was surprised to see my room full of people. My mother was kneeling in front of me. Behind her were eight women. I had been notified of their coming the night before. They were *manfoos,* Imperial ladies of honor, the wives of well-respected clansmen. They came at Emperor Hsien Feng's request to help me dress for the ceremony.

I tried to keep a cheerful face, but tears welled up in my eyes.

The *manfoos* begged to learn what was bothering me.

I said, "It's hard for me to rise when my mother is on her knees."

"Orchid, you must learn to get used to the etiquette," Mother said. "You are Lady Yehonala now. Your mother is honored to consider herself your servant."

"It's time for Your Majesty's bath," one of the *manfoos* said.

"May I now rise, Lady Yehonala?" Mother asked.

"Rise! Please!" I cried, and jumped off the bed.

Slowly Mother rose. It was obvious that her knees were killing her.

The ladies of honor quickly moved to a side room and started to prepare my bath.

Mother led me to the tub. It was a giant bucket, which had been delivered by the head eunuch. Mother closed the curtain and dipped her hand into the water to feel the temperature.

The *manfoos* offered to undress me. I pushed them away and insisted that I undress myself.

Mother stopped me. "Remember, it will be considered an embarrassment to His Majesty if you do any labor yourself."

"I'll follow the rules once I am inside the palace."

Mother wouldn't listen, and the *manfoos* finally stripped me, then excused themselves and retreated quietly.

Mother applied the soap to my skin. She started to rub my shoulders and back and ran her fingers through my black hair. It was the longest bath I had ever had. By her touch it felt as if she were having me to herself for the last time.

I studied her face: her skin pale as a radish, her neatly combed hair, the wrinkles spreading around her eyes. I wanted to get out of the tub and embrace her. I wanted to say, "Mother, I am not leaving!" I wanted her to know that without her there would be no happiness.

But I uttered not one word. I was afraid of disappointing her. I knew that in her mind I represented my father's dream and the honor of the entire Yehonala clan. The night before, the rules had been explained to me by the head eunuch. I would not be permitted to visit my mother after I entered the Forbidden City. Mother had to apply for and obtain permission to see me, but only in an emergency. The minister of the Imperial household had to verify whether the matter was urgent or serious enough before granting permission. The same rule applied if I wanted to leave the palace to visit my family.

The idea of not being able to see my family frightened me, and I began to cry.

"Chin up, Orchid." Mother took a towel and began to dry me. "You should be embarrassed for weeping like this."

I put my wet arms around her neck. "I hope that happiness shall enhance your health."

"Yes, yes." Mother smiled. "The tree of my longevity has shot up a foot since last night."

Rong entered the room dressed in a pale green silk robe with golden butterflies on it. She got down on her knees and bowed to me. Her voice was filled with delight when she said, "I am proud to be an Imperial relative."

Before I could speak with Rong, a eunuch outside announced, "Duke Kuei Hsiang is here to see Lady Yehonala."

"Honored." This time the words got out of my mouth smoothly.

My brother stumbled in. "Orchid—uh, Lady . . . Lady Yehonala, His uh . . . His Majesty Emperor Hsien Feng has . . ."

"On your knees first." Mother corrected his manners.

Kuei Hsiang clumsily adjusted his pose. His left foot caught the corner of his robe and he fell.

Rong and I started to giggle.

Kuei Hsiang made sloppy bows. His hands were folded below his chest, which made him look like he was nursing a stomachache.

"About one candle-time ago," Kuei Hsiang said after he settled himself, "His Majesty finished dressing and entered his dragon chair."

"What does his chair look like?" Rong asked with excitement.

"It has nine dragons under straight-handled canopies of yellow satin. His Majesty went to the Palace of Benevolence to meet with the Grand Empress. By now he should have completed the ceremony in the Hall of Supreme Harmony and should be inspecting the Record Book of Imperial Marriages. After that, he will receive congratulations from the ministers. And after that . . ."

A loud noise cracked the sky.

"The outer-court ceremony has begun!" Kuei Hsiang cried. "His Majesty must be putting his signature in the record book. In a moment he will be giving the order to the guards of honor to fetch the Imperial brides!"

I sat like a peony blooming in the morning light. My dress was a medley of many reds. Rich magenta spiked with yellow, wine sparked with cream, warm lavender spilling to nearly blue. The dress was constructed with eight layers of silk and was embroidered with vigorous spring flowers, real and imaginary. The fabric was woven with gold and silver threads. It bore large clusters of jade, pearls and other jewels. I had never worn anything so beautiful, or so heavy and uncomfortable.

My hair was piled a foot high and draped with pearls, jade, coral and diamonds. In the front were three large fresh-picked purple-pink peonies. I feared that it would all come loose and the ornaments would fall. I dared not move, and my neck already felt stiff. Eunuchs walked around and talked in low voices. Court officers whom I had never seen before filled the house. As if on a stage, everyone was dressed and moved according to an invisible script.

Mother kept grabbing the head eunuch's sleeves, asking repeatedly if something had gone wrong. Irritated, the eunuch sent his assistants, teenage boys, to distract her. The boys held her to a chair. They smiled and begged her not to give them a hard time.

The main room of the house had been cleared for the *chieh-an,* a table specially made to hold the Emperor's record book and the stone Imperial stamp. The left and right chambers were also cleared and set with tables for incense burners. In front of the tables were mats on which I would kneel when receiving the marriage decree. On each side of the mats stood eunuchs dressed in shiny yellow robes. I felt exhausted, but the head eunuch said we still had a long way to go before the ceremony would start.

Two candle-times passed. Finally I heard the sound of hooves. The eight ladies of honor quickly retouched my makeup. They sprayed me with a strong-scented perfume and checked my dress and headwear before helping me out of my chair.

As I lifted myself, I felt like a big rusty carriage. My jewel-laden belts clanked as they dragged over the chair and fell to the floor.

Imperial Guards and eunuchs filled the street. Kuei Hsiang, who had been waiting by the front gate, received His Majesty's ambassador. On his knees, Kuei Hsiang stated my father's name and recited a brief welcome speech. As he spoke, he knocked his forehead on the ground three times and bowed nine times. A moment later I heard my name called by the ambassador. The ladies of honor quickly formed a wall on either side of me. I stepped out the door and moved slowly toward the *chieh-an.*

Standing before me was a rabbit-faced eunuch in heavy makeup. He was the ambassador, dressed in a glittering yellow gown. On his hat was a peacock feather and a red diamond. He avoided looking at me. After offering me three deep bows, he "invited in" three objects. One was a little yellow case from which he took a yellow silk scroll. It was the decree. The second one was the Record Book of Imperial Marriages. The last one was a stone stamp with my name and title carved on the surface.

Following the eunuch, I performed the ceremony in front of the tables. I bowed and knocked my forehead on the ground so many times that I became dizzy. I worried that things would start to fall from my hair. After this, I received blessings from my family.

My mother came first, followed by Rong, my uncle and Cousin Ping. They got down on their knees and bowed to the ambassador and then to me. Mother trembled so much that one of her headpieces began to slide from its place.

"Rise," I quickly said, trying to stop the piece from slipping.

The eunuchs carried the record book and the stone stamp over to the incense-burner tables. The eunuchs seemed to strain under their weight.

I took off my satin cape as the etiquette instructed and bowed toward the book and the stamp. Afterward I stayed in the kneeling position and turned to face north.

The ambassador opened the scroll and began to read from the decree. He had a deep, resonant voice, but I couldn't understand a word he said. It took me a while to realize that he was reading the decree in two languages, Manchu and Mandarin, both in stylized ancient tones. My father once told me that when he worked in his office, he usually skipped the Manchu parts of reports and moved directly to the Chinese parts to save time.

The weight on my head made me feel like I was a snail carrying a house on my back. As the reading went on I glanced toward the hallway. It was packed with guards. On the center terrace two palanquins were waiting. Why two, I wondered. Wasn't I the only one to be picked up from this house?

When the ambassador finished his reading I discovered the reason for the second palanquin. The eunuchs put the decree, the record book and the stone stamp back into their cases. Then these objects were "invited" to "sit" in the second palanquin. The ambassador explained that these things were now considered part of me.

"The Imperial phoenix walking!" At the ambassador's call my family fell to their knees for the last time. By now Mother's makeup was a mess, and she wiped her tears with her hands, forgetting her appearance.

A band started to play. The sound of Chinese trumpets was so loud that my ears hurt. A group of eunuchs ran in front of me throwing firecrackers. I stepped on "cracked" red paper, yellow straws, green beans and colorful dried fruit. I tried to hold my chin up so my headwear would stay in place.

I was gently ushered into my palanquin. Now I was a real snail. With a motion that nearly knocked me from my seat, the bearers hoisted the chair.

Outside the gate the horses had begun to move. Bannermen carried dragon flags and yellow umbrellas. Among them were lady riders dressed in sixteenth-century Manchu warrior costumes. Hanging from the sides of their mounts were yellow ribbons tied to cooking ware.

Behind the ladies was a flock of animals dyed red. It seemed like a rolling river of blood. When I looked again, I saw sheep and geese. It was said that these animals symbolized fortune well kept, and the red the passion for life.

I let down the curtain to hide my tears. I was preparing myself to not see my family for a long time. This was what Mother wanted, I convinced myself. A poem she read to me when I was little came to mind:

> *Like a singing river*
> *You break out to flow freely*
> *I am the mountain behind*

Happily I watch you
Memory of us
Full and sweet

My memories were full and sweet indeed. They were all I had, and I was taking them with me. As soon as I felt that the palanquin was moving steadily, I opened a slit in the back curtain and looked out.

My family was no longer in sight. Dust and ceremonial guards blocked my view.

Suddenly I saw Kuei Hsiang. He was still on all fours with his head glued to the ground.

My heart betrayed me and I cracked like a Chinese lute broken in the middle of its happy playing.

Six

I DIDN'T GET TO SEE much of the celebration the day I became an Imperial concubine. I sat inside my palanquin and heard the bells struck from the towers of the Gate of Zenith.

Nuharoo was the only one who went through the Gate of Celestial Purity, the main entrance into the Imperial backyard. The rest of us were carried through courtyards from side gates. My palanquin crossed the Golden Water River on one of the five bridges that spanned it. The river marked the boundary of the forbidden landscape; the bridges each represented one of the five Confucian virtues: loyalty, tenacity, honesty, modesty and piety. I then passed through the Gate of Correct Conduct and entered another courtyard, the largest in the Forbidden City. My palanquin skirted the Throne Hall, whose enormous carved columns and magnificent tiered roof rose above the pure expanse of white marble of the Dragon Pavement Terrace.

I was let off at the Gate of Heavenly Bustling. By this time it was midafternoon. Other palanquins had arrived. They were the chairs of Ladies Yun, Li, Soo, Mei and Hui. The girls got out quietly. We acknowledged one another's presence and then waited.

Eunuchs came to tell us that Emperor Hsien Feng and Empress Nuharoo had begun the wedding ceremony.

It felt strange. Although it had been made more than clear to me that I was only one of Emperor Hsien Feng's three thousand ladies, I couldn't help but wish that I were in Nuharoo's place.

Soon the head eunuch reappeared and informed us that it was time to go to our own living quarters. Mine was called the Palace of Concentrated Beauty, where I would live for many years. It was here that I learned that Emperor Hsien Feng would never distribute his essence equally among his wives.

The Palace of Concentrated Beauty was embraced by age-old trees. When the wind blew, the leaves would roar. The sound reminded me of my favorite poetic line: "The wind shows its body through the trembling leaves." I tried to locate the gate I had come through. It was on the west side and seemed to be the only entrance. The building in front of me was like a temple, with a wing-like roof and high walls. Under the yellow glazed tiles the beams and columns were brightly painted. The doors and window panels were carved with symbols of fertility: round-shaped fruit, vegetables, Buddha's hand, budding flowers, ocean waves and clouds.

A group of well-dressed men and women quietly appeared in the courtyard. They threw themselves at me and got down on their knees.

I looked at them and didn't know what was expected of me.

"The lucky moment is here, Lady Yehonala," one of them finally said. "Please allow us to help you into your chamber." I realized that they were my servants.

I lifted my robe and was about to take a step when I heard a tremendous noise beyond the walls.

My legs nearly gave out and the servants rushed to hold me up. I was told that the sound was from a Chinese gong. This was the moment when Emperor Hsien Feng and Empress Nuharoo entered the Grand Nuptial Chamber.

I had heard about Imperial wedding rituals from Big Sister Fann. I was familiar with the nuptial bed and its sun-colored gauze curtain, covered with fertility designs. I remembered Fann's description of the bright yellow satin quilt, which was embroidered with a hundred children playing.

Many years later Nuharoo told me that the scent in the Imperial chamber was the sweetest she had ever known. The smell came from the nuptial bed itself, which was made of fragrant sandalwood. She described how she was received. She had three golden phoenixes on her head, and she was accompanied by Chief Eunuch Shim, who carried her insignia.

After she stepped down from her palanquin, she walked through the Hall of Maternal Blessing. She then entered the nuptial chamber, which was in the Palace of Earthly Tranquility. It was in this sweet-smelling room that Nuharoo changed her costume from cool yellow to warm. With a piece of sun-colored silk over her head and eyes, she pledged herself to Emperor Hsien Feng and drank from the wedding cup.

"The walls of the chamber were so red that I thought something had gone wrong with my eyes," Nuharoo recalled years later, smiling. "The room felt empty because it was extremely large. On its north side were the thrones, and on the south a great red brick bed was warmed by a fire underneath."

I had correctly imagined it all. The setting and ritual matched Nuharoo's account. But while I was living it, I merely tried to survive the moment. I was not prepared for my own disappointment.

I told myself that I had no reason to weep. I told myself that it was greedy of me to feel that I needed more than what was granted. Yet sadness refused to leave me. I tried to picture Ping and his disgusting opium-stained teeth. But my mind went on its own path. It brought me the melody of my favorite opera, *The Love of Little Jade*—the story of a housemaiden and her soldier lover. When I thought of how the soldier brought his bride a piece of soap as a wedding gift and how happy it made her feel, my tears ran.

Why did my eyes fail to find pleasure in this room filled with treasure? My servants dressed me in a gorgeous apricot-colored satin robe dotted with sweet plum blossoms—a dress I had worn many times in my dreams. I walked toward the dressing mirror and saw an astonishing beauty. On my head was a dragonfly hairpin inlaid with rubies, sapphires, pearls, tourmalines, tiger-eyes and kingfisher feathers. I turned around and looked at the room's furnishings, its mosaic panels of gems and abundant harvests. On my left were cabinets of red sandalwood ornamented with jade and precious stones, on my right a rosewood washstand inlaid with mother-of-pearl. Behind me were bed screens made of the most valuable ancient paintings.

My heart shouts: *What else would you, could you, dare you want, Orchid?*

I was cold, but I was told to leave my door open during the day. I sat down on my bed, covered with a beige spread. Eight folded comforters made of the finest silk and cotton were stacked against the wall. The floor-length bed curtains were embroidered with white wisteria. The red border had pink and green peonies on it.

I saw Chief Eunuch Shim walk by my window with a group of young eunuchs following him. "Why are the lanterns not lit?" He was displeased. Then he saw me through the window. With a humble smile on his face Chief Eunuch Shim got down on his knees and said, "Lady Yehonala, your slave Shim at your service."

"Rise, please." I stepped out into the yard.

"Have the slaves introduced themselves, Lady Yehonala?" Shim asked, still on his knees.

"Not yet," I replied.

"They should be punished, then. It is their duty." He rose and snapped his fingers.

Two large-framed eunuchs appeared, each holding a leather whip longer than a man.

I was confused. I didn't know what Chief Eunuch Shim intended to do.

"The guilty ones, line up!" he ordered.

Trembling, my servants lined up.

Two buckets of water were brought. The large eunuchs dipped their whips in them.

"Chief Shim," I called. "Please understand that it is not my servants' fault that they haven't introduced themselves. I was not ready until now."

"Are you forgiving your slaves?" Chief Eunuch Shim asked, a wicked smile crossing his face. "You should expect nothing less than perfection from your slaves, Lady Yehonala. The slaves must be punished. The Forbidden City tradition can be summed up in six words: Respect comes out of a whip."

"I am sorry, Chief Shim. I can't see myself whipping anyone who did no wrong." I regretted the slip of my tongue, but it was too late.

"I am sure the servants *are* guilty." Shim was annoyed. He turned around and kicked a young eunuch.

I felt violated and retreated to my room.

Chief Eunuch Shim took his time to reveal the purpose of his visit. We were in my sitting room with more than twenty servants and eunuchs present. With an air of concerned patience he explained to me how the Forbidden City was run. He introduced the various departments and craft shops, most of which seemed to fall under his authority. He was in charge of the departments that supervised the vaults of gold and silver bullion, furs, porcelain, silk and tea; he was also responsible for those who provided the court with the sacrificial animals, grain and fruit for religious ceremonies. He controlled the eunuchs who looked after the kennels where Pekingese were bred. He oversaw the departments that maintained the palaces, temples, gardens and herb farms.

I stood with my back straight and my chin slightly raised. Even if Chief Shim was merely displaying his own power, I was glad to be informed. Besides the locations of the courts and the schools that educated the princes, he told me about the Imperial armory, which served as the palace police. "My duties extend to the Imperial buttery, the Imperial weaving and dye shops, also the bureaus that take care of the Emperor's boats, wardrobes, games, the printing offices, the libraries, the silkworm and honey farms."

Of all the departments, the royal theatricals interested me the most. Also the Imperial craft workshops, which produced the work of China's most talented artists and craftsmen.

"I have many responsibilities," Chief Eunuch Shim concluded. "But above all, I exist to safeguard the authenticity of Emperor Hsien Feng's succession."

I realized that he expected me to acknowledge his power. "Guide me, Chief Shim, please," I began, "for I am a naïve girl from the countryside of Wuhu, and I shall be grateful for your advice and protection."

Satisfied with my manners, he revealed that he was here to fulfill two orders from my mother-in-law. First was to reward me with a cat.

"The days will be long for you, living in the Forbidden City," Chief Eunuch Shim said, waving for a eunuch to bring up a box. "And the cat will be your companion."

I opened the box and saw a beautiful white creature. "What is its name?" I asked.

"Snow," Shim replied. "It's a she, of course."

I gently picked up the cat. It had a pair of lovely tiger's eyes. It looked frightened. "Snow, welcome!"

Second, Chief Eunuch Shim notified me of my yearly allowance. "It will be five bars of gold, one thousand taels of silver, thirty bolts of satin, silk and cotton cloth, fifteen sheets of buffalo, sheep, snake and rabbit skin, and one hundred silver buttons. It sounds like a lot, but you will run short by the end of the year, because you are responsible for paying the salaries of your six eunuchs, six ladies in waiting, four maids and three chefs. The maids attend to your personal needs, while the eunuchs clean, garden and deliver messages. The eunuchs are also responsible for tending your sleep. For the first year they will take turns, with five sleeping outside your bedchamber and one inside. You will not get to pick the eunuch who will sleep in your room until the Grand Empress thinks you are ready."

The servants stared blankly at me. I had no idea what was on their minds.

"I have assigned you the best servants." Chief Eunuch Shim smiled a crooked smile. "The ones who snore I have given to Lady Mei, and the ones who are lazy I have given to Lady Hui. I have assigned the wicked ones to Lady Yun and . . ." He glanced at me and paused, as if expecting me to say something.

It was the court's unspoken tradition to reward a eunuch for such a display of loyalty. This of course I knew, but my mistrust of Shim prevented me from seizing the opportunity. I wondered what he would say about me in front of Nuharoo and Ladies Yun, Li, Soo, Mei and Hui. I was sure he had enough tricks in his bag to fool everybody.

"May I know the treatment of His Majesty's other wives?" I asked. "Where will they be living?"

"Well, Empress Nuharoo will spend the remainder of this week with Emperor Hsien Feng in the Palace of Earthly Tranquility. She will then move to the Palace of Reception of Heaven to live. Lady Yun has been given the Palace of Universal Inheritance, Lady Li the Palace of Eternal Peace, Lady Mei the Palace of Great Mercy and Lady Hui the Palace of Prolonging Happiness."

"What about Soo?"

"Lady Soo has been sent back to her parents in the south. Her health needs to be attended to. The Palace of Pleasant Sunshine is reserved for her when she returns."

"Why are the other ladies' palaces all located on the east side of the Forbidden City? Who else besides me lives on the west side?"

"You are the only one who lives on the west side, Lady Yehonala."

"May I know why?"

Chief Eunuch Shim lowered his voice to a whisper. "My lady, you may get yourself in trouble by asking too many questions. However, I am willing to risk losing my tongue to satisfy you. But first I need your total trust. May I have your word?"

I hesitated and then nodded.

Shim leaned toward me and placed his mouth near my earlobe. "It could be either Emperor Hsien Feng's or the Grand Empress's idea to place you where you are. You see, if it was the Grand Empress's idea . . . Forgive me, I am nervous about telling you this . . . Her Majesty has a habit of placing her favorites near her on the east side. It is for her convenience, so that she may summon them whenever she needs a companion."

"Are you saying that she disfavors me and doesn't want me near?"

"I didn't say that. You made the deduction yourself."

"Is it not true?"

"I won't answer that."

"What about Emperor Hsien Feng? What if it was his idea?"

"If the idea came from His Majesty, it is a sign that he adores you—therefore he wants you as far away from his mother as possible. In other words, he makes it inconvenient for the Grand Empress to spy on him if he decides to visit you. Go on and congratulate yourself, my lady."

Soon after he left, I sent a servant with two hundred taels of silver as a gift. It was a lot, but I felt it necessary. Without Chief Eunuch Shim I would be a blind person walking on a path filled with traps. Nonetheless, I sensed that he was a man to be feared.

Evening was coming on. The sky darkened. The leaves on the trees turned black, as if the green was stained with ink. The edges of the clouds wrinkled and folded out of one shape and into another. Crows returned to their nests on high branches. They sounded shrill, as if their day had been hard.

I called in my servants and said that I would like to have dinner. The eunuchs and ladies in waiting bowed and took my order to the kitchen. The last eunuch in the line didn't rise. He stayed on his knees demanding attention. I was annoyed and told him to remove himself.

But when he raised his eyes, I recognized him. He was the young eunuch I had met on the day of my selection, the one who had brought me water.

"An-te-hai?" I called, almost excitedly.

"Yes, my lady!" He answered with equal enthusiasm. "An-te-hai, your faithful slave."

I stood and offered him both of my arms.

He pushed himself a few steps back, reminding me of my status.

I sat back down and we both smiled.

"So, An-te-hai, what do you want?"

"Lady Yehonala, I understand that you can order my death any time if my words upset you. But there is something I must say."

"You have my permission."

He hesitated and then raised his gaze to look me directly in the eye.

"I am good for you," he said.

"That I already know."

"Will you make me your first attendant?"

I stood up. "How dare you make such a request when I've just arrived."

An-te-hai knocked his forehead on the ground. "Punish me, Lady Yehonala." He raised his hand and began to slap his cheeks left and right.

I didn't know what to do. He kept on, as if what he was slapping was some other face, not his own.

"Enough!" I yelled.

The eunuch stopped. He looked at me with a strange longing, his eyes filling with the tears of a worshiper.

"What makes you think you can serve me better than the others?" I asked.

An-te-hai raised his eyes from the floor and said, "Because I offer what others don't."

"And what is that?"

"Advice, my lady. In my humble opinion, time and luck are not necessarily on your side at the moment. My advice can help you get ahead in this place. I am an expert on Imperial etiquette, for example."

"You are very confident, An-te-hai."

"I am the best in the Forbidden City."

"How would I confirm this?"

"Test me, my lady. You will find out."

"How many years has it been since you entered the Forbidden City?"

"Four years."

"What have you achieved?"

"A belief, my lady."

"A belief?"

"It is that the big melon I carry between my shoulders is a tough one. I have equipped myself with knowledge of Imperial society. I know the names of the builders of the Forbidden City, the Summer Palace and the Grand Round Garden. I know their locations even on the astrological map. I can explain why there are no trees planted between the Palaces of Supreme Harmony, Central Harmony and Preserving Harmony."

"Keep going, An-te-hai."

"Concubines of Emperor Hsien Feng's father and grandfather are my friends. They live in the Palace of Benevolent Tranquility. I know each of their stories and their relationship to His Majesty. I can tell you how the palace gets its heat in the winter and how it stays cool in the summer. I can tell you where your drinking water is from. I am familiar with the Forbidden City's murders and ghosts, the stories behind the mysterious outbreaks of fire and sudden disappearances of people. I know the sentinels at the gates, and I am a personal friend of many of the guards, which means that I can go in and out of the palaces like a cat."

I tried not to show that I was impressed.

He told me that Emperor Hsien Feng had two beds in his bedroom. Each night, both beds were made and the curtains drawn so no one would know in which bed His Majesty lay. An-te-hai let me know that his knowledge extended beyond the Imperial household, to the outer court and the functioning of the government. His secret for gaining information was to lead everyone to believe that he was harmless.

"So you are a natural spy."

"For you, my lady, I'm willing to be anything."

"How old are you exactly?"

"I'll be sixteen in a few months."

"What is the truth behind this proposal, An-te-hai?"

The eunuch paused for a moment and then answered, "I want a chance. I have been looking for a worthy master for a long time. As a eunuch, I understand that I ought not to think about my future, because there isn't any. But I don't want to live in hell for the rest of my life. All I am asking, my lady, is to be given an opportunity to prove my loyalty."

"Rise," I said. "Leave me now, An-te-hai."

He rose and quietly stepped back toward the door.

I noticed that he was limping a bit, and I remembered that he was the one Chief Eunuch Shim had kicked in the courtyard.

"Wait," I called. "From now on, An-te-hai, you'll be my first attendant."

I changed into a beige robe before I was ushered to my eating chair. My dining table was as big as my gate. The carvings on its surface and legs were remarkable. As I was waiting to be served, I learned the names of my eunuchs and ladies in waiting.

My eunuchs had unique names. They were Ho-tung, River of the East; Ho-nan, River of the South; Ho-tz'u, River of the West; Ho-pei,

River of the North; Ho-yuan, Riverhead; and Ho-wei, River End. Although their names began with *ho,* which meant "river," they were by no means related. The names of several of my ladies in waiting began with *chun,* meaning "spring." They were Chun-cheng, Spring Dawn; Chun-hsia, Spring Sunset; Chun-yueh, Spring Moon; Chun-meng, Spring Dream. All of them were reasonably good-looking and clean. They answered my calls promptly and demonstrated no particular characteristics. Their hair was done in a uniform style. While the eunuchs wore queues, the ladies wore buns on the back of their heads. In my presence, they kept their hands by their thighs and their eyes fixed on the floor.

I sat at the giant table for so long, surrounded by eunuchs and ladies in waiting, that my stomach started grumbling. Dinner was still nowhere to be seen. I turned my attention to the hall. It was large and empty of warmth except for the opposite wall, where hung a painting depicting a village family. A lovely poem was written in its upper right corner.

> *The thatched roof is slanting low,*
> *Beside the brook green grasses grow,*
> *Who talks with a drunken southern voice so sweet?*
> *A gray-haired man and wife in their retreat.*
>
> *East of the brook their eldest son is hoeing weeds;*
> *Their second son now makes a cage for hens he feeds.*
> *I like their youngest son, who, having nothing to do,*
> *Lies by the brook podding lotus seeds one by one.*

Who had lived here before me? I wondered. She must have been one of the Imperial concubines of the late Emperor Tao Kuang. She must have loved paintings. The style was simple, refreshing. I marveled at the contrast between the grand setting and the humble image.

The painting reminded me of the warmth of my own family. I remembered when my sister, brother and I would gather at the dinner table to await our father's arrival. I remembered a time when our father cracked a joke. When we all burst into laughter, rice sprayed out our mouths. Rong choked on her tofu soup, and my brother fell under the table and broke his ceramic bowl. My mother failed to maintain her composure. She too burst into laughter, calling her husband "a crooked beam that leads the house to fall."

"Your dinner's here, my lady." An-te-hai's voice woke me from the memory.

As if in fantasy, I saw a parade coming out of the kitchen. A line of eunuchs, each holding a steaming dish, moved gracefully toward me. The pots and terrines were covered with silver lids. Soon the table was full of dishes.

I counted the dishes. The number was ninety-nine!

Ninety-nine dishes just for me?

An-te-hai announced what I was served: "Stewed bear claws, vegetables mixed with deer liver, fried lobster with soybean sauce, snails with cucumbers and garlic, marinated quail roasted with sweet-and-sour sauce, shredded tiger meat wrapped in pancakes, deer blood with ginseng and herbs, crispy duck skin dipped in spicy onion sauce, pork, beef, chicken, seafood . . ."

There were dishes I had never seen or heard of.

The parade went on. My servants' expressions told me that this was ordinary. I tried to hide my shock. After the plates were set down, I waved my hand. The servants retreated and stood quietly against the walls.

I felt awkward facing the monstrous table.

"We wish you a great meal!" my servants sang in one voice.

I lifted my chopsticks.

"Not yet, my lady." An-te-hai rushed to my side.

The eunuch went around the table with a pair of chopsticks and a small plate. He picked pieces from every dish and stuffed them into his mouth.

As I watched An-te-hai chewing, I was reminded of the story Big Sister Fann had told me about Emperor Hsien Feng's mother, Chu An, who attempted to poison Prince Kung. The thought took away my appetite.

"It's safe to dine now." An-te-hai wiped his mouth and stepped away from the table.

"Am I supposed to eat all this by myself?" I asked.

"You are not expected to, my lady. It is the court's etiquette that you are served with ninety-nine dishes at each meal."

"But it is a big waste!"

"No, you won't waste a thing, my lady. You can always reward dishes to your attendants. The slaves are hungry, and they are never given enough to eat."

"Will people mind?"

"No. They will feel honored."

"Doesn't the kitchen prepare food for you as well?"

"We eat what horses eat, only the amount is meager by comparison. Three yams a day is my share."

I finished as much as I could. I heard the sound of my jaw crunching cucumbers, chewing bear tendons and sucking on pork ribs. The servants continued to look at their feet. I wondered again what was cooking inside their heads. As I became full, I put down my chopsticks and picked up my dessert, a sweet bun made of red beans and black sesame.

An-te-hai came near, as if he knew I had something to say.

"I don't feel like having people staring at me while I am eating," I said. "Is there any way I can dismiss them?"

"No, my lady, I am afraid not."

"Are mistresses of other palaces being served the same way?"

"Yes, they are."

"By the same kitchen?"

"No, by their own kitchens. Each palace has its own kitchen and chefs."

"Please get a stool and come and keep me company while I am eating."

An-te-hai obeyed.

When I picked up a cup, An-te-hai reached for the teapot on the far corner of the table. He filled my cup with chrysanthemum tea.

It didn't take long for me to see that An-te-hai had a gift for anticipating my needs. Who was he? I wondered. What had caused a sweet and clever boy like him to become a eunuch? What was his family like? How had he grown up?

"My lady." As I finished the last bite of the bun, An-te-hai leaned over. His voice was soft. "It might be a good idea for you to send a message to Emperor Hsien Feng and Empress Nuharoo to wish them a good dinner."

"Wouldn't Nuharoo want her time with Emperor Hsien Feng undisturbed?" I asked.

From An-te-hai's silent response, I realized that I'd better follow his advice.

"It is not about sending a good wish," An-te-hai explained after a beat. "It is to make an impression. It is to have your name appear on one of Emperor Hsien Feng's bamboo message chips. It is to remind His Majesty of your existence. The other ladies in their palaces are doing the same."

"How do you know?"

"I have sworn brothers who report to me from all the palaces."

I rinsed my mouth with a cup of green tea. I was supposed to nap after a meal, but my mind wouldn't relax. I visualized a battle in which every concubine was a soldier in disguise. According to An-te-hai, my rivals had already started to build defenses. Many of them had presented the Grand Empress with small but thoughtful gifts, thanking her for selecting them.

I hoped that Emperor Hsien Feng was a man of fairness. After all, he was called the wisest man in the universe. I would be satisfied if he would summon me once a month. I would never expect to have him all to myself. I would take pride in helping him build the dynasty, like the virtuous women displayed in the Imperial portrait gallery. Providing His Majesty with a harmonious home was an appealing idea. I would like to see the seven of us unite against the rest of the court-lady population. As the chosen wives I saw us respecting and helping one another in the interest of making the household a home for us all.

An-te-hai didn't say that he disagreed with me. But I came to know his feelings by the way he knocked his head on the floor. If the sound of his knocking was *tunk, tunk, tunk,* which meant a slight disagreement, we would have a discussion. But if it was *ponk, ponk, ponk,* I'd better listen, because that meant I had no idea what I was talking about. This time the sound was *ponk, ponk, ponk.* An-te-hai tried to convince me that the ladies in the other palaces were my natural enemies. "It is like bugs to plants—they need to eat you to survive." He suggested that I work on gaining the upper hand. "Somebody is thinking about strangling you at this very moment," he said.

I could hardly move when the eunuchs came to clear the dinner table. My nap forgotten, the next thing I was expected to do was bathe. My tub was set three feet above the floor like a stage, with hot and cold water buckets and stacks of towels around it. The tub was so big it would be called a pond in my village. It was made of fine wood in the shape of a giant lotus leaf. The painting on the tub was beautiful. The details of the lotus flower were astonishingly vivid.

I wasn't in the habit of bathing daily. In Wuhu I washed myself once every couple of months during the winter, and I swam in the lake in the summer. I asked An-te-hai if I could swim in the Imperial lake when the weather got warm.

"No," the eunuch replied. "His Majesty wants his ladies' bodies covered at all times."

The ladies in waiting announced that the bath was ready.

An-te-hai told me that I had a choice of being bathed by either the eunuchs or the maids. Of course the maids, I said. It would be awkward to expose my body to eunuchs. By appearance they looked no different from ordinary men. I couldn't imagine them touching my body. It would take me a while to get used to An-te-hai sleeping at the foot of my bed.

I wondered if An-te-hai had a man's needs. He seemed to be indifferent during my changing. Was he pretending? If so, he must have great discipline. What I was beginning to like about him was that he managed to rise above his personal tragedy. Perhaps I spoiled my eunuchs, a weakness many considered evil. I couldn't help but feel for their suffering. The truth was that I myself desired the same compassion.

Women in China dreamed about becoming me without knowing my suffering. By identifying with the eunuchs, I tended my heart's wound. The eunuchs' pain was written on their faces. They had been gelded and everyone understood their misfortune. But mine was hidden.

It felt funny to be held by so many hands. These people begged me not to lift a finger. If I were to help myself in any way, it would be considered an insult.

The water was warm and soothing. As I lay against the rim of the tub, the maids got down on their knees. Three of them threw their hands on me at the same time. They rubbed and scrubbed. I was supposed to enjoy this, but my mind kept seeing a hen being dipped in hot water and then her feathers being pulled off.

The maids' hands moved up and down my body. Although they were gentle, my body suffered intrusion. I tried to remember what An-te-hai had told me, that I lived to please Emperor Hsien Feng, not myself. I wished that the Emperor could see this. I wondered when he would appear.

My body fermented like a steamed bun. The maids were sweating. They had been massaging my shoulders, fingers and toes. Their robes were wet, their hair messy. Just watching them tired me, and I couldn't wait for this to end. An-te-hai had warned me that I was not to thank my maids. He emphasized that I was not to express my feelings. I must not remind people that I was as ordinary as they were.

After they patted me dry and dressed me in a red nightgown, the maids retreated. The eunuchs then wrapped me in warm blankets and ushered me back to my bedroom.

. . .

My palace was divided into three areas. The first was the living quarters, which included three large rooms with windows facing south. The rooms were connected in a rectangular shape. The middle room was a receiving hall, with a small-scale throne for my husband to sit on when he came. Behind the throne, against the wall stood an altar. Above the altar was a large Chinese landscape painting. The left chamber was called the western chamber. This was where I slept. There was a table with two chairs on the side by the window. Two green bamboo plants stood next to the chairs. On the right was the eastern chamber. This was my dressing room. It had a bed in it. I would sleep there if His Majesty decided to stay overnight. The rule stated that in order for him to have a proper sleep, he must not share a bed with any of his wives through the night. The bed in the eastern chamber was always prepared, cooled or warmed according to the season. Behind these chambers were my dining room, bathroom, sitting room and storage rooms.

The second part of my palace was the garden, which would become my favorite spot. It had natural meadows and creeks and also a tiny pond called the Heavenly Lake. I purposely let the water reeds grow wild in it because I liked to be reminded of Wuhu. I had always adored plants and was a passionate gardener. I filled my garden with nature's splendor. Besides large flower-bearing trees like red silk-cotton and magnolia, I had bowl-sized peonies in every color imaginable. I also had deep red roses with purple hearts, hoof-shaped white lilies, fire-colored mountain tea flowers and yellow winter plum flowers, which I called "leg-pullers." Plum flowers had waxy petals and bloomed only on snowy days, as if they loved the cold. Their strong scent wafted into my bedroom in the morning when An-te-hai opened the window. They "pulled my legs" to the garden, and I couldn't help but admire their beauty while still in my pajamas. To prevent me from catching a cold on freezing days, An-te-hai would cut a branch of winter plum before I rose, or put a single flower in a vase by my breakfast table.

My taste in flowers was broad. I loved the elegant ones as well as those that I called "the small people." I loved butterfly-shaped morning glories, tiger-faced purple ground cover. My expertise was in peonies and chrysanthemums. Although royal society considered chrysanthemums fit only for peasants, I grew them enthusiastically. I had every kind of chrysanthemum. "Golden Claws" was the one I prized the most. Its blossoms opened like dancers' hands, holding the morning sunlight in their palms. No one had ever seen this variety anywhere else but in my garden. The plants shot up to my shoulders in late autumn, and I never tired of looking at them.

I visited my garden when I was unable to sleep at night. I came to listen to the sounds of my childhood. I could hear the fish talking in the water. I wandered around the bushes with my hands brushing the leaves and flowers. I loved to feel the dew on my fingertips.

Many years later a story was told about a eunuch who once witnessed a fairy in my garden at midnight. The "fairy" was probably me. There was a period during which I felt I was unable to go on living. It might have been one of those nights when I had been planning to end my life.

The third part of my palace was the compound on either side of the main chambers. This part was for my eunuchs, ladies in waiting and maids. Their windows faced the courtyard, which meant that if I walked toward the gate, they would notice immediately, and also see anyone who attempted to enter. The eunuchs patrolled my palace in shifts, so there was always someone awake.

An-te-hai was sound asleep on the floor. Chief Eunuch Shim had lied to me when he said that he gave me people who didn't snore. An-te-hai snored like a burbling teapot. However things would change later on, after years of isolation, agony and fear, An-te-hai's snoring became the song of Heaven to me. Without hearing it, I would be unable to sleep.

As I lay awake, my thoughts went to Emperor Hsien Feng. I wondered if he and Nuharoo were enjoying each other. I wondered when he would summon me. I felt a bit cold, and I remembered that An-te-hai had told me that he had trouble warming my bed. The heater under my *kang* was not working properly. He believed it was Shim's doing, that the chief eunuch was sending me a message: either I would live a comfortable life by tipping him on a regular basis, or I would be cold in winter and hot in summer. Easy or difficult, Shim was telling me: it was my choice.

"As long as you are one of the three thousand concubines, you can't escape him," An-te-hai had said.

I didn't have any trouble sleeping in a bed that was not warmed to the Imperial standard. However, it was important to work toward the goal of becoming Emperor Hsien Feng's favorite. It was the only way to gain respect. I had no time to lose. I was turning eighteen. In the Imperial garden of beauty, eighteen was considered a flower on its way to withering.

I tried not to think about what I truly desired from life. I got up and copied a verse from a poetry book.

The east branch of the Yangtze keeps flowing,
Love seeds we once sowed forever keep growing.
Your face in dreams grew blurred to my eyes,
I stayed up and listened to night birds' cries.

Spring not yet green,
My gray hair seen,
Our separation too long for my heart to grieve.

The past appears again and again
On the night of the fabulous Lantern Festival.

Seven

THE FIRST MONTH passed quickly. Every morning when the sun's rays touched my curtain I rose to find my cat, Snow, beside me. I had become attached to this soft creature. I knew what my day would be like. It would be another day of waiting and hoping that His Majesty would visit.

An-te-hai said that I should find things to do in order to occupy myself. Embroidery, fishing and playing chess were his suggestions.

I picked up chess, but lost interest after a couple of games. The eunuchs let me win every time. I felt that my intelligence was insulted, but they were too afraid to play as equals with me.

I became fascinated by the Imperial clocks, which were part of the furniture and wall displays throughout the Forbidden City. My favorite one was the woodpecker. It lived inside a ceramic tree trunk and came out only to peck the hour. I loved its chiming sounds. An-te-hai liked its pecking motion because it reminded him of a bowing head. When he could, he tried to be there to receive the "bows."

My other favorite clock was strange in shape. It looked like a family of wheels embracing together. It sat in a clear glass box, which allowed me to look at its inner workings. Like a harmonious family, every wheel performed its duty and delivered its energy so that the hour could sing.

I studied the clocks and wondered about their places of origin. Most were from faraway lands. They were gifts from foreign kings and princes to the Chinese emperors of previous dynasties. The designs showed the makers' love for life, which made me wonder whether all the stories I had been told about the savage barbarians were true.

My enthusiasm for the timepieces was quickly spent. I began to have trouble looking at their needle-like hands. The way they crawled so slowly made me want to push them forward. I told An-te-hai to cover their faces with cloth. "No more bows," I heard him say to the wood-pecker.

Today I was bored even before I got out of bed.

"Did my lady have a good night's sleep?" An-te-hai's voice came from the courtyard.

I sat on the bed and didn't bother to answer.

"Good morning!" The eunuch stepped in with a sweet smile. "Your slaves are ready to attend your wash, my lady."

My morning wash was an event. Before I got out of bed, the eunuchs and maids made a parade of dresses. I had to pick one among three dozen. So many fine dresses, although half of them were not to my taste.

Then I had to pick out shoes and hats and jewelry. After I got out of bed I went to a room to use the chamber pot. I was followed by six maids. It was no use that I demanded to be left alone. These people were trained by Chief Eunuch Shim to be deaf and mute in situations like this.

It was a large room without furniture. A finely carved and painted yellow pot was placed in the center. It looked like a big pumpkin. Small lanterns stood in the corners of the room. The walls were draped with curtains, which were embroidered with blue and white flowers.

I was in a hurry but couldn't let myself go. There was no window to let out the odor. The maids stood around me, staring. I told them again and again to leave me alone, but they refused. They begged me to let them serve. One of them held a wet towel to wipe me afterward, an-other carried a dish of soap, the third one a handful of silk paper on a tray, the fourth one a silver basin. The last two each carried a bucket filled with water, one hot and the other cold.

"Leave your stuff on the floor," I said. "You are dismissed."

Everyone murmured "Yes, my lady," but no one moved.

I raised my voice. "I am going to stink."

"No, you don't stink," they replied in unison.

"Do me a favor!" I shouted. "Out!"

"We don't mind. We love your stink."

"An-te-hai!"

An-te-hai rushed in. "Yes, my lady."

"Call Chief Eunuch Shim immediately and tell him that my servants are not obeying me."

"It won't work, my lady." An-te-hai put his hands together to form a tube as he whispered into my ear. "I am afraid Chief Eunuch Shim wouldn't do anything about this."

"Why?"

"It is the rule that the Emperor's wives be served this way."

"Whoever invented the rule must be an idiot."

"Oh, no, my lady, don't ever say that!" An-te-hai was shocked. "It was Her Majesty the Grand Empress who invented the rules!"

I pictured the Grand Empress sitting on her chamber pot, attended by a roomful of maids. "She must think that her shit is diamonds and her farts perfume. Does Her Majesty have rules about the size, shape, length, color and odor of stools?"

"Please, my lady." An-te-hai became nervous. "You want to bring no trouble to yourself and me."

"Trouble? All I want is to be able to shit by myself!"

"It is not about shitting, my lady," An-te-hai murmured, as if his mouth was stuffed with food.

"What it is about, then?"

"It is about grace, my lady."

"Grace? How can anyone shit gracefully?"

Getting my face made, my hair oiled and combed and my dress put on and tightened around my waist, only to be taken off in the afternoon, became not only boring but also tiring. The eunuchs and ladies in waiting held trays and marched back and forth in front of me with dresses, underwear, accessories, ornaments, belts and hairpins. I couldn't wait for the ritual to be over. I would have preferred to have them tell me where these things were and pick them out myself. But I was not entitled to change the rules. I started to see that the Imperial life was about nothing but elaborate detail. My biggest problem was patience.

An-te-hai kept me company when my hair was being done. He amused me with stories and jokes. He stood behind me as I sat facing the mirror.

First the hairdresser smoothed my hair with scented water. Then he oiled it with mountain sunflower extract. After combing it through, he coiled it up. He tried to fashion it into the shape of a swan on this particular morning.

The process annoyed me and I was becoming irritated.

To ease the tension, An-te-hai asked if I would like to learn the details of Emperor Hsien Feng's belt.

I told him that I was not interested.

"The belt is the Imperial color, bright yellow, of course," An-te-hai began, ignoring me. "A work of original Manchu craftsmanship, functional but exquisite." Seeing that I didn't object, he went on. "It is reinforced with horsehair and ornamented with white folded silk ribbons. The belt has been passed down from His Majesty's ancestors and is worn during important ceremonies. The court's astrologer has exact specifications about how His Majesty should wear such items. Usually Emperor Hsien Feng will also wear an ivory tube with toothpicks, a knife in a sheath of rhinoceros horn and two perfume sachets embroidered with tiny pearls. Originally these were made of tough linen used to replace a broken bridle."

I smiled, appreciating the eunuch's intention. An-te-hai always knew how to set off my craving for knowledge.

"Does Nuharoo know what you know?" I asked An-te-hai.

"Yes, my lady, she does."

"Was it part of the reason that she was chosen?"

An-te-hai went quiet. I could tell that he didn't want to offend me.

I dropped the subject and said, "An-te-hai, from now on you are responsible for refreshing my knowledge of royal life." I avoided saying the words "teach me." I noticed that An-te-hai would be more at ease and provide me with better information if I acted like his master instead of his pupil.

"I want you to suggest what I should wear during the coming Chinese New Year's celebration."

"Well, first you have to be sure that you never dress above your rank. Yet you don't want to appear unimaginative. That is to say, you have to be able to foretell what the Grand Empress and Empress Nuharoo might wear."

"Yes, that makes sense."

"I would assume that their jadeite pendants will be in the shape of lotus leaves, their other ornaments of pearl and pink tourmaline. They will take care not to step over Emperor Hsien Feng. His pendant is a carving of a triple goat, an auspicious sign he wears only on the eve of the Chinese New Year."

"What should my pendant be?"

"Any sign or symbol you please, as long as you don't outshine the two ladies. As I said, you don't want to underdress either, because you don't want to forfeit His Majesty's attention. You must do everything in your power to stand out among thousands of concubines. You might not get to see your husband at all except on those occasions."

I wished that I could invite An-te-hai to join me for breakfast instead of serving me, watching me eat and then going to his quarters to have a cold yam.

He appreciated my feelings and was happy to enslave himself. I knew that he was weaving his future around me. If I became Hsien Feng's favorite, his position would be elevated. But I was getting no attention from His Majesty. How long did I have to wait? Would I ever get a chance? Why was I not hearing anything from Chief Eunuch Shim?

It had been seven weeks since I entered the Palace of Concentrated Beauty. I no longer looked at the yellow glazed roofs. Their brilliance had faded in my eyes. The task of picking out dresses to wear in the morning bored me to tears. I realized by now that I would dress up for no one else to see. Even my eunuchs and ladies in waiting would not be there to witness the perfection of my beauty. They were instructed to hide themselves when not called. I usually ended up alone after I was fully dressed.

Every day I found myself standing in the middle of the splendid but empty palace, my neck stretched long and hard from morning to noon. Countless times I dreamed of Emperor Hsien Feng's visit. In my fantasies he came, took my hand and passionately embraced me.

Lately I had been sitting by my pond. Dressed up like a fool, I watched the turtles and toads. In the morning the sun lingered over the garden, and two turtles would swim up lazily. They floated on top of the water for a time and then crawled over to a flat rock to relax. Slowly one would get on top of the other. They would lie motionless in this position for hours, and I would sit with them.

The beautiful wide-open eyes look dead, although her posture is erect and her costume magnificent—lines from old operas repeated themselves inside my head.

An-te-hai appeared from the bushes holding a cup of tea on a tray.

"Is my lady having a good day?" An-te-hai placed the tea in front of me.

I sighed and told him that I didn't feel like having tea.

An-te-hai smiled. He leaned over and pushed the turtles gently back into the water. "You are too anxious, my lady. Don't be."

"Life is too long in the Forbidden City, An-te-hai," I said. "Even the seconds are hard to pass."

"The day will come," An-te-hai said. His expression showed a sincere belief. "His Majesty will summon you, my lady."

"Will he?"

"You must believe that he will."

"Why would he?"

"Why wouldn't he?" An-te-hai rose from his knees.

"Speak no more of false hope, An-te-hai!"

"You can't afford to lose your confidence, my lady. What else do you own besides hope? His Majesty has placed you on the west side of his palace. I believe that is the sign of a strong interest. All the fortune-tellers I have consulted predict that he will summon you."

My mood lightened and I picked up the tea.

"May I ask"—the eunuch smiled as if he felt better himself—"if my lady is prepared if the summons comes tonight? In other words, is my lady familiar with the mating ritual?"

Embarrassed, I replied, "Of course I am."

"If you desire an explanation, I am here to help."

"You?" I couldn't help laughing. "Watch your behavior, An-te-hai."

"Only you know whether or not I was behaving, my lady."

I went quiet.

"I will be glad to drink the poison you hand me," An-te-hai said softly.

"Perform your duty and waste no words." I smiled.

"Wait for me, my lady. I'll show you something." Quickly An-te-hai collected the tea set and left. Moments later he returned with a paper box in his hand. Inside was a pair of silkworm moths.

"I got this from the garden of the Palace of Benevolent Tranquility," An-te-hai said. "It is where the elder concubines live—twenty-eight of them, left by Emperor Hsien Feng's father and grandfather. These are their pets."

"What do they do with moths?" I asked. "I thought they spent their days doing embroidery."

"Well, the ladies watch and play with the moths," An-te-hai said. "It is the same as the emperors and princes indulging themselves with crickets. The only difference is that there is no competition between silkworm moths."

"What's the fun in watching moths?"

"You have no idea, my lady." As if revealing a mystery, An-te-hai became excited. "The ladies love to watch the moths couple, and then they tear them apart in the middle of their mating ritual. Would you like me to show you?"

Imagining what An-te-hai would do, I raised my hands in the air. "No! Take the box back. I am not interested!"

"All right, my lady, I won't show you today. But someday you will want to see this. You will then understand the fun of it, just like the other ladies."

"What happens when you tear the moths apart?" I asked.

"They bleed to death."

"And that is the 'fun' you were talking about?"

"Precisely." An-te-hai smiled, misreading, for the first time, my thoughts.

"Whoever does this must have a sick mind," I said, turning my head toward the distant mountains.

"Well, to those in despair it helps healing," the eunuch said quietly.

I turned and stared into the open box.

Two moths were becoming one. Half of the male's body was inside the female's.

"Would you like me to remove the box, my lady?"

"Be gone, An-te-hai, and leave the moths to me."

"Yes, my lady. The moths are easy to feed. In case you need to have more than one pair, the silkworm seller comes to the palace the fourth day of every month."

The pair rested peacefully on a mat of straw. Next to them were two broken cocoons. The two little white bodies had wings covered with thick ash-colored powder. Once in a while their wings trembled. Were they having fun?

The sun shifted. The flat rock was now in shade. The garden was warm and comfortable. I noticed my reflection in the water. My cheeks were the color of a peach flower, and my hair reflected the light.

I tried to block my mind from traveling further. I didn't want to ruin the moment by picturing my future. But I knew that I envied the pair of moths and the turtles. My youth told me that I couldn't extinguish my desire, just as I couldn't force the sun not to shine or the wind not to blow.

Afternoon came. A rickety cart dragged by a donkey appeared in my view. It was a rusty water cart. An old man with a whip walked behind it. There was a little yellow flag on top of the giant wooden cask. The old man was coming to fill the water jars in my palace. According to

An-te-hai, the water cart was over fifty years old. It had served since Emperor Chien Lung. To procure the best spring water, the Emperor had ordered experts to come to Peking to study and compare the quality of water samples gathered from springs across the country. The Emperor had personally conducted the measuring and weighing of the water, and he had analyzed the mineral content of each sample.

The water from Jade Mountain Spring was given the highest rating. From then on, the spring was set aside for the exclusive use of residents of the Forbidden City. The gates of Peking closed by ten at night, and nothing was allowed to pass through except the water cart with the little yellow flag. The donkey traveled in the center of the boulevard. It was said that even a prince on a horse had to make way for the donkey.

I watched the water man finish his task and then disappear behind the gate. I listened to the fading sound of the donkey's steps. I felt sucked back into the darkness. Misery settled in like wetness from the rainy season.

The next time I opened the silkworm box, I found the moths gone. In their place were hundreds of brownish dots all over the straw.

"The babies! The moths' babies!" I cried like a crazy woman.

Another week passed and there was no news. No one visited me either. The silence around my palace grew enormous. When Snow came to my arms I was moved to tears. As the day went on, I fed the cat, bathed and played with her until I was bored. I read books and copied more poems from ancient times. I began to paint too. The paintings reflected my mood. They were always of a single tree in the landscape, or one blossom in a vast field of snow.

Finally, on the fifty-eighth day after my arrival in the Forbidden City, Emperor Hsien Feng summoned me. I could hardly believe my ears when An-te-hai brought me His Majesty's invitation, asking me to join him at an opera.

I studied the invitation. Hsien Feng's signature and stamp were grand and beautiful. I kept the card under my pillow and touched it over and over before I went to sleep. The next morning I got up before dawn. I sat through the makeup and dressing ritual feeling alive and excited. I imagined myself being appreciated by His Majesty. By sunrise everything was set. I prayed that my beauty would bring me luck.

An-te-hai told me that Emperor Hsien Feng would send a palanquin. I waited, burning with anxiety. An-te-hai described where I would be going and whom I would be meeting. He pointed out that theatrical performances had been a favorite royal pastime for generations. They had been most popular during the early Ch'ing Dynasty, in the 1600s. Grand stages were built in royal villas. In the Summer Palace alone, where I would be going today, there were four stages. The grandest one was three stories high. It was called the Grand Changyi Magnificent-Sound Stage.

According to An-te-hai, performances were held each Lunar New Year's Day and on the birthdays of the Emperor and Empress. The performances were never less than extravaganzas, usually lasting from early morning till late into the night. The Emperor invited princes and high officials, and it was considered a great honor to be asked. On the eightieth birthday of Emperor Chien Lung, ten operas were performed. The most popular performance was *The Monkey King*. The character of Monkey had been adapted from a classic Ming Dynasty novel. The Emperor loved the opera so much that he exhausted every variation of the story. It was the longest opera ever produced, lasting ten days. The presentation of an imaginary Heaven mirroring humanity's earthbound existence cast a spell over the audience, not broken until the very end. Even then, it was said that some desired the troupe to immediately repeat certain scenes.

I asked An-te-hai if those in the royal family were truly knowledgeable or merely enthusiastic fans.

"Most of them, I would say, have been false experts," he replied, "except Emperor Kang Hsi, Hsien Feng's great-great-grandfather. According to the book of records, Kang Hsi oversaw scripts and musical scores, and Chien Lung supervised the writing of quite a few librettos. Most people, however, come for the food and the privilege of sitting with His Majesty. Of course it is always important to demonstrate a cultured sensibility. It is fashionable to exhibit one's taste in a culture of delicacy."

"Would anyone dare to show off his knowledge with the Emperor present?" I asked.

"There is always one who doesn't understand that others will consider him a ringdove doing a somersault—showing his fancy behind."

An-te-hai told a story to give me an example. It took place in the Forbidden City during the reign of Emperor Yung Cheng. The Emperor was enjoying a performance, a story about a small-town governor who overcame his weakness and set his spoiled son straight by punishing him. The actor who played the governor was so accomplished that the Emperor granted him a private audience after the performance. The man was rewarded with taels and gifts, and His Majesty was lavish with his praise. The actor got carried away and asked if His Majesty knew the real name of the governor in history.

"'How dare you ask questions!'" An-te-hai mimicked the Emperor, his right hand giving a flourish to an imaginary dragon robe. "'Have you forgotten who you are? If I allow myself to be challenged by a beggar like you, how would I run the country?'" An edict was issued and the actor was dragged out and beaten to death in his costume.

The story made me see the true face of the splendid Forbidden City. I doubted that the execution of the foolish actor benefited the image of His Majesty. Such punishment achieved nothing but terror, and terror only increased the distance between the Emperor and the hearts of his people. Terror would bring him the greatest loss in the end. Who would stay with you down the road if all you were known for was instilling fear?

In retrospect, the story must have influenced my actions in a rather minor incident that occurred during my reign, an incident of which I was particularly proud. I was seated in the Grand Changyi Magnificent-Sound Stage celebrating my sixtieth birthday. The opera was called *The Yu-Tang Hall*. The renowned actor Mr. Chen Yi-chew was playing the character Miss Shoo. He was singing, *Coming to the judge's hall I look up / On both sides stand executioners carrying arm's-length knives / I am like a sheep finding herself in a lion's mouth* . . . But at the word "sheep" Chen suddenly stopped. He realized that my birth sign was a sheep, and that if he went on to finish his line, others might think that he was cursing me. Chen tried to swallow the word, but it was too late — everybody had already heard it, for it was a famous opera and the lyrics were well known. The poor man attempted to rescue himself by manipulating the syllable "sheep." He dragged his voice and held the tail sound until he completely exhausted his breath. The orchestra was confused and the drummers beat their instruments to cover the flaw. Then Chen Yi-chew proved himself to be a veteran of the stage — he came up with a line on the spot, which replaced "a sheep finding herself in a lion's mouth" with "a fish ending up in the fisherman's net."

Before the court had a chance to report that an "accident" had taken place and the actor must be punished, I praised Chen for his brilliance. Of course nobody mentioned the changing of the lyrics. In memory of my kindness, the artist decided to keep the new line forever in his text. In today's *Yu-Tang Hall* you will find "a fish ending up in the fisherman's net" instead of "a sheep finding herself in a lion's mouth."

· · ·

As we continued to wait for His Majesty's palanquin, I asked An-te-hai what type of opera was popular in the Forbidden City.

"The Peking opera." An-te-hai's eyes brightened. "Its main melodies have been drawn from the *Kun* and *Yiyang* operas. Each emperor or empress has had his or her favorite. Opera styles evolve over time, but the librettos remain mostly *Kun*."

I asked him what the royal family's favorite operas were and hoped that there would be one I knew.

"*Romance of the Spring and Autumn*." An-te-hai counted with his fingers. "*The Beauty from Shang Dynasty, Literature of Peacetime, A Boy Wonder Who Wins the Imperial Examination, The Battle of Iron Bannermen*..." He named close to thirty operas.

I asked An-te-hai which one might be performed today. His guess was *The Battle of Iron Bannermen*. "It is Emperor Hsien Feng's favorite," he explained. "His Majesty doesn't care much for classics. He thinks they're boring. He prefers those that contain lots of martial-arts and acrobatic skills."

"Does the Grand Empress enjoy the same?"

"Oh, no. Her Majesty favors stylized voices and star actors. She takes opera lessons herself and is considered an expert. There is a possibility that Emperor Hsien Feng will be in the mood to please his mother. I have heard that Nuharoo has worked him toward thoughts of piety. His Majesty might order the troupe to play the Grand Empress's favorite, *Happy Time for Ten Thousand Years*."

An-te-hai's mention of Nuharoo with Emperor Hsien Feng stirred my thoughts and roused my jealousy. I didn't like myself to be small-hearted, but I couldn't help my feelings. I wondered how other concubines were coping with their envy. Had they shared the bed with Hsien Feng yet?

"Tell me about your dreams, An-te-hai." I sat down. I had a sudden realization that the road to salvation was inaccessible. Despair seeped through me. I felt I had been pushed into a sealed room where my breathing became difficult. It was not true that I would be happy once my stomach was full. I couldn't escape who I was, a woman who sensed that she lived to love. Being an Imperial wife offered me everything but that.

The eunuch threw himself on the floor and begged for forgiveness. "You are upset, my lady, I can tell. Have I said something wrong? Punish me, for anger will ruin Your Majesty's health."

The feeling of an underdog came over me. My frustration turned into sadness. Where would I go from here? *But I still want to try to grow tomatoes in August, although it is too late,* a voice inside my head sang.

"You have said nothing wrong," I said to An-te-hai. "Now let's hear your dreams."

After he made sure that I was not upset with him, the eunuch began. "I have two dreams, my lady. But the chance of realizing them is like catching a live fish in boiling water."

"Describe the dreams."

"My first dream is to get my member back."

"Member?"

"I know exactly who owns my penis and where he stores it," An-te-hai said. As he spoke, he turned into a young man I had never seen. His eyes were full of light and his cheeks flushed. There was a strangeness to his voice. It was charged with hope and determination.

"The man who butchered me has collected a lot of penises. He keeps them in jars of preservative and hides them away. He is waiting for us to find success so he can sell the penises back to us for a fortune. I want to be buried in one piece when I die, my lady. All eunuchs do. If I don't get buried in one piece, I will come back handicapped in the next life."

"Do you really believe that?"

"I do, Your Majesty."

"What about your other dream?"

"My other dream is to honor my parents. I want to show them that I have succeeded. My parents have fourteen children. Eight of them died of hunger. My grandmother, who raised me, never had a full meal in her life. I don't know if I will ever see her again ... She is very sick and I miss her terribly." An-te-hai made an effort to smile while trying to hold back his tears. "You see, my lady, I am a squirrel with a dragon's ambition."

"That's what I like about you, An-te-hai. I wish my brother Kuei Hsiang had your kind of ambition."

"I am flattered, my lady."

"I suppose you know my dream by now," I said.

"A little, my lady. I dare to admit that."

"It seems as unreachable as yours, doesn't it?"

"Patience and faith, my lady."

"But Emperor Hsien Feng hasn't called me to his bed. And I am beyond pain and shame." I didn't bother to wipe my tears, which were streaming down my cheeks. "I have made my way into the Forbidden City, but it feels like there's never been a greater distance between my bed and His Majesty's. I don't know what to do."

"You are getting thinner each day, my lady. It hurts me to see you pushing your dinner away."

"An-te-hai, tell me, what do you see me turning into?"

"Isn't it a blossoming peony, my lady?"

"It was. But I am withering, and soon spring will vanish and the peony will be dead."

"There is another way to look at it, my lady."

"Show me."

"Well, to me, you are no dead flower but rather a camel."

"Camel?"

"Have you ever heard of the saying 'A dead camel is bigger than a live horse'?"

"What does that mean?"

"It means that you still have a better chance than the smaller people."

"But the truth is that I have nothing."

"You have me." On his knees, he came near. He raised his eyes and stared at me.

"You? What can you do?"

"I can find out which concubines have shared the bed with His Majesty and how they got there."

Eight

THE FIRST THING that caught my eye at the Grand Changyi Magnificent-Sound Stage was not Emperor Hsien Feng, or his guests, or the fabulous opera sets and actors in costume. It was the diadem on Nuharoo's head, which was made of pearls, coral and kingfisher feathers in the pattern of the character *shou*, longevity. I had to look away in order to keep the smile on my face.

I was ushered through a heavily guarded gate and hallway and then entered the open theater, which was in a courtyard. The seats were already filled. The audience dressed magnificently. Eunuchs and ladies in waiting walked up and down the aisles carrying teapots, cups and food trays. The opera had begun, gongs and chimes rang out, but the crowd had not quieted down. Later I would learn that it was customary for the audience to continue talking during the performance. I found this distracting, but it was the Imperial tradition.

I looked around. Emperor Hsien Feng was sitting next to Nuharoo in the center of the first row. Both he and Nuharoo were in Imperial yellow silk robes embroidered with dragon and phoenix motifs. His diadem was crowned by a large Manchurian pearl, and it had a silver inlay of trapped ribbons and tassels. His chin strap was made of sable.

Hsien Feng watched the performance with great interest. Nuharoo sat elegantly, but her attention was not on the stage. She glanced around without turning her neck. On her right side sat our mother-in-law, the Grand Empress. She was in a vermilion silk robe embroidered with blue and purple butterflies. The Grand Empress's makeup was more dramatic than that of the actors onstage. Her eyebrows were painted so dark and thick that they looked like two pieces of charcoal. Her jaws rocked from side to side as she chewed nuts. Her painted red mouth reminded me of a spoiled persimmon. Like a broom, her eyes swept back and forth over the audience. Behind her were the Imperial daughters-in-law, Ladies Yun, Li, Mei and Hui. All gorgeously dressed, they sat stone-faced. In the back and on the sides sat the royal princes, their families and other guests.

Chief Eunuch Shim came to greet me. I apologized for being late, even though it was not my fault—the palanquin had failed to arrive on time. He told me that as long as I made it to my seat without disturbing my husband and mother-in-law, I would be all right. "His Majesty never truly demands his concubines' presence," Shim said. It made me realize with crushing disappointment that I was only there out of formality.

Chief Eunuch Shim helped me into my seat between Lady Li and Lady Mei. I apologized for distracting them, and they politely returned my bows, saying nothing.

We turned our attention to the opera. It was called *The Three Battles Between the Monkey King and the White Fox*. I was struck by the talent of the actors, who Lady Mei told me were eunuchs. I was especially taken by the White Fox. "Her" voice was unique and beautiful and "her" dancing so sensuous that I forgot that she was a he. To attain this level of skill and flexibility the actors must have started their training when they were young children.

The performance was reaching its moment of action. The monkeys displayed their acrobatic skills. Spinning and somersaulting, the Monkey King executed a flip over the smaller monkeys' shoulders. At the end he threw himself high into the air and then landed smoothly on a tree branch, a prop made of painted wood.

The crowd cheered.

The Monkey King hopped onto a cloud, a board hung from the ceiling by ropes. A large white cloth, which represented the heavenly waterfall, was thrown up, the cloud was lifted, and the actor made his exit.

"*Shang! Tip him! Shang!*" Emperor Hsien Feng clapped and yelled.

The crowd followed, shouting, "Shang! Shang!! Shang!!!"

Hsien Feng's head rocked like a merchant's drum. With each beat of the gong he kicked his feet, laughing. "Excellent!" he shouted, pointing at the actors. "You've got balls! Great balls!"

Plates of nuts and seasonal dishes were passed by the Grand Empress. Not having eaten since the previous evening, I helped myself to berry buns, dates, sweet beans and nuts. I seemed to be the only lady who truly enjoyed the opera besides the Grand Empress. The rest of the ladies looked bored. Nuharoo struggled to appear interested. Lady Li yawned and Lady Mei chatted with Lady Hui.

As if to rouse her daughters-in-law, the Grand Empress handed out paper fans.

We got up and bowed in Her Majesty's direction and then sat back down and opened our fans.

It was time for the action scene. The monkeys were led by their king on all fours as they circled their enemy, the dying White Fox, who sang to the audience:

> *If you will take advice, my friend,*
> *For wealth you will not care.*
> *But while fresh youth is in you*
> *Each precious moment spare.*
> *When flowers are fit for culling*
> *Pluck them as you may.*
> *Ah! Wait not till the bloom be gone*
> *To bear a twig away.*

The audience clapped at the singing, and Lady Yun got up. I assumed she needed to go to the chamber pot. But something about her movement caught my eye. She was twisting her bottom, and her belly seemed slightly swollen.

She's pregnant! Nuharoo, Li, Mei, Hui and the others all uttered the same phrase.

After a hard stare, Nuharoo turned away. She picked up her fan and rocked her wrist ferociously. The rest of the Imperial wives did the same.

My mood turned dark. Nuharoo's diadem and Lady Yun's belly were like two burning rods stuck in my skin.

Emperor Hsien Feng did not even bother to say hello to me. He got up and left at intermission. I watched him exit, followed by eunuchs and ladies in waiting carrying washbasins, spittoons, fans, cracker dishes, soup pots and trays.

Chief Eunuch Shim told us that our husband would be back shortly. We waited, but His Majesty did not return. The crowd turned its attention back to the opera. My mind was like a pot boiling with dead thoughts. I sat till the end, my ears buzzing with the sound of drums.

The Grand Empress was pleased with the performance. "This is much better than the original *Monkey King!*" she said to the troupe leader. "The old version put me to sleep. But this one made me laugh and cry." She praised the acting and told Shim to loosen his money belt.

Her Majesty asked to meet with the leading actors, the young men who played the Monkey King and the White Fox. The actors came from backstage with their makeup still on. Their faces looked like they had been dipped in soy sauce.

The Grand Empress ignored the Monkey King and talked to the White Fox effusively. "I love your voice." She produced a bag of taels and placed it in his hands. "It makes me drunk with happiness." She held his hand and wouldn't let go. "A true songbird. My songbird!" She stared at the actor with the eyes of a young lover, murmuring, "Beautiful boy! Lovely creature!"

The actor was only average-looking, in my opinion, although I greatly admired his singing and dancing. His White Fox possessed the essence of feminine beauty. I had never seen a man playing a woman so poetically. It was amazing what art could do, for the Grand Empress was known as a eunuch-hater.

The Grand Empress turned to us. "How did you enjoy the opera?"

We got the hint: it was time to offer our share. The Imperial wives and concubines, myself included, reached into the small string bags we all carried.

The actors kowtowed and retreated.

Her Majesty rose from her seat, and we understood that it was time to depart.

We got down on our knees and said, "Until next time, we wish you a peaceful season!"

Our mother-in-law marched out without a nod.

"The Imperial palanquins walking!" Chief Eunuch Shim called, and the bearers came with our chairs.

We bowed to Nuharoo and then to each other in silence.

The curtain of my palanquin was put down. I fought hard with my bitterness and was ashamed of my weakness. It did no good when I told myself that it had been my choice to enter the Forbidden City, and that I had no right to complain or feel miserable.

An-te-hai's image appeared in the mirror as I was taking off my makeup. He asked if I needed my dresser to help me undress. Before I could reply, he said that he could assist me if I didn't mind.

I let him.

An-te-hai picked up a comb and carefully began to loosen the ornaments in my hair.

"My lady, would you care to go to the east garden tomorrow?" he asked. "I have discovered some interesting plants . . ."

I stopped him because I could feel my anger looking for an outlet.

An-te-hai closed his mouth. His fingers worked steadily through my hair. He pulled out a jade flower and then took off my diamond necklace. He set the pieces on the dressing table one after another.

Unable to bear my feelings, I started to weep.

"The knowing mind is powerful enough to rescue one from disaster," An-te-hai said quietly as if to himself.

The dam inside me broke and the angry water surged. "But for me, knowing is hurting."

"Hurting is the beginning of healing, my lady."

"Go ahead and deepen my wound, An-te-hai. The truth is that I have failed utterly."

"No lady in this place can make things happen without paying a price."

"Nuharoo did, and so did Lady Yun!"

"But it is not the whole truth, my lady. Your perspective needs adjusting."

"What perspective are you talking about? My life has been uprooted by a tornado, I have been thrown into the air, and now I'm crashing. What can I do but give up?"

An-te-hai stared at me in the mirror. "Nothing, my lady, nothing is more terrible than giving up."

"How will I go on, then?"

"By studying the way the tornado runs its course." He picked up a brush and resumed combing my hair.

"What course?"

"A tornado is at its strongest around the edges." The eunuch held up my hair with one hand and brushed it in a quick motion with the other. "The wind has the strength to lift cows and carriages and fling them back to earth. But the center of the tornado is quiet . . ." He stopped, and his eyes traced the length of my hair. "Beautiful hair, my lady. It is silky black, which promises strong health. This is hope in its most basic sense."

"What about the tornado?"

"Oh, the tornado, yes, the quiet center. It is relatively still. This is where you should be, my lady. You must avoid certain paths where you know opportunities are few, and concentrate on creating new paths where no one has walked and where thorns are seemingly thick."

"You have been thinking well, An-te-hai," I said.

"Thank you, my lady. I have thought of a way for you to create a real-life opera, with yourself as the leading lady."

"Let me hear it, An-te-hai."

Like an advisor offering his strategy to a general, An-te-hai revealed his plan. It was simple but seemed promising. I would perform an Imperial ceremony of sacrifice—a duty that belonged to Emperor Hsien Feng.

"I think you should go and perform in His Majesty's name, my lady," An-te-hai said, closing my ornament boxes. He sat down and faced me. "The sacrifice will add to His Majesty's piety and serve him well in Heaven."

"Are you sure that this is what His Majesty desires?"

"Positive," the eunuch replied. "Not only His Majesty but also the Grand Empress."

An-te-hai explained that the dates on which the Imperial ancestors had to be honored were numerous and the royal family was behind schedule. "His Majesty rarely has the energy to attend the ceremonies."

"Have the Grand Empress and the other concubines done so?"

"They have, but they have no interest in doing it every year. Emperor Hsien Feng is afraid of upsetting his ancestors, so he has asked Chief Shim to send Nuharoo and Lady Yun. But they have refused his request with excuses of poor health."

"Why didn't Chief Shim send me?"

"Well, he doesn't want to give you any opportunity to please His Majesty."

"I have tried my best to please him!"

"Well, it is your right to perform the ceremony for your husband."

"Prepare my palanquin first thing tomorrow."

"Yes, my lady."

"Wait, An-te-hai. How will the Emperor learn of my act?"

"The eunuch in charge of the temple will take down your name. It is his duty to inform His Majesty every time someone pays respect to his ancestors on his behalf."

I had no knowledge of how to honor the Imperial ancestors. According to An-te-hai, all I had to do was to throw myself on the ground and bow toward various portraits and stone statues. It didn't sound challenging.

Next dawn I rode in the palanquin with An-te-hai walking beside me. We went through the Lodge of Fresh Fragrance and then the Gate of Spiritual Valor. Within an hour, we arrived at the Temple of Eternal Peace. In front of me was a spacious building with hundreds of birds nesting under its eaves.

I was received by a young monk who was also a eunuch. He was red-cheeked and had a mole between his eyebrows. An-te-hai announced my name and title, and the monk brought out a large record book. He took up a brush pen, dipped it in ink and wrote my name in block style in the book.

I was guided into the temple. After we passed a few arched doorways the monk said that he had some business to take care of and disappeared behind a row of columns. An-te-hai followed him.

I looked around. The giant hall, several stories high, was filled with gold-colored statues. Everything was painted in shades of gold. There were temples inside the temple. The small temples matched the design of the main one.

A senior monk appeared from a side arch. He had a snow-white beard that nearly reached his knees. Without speaking, he gave me a bottle filled with incense sticks. I followed him to a series of altars.

I lit the incense, got down on my knees and bowed to the various statues. I had no idea which ancestor I was worshiping. Moving through the temple, I repeated the act over and over. After paying homage to a dozen ancestors, I was tired. The monk sat in the corner with his eyes closed. He chanted with one hand tapping his chanting instrument, a *mooyu,* or wooden fish. His other hand fumbled with a string of prayer beads. His toneless chant reminded me of the professional mourner we had hired in the village for funerals.

It was very warm in the temple. Since no one was watching, I allowed my bows to become less deep. Gradually the bows were replaced by nods. My eyes made sure that the monk didn't discover my mischief. I kept looking at him until the sound of his *mooyu* faded into silence. He must have fallen asleep. I wiped off my sweat but remained in the bowing position just in case. My eyes traveled from corner to corner. The temple was filled with gods of all kinds. Besides the official Manchu god, which was called Shaman, there were Taoist gods, Buddhist gods and Kuan Kong, a Chinese folk god.

"There was a prince who during his worship discovered that the

Chinese god's clay horse had been sweating." The monk suddenly spoke as if he had been watching me all along. "The prince concluded that the god must be working hard riding his horse, patrolling the palaces. From then on Kuan Kong became a key figure for worshipers in the Forbidden City."

"Why does each god sit in his own booth?" I asked.

"Because they deserve attention for who they are," the monk replied. "For example, the venerable Tsongkapa was the founding father of Yellow Sect Buddhism. He is the one who sits on a golden chair against that wall with a hundred small copies of himself. Beneath his feet is a Buddhist sutra in Manchu."

My eyes went to the deep end of the hall where a large vertical silk painting was on display. It was a portrait of Emperor Chien Lung in a Buddhist robe. I asked the monk if Chien Lung, my grandfather-in-law, had been a believer. The monk informed me that not only was he a devoted Buddhist, he was also an adept in the Mee Tsung religion, which originally was a branch of Buddhism. "His Majesty spoke Tibetan and read sutras in the Tibetan language as well," the monk said, and went back to tapping his *mooyu*.

I was exhausted. Now I understood why the other concubines wouldn't come.

The monk rose from his chanting mat and said that it was time to move on. I followed him to an altar in an open court. He led me to kneel in front of a block of marble and started chanting again.

It was noon and the sun beat directly on my back. I prayed for the ceremony to be over.

According to An-te-hai, this should have been the last act. The monk was beside me on his knees, and his beard was touching the ground. After three deep bows he got up. He opened a manuscript of recorded deeds and began to read, in Mandarin, the names of ancestors followed by descriptions of their lives. The descriptions were almost uniform, all praise and no criticism. Words like "virtue" and "honor" were in every paragraph. The monk told me to knock my forehead on the ground five times for every new name. I followed his instructions.

The names on the monk's list seemed endless and my forehead was becoming raw. The strength to continue came only from my understanding that the end was near.

But I was wrong.

The monk continued his reading. My nose was a few inches from his feet, and I could see their calluses. My forehead must be bleeding by now, I thought. I bit my lip. Finally he was done with his list, but then he said that I had to repeat the same ceremony in the Manchu language.

I prayed that An-te-hai would rescue me. Where was he?

The monk had begun in Manchu. He droned on, and I could understand nothing except for the names of the emperors. Unconsciousness was about to claim me when I saw An-te-hai. He rushed toward me and helped me rise.

"I am sorry, my lady. I didn't know that this monk would keep reading until his victim passed out. I thought my brothers were joking when they told me about him."

"May we leave now?" I asked.

"I am afraid not, my lady. Your good deed will not be recorded unless it is completed properly."

"I shall not survive this!"

"Don't worry," An-te-hai whispered. "I have just offered a handsome bribe. He assured me that the rest of the ceremony will take little time."

Stone gods lined the edge of the site, an open space with one wall to the west. A fifty-foot flagpole stood to the southeast. On top of the pole was a bird feeder. Birds were said to deliver the Emperor's messages to the spirits. There was a strange object hanging on the wall. As I walked closer I was able to tell that it was a dust-colored cotton bag.

"The bag belonged to the dynasty's founding father, King Nurhachi," the senior monk explained. "Inside are the bones of the king's father and grandfather. Nurhachi carried them back to the tribe to be buried after the two men were slaughtered by the enemy."

The monk clapped his hands. Two women whose faces were caked with mud appeared. "The witches of the Shaman tribes," the monk introduced. The women's robes were thick with patterns of black spiders. Their hats were covered in fish scales made of copper. Dangling over their heads, ears and necks were beads made from fruit pits. Bells were tied to their limbs. Drums of different sizes hung from their necks and waists. They each had a three-foot-long brown "tail" made of braided leather strips hanging from their behinds. As they started to dance they encircled me. Their mouths smelled of garlic. They sang by imitating animal sounds.

I had never seen such a disturbing dance. The women were in a squatting position most of the time. The "tails" looked more like stringy excrement.

"Don't you move!" the monk called when he saw that I was attempting to stretch my legs.

The dancers sprang away and went to encircle the flagpole. They spun around like headless chickens with their arms waving at the sky. They shouted, "Pig! Pig!"

A trussed pig was carried over by four eunuchs. The animal wailed. The dancers hopped back and forth across its body. The pig was carried away. A golden plate was brought over with a flopping fish on it. The monk told me that the fish had been caught from the nearest pond. The young monk returned and skillfully trussed the fish with a red ribbon.

"On your heels!" The senior monk dragged me up and grabbed my right hand. Before I realized what was going on, a knife was put in my hand and I was forced to slice open the fish.

An-te-hai and the young monk supported me with their knees and arms so I wouldn't collapse.

A blanched pig's head was carried in on a large tray. The senior monk told me that it was the wailing pig I had seen a moment ago. "Only a freshly slaughtered and boiled pig will guarantee the magic."

I shut my eyes and took deep breaths. Someone gripped my left hand and tried to loosen my stiff fingers. I opened my eyes and saw the dancers, who offered me a golden bowl.

"Hold it!" the senior monk commanded.

I was too weak to protest.

A rooster was brought before me. Once again I was handed a knife. The knife kept slipping through my fingers. The monk took the bowl into his own hands and told me to grab the rooster. "Cut its throat and pour its blood into the bowl!"

"I . . . can't . . ." I felt that I was about to faint.

"Steady, my lady," An-te-hai said. "It is the end!"

The last thing I remembered was that I poured wine upon the cobblestones where the fish, the pig's head and the rooster lay in their blood.

On my way back in the palanquin I threw up. An-te-hai told me that every day a pig was brought through the Gate of Thunder and Storm and was sacrificed by noon. The headless pigs were supposed to be discarded after the ceremony, but they were not. The eunuchs of the temple hid them, chopped them up and sold them for a good price. "For over two hundred years, the broth in the giant wok that the pigs were boiled in has never been changed," An-te-hai told me. "The fire in the stove has never been allowed to die. The eunuchs hawked the pig meat: 'This is no ordinary meat. It has been dipped in the heavenly soup! It will bring you and your family luck and great fortune!'"

Nothing changed after my visit to the temple. By the end of autumn my hope to gain Emperor Hsien Feng's attention was completely crushed. All night long I listened to crickets singing. The crickets in the Imperial backyard did not sound the same as the ones in Wuhu. Wuhu crickets carried short tunes, with three beats between each interval. The Imperial crickets sang without rest.

An-te-hai told me that the senior concubines who lived in the Palace of Benevolent Tranquility raised the crickets. When the weather was warm the crickets began to sing right after dark. Thousands of crickets lived in *yoo-hoo-loos*, bottle-shaped gourds made by the concubines.

The storm season started early this year, and the flowers were beaten. White petals covered the ground, and their fragrance was so strong that it filled my room. The roots of my peonies were soaked by the daylong rains and began to rot. Bushes were sick with brownish spots. Puddles were everywhere. I quit walking outside after An-te-hai stepped on a water scorpion. His heel swelled to the size of an onion.

Every day I went about the same routine. I put on makeup and dressed in the morning and took it all off in the evening. I waited for His Majesty and did nothing else. The sound of the crickets got sadder and sadder in my ears. I tried not to think of my family.

An-te-hai went to the Palace of Benevolent Tranquility and came back with a basketful of beautifully carved *yoo-hoo-loos*. He wanted to show me how to grow and carve the gourds. He promised that it would help lift my loneliness, as it had for many other concubines. The gourd, he pointed out, was an auspicious symbol, implying a wish for "numerous descendants."

"Here are the seeds from last year." An-te-hai offered me a handful, which looked like black sesame seeds. "You plant them in the spring. After they blossom, the gourds will begin to form. You can design a cage that will force the gourd to grow into a desired shape—round, rectangular, square or asymmetric. When it is ripe, the shell will turn hard. You then pick the gourd off the vine, empty out the seeds and carve it into a piece of art."

I studied the gourds An-te-hai had brought. The designs and colors were intricate and rich. A spring motif was used over and over. I was especially moved by one piece showing babies playing in a tree.

• • •

After dinner An-te-hai took me to visit the Palace of Benevolent Tranquility. We each carried gourds. Instead of calling for the palanquin I walked. We crossed several courtyards. As we approached the palace, there was a strong smell of incense. We entered clouds of smoke. I heard mourning sounds and figured that it might be monks chanting.

An-te-hai suggested that we first stop at the Pavilion of Streams to return the gourds. As we passed the gate and entered the garden, I was struck by the grand temples covering the hills. Statues of Buddha were everywhere. The small ones were egg-sized; I could sit on the feet of the big ones. The names of the temples were carved on golden boards: *Palace of Excellent Health, Palace of Eternal Peace, Hall of Mercy, Mansion of Lucky Cloud, Mansion of Eternal Calm.* Some were built from existing pavilions, others from existing rooms and gardens. Every space was crowded with pagodas and altars.

"The elderly concubines have turned their living quarters into temples," An-te-hai whispered. "They spend their lives doing nothing but chanting. Each has a small bed behind the statue of a Buddha."

I wanted to know what the concubines looked like, so I followed the sound of their chanting. I descended a path leading to the Hall of Abundant Youth. An-te-hai told me that it was the largest of these temples. As I entered, I saw that the floor was covered with praying figures. The incense smoke was thick. The worshipers rose and fell on their knees like an ocean wave. They chanted tonelessly, their hands busy moving beads strung on waxed threads.

I realized that An-te-hai was not with me. I had forgotten that eunuchs were not allowed in certain religious areas.

The sound of chanting became louder. The huge Buddha in the middle of the hall smiled ambiguously. For a moment reality escaped me. I became one of the concubines on the floor. I could see myself carving gourds. I could see my skin wrinkle and then crease into folds. My hair was turning white and I could feel my teeth falling out.

"No!" I screamed.

The *yoo-hoo-loos* I carried fell from my hands.

The chanting stopped. Hundreds of heads turned in my direction.

I was unable to move.

The concubines stared at me. Their toothless jaws cracked open. Their hair was so thin that they looked bald.

I had never seen such grave-looking ladies. Their backs were hunched and their limbs reminded me of gnarled trees on the tops of mountains. There was no trace of past beauty on these faces. I couldn't imagine any of them being the subject of an emperor's passion.

The women raised their stick-thin arms toward the sky. Claw-like hands made scratching motions.

I felt an overwhelming sense of pity for them. "I'm Orchid," I heard myself say. "How do you do?"

They rose, narrowing their eyes. Their expressions were predatory.

"We have an intruder!" came an ancient, trembling voice. "What do we do with her?"

"Pinch her to death!" was the crowd's shrill response.

I threw myself on the floor and kowtowed repeatedly. I explained that it was wrong for me to intrude. I apologized and promised that they would never see me again.

But the women were determined to reach me and tear me apart. One woman pulled my hair, another punched my chin. I begged to be forgiven as I tried to back up toward the gate.

The women laughed hysterically, kicking, pushing and tossing me back and forth.

I was pinned to a wall. Several strong hands grabbed my throat. I could feel the long-nailed fingers pressing and cutting off my breath. The old faces crowded in on me like black clouds rolling over a sky. "Slut!" they cursed. "Now pray to Buddha before you die."

Suddenly the crowd was distracted. An-te-hai had climbed on top of the gate and was now throwing down gourds loaded with rocks. "Toothless ghosts!" he yelled. "Go back! Back to your coffins!"

Nine

I SENT An-te-hai for Chief Eunuch Shim. When Shim arrived, I received him in my official court robe with full makeup and headdress. He was surprised.

"Lady Yehonala." Shim got down on his knees and kept his eyes on the floor. "You needn't be so formal. As your slave, Shim doesn't deserve such respect." He paused and raised his eyes to my knees. The half-revealed pupils made him look like a lizard. "I don't mean to criticize, but Lady Yehonala, you should be careful. You can get both of us in trouble."

"I am desperate, Chief Shim," I said. "Please rise and have a seat."

As I spoke, I signaled to An-te-hai, who brought out a carved golden box.

"Chief Shim, I have a humble gift for you." I opened the box and took out the *ruyi* that Emperor Hsien Feng had given me.

Upon seeing the *ruyi* Shim nearly jumped. His eyes were so wide I thought his eyeballs would fall out of their sockets. "It is . . . it is His Majesty's engagement gift to you, Lady Yehonala! It is an authenticated piece, a pledge. If you don't know its value, allow me to —"

"I'm glad that you recognize the value." I smiled. "However, I still would like you to have it."

"Why, Lady Yehonala? Why?"

"I'd like to exchange it for a favor, Chief Shim." I made him look me in the eye. "To tell you the truth, this *ruyi* is the last thing I own. I want to give it to you because I understand the value of your help."

"Lady Yehonala, please. I . . . can't accept it." He got up, only to crash down on his knees again.

"Rise, Chief Shim."

"I dare not!"

"I insist."

"But Lady Yehonala!"

I waited until he was on his feet. "The *ruyi*"—I uttered each word with deliberation—"will be more valuable when I become the mother of Emperor Hsien Feng's child."

The expression on Chief Eunuch Shim's face froze. He seemed to be transfixed by the possibility.

"Yes, Lady Yehonala." He knocked his forehead on the floor.

I let him go on for a while and then said, "Thank you for helping me."

Slowly Chief Eunuch Shim got up. He shook his sleeves and breathed deeply. A moment later, he was himself again. He seemed to be pleased and frightened at the same time. He took the *ruyi* from my hand and held it to his chest.

"Which date, my lady, would you like me to schedule you with His Majesty?" he asked, putting the *ruyi* in the inner pocket of his robe.

"Does the date make a difference?" I had not been prepared for such a quick response.

"A big difference, my lady. You want to see His Majesty on your most fertile days, don't you?"

"That's right." I quickly calculated the dates.

"And the date is?"

"The fourteenth day of the next full moon."

"Perfect, my lady. I'll mark the date in my book right away. If you don't hear from me, we are set. If everything goes right with His Majesty, you will be summoned on the fourteenth day of the next full moon. Until then, my lady." He took a step back and then motioned toward the door.

"Wait." I didn't trust him. How could a date with Emperor Hsien Feng be so easily arranged? "Chief Shim, please bear with my questions. What if His Majesty wants to see other ladies on that day? How can you be sure to make him want me instead?"

"Don't worry, my lady." He smiled. "I have a way to bend the wind in the Forbidden City."

"And that is to say . . ."

"That is to say if Emperor Hsien Feng expresses a desire to see any other lady—for example, Lady Li—I'll say to him, 'Your Majesty, Lady Li is unclean.'"

"Well, what about Lady Mei?"

"'I'm sorry, your Majesty, Lady Mei is unclean too.'"

"So, everyone will have their cycle except the one you want to sleep with the Emperor?"

"Yes. I have succeeded many times."

"I am counting on you to make it work for me, Chief Shim."

"You needn't worry, my lady. I'll whet His Majesty's appetite by telling him how delicious you are."

But I did worry, and now I had only twelve days to prepare myself. I had no idea how to please a man in bed. I needed to be instructed immediately. I thought of Big Sister Fann and wished that I could speak with her, but there was no way I could get out of the Forbidden City. To ask for permission to leave, I had to lie. I sent An-te-hai to the Imperial household to report that my mother was ill and I needed to go home. Two days later, permission was granted for a ten-day leave. An-te-hai told me that I was lucky. Just a few weeks ago Lady Li had made the same request—her mother was truly ill—and been refused. Emperor Hsien Feng was taking his pleasure, and he would not release her. Lady Li's mother had died.

"That shows how unimportant I am to His Majesty," I said bitterly.

I arrived home at noon and immediately sent An-te-hai to fetch Big Sister Fann. My mother, Rong and Kuei Hsiang were thrilled to see me. Mother planned to take me shopping, but I begged her to stay home and not to leave the bed until my visit was over. I explained that I had lied to the Emperor, and that I could be beheaded if found out.

Mother was shocked and thought my behavior unforgivable. But after I described my situation, she had no trouble staying in bed. She said she felt sick and asked Rong to place some towels by her bedside. Rong put a pot of strong-scented herb medicine on the stove in case the Forbidden City sent its spies.

Big Sister Fann came. "Impressive, Orchid! Impressive! You are like a pepper in autumn—turning redder and hotter each day!" She had no time to tell me how much she missed me. "I have a place for you to learn what is required, but you must disguise yourself." I exchanged clothes with Rong. Big Sister Fann handed a set of women's clothes to An-te-hai.

"I am taking Orchid to visit a friend," Big Sister Fann told my mother.

We were out in the street when Fann told me that we were heading for the House of Lotus.

"Big Sister Fann!" I knew the nature of the house and hesitated.

"I wish we had a choice, Orchid," she said apologetically.

I stood in the middle of the road, unable to make a decision.

"What are you thinking, Orchid?"

"To win His Majesty's heart" were the words that jumped out of my mouth.

"Then come, Orchid. We will use the house only for what it can teach us — the ways of pleasing men."

We hired a donkey cart. After half an hour we arrived in the west corner of Peking. The streets narrowed and the air smelled sour. We dismounted in the back of a busy street where shopkeepers stacked their rotten fruit and vegetable baskets. I hid my face behind a scarf and walked quickly with Big Sister Fann and An-te-hai. We stopped in front of an old building. A lantern sign hung down from the second floor that read *House of Lotus.*

The three of us entered a dimly lit hallway. The interior was covered with murals depicting elaborate bedrooms where lavishly dressed people indulged themselves in every way imaginable. The characters were stylishly drawn. After my eyes adjusted to the light I began to see the shabbiness — chipped paint and falling plaster everywhere. The place had an odd odor, a mixture of perfume and stale tobacco.

A frog-faced woman appeared behind a counter. She had a smoking pipe sticking out of her mouth. She greeted Big Sister Fann with a broad smile. "What wind has brought you here, my friend?"

"The southern wind, Mistress," answered Fann. "I am here to ask you a favor."

"Don't be modest about your intention." The Mistress patted Big Sister Fann's shoulder with one hand. "I know you are with the spirit of the god of money or you wouldn't be here. My temple is too small for a big worshiper like you."

"Don't be modest yourself, Mistress," Big Sister Fann said. "Your small temple happens to have the god I need to talk to. Come." She pulled me over and introduced me as her niece from the countryside, and An-te-hai as my sister.

The Mistress looked me up and down. She turned to Big Sister Fann. "I am afraid I can't offer much. This girl is too skinny. How can you expect a spider to spin when it has no butt? It'll take me too much money just to fatten her up."

"Oh, don't worry." Big Sister Fann leaned toward the Mistress. She pulled her ear and whispered, "My niece is here for a consultation only."

"I don't do small business anymore, sorry." The Mistress took a toothpick from a shelf behind the counter and started to run it over her teeth. "The market has been bad, you know."

Big Sister Fann winked at me.

I cleared my throat.

An-te-hai stepped up and passed me a bag.

I went to the counter and removed what was in the bottom of the bag.

My dragonfly hairpin, inlaid with jewels and pearls, glistened in the light. I put it on the counter.

"Oh, my heavens!" The Mistress drew a breath and tried not to show surprise. Covering her mouth with both hands, she studied the hairpin. Raising her chin, she looked at me suspiciously. "You stole this."

"No, I didn't," I said calmly. "It was an inheritance."

"That's right," Big Sister Fann echoed. "Her family have been jewelry makers for . . . centuries."

"I am not doubting whether it is real," the Mistress said as her eyes continued to search me. "I only wonder why such a rare treasure is outside of the Forbidden City."

To avoid the Mistress's stare, I turned to look at the murals.

"Is that enough for your consultation?" Big Sister Fann asked.

"You are too kind." The Mistress picked up her pipe and stuffed dry leaves in it. "My only hesitation is that I am not sure it is safe for me to keep. If it is a stolen piece . . ." She paused. Her hand drew a hanging rope in the air.

"Let's go to another house, Aunt." I reached for the hairpin.

"Wait!" The Mistress put her hand on top of mine. Gently but firmly she picked up the hairpin. Her face turned into a smiling rose. "Oh, my dear child, don't dare make a fool of your aunt. I didn't say I didn't want it, did I? It is good that you were brought to me, because I am the only lady in town who can offer what you want. My child, I am going to give you the lesson of a lifetime. I am going to be worthy of your priceless hairpin."

We sat in the master chamber. It had a large bed with decorative posts up to the ceiling. Made of redwood, the bed had been carved with peonies, eggplants, tomatoes, bananas and cherries, which suggested male and female sexual organs. The curtains were washed white and perfumed. The side walls had built-in shelves displaying miniature sculptures. Most were Buddhist gods in the middle of coupling. The actions were cleverly depicted, the poses elegant. Females mounted males in positions of meditation. The lovers' eyes were either half open or closed. Between each couple were displayed plates painted with individual pink peonies and eggplants. The peonies had dark, hair-like pistils and the eggplants had cap-like tops painted in light purple.

"It is all about arousing the mind," the Mistress commented as she served tea. "When girls first come to my house, I teach them a skill called the fan dance. "The Mistress opened a chest and pulled out a set of props: a small round pillow, a stack of paper money, and a dozen eggs on a bamboo tray.

"I lay these objects on top of one another, with the money on the bottom, the pillow in the middle and the eggs on top. The girl sits on the arrangement. She is given one minute to turn the stack of money into the shape of a fan. The rule is that the eggs cannot be broken."

How was this possible?

The Mistress snapped her fingers.

Two girls entered from a side door. They were in their late teens and were dressed in thin brocaded robes. Although they had pleasant features, they showed no hospitality. They spit out sunflower seeds, kicked off their slippers and climbed onto the bed. Opening their legs, they squatted over the eggs like two hens.

The Mistress snapped her fingers again, and the girls started to rock their bottoms.

The view was unbearably comic and I failed to suppress a giggle.

Big Sister Fann jabbed me with her elbow.

I apologized but could hardly control myself.

"You won't be laughing when you start practicing yourself, believe me," the Mistress said. "It takes a great deal of effort to master the trick."

I asked what this movement was for.

"It is to help you gain power and control of your body," the Mistress replied. "It is to add sensitivity to your bottom lips."

Bottom lips?

"Follow my advice and practice, and you will understand what it is for. When the skill is mastered, you will drown the man beneath you in pleasure and he will remember your name."

The words got me. Yes, I would like to have Emperor Hsien Feng remember my name. I would like His Majesty to remember the pleasure along with its deliverer.

I looked at the ivory-colored rocking behinds and tried to picture the girls in bed with men. My cheeks started to burn. It was not out of shame but from the knowledge that I was going to try this myself.

"We have been in business a long time," the Mistress said, trying to brush away my doubts. "Men come at all costs. We bring life back to them. We release the beast out of younger men and make older men know their youth once again."

My eyes were on the girls, who were now balanced on their limbs.

"This is a time-tested position." The Mistress gave a mysterious smile. "You see, the girls from good families are taught to despise my house. Such girls don't know that it is because of them I am in business. The good girls never know what my girls know; therefore they end up keeping their house, and my girls their husbands and their money!"

"How long does it take to master the . . . dance?" I asked, wanting to get out of here as soon as I could.

"Three months." The Mistress pulled over a chair and sat down.

I had only ten days!

"Every day you squat on top of the eggs and rock your behind." The Mistress lit her pipe and inhaled. "After three months, your bottom lips will grow a little thicker and fatter than a normal woman's. When a man wears those lips, you will drive him wild. He will want to die for you, and you will be able to empty his pockets."

I tried to forget where I was, but it was hard.

Big Sister Fann gave me an I-didn't-hear-it look.

An-te-hai stared boldly. He was spellbound by what he was watching.

The girls lifted themselves off the eggs. Their bodies glistened with sweat.

"Take a look at what they have done." The Mistress waved at me.

I went over to see.

The Mistress removed the egg tray and the pillow. A perfect fan presented itself—the stack of paper money had been moved into the intended shape.

"Now try it yourself," the Mistress said, putting down the tray and the pillow.

I couldn't move.

"You might as well face it," the Mistress said. "It is a man's world."

The girls offered to help take off my clothes.

I felt foolish. My body became tense.

"Your future depends on your performance." The Mistress's voice was flat, without emotion. "You must make the man think of you as magical or he will not call you back."

"Yes," I replied in a weak voice.

"Then quit fighting and let go. A good life doesn't come free." The Mistress led me to the bed and motioned for me to squat. "The fact is, life comes easy to nobody."

Embarrassed, I told An-te-hai and Big Sister Fann to leave the room. The two exited without a word.

I got down and squatted like a hen. The position was so awkward that my limbs became sore almost instantly. I moved my behind in circles. The touch of the eggs brought with it an odd sensation. I struggled with my knees and ankles to stay in position.

"Keep going." The Mistress reached out and stabilized the egg tray underneath me. "Perfection needs time."

"I don't have time." I rocked my behind and began to gasp. "Ten days is all I have."

"You've got to be crazy to think you can master the trick in ten days."

"I wouldn't be here if I was not crazy."

"Only a fool would expect herself to drink hot porridge in one gulp."

"I understand, but I must get it done before . . ." Before my sentence ended, a cracking sound came from my bottom.

It was the eggs. I had crushed them.

The Mistress grabbed a towel to keep the yolks from spilling. Quickly, she replaced the broken eggs with new ones.

Getting back into position, I balanced myself on both hands. My body felt like a strange object. I rocked, bearing my developing muscle pain.

"Ten days is definitely a torture." The Mistress now was admiring my strength. "You need to take breaks. You don't want to crush the eggs again."

"No, I don't. However, I can't afford not to keep going."

"There is another way to attract men." The Mistress got off her chair. She took the pipe out of her mouth and knocked it on her sole to empty the ash. "Care to hear it?"

I nodded.

The girls came and handed me a hot towel.

I crawled off the bed and wiped my behind.

"I can't teach you to beat your fate." The Mistress refilled the pipe with dry leaves and lit it. She made a sucking sound as she inhaled the smoke. "Because you can't. But it helps a great deal if you have an understanding of men as creatures. You must come to see why 'Roses in one's own backyard don't smell as good as roses in the wild.'"

"Go on, madam, please," I said.

"You are a pretty girl, all right, but when the lamp is out, a beautiful girl or a beast of a girl — it makes no difference to a man. Over the years I have seen so many men abandon their good-looking wives for ugly concubines, and then abandon the concubines for uglier prostitutes."

"How can a woman make a difference?"

"I told you, it is the mind's game. The truth is that men need encouragement no matter how strong they appear to be," the Mistress said.

Looking at an erotic painting in which a man gazed intently at a woman's breasts, the Mistress continued. "Be blind about his looks and habits. Try to ignore his manners as well. Be prepared: he may have the features of a panda, the smell of a barn, his sun instrument may be small like a walnut, or too large like a daikon instead of a carrot. He might demand hours of service before reaching satisfaction. You must concentrate on the music inside of his head. You must keep the pot boiling. You must remember the paintings in my house. They will help to create the magic. Look at this gentleman, holding his lady's breasts like they are sweet peaches. Praise him with your noises. No actual words. Just the sounds. Wipe it on him like honey. Make flavors. Turn *uhn* into *woo* and back. Let him know he's fantastic."

"Doesn't he already know? Doesn't my willingness tell him so? I would have told him a thousand times by the time I am in bed with him, wouldn't I?"

"You will be surprised, young lady."

"How is that?"

"You haven't spoken with your bottom lips, have you?"

"Oh, that's right."

"Put your skill to use!"

"Yes, of course." My embarrassment turned into amusement.

"You might end up pleasing yourself too." The Mistress smiled.

"What if . . ." I paused, because I didn't know if I could make my question comprehensible. I decided to ask anyway. "What if he doesn't like what I do?"

"There is no such thing. Men like it," the Mistress said confidently. "But timing counts a great deal, and of course the condition of his health too."

"What if I don't like him?"

"Didn't I already tell you? Pay attention to just the business. You are not after him, but his pockets."

"What if he insults me and tells me to leave his bed? What if I fail to hide my feelings of disgust?"

"Listen, this business is not about how one feels. It never was, is or will be. Such is the fate of a woman. You've got to make a dish with whatever you've got in the kitchen. You can't dream only about the fresh vegetables in the market!"

"How can I pretend to be excited when I am not?"

"Fake it! It is a son-of-a-dog act! The worst part is, by the time you reach perfection, you are too old. Youth evaporates like dew, born in the morning and dead in the afternoon."

The Mistress threw herself into a chair. Her chest pumped as if she had just been revived after nearly drowning.

The two girls sat by themselves and remained stone-faced.

I put my clothes back on and got ready to leave.

"One last thing," the Mistress uttered from the chair. "Don't ever voice your disappointment, no matter how hurt or angry you are. Don't try to argue with him."

"I don't even know if there will be a conversation."

"Some men like to chat afterwards."

"Well, as long as he is interested, I intend to continue my act."

"Good."

"I also would like to—I mean, if the situation permits—ask him questions. Can I?"

"Be sure to ask dumb questions."

"Dumb questions? Why?"

"Without exception, a woman who tries to show that she's got a brain gets abandoned."

"Why?"

"Why? Men hate to be challenged. It's simply demeaning to them."

"So I should act dumb?"

"You'll be doing yourself a favor."

"But . . ." I couldn't imagine myself acting dumb on purpose. "It is not part of my nature."

"Make it yours!" The Mistress stared at me with wide eyes. Her skin was bleached out by the light and became pale, almost bluish.

"Thank you, madam," I said.

Taking out the hairpin from her inner pocket, she wiped it with her sleeve. "We are talking about survival. Like I said, I want to be worthy of your hairpin."

"It was a good lesson." I bowed lightly. "Goodbye and thanks."

The Mistress licked the hairpin with her tongue. "What kind of man are you seeing, if you don't mind my asking?"

"I wish I knew." I walked toward the door and lifted the curtain.

Ten

P URPLE WISTERIA fell in cascades from the roof. Birds and crickets and other insects chirped in the bushes. The moment had come. Emperor Hsien Feng had summoned me.

To calm my excitement, I went to sit by the peony garden. The terraces were the most beautiful architectural ornament of my palace. The flowers of a deeper hue were planted near the shore of the pond. The blooms became lighter as the garden rose on the hillside, creating the illusion of a landscape fading away into the far distance. The view inspired me as an example of what one could achieve with what was offered in life.

At lunch I ordered my favorite food, Yang-chou noodles. An-te-hai and I celebrated my good luck. I wrote a poem entitled "Yang-chou Noodles."

> One leaf lands in the wok, the other dances in the air
> Leaves grow out of the tip of the chef's knife
> One moment I see silver fish splash in white waves
> Another moment willow leaves riding the east wind.

My official preparations took several hours. Eunuchs were sent from the Emperor's palace to help. Together my eunuchs and ladies in waiting bathed and perfumed me. I was wrapped naked in a white silk cloth and carried by four eunuchs on a litter. I was on my way to His Majesty Emperor Hsien Feng's bedchamber in the Hall of Spiritual Nurturing, three palaces south of the Palace of Concentrated Beauty, where I lived.

We passed the Palace of Grand Harmony and the Palace of Luminous Virtue and moved through the grand hallways of the Palace of Peace and Longevity. The temperature dropped as night fell, and I was cold under the thin cloth. An-te-hai had been thoughtful enough to bring an extra blanket, and he covered me with it.

The moment we arrived at His Majesty's inner chambers, An-te-hai was ordered to retreat. Chief Eunuch Shim received me and quietly guided the litter bearers in. After a few turns I entered a room brightened with large red candles and wall-to-wall yellow silk curtains. In the middle of the room was His Majesty's bed.

The eunuchs who had brought me departed and were replaced with a group of Hsien Feng's eunuchs, dressed in fine yellow silk robes. They quickly pulled out embroidered sheets, blankets and comforters. After the bed was prepared they gently lifted me to the edge of its huge surface and then left the room.

Another group of eunuchs entered. They each held heated copper pots in their hands. They warmed the sheets and comforters with the pots. Then they unwrapped me. Laying me on the side of the bed nearest the wall, they covered me with warm sheets. From beginning to end, their faces remained expressionless. When their hands touched my body, it made me feel like just another pillow. When all was set, they let down the bed curtain and retreated.

The room was deadly quiet. The smell of incense grew strong. Through the curtain I observed the room, which was filled with works of calligraphy and paintings. The largest painting was of a Buddha crossing a river. The Buddha was painted in pure gold. He was a giant with a huge belly and he rode on a thin lotus leaf. He showed no concern over the possibility of sinking, for his eyes were fully closed and his mouth revealed a faint smile. In his hands was the famous jar of wisdom. To the right of the painting was a blue bookshelf stacked with books. Two floor-length lanterns decorated with calligraphy hung from the ceiling. Everything was carved and coated with gold. Images of dragons and cranes were repeated throughout the room. Panels on both sides of one of the windows read: *Luck year in, year out* and *Peace with all matters.* A *qin,* a seven-stringed instrument of polished wood, lay on a shelf behind the bed.

I was thirsty and realized that I had barely eaten that day. Lately I had been having trouble eating and sleeping. All my energy had gone into imagining what it would be like to sleep with His Majesty. I wondered how he would begin with me, which part of my body he would explore first, and if everything about me would please him enough. I wondered if he would compare me with other women. What would happen if he found that I was not to his taste? Would he order me to leave? Would he leave me?

Chief Eunuch Shim made it clear that once I was found unsuitable, the abandonment would be entirely my own responsibility. Recently, His Majesty was said to be prone to mood swings. An-te-hai heard from another eunuch that one evening the Emperor had summoned six concubines, one after the other, and all were found wanting. He kicked them out and told Shim that he never wanted to see the women again. The word "never" from the Son of Heaven carried great weight —they were removed from their palaces and banished to the deep end of the Forbidden City, where they would grow and carve *yoo-hoo-loos* for the rest of their lives.

Would the same happen to me tonight? What would or could I do if it did happen? I remembered Big Sister Fann telling me that His Majesty considered concubines to be dishes forced down his throat. The thought disturbed me so much that I failed to pray for Heaven's blessing. I lay in the bed with my face to the wall. I was cold from head to toe.

The red candles produced a sweet jasmine scent. Exhaustion hung upon me like a heavy lid. Why add additional weight to a burden that was already heavy? The youth in my spirit rose. It called me a "walking stick made of ice." I rebuked myself for creating my own frosty weather. *Feel the sunlight!* my youthful wisdom cried. *Why betray your courage, Orchid? Since your father's death there hadn't been a path until you walked on the weeds!*

I heard a man's voice. It came from the right side of the connecting hall. It could be no one but His Majesty Emperor Hsien Feng.

My fear intensified. The voice sounded unpleasant, as if His Majesty was arguing with someone. The words were strained and the mood dark. There was a moment of silence, and then the voice cursed, "Imperial sewage grease!"

I heard approaching steps. I covered myself with blankets and pillows, trying to gather the courage to greet my husband for the first time. It had been weeks since I last saw him. Honestly, I couldn't recall his features. Chief Eunuch Shim had instructed me not to greet my husband. My nakedness only increased my nervousness. My nightgown lay on a stool next to the bed. Beside it was His Majesty's blue silk gown, which he would change into for the night.

"No! Who do they think I am? Go to hell! I won't permit it!" The man I was now sure was Emperor Hsien Feng shouted from the other room. ". . . Well, if they hadn't come with troops. What have the British and the French done? They have forced me to pay eight hundred thousand taels more than I was already required to pay. Now they want me to open Tientsin. Tientsin is the gate of Peking, for heaven's sake! They are strangling me with a rope . . . What do they mean by amending the treaty? It's a savage's excuse! I have already opened ports in Canton, Shanghai, Foochow and Taiwan. I don't have any more to open . . ."

Gradually his voice grew weak. He broke down. He was crying. "I am so ashamed . . . China's dignity has been sacrificed. I have no face to go to the altar anymore. Why can't you do something? Sleep has become impossible. I have been drinking, yes. How else am I to escape my nightmares! What do you mean, it was up to me?"

There was a pause, followed by the sound of porcelain crashing.

The north wind whistled outside the windows. After a long silence I heard Hsien Feng blow his nose. Then came the sound of shuffling feet. I saw the shadow of His Majesty approach the bed curtain and pulled the comforter over my head. He sat down on the edge of the bed and sighed deeply as he took off his robe.

"Tea, Your Majesty?" Chief Eunuch Shim's voice came from the hallway.

"I'll drink my own piss!" was His Majesty's reply.

"We wish Your Majesty an excellent night!"

The footsteps in the courtyard receded.

I was not sure whether Emperor Hsien Feng knew that I was in his bed. I certainly didn't want to surprise him. Should I make some noise to let him know that he was not alone?

His Majesty kicked off his boots and tossed aside his belt with its pendant beads and charms. He was in a white shirt. His black braid coiled around his neck like a snake. Without changing into his nightgown, he slid into bed and leaned against a pillow.

He turned his head and our eyes met.

There was not the slightest hint of surprise in him. Having a girl in his bed was like having an extra comforter. I saw no flicker of interest in his large slanted eyes. He was as handsome as I now began to remember him from our first encounter—a shaved chin, a straight Manchu nose and a boat-shaped mouth with firm lips. I had never seen a man with such perfect features and delicate skin.

We continued to stare at each other and I could feel my blood pumping in my veins.

"May His Majesty live for many many years and may your descendants be counted in the hundreds." I recited what I had been instructed to say.

"Another parrot!" He turned away and rubbed his face with both of his hands. "Parrots all trained by the same eunuch . . . You all bore me to death."

"Your Majesty . . ."

"Don't dare get near me!"

What should I do? My chance had been ruined before I could begin. My tears welled up. I was afraid to move.

The man lying next to me was absorbed by his own thoughts, and I could sense nothing but tremendous pain and anger in him.

I decided to quit thinking about attracting him. What could a single move of a chess piece do if the game had already been lost? For the past nine days I had stayed up every night practicing the fan dance. I had also taken lessons from An-te-hai on playing the *qin*. I had managed to learn enough to accompany myself in a few songs. My voice was not that of a nightingale, but it was naturally pleasant and sweet. I never lacked confidence in my voice. If my parents had allowed, I would have pursued a life in opera. When I was about ten, a singer who performed in my house told me that I had potential if I was willing to work hard.

What would I tell my father? How often had he said, "In order to get cubs, one must be daring and enter the tiger's cave"? *I was inside the cave but there were no cubs.* I remembered another story he had told me. It was about a family of monkeys who tried to catch the moon's reflection in the water. The monkeys gathered in a large tree and turned themselves into a long chain reaching from the tree to the water. The lowest monkey tried to scoop up the moon with a basket. It was an ingenious plan, but Father's point was that certain things are simply impossible, and there is wisdom in accepting one's limitations.

Was anything up to me at this moment? The silk pillow felt soft and cool against my cheek. I could no longer drag my thoughts along this path. I heard an aria inside my head: *Like a river rock that rolls uphill, like a rooster that grows a set of teeth . . .*

A touch on my shoulder woke me.

"How dare you fall asleep while His Majesty is awake!"

I sat up. I couldn't quite tell where I was.

"Where have you been?" the man in front of me mocked. "Soochow or Hangchow?"

I was shocked. "Pardon me, Your Majesty, for I haven't been myself. I didn't mean to upset you. I was tired and I fell asleep carelessly."

"That doesn't make any sense!"

I pinched my thigh, trying to get my mind to work.

"How can you possibly be tired?" Emperor Hsien Feng sneered. "What have you been doing besides embroidery?"

I remained silent, but my mind's wheel rolled.

"Answer my question." His Majesty got up from the bed and began to pace with his shirt open in the front. "If you have been doing embroidery, tell me about it. I need distraction."

I sensed that His Majesty was uninterested in hearing me talk about embroidery or anything else. I would be looking for trouble no matter what I said. The man was a smoking hut. I wanted to tell him that I had expected our coupling, not conversation.

His Majesty looked at me.

Realizing that I was naked, I reached toward the stool to grab my gown.

He kicked the stool and my gown fell to the floor. "Wouldn't you like to be out of your costume for a while?"

I looked at him, amazed by his words. His voice reminded me of certain village boys I had known, boys in their late teens who still sounded like young roosters.

"I would." The Son of Heaven answered his own question. "I might even be happy for a moment."

I was overwhelmed by curiosity and decided to take a risk. "Your Majesty, may I have your permission to ask a question?"

"Yes, you may ask for anything except my seeds."

I understood what he meant and felt insulted. I lost interest in speaking further.

"Go ahead, slave, I have given you my permission."

My voice left me. Despair flooded my heart's bank. I thought about what I had done to gain this one chance. I could hear the clock ticking and Chief Shim's voice: "Your time is up, Lady Yehonala!"

I tried to convince myself to make peace with the loss, but my spirit wouldn't obey. Every nerve in my body rebelled against my will to perform what I was taught.

"I'll send for someone to replace you." His Majesty leaned over. He smelled of orange peel. "I am in the mood to be pleased." His breath touched my cheek and he seemed to enjoy the threat. "I want a parrot. Coo-coo! Coo-coo! Sing or sink. Coo-coo!"

Hopelessness came to wrap me and I still could find no words.

"Chief Eunuch Shim is waiting right behind the door," His Majesty continued. "I shall call him to take you away." He made a move toward the door.

I allowed my nature to take over. Despair had aroused my desire to fight, and suddenly my fear cleared. In my mind's eye I saw a suicide rope hanging down from the Imperial palace beam, dancing like the sleeves of the moon goddess. The joy of taking control was unexpected but real. I got off the bed and slipped into my gown. "Have an excellent night, Your Majesty," I said, and then I lunged toward the door.

I would have regretted it if I had been older or more experienced, but I was young and my blood was a hot spring. The situation had maddened me. Understanding that I would be beheaded for my behavior, I wanted to perform the final act my way.

"Halt!" Emperor Hsien Feng called from behind. "You have just offended the Son of Heaven."

I turned around and saw a grin on his face.

"If you are to order my punishment," I said, standing straight and tall, "my only wish is that you have the mercy to make it quick."

As I spoke, I tightened the laces on my gown. What more could I achieve? Since moving to the Forbidden City I had ceased being an ordinary person. What would Big Sister Fann's reaction be when she learned that I had addressed the Son of Heaven as one equal spirit to another? I smiled just thinking about Big Sister Fann's face. She would spread the story of the "legendary Orchid" until her lips grew blisters.

Almost with elation I told His Majesty that I was ready for the eunuchs to remove me.

Hsien Feng made no move. He seemed surprised at the situation. But what he felt no longer mattered to me. All my waiting for tomorrow's luck was over. My soul was set free.

"You interest me," the Emperor said, and a smile traveled across the sealed lips.

This seemed to be the Imperial style of torture.

"Tell me that you feel remorse for what you have done." He walked up to me until his face was inches away. There was a gentleness in his gaze. "It is too late even if there is regret. Begging is of no use. I am in no mood to grant mercy. Not one ounce. I have no more mercy to give."

For that reason alone I pity you. I shot my words at him with my eyes. I was glad that I was not in his position. He could order my death, but he couldn't order himself one. What kind of power was his, then? He was his own captive.

His Majesty insisted on learning my thoughts. After a moment's hesitation I decided to reveal them. I told him I pitied him although he appeared to be powerful. I told him it was not impressive that he picked not an equal but me, a defenseless slave, to punish. I told him I wouldn't resent him for punishing me, because I could see he had to find someone on whom to take out his frustration, and there was nothing easier than beheading a concubine.

As I spoke, I expected him to become enraged. I expected him to call the eunuchs to drag me out and the guards to poke me with their swords. But His Majesty did just the opposite. Instead of bursting with rage, he became calm. He seemed to be truly affected by my words. His expression became the work of a poorly skilled clay sculptor who intended to make a cheerful face but instead made a bitter one.

His Majesty slowly sat himself down on the edge of the bed and waved for me to sit by him. I obeyed. The sound of the *yoo-hoo-loo* outside the window was loud but not unpleasant. The moonlight threw shadows of a magnolia on the floor. I felt strangely peaceful.

"How about a simple conversation?" he asked.

I didn't feel like responding, so I remained silent.

"You don't have anything more to say?"

"I have said it all, Your Majesty."

"You . . . are smiling!"

"Are you offended?"

"No. I like it. Keep smiling . . . Did you hear what I said?"

I felt my facial expression freeze at his order.

"What's wrong? Your smile has disappeared. Get it back! I want to see that smile back on your face. Put it back. Now!"

"I am trying, Your Majesty."

"It is not there! You have taken my smile away! How dare . . ."

"How about this, Your Majesty?"

"No, that is not a smile. That is a grin. An ugly one. Do you need help?"

"Yes."

"Tell me how, then."

"Your Majesty could tell me my name."

"Your name?"

"Do you know my name?"

"What a wicked question! No, of course I don't."

"I am your wife. I am your consort of the fourth rank."

"Indeed?"

"My name, Your Majesty?"

"Would you kindly remind me?"

"Would I? Has anyone in this realm had the luck to hear the Son of Heaven say 'Would you kindly'?"

"What's your name? Come on!"

"Why bother?"

"His Majesty wants to bother!"

"He'd better not. It'll give him nightmares."

"How so?"

"I have no idea whether I shall turn into a good ghost. And a bad ghost chases after the living. I assume you are aware of that."

"I see." He got up and walked barefoot to a golden tray on his desk. On the tray was a bamboo chip with my name on it. "Lady Yehonala." He picked up the chip and cupped it in his hand. "How does your family call you, Yehonala?"

"Orchid."

"Orchid." He nodded and murmured the name repeatedly as he dropped the chip back onto the tray. "Well, Orchid, maybe you'd like to ask me to grant you a last wish."

"No, I would like to get my life over with as soon as possible."

"I shall certainly honor that. Anything else?"

"No."

"Well then," the Emperor said, "perhaps before you die you may wish to know how you came to be here tonight." The Emperor's effort to appear stern could not hide a faint smile.

"I wouldn't mind, no," I managed.

"Well, it all began with Chief Eunuch Shim telling me a story . . . Come, Orchid, lie here with me. It wouldn't hurt, would it? Maybe this will turn you into a good ghost."

As I climbed into the bed, my gown became tangled.

"Off, take your dress off." Emperor Hsien Feng pointed his finger at my gown.

I revealed my body with embarrassment. What a strange play to be part of!

"It was a story about the Emperor Yuan Ti of the Han Dynasty." His Majesty's tone was warm and charged with energy. "Like myself he owned thousands of concubines whom he never saw. He had time only to pick them from their portraits, which were painted by the court artist, Mao Yen-shou. The concubines showered gifts on the painter in the hope that he would make them look as desirable as possible. The loveliest of all the concubines was an eighteen-year-old girl named Wang Ch'ao-chun. She possessed a strong character and didn't believe in bribery. She thought that it would be all right if the artist painted her as she really was. But of course Mao Yen-shou painted a terrible portrait of her. The painting failed to do justice to her beauty. As a result, Emperor Yuan Ti knew her not.

"In those days many dignitaries came to pay homage at the court, among them Shang Yu, the Great Khan, who reigned over the Turkomans of the Huns. Wishing to strengthen the ties of friendship with this powerful neighbor, Emperor Yuan Ti offered him one of his own concubines as a wife. And Emperor Yuan Ti gave him Wang Ch'ao-chun, whom he had never seen.

"When the bride, who had come to bid farewell, appeared before Yuan Ti, the Emperor was struck dumb by her beauty. He had not known that his harem contained a maiden of such transcendent loveliness. He desired her right on the spot, but it was too late—Wang Ch'ao-chun was his no longer.

"As soon as the couple departed, Yuan Ti ordered Mao Yen-shou's beheading. Even so, the Emperor was forever haunted by the memory of the maiden and by regret for the happiness that might have been his."

Emperor Hsien Feng gazed at me. "I summoned you because I didn't want to suffer the regret Yuan Ti did. You are as beautiful as Chief Eunuch Shim described. You are Wang Ch'ao-chun's incarnation. But Shim failed to tell me that you are also a lady of character. You are better than the orange-peel tea they make me drink. It is delicious, but I find no pleasure in its taste.

"It is the same with everything these days. I wouldn't be able to enjoy Wang Ch'ao-chun even if she existed. And I am wondering about you. All I can think of, I'm afraid, is the shrinking map of China. Enemies are coming from all directions. They have grabbed me by the throat and spit in my face. I am beat up and shot through. Why should I —how can I—sleep with you or any concubine? To pass on a living man's worst nightmare? I am incapable of producing an heir. I am no different from a eunuch."

He began to laugh. There was a wrenching sadness in his manner and voice, which touched me. I knew the map he was talking about. It was the same map my father had shown me. The man in front of me reminded me of my father. He too had desperately desired to bring back the honor of the Manchus, and yet he ended up deserting his post. I felt the shame His Majesty bore. It was the same shame that killed my father.

I looked at Hsien Feng and thought that he was a true Bannerman. He could have sat back and enjoyed the garden and the feast of concubines, but he chose to worry himself to impotency.

An urge to comfort him overcame my fear. I moved to sit on my knees. I opened my arms and pulled him to my chest as a mother would an infant. He offered no resistance, and I held him this way for a long time.

He sighed and drew back to look at me.

I reached for the sheet to cover my exposed breasts.

"Leave it," he said, pulling away the sheet. "I enjoy what I see."

"My death sentence?"

He grinned. "You'll have a chance to live if you help me get a good night's sleep."

Sunlight filtered through my heart's darkest chamber, and I smiled.

"The smile is back!" he cried happily, like a child discovering a shooting star.

"Is it time for Your Majesty to sleep?"

"It is no longer an easy job." He sighed.

"It will help if you let go of your thoughts."

"Impossible, Orchid."

"Does Your Majesty like games?"

"Games no longer interest me."

"Does Your Majesty know 'Joy at Meeting'?"

"That is an old song. By Chu Tun-ju of the Sung Dynasty?"

"What an excellent memory Your Majesty has!"

"Let me warn you, Orchid, no doctor has succeeded in helping me with my sleep."

"May I have your *qin*?"

He reached for the instrument and passed it to me.

I plucked the strings and began to sing.

> *I lean on the western railing of the city wall*
> *Of Ching-ling in the fall.*
> *Shedding its rays over the land, the sun hangs low*
> *To see the great river flow.*

The central plain is a mess,
Officials disperse in distress.
When to recover our frontiers?
The winds of Yang-chou came to blow away my tears.

Emperor Hsien Feng listened quietly and started to weep. He asked me to sing another song. "If you were an actor from the royal troupe, I would reward you with three hundred taels," he said, taking hold of my hand.

I sang. I no longer wanted to think about how strangely things had turned out. After I finished "Farewell, Black River" and "The Drunken Concubine," His Majesty wanted more. I begged his pardon and explained that I was not prepared.

"One last song." He held me close. "Anything that comes to your mind."

My fingers wandered over the strings. A moment later a tune came to me.

"It is called 'Immortal at the Magpie Bridge,' composed by Ch'in Kuan." I cleared my throat and started.

"Wait, Orchid. 'Immortal at the Magpie Bridge'? Why have I never heard of this? Is it popular?"

"Was."

"That's not fair, Lady Yehonala. The Emperor of China should be informed about everything."

"Well, that's why I am here, Your Majesty. For me, this lyric eclipses all other love poems. It tells the old legend of the Cowherd and the Maiden—or the Weaver—two stars separated by the Milky Way. They were to meet on the Magpie Bridge once a year, on the seventh day of the seventh lunar month, when the autumn wind embraces the dew."

"The pain of separation is known to many," the Emperor said quietly. "The story reminds me of my mother. She hanged herself when I was a child. She was a beautiful woman, and we are separated by the Milky Way."

I was moved to hear him say this, but managed not to comment. Instead, I sang.

Clouds float like works of art,
Stars shoot with grief at heart.
Across the Milky Way the Cowherd meets the Maiden.
When autumn's golden wind embraces the dew of jade,
All the love scenes on earth, however many, fade.

Their passion flows like a stream.
This happy date seems but a dream.
Can they bear a separate homeward way?
If love between both sides can last,
Why need they stay together night and day?

Before my last note ended, Emperor Hsien Feng was asleep.

I put the instrument down beside the bed, wishing that this moment would go on forever. But it was time for me to depart. According to custom, I had to be sent back to my own palace at midnight. The eunuchs would soon come and remove me. Would I be summoned again? Most likely Emperor Hsien Feng would forget about me when he woke up.

A sense of melancholy descended. Fortune had not led to intimacy. I tried not to think about my *ruyi* and my lost hairpin and the energy and hope that went into my preparation. I hadn't been given a chance to perform my fan dance. If Emperor Hsien Feng had desired me, I felt I could have made him happy.

Lying next to him, I watched the candles inside the red lanterns die out one after another. I tried not to feel beaten. What good would it do if I allowed myself to break down? The Emperor would only be irritated.

Sorrow drowned me in silence. My heart floated in an ocean strangled by seaweed. The candle in the last lantern flickered and went out. The room turned black. I hadn't noticed until now that the clouds had blocked the moon completely. The singing of the *yoo-hoo-loos* was joined by other insects. The symphony of this night was marvelous. I lay in the dark and watched Emperor Hsien Feng breathing peacefully in his sleep. Like a pen, my eyes traced the contours of his body.

A shaft of moonlight cut the floor. The color was white with a touch of yellow. It recalled my mother's complexion as she watched my father die. Each day the wrinkles chewed away a bit of her, biting deeper into her skin. Then suddenly one day the lines changed the entire landscape of her face. Her skin hung as if pulled by the earth. My mother was no longer a young woman.

Slowly and silently, I removed myself from the bed. I placed the *qin* on the table against the wall. I put on my gown and looked out the windows. I stared at the moon and saw myself in it—a large tear-washed face.

Hsien Feng lay curled in sleep, a man dreaming a man's dreams. Like everyone in China, I used to think of the Son of Heaven as a godlike figure, the dragon who penetrated the universe. Today I saw a man whose delicate shoulders were having trouble carrying the nation's burden; I saw a man who sobbed over my songs, a man who grew up without a mother's love. What was misfortune if this was not? How terrible it must have been for him when his mother hanged herself in shame and everyone lied to him while all along he knew the truth! The irony was that he would never get to be the simple man he desired to be. Tomorrow morning, in front of his audience, he had to fake himself.

Tonight had been worthy of my *ruyi* and my hairpin. I was glad for what I had achieved. If His Majesty forgot me tomorrow, he couldn't erase my memory of tonight. It belonged to me. If I were to see my grave tomorrow, I would carry this night with me.

The moonlight shifted and now shone through the carved window frames. The shadows looked like embroidery spilling onto the floor. I put my cheek against the soft silky sheet of the Imperial bed and my skin against the body of the Son of Heaven. I wanted to thank him for stripping us of our titles and allowing us to touch each other the way common souls did.

At this thought I relaxed, although my fear still lingered. I prepared myself to leave the Hall of Spiritual Nurturing and never return.

Emperor Hsien Feng turned. His left arm was exposed. In the moonlight it looked as thin as a young boy's. I would let him sleep. He was facing me now. His eyebrows were no longer furrowed. His dream must be sweet.

The *yoo-hoo-loos'* singing had become discordant. It was a sign (so An-te-hai told me) that the males were finished mating and were now struggling to leave the females' bodies. The high-pitched sounds, those of the females, were disturbing. The longer I sat, the harder they were to bear. I was forced to admit that I had fallen in love with the moment, and was dreading its end. An ache started to take hold of me. I grew more desperate with each fleeting instant.

I could kiss him, I thought. I could kiss him the way I had learned at the House of Lotus. I wished that His Majesty were the same as the customers who visited that house, for they knew pleasure and sought it at every opportunity. I wondered if Emperor Hsien Feng had ever experienced true pleasure. I sensed that he hadn't. He didn't seem familiar with affection. But how could I blame him? He had to rule the country, and every night it was his duty to deposit his seeds in womb after womb. Wouldn't I be impotent too?

I heard soft footsteps. The eunuchs were coming for me.

Emperor Hsien Feng remained still. I bid a silent farewell.

There was a light knock at the door.

I stood in the moonlight.

The door was gently pushed open. Chief Eunuch Shim's figure blocked the moon. He threw himself on the ground and bowed toward the sleeping Emperor. "It's time for me to fetch Lady Yehonala, Your Majesty."

No response came from the bed.

Chief Eunuch Shim repeated himself.

Snoring was Emperor Hsien Feng's reply.

With no hesitation, Shim waved and four other eunuchs stepped in. They approached me with the litter. They took me by the arms and placed me on it and carried me outside.

Just as Shim was about to close the door, a sudden wailed "No!" erupted from the room.

Signaling his people to halt, Shim went back. He stuck his head inside the bedroom. "Your Majesty?"

There came no answer.

He hesitated for a moment and then signaled for the eunuchs to free me.

I got off the litter and slipped barefoot back into His Majesty's room.

Chief Eunuch Shim pulled the door closed.

I was beyond my good senses.

His Majesty cuddled up behind me. The touch of his skin was exciting. He was still sound asleep. I stayed awake for another hour before I drifted off. In my dream I was being swallowed by a dragon with a shark's mouth. The clouds rolled around me. I struggled to get away from the monster. My shoulders were caught and my chest was pressed. The dragon held me in its claws. "I am potent," it whispered.

I woke. Emperor Hsien Feng was touching me. I had the sensation I felt when I sat on eggs. His hands were cold but his body warm and his movements gentle. He explored.

I wrapped him like a vine around a tree.

He fumbled and his breath grew thick. He seemed to be surprised by his own excitement. One moment he pushed me away, and the next he threw himself back at me.

I tried to recall the steps I had learned from the House of Lotus. But my mind was a stewing pot where my thoughts turned into mushy beans.

"Take it," he whispered. "Are you ready?"

"Ready . . . for what, Your Majesty?"

"Don't disgust me. Stick up your behind. Aren't you after my seeds?"

"What does His Majesty expect me to say?"

"Say the lines."

"Lines? What lines? I have . . . lost the lines. You don't want to be bored with something you have heard said hundreds of times."

"Be quiet for my ancestors' sake!" Hsien Feng pulled himself away.

I looked at him and found him attractive in his nakedness. I'd better enjoy this, I thought, since I'll never be allowed to see another naked man in my life.

He asked for my thoughts and I reported honestly.

"What a wicked spirit!" he said slowly. "You are calm and unafraid. You look at the Son of Heaven as if he were a tree."

I decided not to interrupt.

"Look, I am obligated to produce the bloody sheet. Shim is waiting to collect it. He is waiting to pass it on to the household officials for examination and the record book. Then they will wait for the sign of an heir. They will calculate the dates on their fingers. The doctors will be called to stand by, day and night, for a sign of pregnancy."

His droning explanation somehow aroused me and I became unafraid.

"You come in armies," he continued. "You don't care how I feel. You come to fill up my bedroom and rob me of my essence. You selfish, greedy, bloodsucking female wolves!"

"I would enjoy our business." Words were pushed out of my chest as if by a strange force.

He was astounded. "You . . . would?"

"I am not afraid to stick up my behind." My voice demanded me to release it. "I am here to be your lover. I have paid for this moment dearly. It has not only cost me my *ruyi* and hairpin, but has also taken me from my family." My tears came and I had no desire to hold them back. "I haven't allowed myself to miss my mother and my siblings, but I do now, terribly! I haven't cried despite the fact that I've had to spend my days in loneliness, but I do now. I might be selfish, but I am not greedy or a bloodsucking wolf! I am after nobody's essence, but I *am* hungry for affection!"

"You . . ." He came closer and gently pulled me toward him "These are not the official lines. Who prepared the lines for you? You did? Yourself? Do you have more?"

An urge to perform pleasure rose inside me. "Your Majesty, spare me from answering the question. I was thinking . . . if you like, there are dances I know."

Against my will, my mind started to picture a pair of mating silkworms, the moment when half of the male moth's body was swallowed by the female's. I lay half in excitement and half in disgust.

On top of me he groaned, murmuring words I didn't understand. I couldn't believe that the expected pain was not taking place. My body welcomed its intruder.

Emperor Hsien Feng struggled as if performing a difficult task.

I was awkward too. Sticking up my behind was not part of the fan dance. We were like two monkeys exploring ways to settle ourselves. Eventually I was exhausted and lay down on my back. His face appeared above me. His sweat dripped into my mouth. I arched my rib cage and stuck out my breasts.

"Keep going," he cried as his breath came to a halt.

I could hear my own thought: *Apply what you learned at the House of Lotus!* But I was unable to move my behind. I fumbled and flipped and was on my stomach.

Hsien Feng sprawled himself on me like a blanket. I felt so surprisingly at home that I wept.

His movements had a rhythm. The lines from an opera came into my head: *Cease yearning for the future, my love, for sun will not be brighter and day will not be happier* . . . Pleasure grew and gradually seized me.

The Son of Heaven whispered between breaths. I was not sure if I heard the word "seeds."

Before dawn he wanted more. It was then that I had a chance to try my fan dance. I was curious about the effect. It worked. His Majesty praised me as magical. He especially appreciated my calling him "love" in the midst of passion, rather than "Your Majesty."

For the next few nights I continued to be summoned. My lover was amazed that he was repeatedly able to plant his seeds. Indulging himself, he begged me to explore. I became anxious about the Grand Empress. She would accuse me of keeping him all to myself, of robbing her of grandchildren "counted in the hundreds." The pleasure of love made us stay up all night. His Majesty held me close. My energy seemed inexhaustible, and I let myself be carried away again and again.

In the mornings we looked at each other as if we had been lovers for years.

"'Magpie Bridge,'" His Majesty uttered one day. "It is the most beautiful tale I have ever heard. The Imperial tutors would never have taught it to me. My head has been stuffed only with rubbish. My studies have been limited to pictures of a broken empire. The lessons never made sense to me. How could all be lost when every emperor has been wise? The tutors could never explain how we have come to owe so much to those who have stolen from us."

I listened attentively.

"The tutors told me that my mission in life was revenge," he continued. "So I was taught hatred. They threatened that I would be given no place in the temple of my ancestors if I didn't perform my duty. My duty is to restore the map of China. But how can I possibly achieve that? China is torn and I am sent to do battle without weapons! This is what my life is about: to be humiliated by barbarians."

He made me feel that I was his friend. Then one night he asked, "What would you like me to grant you?"

"I don't want to say 'to see you again,' but I am afraid that I am beginning to desire that." I tried to take hold of myself, but my tears betrayed me.

"Orchid, don't be distressed. I have the power to give you anything."

My heart took comfort in his promise, but my head warned me not to trust his words in a moment of passion. I told myself that tomorrow another concubine would be sent. Another concubine who was as desperate as I was; another concubine who had also offered her life savings to Chief Eunuch Shim.

By the time the sun rose I was back in the Palace of Concentrated Beauty. After washing, I stepped out of the room into the garden.

The weather was clear and the sun bright. The roses and magnolias were just beginning to bloom. In the courtyard, dozens of birdcages hung from the branches of trees. At this hour the eunuchs came to train the Imperial birds. The birds were from all over the country. After a period of training, the best would be sent to Emperor Hsien Feng. He would then distribute them as gifts to his late father's concubines in their palaces.

The eunuchs taught the birds to sing, talk and do tricks. Most of the birds were exotic and had funny names, such as Scholar, Poet, Doctor and Tang Priest. Those who performed were rewarded with crickets and worms. Those who didn't were starved. There were pigeons too. These were all white and allowed to fly freely. An-te-hai's favorite hobby was training pigeons. He tied whistles and bells on the birds' ankles, then let them go. They circled above my palace producing lovely sounds. When the wind was strong the sounds made me think of ancient music.

There was one highly intelligent parrot An-te-hai named Confucius. The bird could recite three-character phrases from the *San Tzu Ching*. For example, it said, "Men were kind-natured when they were born." An-te-hai gave Confucius to Chief Eunuch Shim as a birthday gift, and he in turn presented it to Emperor Hsien Feng as *his* birthday gift, and then the Emperor rewarded me with the bird. By that time the bird didn't know what it was talking about. It garbled a word, which twisted the meaning. What the parrot Confucius was now saying was "Men were evil-natured when they were born." I wondered if this was the work of His Majesty. I told An-te-hai to spare the bird from correction.

I also loved the peacocks An-te-hai raised. Peacocks roamed everywhere in my palace. An-te-hai trained them to follow me. He called them "my Imperial ladies." They lived and bred in my garden. When An-te-hai saw me step out, he would blow a whistle and the peacocks would gather and greet me. It was wonderful. The birds made a kind of cackling noise that sounded as if they were chatting. If they were in the right mood they would open their blue and green "dresses" and compete to show off their beauty.

"May luck stay with you, my lady." An-te-hai greeted me with deep bows this morning.

"May luck stay with you!" Other eunuchs, ladies in waiting, maids and even the chefs echoed the sentiment in every corner of the palace — everybody knew by now that I had become His Majesty's favorite.

"Has the morning boat gone out on the canal yet?" I asked An-te-hai. "I'd like to visit the temple on Prospect Hill."

"You can go anywhere, anytime, my lady," An-te-hai said. "This morning Emperor Hsien Feng has ordered that you be sent to him every night. You are on top of the Forbidden City, my lady. If you wish, the court will make a petrified tree bloom and a rotten vine climb."

It was from the top of Prospect Hill that the secret, tranquil, elegant Imperial capital of Peking was best revealed. The hill was actually an artificial mound built to obstruct the descent of the noxious and unpropitious spirits of the north onto the Forbidden City. From its crest the city looked like a magical forest filled with flowering trees and shrubs, more wooded than the countryside itself. Through the foliage the gleaming old yellow-gold tiles showed, and also the bright enameled temple roofs, gatehouses and palaces. The scarlet and emerald pavilions exhibited their fantastically ornate and upturned eaves.

Standing on top of the hill, I was overwhelmed by the idea that I had been blessed by celestial energy. I had been made love to by the Son of Heaven. More important, it was continuing to happen.

As I took a deep breath of fresh air, the golden roof of the Palace of Benevolent Tranquility caught my eye. I remembered the jealous elderly concubines. I remembered the way they stared at me like hungry vultures. One story An-te-hai told would not leave my mind: the fate of a favorite concubine of the Ming Dynasty after the Emperor died. She was trapped in a court conspiracy orchestrated by fellow concubines, and she was buried alive.

I received an unexpected guest: Nuharoo. She had never visited before. I was sure that it had to do with Hsien Feng's spending his nights with me. I had no doubt that her eunuchs spied for her, as An-te-hai spied for me.

Nervous but without panic, I greeted her.

Standing like a gorgeous magnolia, she performed her greeting by bending her knees slightly. I couldn't help but admire her beauty. If I were a man, I would desire her endlessly. Dressed in an apricot-colored satin robe, she was as graceful as a goddess descended from the clouds. Her sense of nobility seemed inborn. Her lacquered black hair was combed back in a goose-tail shape. A golden hairpin with a string of pearls dangled inches from her forehead. In her presence I lost confidence in my own beauty. I couldn't help but believe that I would lose Emperor Hsien Feng's affection if he took another look at her.

According to custom, I had to get down on my knees and kowtow to receive her. But she walked up and held my arms before I had a chance.

"My dear younger sister," she said, as befitted her rank. She was in fact a year younger than me. "I have brought you some good herbal tea and wild mushrooms. They were sent here from Manchuria. You will need it now." She waved her hand and her eunuchs came and presented me with a beautifully wrapped yellow box.

There was no sign of jealousy, I observed. Her voice bore no disturbance.

"This is the best kind of *tang kuei*," Nuharoo explained, picking up a dry root. "It is picked from cliffs high above the clouds. It grew from the freshest air and rain. Each is thirty years old or more." She sat down and took the teacup An-te-hai served her.

"You have grown taller since I saw you last." She smiled at An-te-hai. "I also have a gift for you." She waved again and her eunuch brought over a small blue silk box.

An-te-hai threw himself on the floor and kowtowed before taking the box. Nuharoo encouraged him to open it. Inside was a bag of taels. I was sure An-te-hai had never had that much money given to him all at once. He held the box and walked on his knees toward Nuharoo. "An-te-hai doesn't deserve this, Your Majesty!"

"Go and please yourself with it." Nuharoo smiled.

I waited for her to speak about the husband we shared. I waited to hear the words that expressed her frustration. I almost wished that she would say something to insult me. But none came. She sat calmly sipping her tea.

I wondered what made her hold herself so upright and calm. If I were she, I would find it difficult. I would resent my rival and wish myself in her place. Was she putting up a front? Or had she already developed a scheme to destroy me and was now only playing peace to deceive me?

Her quietness bothered me. Eventually I could bear it no longer. I began to confess. I reported that Emperor Hsien Feng had been spending nights with me. I begged Nuharoo for forgiveness, and I worried that my voice lacked sincerity.

"You have done nothing wrong," she said in an even tone.

Confused, I went on. "But I have. I have failed to ask for your advice." I had difficulty continuing. I was unused to faking my emotions. "I was . . . was afraid. I was not sure how to report to you. I am inexperienced in court etiquette. I should have kept you informed. I am ready to accept your censure." My mouth was dry and I took up my tea and poured it down my throat.

"Yehonala." Nuharoo put down her cup and wiped her mouth lightly with the tip of her handkerchief. "You have been worrying for the wrong reason. I am not coming to demand Emperor Hsien Feng back." She got up and took my hands in hers. "I have come for two matters. First, of course, is to congratulate you."

A small voice spoke inside my head: *Nuharoo, you can't possibly have come to thank me for taking Hsien Feng away. I don't believe you are sincere.*

As if reading my mind, Nuharoo nodded. "I am happy for you and for myself."

In accordance with etiquette, I thanked her. But my expression betrayed me. I fear it said, *I don't believe you,* a sentiment she may have detected but to which she chose not to respond.

"You see, my sister," Nuharoo's voice was gentle and soft, "in my position as the Empress, my concern is broader than you might imagine. I was taught that once I entered the palace, I would not only be married to His Majesty, but also to the entire Imperial society. The dynasty's welfare is my only concern. It is my duty to see my husband live to meet his obligations. And one such obligation is to produce as many heirs as possible." She paused, and said with her eyes, *Yehonala, can you see now that I have come to thank you?*

I bowed to her. I believed that she was conducting this act out of pain. I should offer her, if nothing else, words of understanding.

As if knowing what I was going to say, she raised her right hand. "The second matter of my visit is to tell you the news that Lady Yun has given birth."

"She has? How . . . wonderful!"

"It is a girl." Nuharoo sighed. "And the court is disappointed. So is the Grand Empress. I have been feeling sorry for Lady Yun, but sorrier for myself. I haven't been granted fortune by Heaven to conceive a child." Moisture filled her eyes and she took out her handkerchief and began to dab.

"Well, there is time." I comforted her, took her hand. "After all, the Emperor has been married just a year."

"That doesn't mean he hasn't been offered women since his teens. By Hsien Feng's age, twenty-two, Emperor Tao Kuang had produced seventeen children. What concerns me" — she looked around and made a gesture to dismiss the eunuchs — "is that His Majesty has been impotent. This is not just my experience, but Lady Li's, Mei's and Hui's as well. I don't know what you have experienced. Would you tell me?" She looked at me eagerly, and I sensed that she wouldn't desist until her curiosity was satisfied.

I didn't want to share what had happened, so I nodded in silent confirmation of the Emperor's condition.

Relieved, Nuharoo leaned back. "If the Emperor remains son-less, it will be my responsibility and misfortune. I can't imagine the throne being passed on to a different clan because of that. It would be a disaster for both of us." She let go of my hand and stood up. "I would like to count on you to bear His Majesty an heir, Yehonala."

I found myself unwilling to trust her words. On the one hand, she wanted to be who she would like to be — an empress who would go down in history as a woman of virtue. On the other hand, she couldn't hide her relief when she found out that Emperor Hsien Feng had been impotent when with me. What would have happened if I had told the truth?

The night after Nuharoo's visit I had a series of nightmares. In the morning An-te-hai woke me up with terrible news. "Snow, my lady— your cat has disappeared!"

Eleven

I TOLD Emperor Hsien Feng about Snow's disappearance and that I had been unable to solve the mystery. "Get another one" was his response. I revealed the incident to him only after I found myself too anxious to comply with his request that I sing for him.

"It can't be Nuharoo," he said. "She may not be terribly intelligent, but she is not the vicious type."

I agreed with him. More than once Nuharoo had surprised me with her remarks or behavior. After an audience the week before, the Emperor told us that a large portion of the country was in the midst of a serious drought. People in the provinces of Hupeh, Hunan and Anhwei were dying of starvation.

"Four thousand new deaths since winter." His Majesty paced back and forth between the standing basin and the throne. "Four thousand! What else can I do besides order the beheading of the governors? The peasants have begun looting and robbing. Soon it will be a nationwide uprising."

Nuharoo removed her necklace and bracelets and took down her hairpins. "Your Majesty, they are yours from now on. Auction them off so the peasants can eat." She spoke with a noble glow on her face.

I could tell that Hsien Feng didn't want to hurt her feelings. He asked Nuharoo to take back her belongings. Then he turned to me. "What would you do if you were me?"

I recalled an idea I once heard my father discussing with his friends. "I would raise taxes on the rich landlords, merchants and government officials. I would tell them that this is an emergency and the country needs their support."

Although Emperor Hsien Feng didn't praise my suggestion in front of Nuharoo, he rewarded me later. That night we had a long conversation. He said that he felt blessed by his ancestors to have a concubine who was not only beautiful but intelligent. I was thrilled, although a little shy. I decided that I must work to live up to His Majesty's praise.

That night was the first night I didn't have to perform the fan dance.

We sat in bed and talked. His Majesty spoke about his mother, and I my father. We shed tears together. He asked what I remembered most about my life as a child in the country. I told him about an experience that changed my view of peasants. When I was eleven, I participated in an event organized by my father, the *taotai,* to rescue the crops from locust infestation.

"The summer was hot and damp," I recalled. "Green stretched as far as the eye could see. The crops were waist high. The rice, wheat and millet were fattening up day by day. The harvest was fingers away. My father was happy, because he knew if everything went smoothly until the crops were harvested, the peasants living in almost five hundred villages would be able to survive the year."

Then came the sound of swarming locusts. They descended when the crops began to mature. Overnight the entire region was infested. It was as if they had come from the clouds or from deep within the earth. These brown cousins of crickets had two tiny shell-like drums close to their wings. When the wings flapped against the drums, it sounded like fingers tapping on tin. The pests came in dark clouds that blotted out the sun. They swarmed over the crops and chewed up the leaves with teeth like saws. In a few days fields of green disappeared.

My father gathered all of his men to help the villagers fight the locusts. People took off their shoes and beat the locusts with them. My father saw the futility of this and switched tactics.

He declared a state of emergency and told the peasants to dig trenches. He placed people in the path of the locusts as they moved through the crops. When a trench was ready, my father ordered one group of peasants to chase the locusts. "Hold up your clothes and wave," he said. The idea was to push the locusts toward the trench, while another group lined up behind the trench, which was piled high with dry straw.

Thousands of people waved and shouted at the top of their lungs, and I was one of them. We chased the locusts into the trench. Once they were in, my father ordered the straw to be lit. The locusts were roasted. I beat at the locusts as fast as I could to prevent them from flying away. We fought for five days and nights and were able to save half our crops. By the time my father pronounced victory, he was covered with locusts and their broken shells. I even picked locusts out of his pockets.

Emperor Hsien Feng listened to me with fascination. He said that he could imagine my father. He wished that he had known the man.

The next day I was ordered to move in with His Majesty. I would stay with him for the rest of the year. He put me in a compound connected to the audience hall, and he came to me during breaks and between audiences.

I dared not wish for my good fortune to last forever. I tried hard not to expect anything. But deep down I desired to keep what I had sprouted.

When Emperor Hsien Feng left me for work, I missed him immediately. I became easily bored and was impatient for his return. Walking around the garden, I could think of little to do but reflect on what had happened the night before. I fed on the details of our time together.

Each day I checked the calendar to remind myself that I had gained another lucky day. May of 1854 was the best time of my life. Everything was too good to be true for a girl of my background. However, I had never allowed the Emperor's adoration to alter my sense of reality. Whenever I got carried away, I caught myself the moment I saw Nuharoo and the other concubines. I told myself to remember that my luck could end in an instant. I tried to make the best of my time.

When the season turned, His Majesty moved to Yuan Ming Yuan, the Grand Round Garden, and took me with him. It was the loveliest of his many summer palaces. Generations of emperors had come here to nurture solitude. The place was itself a fable. It was located to the northwest of the Forbidden City, eighteen miles from Peking. There were gardens within gardens, lakes, meadows, misty hollows, exquisite pagodas, temples and of course palaces. One could wander from sunup to sundown without seeing the same view twice. It took me a while to realize that Yuan Ming Yuan stretched for twenty miles!

The main gardens had been built by Emperor Kang Hsi in 1709. There was a story about how Kang Hsi discovered the site. Out riding one day, he had come across a mysterious ruin. He was enchanted by its wildness and vastness, and certain that it was no common place. And he was right. It was an ancient park that had been buried in sand blown from the Gobi Desert. He found out that it had belonged to a prince of the Ming Dynasty and had been the prince's hunting park.

Thrilled by his discovery, the Emperor decided to build a garden palace on the ruins. Later it became his favorite retreat, and he lived there until his death. Since then his successors had continued to adorn and increase its wonders. More and more pavilions, palaces, temples and gardens had been added in the many years since.

What amazed me was that no single palace resembled another. Yet the whole gave no sense of disharmony. To contrive something so perfect that it looked accidental was the aim of Chinese art and architecture. Yuan Ming Yuan reflected the Taoist love of natural spontaneity and the Confucian belief in man's ability to improve on nature.

The more I learned about the architecture and craftsmanship, the more I was drawn to individual works of art. Soon my sitting room became a gallery. It was crowded with beautiful objects ranging from floor vases to grain carvings—sculptures cut from single grains of rice. Also in my room were long-legged basins set with diamonds. Wall cases became my display windows, which were filled with lucky locks of hair, fancy watches, pencil cases and decorative perfume bottles. An-te-hai framed every piece for the pleasure of my eyes. My favorite of all was a tea table inlaid with pearls the size of marbles.

Emperor Hsien Feng had fallen ill from the strain of rule. After audiences he came to me sad-faced. His mood had swung back to darkness. He hated to rise in the morning, and he wished to avoid the duty of giving audiences. He was especially reluctant when his signature on decrees and edicts was required.

When the peach flowers began to blossom, His Majesty's desire for intimacy began to fade. The peasants had started to rebel openly, he informed me. He was ashamed of his inability to reverse the situation. His worst nightmare had become a reality—the peasants had begun to join the Taiping uprising. Reports of looting and destruction came from every corner. On top of this, and perhaps most troubling of all, the foreign powers continued to demand that he open up more ports to trade. China was behind in its reparation payments for the Opium Wars and was threatened with further invasions.

Soon Emperor Hsien Feng was too depressed even to leave his room. The only time he came to me was to ask me to accompany him to Imperial worship sites. On clear days we took trips to outer Peking. I spent hour after hour inside my palanquin and could eat nothing but a bitter leaf diet—the ceremonies required "an uncontaminated body."

When we arrived at the sites, we begged the Imperial ancestors for help. I followed my husband and threw myself on the ground and bowed until my knees were bruised.

His Majesty always felt better on the way back to the palace. He believed that his prayers would be heard and he would soon expect good news. But his ancestors failed to help him — the barbarians' ships were reported to be closing in on the ports of China with weapons capable of wiping out our army in the time it took to eat a meal.

Fearing for Hsien Feng's health, the Grand Empress ordered him to slow down. "Leave your office, my son. The sick roots of your being need to rejuvenate."

"Would you come to bed with me, Orchid?" His Majesty let fall his heavy dragon robe and took me to bed. But he was no longer his past self. His sense of pleasure had left him. I couldn't arouse him.

"There is no more *yang* element left in me." He sighed and pointed to himself. "This is a skin bag. Look how pitifully it extends from my neck."

I tried everything. I did the fan dance and turned our bed into an erotic stage. Each night I invented a different goddess. I stripped and did bedroom acrobatics. The poses were borrowed from an Imperial pillow book An-te-hai had found for me.

Nothing I did had any effect. His Majesty gave up. The look on his face broke my heart. "I am a eunuch." His smiles were worse than his tears.

After he fell asleep, I went to work with the chefs. I wanted His Majesty to have a more healthful, nutritious diet. I insisted on country-style fresh vegetables and meat instead of deep-fried and preserved foods. I convinced His Majesty that the best way to please me was to pick up his chopsticks. But he had no appetite. He complained that everything inside him hurt. The doctors told him, "Your inner fire is burning so badly that you have blisters growing along your swallowing pipe."

His Majesty stayed in bed all day. "I won't last long, Orchid, I am sure," he said with his eyes fixed on the ceiling. "Maybe it is for the best."

I remembered that my father had done the same after he had been removed from his post. I wished that I could tell Emperor Hsien Feng how selfish and unmerciful he was to his people. "Dying is cheap and living is noble." I groaned like a drunken lady.

Trying to cheer him up, I ordered his favorite operas. Troupes performed in our sitting room. The actors' swords and sticks and imaginary horses were inches away from His Majesty's nose. It got his attention. For a few days he was pleasantly distracted. But it didn't last. One day he walked out in the middle of the performance. There would be no more opera.

The Emperor had been living on ginseng soup. He was spiritless and often fell deeply asleep in his chair. He would wake up in the middle of the night and sit alone in the dark. He no longer looked forward to sleep for fear of nightmares. He was afraid of shutting his eyes. When it became unbearable, he would go to the piles of court documents, which were brought every evening by his eunuchs. He would work until exhausted. Night after night I heard him weeping in utter despair.

A handsome rooster was brought to his garden to wake him up at dawn. Hsien Feng preferred the singing of a rooster to the chimes of clocks. The rooster had a large red crown, black feathers and emerald green tail feathers. It had the look of a bully, with vicious eyes and a beak like a hook. Its claws were as large as a vulture's. The Imperial rooster woke us with loud cries, often before dawn. The cry reminded me of someone who was cheering: *Ooow, oow, oow . . . Oh. Ooow, oow, oow.* It woke His Majesty, all right, but he didn't have the energy to get up.

One night Hsien Feng threw a pile of documents on the bed and asked me to take a look. He pounded his chest and yelled, "Any tree will bear a rope for me. Why should I hesitate?"

I started to read. My limited schooling didn't allow me to go much deeper than the meanings of primary words. It was not difficult to understand the problems, though. They were all anyone had talked about since I had entered the Forbidden City.

I don't recall exactly when Emperor Hsien Feng began to regularly ask me to read his documents. I was so driven by the desire to help that I ignored the rule that a concubine was forbidden to learn the court's business. The Emperor was too tired and sick to care about restrictions.

"I have just ordered the beheading of a dozen eunuchs who have become opium addicts," His Majesty told me one evening.

"What did they do?" I asked.

"They needed money to buy the drug, so they stole from the treasury. I can't believe that this disease has invaded my own backyard. Imagine what it's doing to the nation!"

He pushed himself out of bed and went to his desk. He flipped the pages of a thick document and said, "I am in the middle of reviewing a treaty that the British forced on us, and I am constantly distracted by things that come up unexpectedly."

I gently asked if I could help. He tossed the treaty to me. "You will get sick to death too if you read too much of it."

I went through the document without a break. I had always wondered what gave foreigners the power to coerce China to do what they wanted, like the opening of ports or the selling of opium. Why, I had asked myself, couldn't we flatly say no and chase them away? Now I began to understand. They had no respect for the Emperor of China. It seemed a given to them that Hsien Feng was weak and defenseless. What really didn't make sense to me, however, was the way our court handled the situation. Those who were supposedly the masterminds of the country simply insisted that China's five-thousand-year civilization was a power in itself. They believed that China was inviolable. Over and over I heard them cry in their writings, "China cannot lose because it represents Heaven's morals and principles!"

Yet the truth was so clear even I could see it: China had been repeatedly assaulted and her Emperor shamed. I wanted to yell at them. Had Emperor Hsien Feng's decrees the power to stop the foreign invasion or unite the peasants? Hadn't His Majesty given enough time for the magic plans of his advisors to work?

I looked at my husband day in and day out when he studied the treaties. Each sentence caused him anguish. His facial muscles twitched, as did his fingers, and he pressed his stomach with his hands as if he wished to pull his guts out. He asked me to heat up his tea to the boiling point. He poured the scalding water down his throat.

"You are cooking yourself!" I cried.

"It helps," he said with a tired look in his eyes.

I hid in the chamber-pot room and wept whenever I boiled Hsien Feng's tea. I saw his pain return the moment he went back to work.

"What am I going to do with this mess of mine?" he said every night before bed.

"Tomorrow morning the rooster will sing again and the sunlight will make a difference." I helped him into the sheets.

"I can't bear the rooster's singing anymore," he said. "Actually, I haven't heard it for quite a while. I hear the sound of my body shutting down. I hear my neck squeak when it turns. My toes and fingers feel like wood. The holes in my lungs must be getting bigger. It feels like there are slugs parked there."

Yet we had to carry on the façade of nobility. As long as Emperor Hsien Feng was alive, he had to attend the audiences. I skipped meals and sleep in order to read the documents and offer him a summary. I wanted to be his neck, his heart and his lungs. I wanted him to hear the rooster sing again and feel the warmth of the sunlight. When I was with His Majesty and he happened to be well rested, I would ask questions.

I asked about the origin of opium. It seemed to me that the decline of the Ch'ing Dynasty had started with the importation of it. I knew parts of the story well, others not at all.

His Majesty explained that the infestation started during the sixteenth year of the reign of his father, Tao Kuang. "Although my father banned opium, the corrupt ministers and merchants managed to carry on a secret business. By 1840, the situation had become so out of control that half of the court were either addicts themselves or the supporters of a policy that legalized opium. Or both. In a rage my father ordered an end to opium once and for all. He summoned his most trusted minister to take up the matter . . ." Pausing, His Majesty looked at me. "Do you know his name?"

"Commissioner Lin?"

His Majesty looked at me with adoration when I told him my favorite part of Lin Tse-shu's story, which was when he arrested hundreds of opium dealers and confiscated more than a hundred thousand pounds of contraband. It was not that His Majesty was ignorant of such details. I simply sensed that it would bring him pleasure to experience the moment again. "In the name of the Emperor, Lin set a deadline and ordered all foreign merchants to turn over their opium." My voice was as clear as a professional storyteller's. "But he was ignored. Refusing to give in, Commissioner Lin collected the opium by force. On April 22, 1840, Lin set fire to twenty thousand cases of opium. He announced that China would stop trading with Great Britain."

Emperor Hsien Feng nodded. "According to my father, the burning pit was as large as a lake. What a hero Lin was!"

Suddenly short of breath, His Majesty hammered on his chest and coughed and fell onto his pillow. His eyes closed. When he opened them again, he asked, "Has something happened to the rooster? Shim told me that yesterday the guards had seen weasels."

I called in An-te-hai and was shocked to learn that the rooster had vanished.

"A weasel got it, my lady. I saw it myself this morning. A fat weasel the size of a baby pig."

I told His Majesty about the rooster, and his expression grew dark. "Heaven's signs are all here. The touch of a finger will put the dynasty out of existence." He bit his lower lip so hard that it began to bleed. There was a hissing sound in his lungs.

"Come, Orchid," he said. "I want to tell you something."

I sat down by him quietly.

"You must remember the things I have told you," he said. "If we should have a son, I expect you to pass on my words to him."

"Yes, I will." I held His Majesty's feet and kissed them. "If we should have a son."

"Tell him this." He struggled to push the sentences out of his chest. "After Commissioner Lin's action, the barbarians declared war against China. They crossed the oceans with sixteen armed ships along with four thousand soldiers."

I didn't want him to go on, so I told him that I was aware of all this. When he didn't believe me, I decided to prove myself. "The foreign ships entered the mouth of the Pearl River and fired at our guards at Canton," I said, remembering what my father had told me.

His Majesty's eyes stared into space. His pupils were fixed on the sculpted dragon head that hung from the ceiling. "July twenty-seventh . . . was the saddest day in my father's life," he uttered. "It was the day . . . when the barbarians destroyed our navy and took Kowloon." The Emperor drew in his shoulders and coughed uncontrollably.

"Please rest, Your Majesty."

"Let me finish, Orchid. Our child must know this . . . In the next few months the barbarians took the ports of Amoy, Chou Shan, Ningpo, and Tinghai . . . Without stopping . . ."

I finished it for him. "Without stopping, the barbarians headed north toward Tientsin and took the city."

Emperor Hsien Feng nodded. "You have managed the facts very well, Orchid, but I want to tell you a bit more about my father. He was in his sixties. He had been in good health, but the bad news destroyed him as no disease ever could. His tears had no chance to dry . . . My father didn't close his eyes when he died. I am a son of little piety and I have brought him nothing but more shame . . ."

"It is late, Your Majesty." I rose from the bed, trying to get him to stop.

"Orchid, I'm afraid we might not have another chance." He grasped my hands and placed them on his chest. "You must believe me when I tell you that I am halfway in my grave. I see my father more than ever lately. His eyes are red and swollen, as big as peach pits. He comes to remind me of my obligations . . . Ever since I was a boy, my father took me with him when he conducted audiences. I remember messengers coming in with their robes wet with sweat. The horses they rode died of exhaustion. So much bad news. I remember the echoing sound the

143

messengers made. They yelled the sentence as if it were the last one of their lives: 'Pao Shan has fallen!' 'Shanghai has fallen!' 'Chiang Nin has fallen!' 'Hangchow has fallen!'

"As a child, I made up a poem with lines that rhymed with 'fallen.' My father could only smile bitterly. When he couldn't bear it any longer, he would withdraw in the middle of an audience. For days on end he would kneel before the portrait of my grandfather. He gathered us, all his children, wives and concubines, in the Hall of Spiritual Nurturing. He then admitted his shame. That was the moment after he had signed the treaty, which included China's first war reparations to Great Britain. The amount was twenty-one million taels. The British also demanded ownership of Hong Kong for a hundred years. From that time on, foreign merchants came and went at will. My father died on the morning of January 5, 1850. Lady Jin had difficulty closing his eyelids. A monk told me that my father's soul was disturbed, and unless I got even with his enemy, he would never rest in peace."

Half asleep, my husband continued his sad story. He talked about the Taiping uprising, which started a month after he was crowned. He described it as a wildfire that jumped from province to province, crossing the country and reaching as far as Chihli. "A nasty wound that wouldn't heal. This is what I inherited from my father. A nasty wound. I can't remember how many battles I ordered and how many generals I beheaded for their inability to bring me victory."

All night long my husband tossed and shouted, "Help me, Heaven!"

I had little sleep and was afraid of being sent away. I had been living with His Majesty for months and had been his only company. He made our bedroom his office and drafted letters and edicts at all hours. I ground the ink for him and made sure his tea was hot. He was so weak that he would doze off in the middle of writing. When I saw his chin drop, I removed the brush from his hand so that he wouldn't ruin the document. Sometimes I came to the rescue too late, and there would be a spreading ink blot on the rice paper. To save the lost work, I would fetch a clean sheet and recopy his words. I imitated his style of calligraphy and eventually became very good. When he woke, he wouldn't notice that the page on his desk was not the original. He wouldn't believe me until I showed him the writing that he had ruined.

We succeeded in sharing intimacy, and he was attentive and engaged. But once our lovemaking was over he would become frustrated again. He said not one bit of good news had come to his court for an entire year. He grew bitter. No matter how hard he would work, he believed China was beyond saving. "Doomed by fate," he said. He began to cancel audiences. Retreating into himself, he spent more and more time imagining himself as an emperor of a different time. A wistful, dreamy look clouded his eyes when he described his reveries.

I became nervous when I saw urgent documents piling up. I couldn't enjoy his attention when I knew that ministers and generals were waiting for his instructions. I feared that I would be held responsible—a concubine who had seduced the Emperor. I begged Hsien Feng to resume his duties.

When my efforts failed, I picked up the documents and started to read to him. I read the questions from the letters aloud. Hsien Feng had to think of a reply. When he did, I wrote the answers down on the decree in his style, using a red brush. *Lan* in the third tone meant "I have reviewed." *Chi-tao-le* meant "It's clear to me." *Kai-pu-chih-tao* meant "I am clear about this part." And *Yi-yi* meant "You have my permission to go ahead." He would review what I wrote and put his signature on top of it.

He came to enjoy this. He praised my ability and quick wit. In a few weeks I became Emperor Hsien Feng's unofficial secretary. I reviewed everything that passed across his desk. I became familiar with his way of thinking and his style of debating. Eventually I managed to draft letters sounding so much like him that even he couldn't tell the difference.

During summer days it was difficult for me to avoid the "walk-in" ministers, since we left the door open to let in cool air. To avoid suspicion, Hsien Feng told me to disguise myself as an ink boy.

I hid my long hair under a hat and dressed in a plain robe, pretending to be the eunuch who ground the ink. No one paid attention to me; indeed, the ministers' minds were preoccupied, so they easily ignored me.

Before the summer ended, we left Yuan Ming Yuan and moved back to the Forbidden City. With my persistence, Emperor Hsien Feng was able to rise before dawn again. After washing and dressing, we would have a cup of tea and a bowl of porridge made of red beans, sesame and lotus seeds. We then rode in separate palanquins to the Hall of Spiritual Nurturing. The court had realized the seriousness of Hsien Feng's illness— they knew his heart and lungs were weak, and that his black moods drained his strength—and accepted his proposal that I accompany him to work.

It was only a half-minute walk from our bedroom to the office, but etiquette must be followed—an Emperor didn't walk on his own legs. To me it was a waste of time, but I soon understood how important ritual was in the minds of our ministers and countrymen. Based on the idea that distance creates myth, and myth evokes power, the effect was to separate the nobles from the masses.

Like his father, Hsien Feng was strict about his ministers' punctuality, but not about his own. The notion that everyone in the Forbidden City lived to attend his needs had been continually reinforced since he was a child. He expected devotion and had little sensitivity to the needs of others. He would schedule his appearances at dawn, forgetting or not caring that the summoned would have to travel through the night. Never was a promise given concerning the exact time of the meetings. The fact was that not every appointment was kept. When matters got complicated and the original schedules were pushed back or canceled, officials were left in the dark and had to wait endlessly. Some waited for weeks, only to be told to return home.

When His Majesty realized that he was canceling too many appointments, he rewarded the disappointed with gifts and autographs. Once, when rain poured and those summoned got soaking wet after nights of traveling and their appointments were canceled, Hsien Feng rewarded each with a bolt of silk and satin to make new clothes.

I sat next to His Majesty as he worked. The room was a resting area to the rear of the throne room. It was now called the library because of its wall-to-wall, floor-to-ceiling bookshelves. Above my head was a black tablet engraved with the large Chinese characters *upright* and *aboveboard*. From the outside, it was difficult to gauge the real size of the building. It was much larger than I had imagined. Built in the fifteenth century, it was near the Palace of Benevolent Tranquility but still within the Gate of Imperial Justice, the Gate of Glorious Virtue and the Gate of Preserved Fortune. This last led to a group of large compounds and side buildings that housed the Imperial offices.

The place was also near the office of the Grand Council, which had grown in importance in recent years. From here the Emperor could summon his councilors to discuss matters at any time. His Majesty usually preferred to receive his ministers in the central room of the Hall of Spiritual Nurturing. For reading, writing or receiving senior officials or trusted friends, he would go to the western wing. The eastern wing had been rearranged during the summer and had become our new bedchamber.

To many, being granted an audience with the Emperor was a lifetime honor. Hsien Feng had to live up to their expectations. There was no end of ceremonial detail. The night before an audience, the eunuchs had to clean the palace thoroughly. A buzzing fly would be cause for a beheading. The throne room was scented with fragrance and incense. The kneeling mats had to be laid out properly. Before midnight, guards came and checked every inch of the room. By two in the morning, the summoned ministers or generals would be escorted through the Gate of Celestial Purity. They had to walk quite a distance to reach the Hall of Spiritual Nurturing. Before being led to the throne room, they were received in the western wing's guest rooms. The court officer of registration would attend them. Only tea would be served. By the time the Emperor mounted his palanquin, the summoned would be notified and told to stand up and face east until His Majesty arrived.

Before Emperor Hsien Feng stepped out of his palanquin, a whip would be snapped three times—the call for complete silence. The moment the whip sounded, everyone was expected to get down on his knees. People lined up according to rank. The grand councilors, princes and other royalty would take the first rows. When the Emperor seated himself, everyone was expected to kowtow nine times, forehead touching the floor.

He didn't like to work in the throne room because the throne was uncomfortable. Its back was a magnificent piece of woodcarving, composed of numerous clusters of dragons. Audiences could take hours, and Hsien Feng would end up with a sore back.

The throne room was like a gallery, with every object on display. The throne sat on a raised stage with staircases on either side. Behind the throne were three sets of carved wood panels, each decorated with golden dragons. The stage enabled the Emperor to meet the eyes of more than a hundred officers. The audience began as the first summoned individual walked up the east staircase and presented the Emperor with a book of printed memos.

Emperor Hsien Feng would not touch the book. His secretary would pick it up and place it on a yellow case near the throne. The Emperor might refer to the book if the need arose. The summoned would then walk away, exiting down the west staircase to return to his mat. He now was permitted to state his business. When the summoned finished his petition, the Emperor would give his comments.

Hsien Feng usually initiated a discussion among the grand councilors, princes and senior clansmen. They would offer their views, each vying to present the best option. Sometimes their words became sharp and their tempers heated. There was one incident in which a minister died of a heart attack in the middle of an argument. The summoned was expected to remain quiet until questioned. Then he would respond accordingly, always deferential and reserved. After a conclusion was reached, Emperor Hsien Feng would be ready to issue a decree. A court scholar of the highest rank would be ordered to draft the decree in both Chinese and Manchu. Then the next in line would be called. The procedure repeated itself until noon.

I was much more interested in learning what was going on in the countryside than in listening to ministers who had never set foot outside Peking. I found most of the discussions boring and the solutions lacking in common sense. I was amazed by the differences among the royal princes, the Manchu clansmen, and the governors and generals, mostly Han Chinese who smelled of gunpowder. I was impressed by the Chinese simply because they injected a note of reality. Officers of Manchu origin loved to argue about ideology. They shouted patriotic slogans like schoolchildren. The Han officers chose to remain silent when there was a conflict in this Manchu court. If they wished to get an idea across, they pressed it dispassionately, providing the Emperor and his court only with facts.

After sitting through a few audiences, I noticed that the Chinese did not attempt to counter the Emperor. If their proposal was turned down, they would accept it humbly. Often they would carry out His Majesty's order even if they knew it would be ineffective. After thousands of lives were lost, the Chinese would come back with the casualty figures, hoping that the Emperor would reconsider their proposal. When he did, they were so relieved they wept. I was much moved by their loyalty, but wished that Hsien Feng would listen to the Manchu noblemen less and the Chinese more.

Still, I began to see why the Emperor behaved the way he did. More than once he told me that he believed that only a Manchu was capable of pure devotion to the Ch'ing Dynasty. He always leaned toward the Manchu officers when there was a difference of opinion. He honored the ruling race's privilege, and made it clear to the court that it would be a minister of Manchu origin that he would trust first. For centuries the Chinese ministers had managed to rise above the humiliation. I was in awe of their strength and patience.

Twelve

I N ASSISTING Emperor Hsien Feng, I became familiar with two people who carried great weight in the court and yet whose views were
diametrically opposed to it. One was Su Shun, the head of the Grand
Council. The other was Prince Kung, the Emperor's half-brother.

Su Shun was an ambitious and arrogant Manchu in his forties. He
was a tall man with a vigorous frame, and his large eyes and thin,
slightly hooked nose reminded me of an owl. His bushy eyebrows were
uneven, one standing higher than the other. He was known for his wit
and explosive temper. He represented the conservative party of the
court. My husband called him "a merchant who sells fantastic ideas." I
admired Su Shun's talent for delivering commanding speeches. He
drew examples from history, philosophy, even from classic operas. I
often caught myself thinking, *Is there anything this man doesn't know?*

Detail was Su Shun's specialty, and he was a great storyteller. His
sense of drama enhanced the effect. With only his voice to go by, as I sat
behind my curtain, I was often won over by his words, even if I disagreed with his politics.

To the court, Su Shun was a living book of five thousand years of
China's civilization. The breadth of his knowledge was unparalleled,
and he was the only minister fluent in Manchu, Mandarin and ancient
Chinese. Su Shun enjoyed great popularity among the Manchu clans,
where his anti-barbarian views received wide support.

As the seventh grandson of a nobleman and as a descendant of the
founder of the Ch'ing Dynasty, Nurhachi, Su Shun had connections in

high places. His power also rested in his friendship with influential men, many of whom were quietly wealthy Chinese. Since his youth he had traveled extensively. His broad tastes allowed him to communicate effectively with society at large. He was known for having a special interest in antique art. He owned several ancient tombs in Hsian, where the first emperor of China was believed to be buried.

Su Shun was regarded as a man of generosity and loyalty. There was a story about when he first began to work for the court as a lowly official's assistant: he sold his mother's jewelry so that he could mount banquets for his friends. Later I learned that Su Shun used these elaborate meals to gather information on all areas of life—from gossip about Peking's most popular actors to who hid the most gold in his backyard, from military reforms to political marriages.

Su Shun's recent promotion as Emperor Hsien Feng's right-hand man had stemmed from His Majesty's frustration over the court's bureaucracy. So corrupt was the court that most officials did little but sit on their titles and take their salaries. Many were descendants of royals who had fought under powerful princes; others were society's wealthy but lowborn Manchus who had purchased their posts with "donations" to provincial governors. Together they formed an elite that ran the court. Over the years they emptied the Imperial treasury. When the country suffered economically, these people continued to thrive. When Emperor Hsien Feng realized the depth of the problem, he promoted Su Shun to "sweep away the debris."

Su Shun was effective and ruthless. He concentrated on a single, highly visible case of corruption involving the Imperial civil service examination. The exam was given annually and touched the lives of thousands throughout the country. In his report to Emperor Hsien Feng, Su Shun charged five high-ranking judges with accepting bribes. Also in his report he presented ninety-one cases in which test scores had been mishandled, and challenged the past year's first-place winner. To restore the reputation of the civil service, the Emperor ordered the beheading of all five judges and the first-place winner. People cheered the action, and Su Shun became a household name.

Another thing Su Shun did brought him even greater honor. He prosecuted bankers who produced fake taels. One of the major counterfeiters happened to be his best friend, Huang Shan-li. Huang had once saved Su Shun from being murdered by an unforgiving creditor, so everyone predicted that Su Shun would find a way to exonerate his friend. But Su Shun showed that his first loyalty was to the Emperor.

The other man whose opinion Emperor Hsien Feng valued was Prince Kung. The Emperor once painfully admitted to me that his own talent was nowhere equal to Prince Kung's. His other half-brothers, Prince Ts'eng and Prince Ch'un, were no match for Prince Kung either. Ts'eng was known as "a loser who thinks himself a winner," and Ch'un as "honest but not too bright."

I disagreed with my husband at first. Prince Kung's seriousness and argumentative nature could be alienating. But as I got to know Kung, my view of him gradually changed. He thrived on challenges. Emperor Hsien Feng was too delicate, sensitive and, most of all, deeply insecure. Not everyone saw this, though, for he usually hid his fear beneath a mantle of arrogance and decisiveness. When it came to dealing with loss, Hsien Feng's mind was rooted in fatalism. His brother looked down a more optimistic path.

It was strange spending time with both men. Like millions of other girls in China, I had grown up hearing stories of their private lives. Before Big Sister Fann filled in the details, I knew the general outlines of Empress Chu An's tragic death. When Hsien Feng described it to me in his own words, it sounded flat and even false. He had no memory of a farewell scene with his mother. "No eunuch stood outside holding the white silk rope to hurry her on her way." His Majesty's tone was plain and undisturbed. "My mother put me to sleep, and by the time I woke they said she was dead. I never saw her again."

To Emperor Hsien Feng the tragedy was a way of life, while to me it was a sad opera. The child Hsien Feng must have suffered grievously, and he continued to suffer as a man. But he would not allow himself to truly feel this; perhaps he no longer could.

The Emperor once told me that the Forbidden City was nothing more than a burning straw hut in a vast wilderness.

The palanquin bearers climbed the hills slowly. Behind us, eunuchs carried a cow, a goat and a deer tied up with ropes. The path was steep. Sometimes we had to get out of the chairs and walk. After we arrived at the ancestral site, the eunuchs set up an altar and laid out incense, food and wine. Emperor Hsien Feng bowed to the sky and spoke the same monologue he had delivered many times before.

Kneeling beside him, I knocked my forehead on the ground and prayed that his father would show mercy. Not long before, Hsien Feng wanted to use An-te-hai's pigeons to send messages to his father in Heaven. He had his eunuchs replace the whistle pipes with notes to his father, which he had carefully composed himself. Naturally nothing came of it.

I hoped that the Emperor would be able to redirect his energy in more practical ways. Returning from the temple, he told me that he would like to visit his brother Prince Kung at the prince's residence, the Garden of Discerning, about two miles down the path. It almost made me think that his father's spirit was at work. I asked if I could continue on with him. When he said yes, I was excited. I had seen Prince Kung but had never spoken with him.

Hsien Feng's palanquin was as large as a room. Its sides were made of satin the color of the sun. Inside we were bathed in soft yellow light. I turned to His Majesty.

"What are you looking at?" he asked.

I smiled. "I wonder what's on the Son of Heaven's mind."

"I'll show you what's on my mind," he said as his hands groped between my thighs.

"Not here, Your Majesty." I pushed him away.

"Nobody stops the Son of Heaven."

"The bearers will know."

"So what?"

"A rumor will be born and walk off on its own legs. Tomorrow morning Her Majesty the Grand Empress will spit when mentioning my name at her breakfast table."

"Didn't she do the same with my father?"

"No, Your Majesty, I am not going to do it with you."

"I'll make you."

"Wait until we get to the palace, please?"

He pulled me to him. I struggled and tried to get away.

"You don't want me, Orchid? Think about it. I am offering you my seeds."

"Are you talking about those cooked seeds? The seeds that you told me won't sprout?"

The palanquin rocked and swayed. I tried to keep still but it was impossible: the Emperor of China was not used to restraining himself. The head bearer and Chief Eunuch Shim began to talk. It seemed that the head bearer was concerned for His Majesty's safety and wanted to stop and check. Shim knew exactly what was going on. The bearer and the eunuch argued.

One of my shoes fell off. It tumbled from the compartment and

Chief Eunuch Shim picked it up. He held my shoe in front of the head bearer, who finally understood. The argument ceased. It was at this moment that Emperor Hsien Feng reached his climax. The whole palanquin shook. Shim delicately slipped the shoe back on my foot.

I was happy that our escapade lifted the Emperor from his depression. He complimented me on my pleasantness. But all was not what it seemed with me. On the surface I was pleasant, strong and self-assured, but behind my mask I felt isolated, tense and, in some vague but very real way, dissatisfied. Fear was always with me and I thought of my rivals constantly. How much longer would it be, I wondered, before another took my place? Their jealousy-pickled faces hung before me like winter fog.

I was sure that my rivals had sent spies to watch over me. The "eye" might be one of the Emperor's own attendants. If so, he would certainly report on our activities in the palanquin. A little scandal might be made to go a long way. To the three thousand females in the Forbidden City, I was the thief who had stolen the only stallion. I was the one who had robbed them of their only chance of motherhood and happiness.

The disappearance of my cat, Snow, had been a warning. An-te-hai had found her in a well not far from my palace. Her beautiful white hair had all been pulled out. No one came forward to name the killer, nor did anyone express sympathy. In a strange coincidence, soon afterward three operas were performed on the Grand Changyi Stage. Was that an expression of victory? A celebration of revenge? I was the only concubine who was not invited to attend. I sat alone in my garden and listened to the music float over my wall.

An-te-hai had also reported another bit of gossip. A fortuneteller had visited the palace and predicted that something terrible would happen to me before the end of winter: I would be strangled to death in my sleep by the hands of a ghost. Whenever we passed one another, the expressions on the other ladies' faces told me their thoughts. Their eyes asked, "When?"

Although I meant no harm, I was in a position to do harm. I was left with the choice of either ruining others' lives or letting them ruin my own.

I knew exactly what was wanted from me. But would I voluntarily withdraw from His Majesty's affection? Before I bribed Chief Eunuch Shim, my bed had been cold for months. I refused to willingly crawl beneath those sheets again.

. . .

At audiences, I discovered that the best solutions often existed between the words of those who reported the troubles. They had spent time with the subject and were able to come up with suggestions. What bothered me was that the ministers often held their true opinions back. They trusted the Son of Heaven to see things "through a god's eye."

It amazed me that Emperor Hsien Feng believed that he *was* the god's eye. Rarely doubting his own wisdom, he sought signs to prove its heavenly source. It might be a tree split by thunder in his garden or a shooting star crossing the night sky. Su Shun encouraged Hsien Feng's fascination with himself, convincing him that he was protected by Heaven. But when things outside the Forbidden City failed to go Hsien Feng's way, he acted like a leaking water bag—his self-confidence spilled away.

The Emperor fell apart. When truth and understanding were kept from him, his moods swung all the more violently. One minute he would be definitive about defeating the barbarians and order the deportation of a foreign ambassador; the next minute he would despair and agree to sign a treaty that would only lead China into deeper economic disaster. In public I tried to maintain the illusion of my husband's power. But I could not fool myself. Beneath my golden dress, I was Orchid from Wuhu. I knew that crops were helpless when locusts invaded.

When audiences went smoothly, Emperor Hsien Feng would tell me that I had helped him restore his magic powers. All I did was listen to people like Su Shun and Prince Kung. If I had been a man and been able to set foot outside the palace, I would have gone to the frontier and come back with my own strategies.

Outside our palanquin we could see nothing but barren hills. Letting down the curtain, His Majesty rested on his pillow and continued speaking about his life. "The Taiping rebels caused destruction everywhere. I have no one but my brother to count on. If Prince Kung can't do it, nobody can, and that I know for sure. In the past I humiliated him knowingly and unknowingly; now I take every opportunity to mend our relationship. My father didn't keep his promise, and I am guilty for him. I granted Prince Kung the highest title the day I was crowned Emperor.

"Then I granted him the best place to live outside the Forbidden City, as you will soon see for yourself." He nodded. "I offered him a fortune in taels and he used it to remodel the palace. I neglected my other brothers and cousins. The Garden of Discerning is not a bit less beautiful than any of the palaces inside the Forbidden City."

I was not unfamiliar with what Emperor Hsien Feng had done for his brother. To make Prince Kung feel welcome, Hsien Feng disregarded the tradition that a Manchu prince was not allowed to hold a military position. He appointed Kung as the chief advisor of the Imperial military cabinet. Prince Kung's power was equal to Su Shun's. Ignoring Su Shun's protests, His Majesty also granted Prince Kung the right to pick whomever he liked to work with him, which included his father-in-law, Grand Secretary Kuei Liang, who happened to be Su Shun's enemy.

We reached the Garden of Discerning just before noon. Prince Kung and his *fujin*—Manchu for "wife"—had been notified and were waiting by the gate. Kung seemed to be delighted to see his brother. Twenty-two years old, he was two years younger than Hsien Feng. They were about the same height. I detected Prince Kung's sharpness when he stole a glance at me. It was an evaluation detached from feeling. I sensed his suspicion and distrust. No doubt he had wondered why his brother was keeping me, especially given the harshness of the rumors in circulation.

Following tradition, Prince Kung performed a ritual of welcome. To me it seemed rather unaffectionate. They did not act like two brothers who had grown up together. The feeling was more like a servant paying tribute to his master.

Emperor Hsien Feng acknowledged his brother's gesture. He was impatient with the formality and rushed through his response. Before Fujin finished her "I wish Your Majesty ten thousand years of life" bows, he took his brother by the arms.

I performed my kowtows and bows and then stood aside to listen and observe. I discovered resemblances in the way the brothers carried themselves: elegant and arrogant at the same time. They both had typical Manchu features: slanting single-lidded eyes, a straight nose and a well-defined mouth. Here was the difference, I quickly decided: Prince Kung had a Mongol rider's posture. He walked with a straight back but was bowlegged. Emperor Hsien Feng's movements were more like those of an ancient scholar.

We exchanged gifts. I gave Fujin a pair of shoes that An-te-hai had only moments before returned with. They featured pearls and green jade beads sewn in a beautiful floral pattern. Fujin was delighted. In return she gave me a copper smoking pipe. I had never seen anything like it. The little pipe bore a sophisticated foreign battle scene, with ships, soldiers and ocean waves. The tiny figures were incised precisely and the surface was polished as smooth as porcelain. Fujin told me that it had been made with the help of a machine invented by an Englishman. It was a gift from one of Prince Kung's employees, a Briton named Robert Hart.

After the greetings, servants came with mats and positioned them at our feet. Prince Kung threw himself down on his mat and kowtowed to his brother all over again. His wife followed. After he was pardoned, he called for his children and concubines, who had been waiting, all dressed up, for their summons. Fujin made sure that the children performed their greetings to perfection.

I was relieved when the ritual was finally over and we were led to the sitting room. Fujin excused herself and exited. Before I sat down, Prince Kung asked if I would like to have Fujin give me a tour of the garden.

I told him that I preferred to stay, if he didn't mind.

He showed surprise but said nothing.

With Emperor Hsien Feng's permission I remained in my seat. The brothers began their conversation. Prince Kung focused completely on his brother, as if I were not in the room.

I had never seen anyone talk as frankly and passionately as Prince Kung. His words carried great urgency, as if his house would catch fire if he didn't speak fast enough.

Before the Emperor had a chance to take the first sip of his tea, Prince Kung placed a letter in front of him. "The news reached me yesterday with a six-hundred-mile priority stamp. It is from the governor of Shantung province. As you can see, it is addressed to both Su Shun and me and is extremely troubling."

Emperor Hsien Feng put down his tea. "What's the matter?"

"The dikes around the Yellow River have collapsed near the border of Shantung and Kiangsu provinces. Twenty villages were flooded. Four thousand people have died."

"Someone will be punished!" Emperor Hsien Feng seemed more annoyed than concerned.

Prince Kung put down the document and sighed. "It is too easy to behead a couple of mayors and governors. Lives will not be gained back. We need the local authorities to take care of the homeless and organize rescues."

Hsien Feng covered his face with his palms. "Let me hear no more bad news! Leave me alone!"

As if he had no time to dwell on his brother's suffering, Prince Kung moved on. "I also need your support to establish a Tsungli Yamen."

"What is this Tsungli Yamen?" Emperor Hsien Feng asked. "I have never heard of the title."

"A national bureau of foreign affairs."

"Ah, the foreign problem. Why don't you go ahead, if you think you need it."

"I can't."

"Who's stopping you?"

"Su Shun, the court, the senior clansmen. I face strong opposition. People say that our ancestors never had it, so why should we."

"Everyone is waiting for our father's spirit to perform a miracle." The Emperor frowned.

"Yes, Your Majesty. Meanwhile, many more foreigners are coming. Our best bet is to put in place some restrictions in order to gradually gain control over the situation. Perhaps we will even be able to drive them out one day. But first we must deal with them according to rules that we both agree on. The foreigners call such rules 'law,' roughly equivalent to what we call 'principle.' The Tsungli Yamen will be in charge of making the laws."

"What do you want from me, then?" Emperor Hsien Feng asked in a less than enthusiastic tone.

"I will get started if you grant me an operational fund. My people need to learn foreign languages. And of course I have to hire foreigners to be the teachers. The foreigners—"

"I can't stand the word 'foreigners'!" the Emperor interrupted. "I resent acknowledging the invaders. All I know is that they come to China to impose their ways on me."

"There is something in it for China, Your Majesty. Open trade will help develop our economy."

Emperor Hsien Feng raised his hand to silence Prince Kung. "I won't offer gifts when my face is shamed."

"I understand and agree with you, my brother," Prince Kung said with gentleness. "But you have no idea what humiliations I have endured. Pressure comes at me from both sides, foreign and domestic. I have been called 'the devil's ass-kisser' by my own officers and clerks."

"You deserve it."

"Well, it is easy to close our eyes, but will reality go away?" Prince Kung paused, then decided to finish what he had set out to say. "The truth is, we are under attack and have no defenses. I worry that our court's ignorant arrogance will cost us the dynasty."

"I am tired," Hsien Feng said after a moment of silence.

Prince Kung rang the servants, who brought in a flat-backed rattan chair.

With assistance Emperor Hsien Feng sat on the chair. Pale-faced and sleepy-eyed, he said, "My thoughts are flying away like butterflies. Make me think no more, please."

"Do I have your permission to open the Tsungli Yamen, then? Will you see the funds issued?"

"I hope that is all you are asking." Hsien Feng closed his eyes.

Prince Kung shook his head and a bitter smile crossed his face. The room was quiet. Through the windows I saw maids chasing children as they hopped over stones in a pond.

"I need an official decree, Your Majesty." Prince Kung sounded almost like he was begging. "Brother, we can't afford to wait any longer."

"Fine." Eyes still closed, Hsien Feng turned his face toward the wall.

"In your decree the Tsungli Yamen must be given true power."

"All right, but in return you must promise," Emperor Hsien Feng said, pushing himself to sit up, "that whoever gets paid must perform or he will lose his head."

Prince Kung looked relieved. "I can assure you that the quality of my people will be second to none. But things are more complicated. The most serious obstacle my officers face is the court. I get no respect from this quarter. They secretly cheered when local villagers harassed foreign ambassadors and murdered missionaries. I can't tell you how dangerous such behavior is. It can ignite a war. The senior clansmen are politically sightless."

"Enlighten the court, then," said Emperor Hsien Feng, opening his eyes. He looked truly tired.

"I have tried, Your Majesty. I called meetings and no clansmen showed up. I even sent my father-in-law to personally invite them, hoping that his age would bring respect. But it didn't work. I got letters calling me names and telling me to hang myself. I'd like to ask you to attend the next meeting if that would be possible. I want the court to know that I have your full support."

The Emperor made no answer. He was falling asleep.

With a sigh, Prince Kung sat back. He looked defeated.

The sun had hit the roof beams and the room felt warm.

The smell of jasmine from the plants in the corners was sweet. Gradually the sunlight changed the shapes of the plants' shadows on the floor.

Emperor Hsien Feng began to snore. Prince Kung rubbed his hands and looked around the room. Servants came and removed our teacups. They brought small plates with fresh loquats.

I had no appetite. Prince Kung didn't touch the fruit either. We stared at the sleeping Emperor. Slowly our eyes met and I decided to make use of the time.

"I was wondering, sixth brother," I began, "if you could kindly tell me about the murder of foreign missionaries. I'm having a hard time believing it."

"I wished that His Majesty had the desire to learn about this," Prince Kung said. "You know the saying, 'A long icicle doesn't form with one night of snow'—well, the roots of the incidents can be traced to the reign of Emperor Kang Hsi. During that time, when Grand Empress Hsiao Chuang reached the autumn of her life, she became friends with a German missionary named Johann Adam Schall von Bell. It was he who converted Her Majesty to Catholicism."

"How could that be possible? I mean, the conversion of Her Majesty?"

"Not overnight, of course. Schall von Bell was a scholar, a scientist and a priest. He was an attractive man and was introduced to the Grand Empress by the court scientist, Hsu Kuang-chi. Schall had been teaching under Hsu at the Imperial Hanlin Academy."

"I know about Hsu. Wasn't he the one who correctly predicted the eclipse."

"Yes." Prince Kung smiled. "That was Hsu, but he didn't do it alone. Father Schall was his teacher and partner. The Emperor appointed him to reform the lunar calendar. When Schall succeeded, the Emperor appointed him as his military consultant. Schall helped manufacture the weapons that led to the suppression of a major peasant uprising."

"How did the Grand Empress get to know Schall?"

"Well, Schall predicted that her son Prince Shih Chung would ascend to the throne, since the boy had survived smallpox while the Emperor's other children hadn't. Of course no one at the time understood what smallpox was, and no one believed Schall. A few years later, Shih Chung's brother Shih Tsu died of smallpox. Her Majesty now believed that Schall had a special connection with the universe, and she asked to be converted to his religion. She became a fervent believer and welcomed the foreign missionaries."

"Did the trouble start when the missionaries built churches?" I asked.

"Yes, when they chose sites the locals considered to have the best *feng shui.* Villagers believed that the shadows cast by churches onto their ancestral graveyards would disturb the dead. The Catholics also denigrated Chinese religions, which offended the local people."

"Why wouldn't the foreigners be more understanding?"

"They insisted that their god was the only god."

"Our people would never accept this."

"True." Prince Kung nodded. "Fights started between the new converts and those who held on to their old beliefs. People of dubious reputation, even criminals, joined the Catholics. Many committed crimes in the name of their god."

"I'm sure that would lead to violence."

"Indeed. When the missionaries attempted to defend the criminals, the locals gathered by the thousands. They burned down the churches and murdred the missionaries."

"Is that why the treaties made clear that China would be fined heavily if it failed to control uprisings?"

"The fines are bankrupting us."

There was a silence, and Prince Kung turned to look at the Emperor, who was breathing deeply.

"Why don't we tell the missionaries to leave?" I asked, wishing that I could help myself not to. "Tell them to come back when things are more stable here?"

"His Majesty did. He even gave them the date."

"What was the response?"

"Threats of war."

"Why do the foreigners force their ways on us? As Manchus, we don't force our views on the Chinese. We don't tell them to stop binding their women's feet."

Prince Kung gave a sarcastic laugh. "Can a beggar demand respect?" He turned to look at me as if expecting an answer.

The room began to feel cold. I watched our teacups being refilled.

"The Son of Heaven has been kicked around," I said. "China has been kicked around. Everyone is too ashamed to admit it!"

Prince Kung gestured for me to keep my voice down.

In his sleep Hsien Feng's cheeks flushed. He must be running a fever again. His breathing was now labored, as if not enough air was entering his lungs.

"Your brother believes in *pa kua*—the eight diagrams—and *feng shui,*" I told Prince Kung. "He believes he is protected by the gods."

Kung took a sip of his tea. "Everyone believes what he wants to believe. But reality is like a rock from the bottom of a manure pit. It stinks!"

"How did the Westerners become so powerful?" I asked. "What should we learn about them?"

"Why do you want to bother?" He smiled. He must be thinking that this was no subject for a woman to discuss.

I told Prince Kung that Emperor Hsien Feng was interested in learning. And that I could be helpful.

A look of recognition passed between us. It seemed to make sense to him. "This is no small topic. But you might begin by reading my letters to His Majesty. We must escape the trap of self-deception and . . ." He raised his eyes and suddenly went quiet.

It was through Prince Kung that I learned of the third important man, the general of the Northern Army and the viceroy of Anhwei province. His name was Tseng Kuo-fan.

I had first heard the name from Emperor Hsien Feng. Tseng Kuo-fan was said to be a level-headed, dogged Chinese in his fifties. He had risen from a poor peasant family and had been appointed in 1852 to command the army in his native Hunan. He was known for his thorough methods of drilling his men. He had successfully suppressed the Taiping strongholds on the Yangtze River, which earned him praise from the anxious and impatient capital. He continued to harden his men, who came to be known as the Hunan Braves. They were the most efficient fighting force in the empire.

It was due to Prince Kung's encouragement that the Emperor granted General Tseng a private audience.

"Orchid," Emperor Hsien Feng called as he put on his dragon robe. "Come with me this morning and let me know your impression of Tseng Kuo-fan." I followed my husband to the Hall of Spiritual Nurturing.

The general rose from his knees and greeted His Majesty. I noticed that he was too nervous to raise his eyes. This was not uncommon during a first Imperial audience. It happened more often among those of Chinese origin. Humble to a fault, they could not believe their ruler was receiving them.

In truth, it was not the Chinese but the Manchus who lacked confidence. Our ancestors may have conquered the mainland by force two centuries before, but we had never mastered the art of ruling. We arrived without the fundamentals, such as Confucian philosophy, which

161

unified the nation through morality and spirituality, and without a system that effectively centralized power. We also lacked a language that allowed the Emperor to communicate with his people, 80 percent of whom were Chinese.

Wisely, our ancestors had adopted Chinese ways. In my view, this was probably unavoidable. The culture was so gracious and broad that it both accepted and served us. Confucian fundamentals continued to dominate the nation. For myself, my first language was Chinese, my eating habits Chinese, my rough schooling Chinese, and my favorite form of entertainment Peking operas!

I had come to realize that the Manchu sense of superiority had betrayed us. Today's Manchus were as rotten as termite-infested wood. Manchu men were generally spoiled. They no longer knew how to win battles on horseback. Most had become their own enemies. Beneath their proud exterior, they were lazy and insecure. They created difficulties for my husband whenever he wished to promote someone of true talent who happened to be Chinese.

Sadly, they remained the dominant political force. Their opinions influenced Emperor Hsien Feng. Tseng Kuo-fan was the best general in the empire, yet His Majesty was afraid to promote him. This was typical. Any high-ranking Chinese could easily find himself cut off at a moment's notice. There was never an explanation.

Prince Kung had repeatedly advised the Emperor to rid his administration of discrimination. Kung's point was that until His Majesty could demonstrate true justice, he would receive no true loyalty. Tseng Kuo-fan illustrated the point. The renowned general didn't believe that he was here to be honored. The man broke down when Emperor Hsien Feng attempted a light-hearted joke: "Is 'Head-Chopper Tseng' your name?"

Tseng Kuo-fan knocked his forehead on the floor and trembled violently.

I tried not to giggle when I heard Tseng's jewelry clanking.

The Emperor was charmed. "Why don't you answer my question?"

"I should be punished and die ten thousand times before I soil Your Majesty's ears with this name," the man replied.

"No, I wasn't upset." Emperor Hsien Feng smiled. "Rise, please. I like the name Head-Chopper Tseng. Would you explain how you got it?"

Drawing a deep breath, the man replied, "Your Majesty, the name was first created by my enemies, and then my men adopted it."

"Your men must be very proud to serve under you."

"Yes, indeed, they are."

"You have honored me, Tseng Kuo-fan. I wish I had more head-choppers as generals!"

When Emperor Hsien Feng invited Tseng to join him for lunch, the man was moved to tears. He said that he could now die and greet his ancestors with pride, because he had brought them great honor.

After a little liquor, General Tseng became relaxed. When I was introduced as the Emperor's favorite concubine, Tseng fell to his knees and bowed to me. I was very pleased. Many years later, after the death of my husband, when Tseng Kuo-fan and I were both old, I asked him what he had thought of me when we first met. He flattered me and said that he had been stunned by my beauty and unable to think. He asked if I recalled his drinking down a bowl of dirty water—the one used to wash our fingers during the meal.

I was glad that Emperor Hsien Feng cared to present me to his high-ranking friends. In their eyes I was still just a concubine, albeit a favored one; nevertheless, the exposure was crucial to my political development and maturity. Personally knowing someone like Tseng Kuo-fan would serve me well in the future.

As I listened to the conversation between Emperor Hsien Feng and the general, I was reminded of the sweetest days of my childhood when my father told me stories of China's past.

"You yourself are a scholar," Hsien Feng said to Tseng. "I have heard that you prefer to hire officers who are literate."

"Your Majesty, I believe that anyone who has been taught Confucius's teachings has a better understanding of loyalty and justice."

"I have also heard that you don't recruit former soldiers. Why?"

"Well, in my experience I find that professional soldiers have bad habits. Their first thought when a battle starts is to save their own skin. They desert their posts shamelessly."

"How do you recruit quality soldiers?"

"I spend taels on recruiting peasants from poor areas and remote mountains. These people have purer characters. I train them myself. I try to cultivate a sense of brotherhood."

"I have heard that many of them are from Hunan."

"Yes. I am Hunanese myself. It is easy for them to identify with me and with each other. We speak the same dialect. It is like a big family."

"And you are the father, of course."

Tseng Kuo-fan smiled, proud and embarrassed at the same time.

Emperor Hsien Feng nodded. "It has been reported to me that you have equipped your army with superior weapons—better than the Imperial Army's. Is that true?"

Tseng Kuo-fan got up from his seat and lifted his robe and got down on his knees. "That is true. However, it is important that Your Majesty see that I am part of your Imperial Army. I can't be seen otherwise." He bowed and remained on the floor to emphasize his point.

"Rise, please," Emperor Hsien Feng said. "Let me rephrase my words so there will be no misunderstanding. What I mean is that the Imperial Army, especially those divisions run by Manchu warlords, have become a pot of maggots. They feed on the dynasty's blood and contribute nothing. That is why I am spending more time learning about you."

"Yes, Your Majesty." Tseng Kuo-fan got up and returned to his seat. "I believe it is important to equip the soldiers' minds, too."

"How do you mean?"

"The peasants are not trained to fight before they become soldiers. Like most people, they can't stand the sight of blood. Punishment won't change this behavior, but there are other ways. I can't let my men get used to defeat."

"I understand. I am used to defeat myself," the Emperor said with a sarcastic smile.

Both Tseng Kuo-fan and I couldn't be sure whether His Majesty was mocking or revealing his true feelings. Tseng's chopsticks froze before his open mouth.

"I bear the unbearable shame," Emperor Hsien Feng said, as if explaining. "The difference is that I can't desert."

The general was affected by the Son of Heaven's sadness. He again got down on his knees. "I swear with my life to bring back your honor, Your Majesty. My army is ready to die for the Ch'ing Dynasty."

Emperor Hsien Feng got up from his chair and helped Tseng Kuo-fan to his feet. "How great is the force under your command?"

"I have thirteen divisions of land forces and thirteen divisions of water forces, plus local Braves. Every division has five hundred men."

Sitting through audiences like this, I entered the Emperor's dream. Working together, we became true friends, and lovers, and something more. Bad news continued, but Hsien Feng had become calm enough to face the difficulties. His depression didn't go away, but his mood swings became less dramatic. He was at his best during this period, however brief. I missed him when business kept him from me.

Thirteen

I HEAR PROMISING BEATS." Doctor Sun Pao-tien's voice came through my curtain. "It tells me that you have a *sheemai*."

"What's a *sheemai*?" I asked nervously. The curtain separated the doctor and me. Lying on my bed, I couldn't see the man's face, only his shadow projected by candlelight on the curtain. I stared at his hand, which was inside the curtain. It rested on my wrist, with its second and middle fingers pressing lightly. It was a delicate-looking hand with amazingly long fingers. The hand carried with it the faint smell of herbal medicines. Since no male but the Emperor was allowed to see the females in the Forbidden City, an Imperial doctor based his diagnosis on the pulse of his patient.

I wondered what he could examine while the curtain blocked his eyes, yet the pulse alone had guided Chinese doctors to detect the body's problems for thousands of years. Sun Pao-tien was the best physician in the nation. He was from a Chinese family with five generations of doctors. He was known for discovering a peach-pit-sized stone in the gut of the Grand Empress Lady Jin. In terrible pain, the Empress didn't believe the doctor but trusted him enough to drink the herbal medicine he'd prescribed. Three months later a maid found the stone in Her Majesty's stool.

Doctor Sun Pao-tien's voice was soft and gentle. "*Shee* means 'happiness,' and *mai* means 'pulses.' *Sheemai*—happy pulses. Lady Yehonala, you are pregnant."

Before my mind recognized what he said, Doctor Sun Pao-tien withdrew his hand.

"Excuse me!" I sat up and reached to pull at the curtain. Fortunately An-te-hai had clipped it closed. I was not sure whether I indeed had heard the word "pregnant." I had been suffering from morning sickness for weeks and didn't trust my hearing.

"An-te-hai!" I cried. "Get me the hand back!"

After a busy movement on the other side of the curtain, the doctor's shadow returned. Several eunuchs guided him to the chair and his hand was pushed in. It was obviously displeased. It rested on the edge of my bed with the fingers curled inward like a crawling spider. I could care less. I wanted to hear the word "pregnant" again. I picked up the hand and placed it on my wrist. "Make sure, Doctor," I pleaded.

"There is success in all fields of your body." Doctor Sun Pao-tien's voice was unhurried, each word spoken clearly. "Your veins and arteries are beaming. Beautiful elements blanket your hills and dales . . ."

"Eh? What does that mean?" I shook the hand.

An-te-hai's shadow merged with the doctor's. He translated the doctor's words for me. The excitement in his voice was unmistakable. "My lady, the dragon seed has sprouted!"

I let go of Sun Pao-tien's hand. I couldn't wait for An-te-hai to remove the clips. I thanked Heaven for its blessing. For the rest of the day I ate almost continually. An-te-hai was so overjoyed that he forgot to feed his birds. He went to the Imperial fish farm and asked for a bucket of live fish.

"Let's celebrate, my lady," he said when he came back.

We went to the lake with the fish. One by one I freed the fish. The ritual, called *fang sheng,* was a gesture of mercy. With each fish that was given a chance to live, I added to my stock of goodwill.

The next morning I woke up to the sound of music in the late-summer sky. It was from An-te-hai's pigeons, flying in circles above my roof. The sound of wind pipes took me back to Wuhu, where I had made similar pipes from water reeds, which I tied to my own birds and to kites too. Depending on their thickness, the reeds would produce different sounds. One old villager tied two dozen wind pipes to a large kite. He arranged the pipes in such a way that they produced the melody of a popular folk song.

I got up, went to the garden and was greeted by the peacocks. An-te-hai was busy feeding the parrot, Confucius. The bird tried out a new phrase it had just learned: "Congratulations, my lady!" I was delighted. The orchids around the yard were still in bloom. The flower's long slender stems bent elegantly. The leaves stood like dancers holding up their sleeves. White and blue petals stretched outward as if kissing the sunlight. The orchids' black velvety hearts reminded me of Snow's eyes.

An-te-hai told me that Doctor Sun Pao-tien had suggested that I keep the news of my pregnancy to myself until the third month. I took his advice. Whenever possible, I indulged myself in the garden. The sweet hours made me miss my family. I ached with the desire to share this news with my mother.

Despite my "secret," before long the Imperial wives and concubines in every palace learned about my pregnancy. I was showered with flowers, jade carvings and good-wish paper cutouts. Every concubine made an effort to visit me. The ones who were unwell sent their eunuchs with more gifts.

In my room the presents piled up to the ceiling. But behind the smiling faces lay envy and jealousy. Swollen eyes were evidence of crying and sleepless nights. I knew exactly how the rest of the concubines felt. I remembered my own reaction toward Lady Yun's pregnancy. I hadn't wished Lady Yun bad luck, but I hadn't wished her well either. I had been quietly relieved when Nuharoo told me that Lady Yun had given birth to a daughter instead of a son.

I was not looking forward to what was coming. I feared that numerous traps would be set for me. It was only natural that the concubines should hate me.

As my belly began to swell, my fear increased. I now ate little in order to narrow the risk of being poisoned. I dreamt of Snow's hairless body floating in the well. An-te-hai warned me to be careful every time I drank a bowl of soup or took a walk in the garden. He believed that my rivals had directed their eunuchs to lay loose rocks or dig holes in my path to make me stumble. When I pointed out that he was overreacting, An-te-hai told me a story about a jealous concubine who instructed her eunuch to break a tile on her rival's roof so that it would slip down and hit the rival on the head, and it did!

Before I got into my palanquin, An-te-hai always checked to see whether there was a needle hidden inside my cushion. He was convinced that my rivals would do anything to shock me into a miscarriage.

I understood the cause of such viciousness, but I wouldn't be able to forgive anyone who tried to destroy my child. If I delivered safely, my status would be elevated at the expense of the others. My name would go into the Imperial record books. If the child should be a male, I would rise to the rank of Empress, sharing the title with Nuharoo.

· · ·

167

The night was deep, and His Majesty and I lay side by side. He had been cheerful since learning of my pregnancy. We had been spending our nights at the Palace of Concentrated Beauty, north of the Hall of Spiritual Nurturing. I slept better in my palace because no one came to wake us with urgent business. His Majesty had been living in both palaces, depending on how late his work kept him. An-te-hai's warnings troubled me and I asked His Majesty to increase the night guards at my gate. "Just in case," I said. "I would feel safer."

His Majesty sighed. "Orchid, you are ruining a dream of mine."

I was startled by this and asked him to explain.

"My dreams of building a prosperous China have been repeatedly crushed. Increasingly, I cannot help but doubt my abilities as a ruler. But my power encounters no resistance in the Forbidden City. The concubines and eunuchs are my faithful citizens. There is no confusion here. I expect you to love me and to love one another. I especially desire serenity between you and Nuharoo. The Forbidden City is poetry in its purest form. It is my spiritual garden where I can lie among my flowers and rest."

But is it possible to love here? The atmosphere in this garden had long been poisoned.

"That wonderful evening when you and Nuharoo walked together in the garden," His Majesty said in a dreamy tone. "I remember the day clearly. You carried the light of the setting sun. You were both dressed in spring robes. You had been picking flowers. With armfuls of peonies you walked toward me, smiling and chatting as sweetly as sisters. It made me forget my troubles. All I wanted to do was to kiss the flowers in your hands..."

I wished I could tell him that I was never part of it. His picture of beauty and harmony did not exist. He had woven Nuharoo and me into his fantasy. Nuharoo and I might have loved each other and been friends if our survival hadn't depended on his affection.

"Nowadays when I see something beautiful I want to freeze it." Rising from his pillow, His Majesty turned to me and asked, "You and Nuharoo cared for each other before—why not now? Why do you have to ruin it?"

In the third month of my pregnancy the court astrologers were ordered to perform *pa kua*. Wooden, metal and golden sticks were thrown on the marble floor. A bucket containing the blood of several animals was brought in. Water and colored sand were spread onto the walls to create paintings. In their long, star-patterned black robes, the astrologers squatted on their heels. With their noses almost touching the floor they studied the sticks and interpreted the ghostly images on the walls. Finally they pronounced that the child I carried possessed the proper balance of gold, wood, water, fire and soil.

The ritual continued. Unlike fortunetellers in the countryside, the Imperial astrologers avoided expressing their true views. I noticed that everything said was aimed at pleasing Emperor Hsien Feng, who would issue rewards. Trying to look busy, the astrologers danced around the stained walls all day long. In the evening they sat and rolled their eyeballs in circles. I found excuses and left. To punish me, the astrologers passed on a dire prediction to the Grand Empress: if I didn't lie absolutely still after sunset, with both of my legs raised, I would lose the child. I was tied to my bed, and stools were placed under my feet. I was upset but could do nothing. My mother-in-law was a strong believer in *pa kua* astrology.

"My lady," An-te-hai asked, noticing that I was in a sour mood, "since you have time, would you like to learn a bit about *pa kua*? You can find out whether your child is a mountain type or an ocean type."

As always, An-te-hai sensed just what it was I needed. He brought in an expert, "the most reputable in Peking," my eunuch said. "He got past the gates because I disguised him as a garbage man."

With the three of us shut up in my chamber, the man, who had one eye, read the sand paintings that he drew on a tray. What he said confused me and I tried hard to comprehend. "*Pa kua* will not work once it is explained," he said. "The philosophy is in the senses." An-te-hai was impatient and asked the man to "cut the fat." The expert was turned into a village fortuneteller. He told me that there was a very good chance that my child would be a boy.

I lost interest in learning more about *pa kua* after that. The prediction set my heart racing. I managed to sit still and ordered the man to continue.

"I see the child has everything perfect except too much metal, which means he will be stubborn." The man flipped the rocks and sticks he had spread out on the tray. "The boy's best quality is that he is likely to pursue his dreams." At this point the man paused. He raised his chin toward the ceiling and his eyebrows twitched. He squeezed his nose and blinked. Yellowish crust flaked from his empty eye socket. He stopped talking.

An-te-hai moved closer to him. "Here is a reward for your honesty," my eunuch said, putting a bag of taels into the man's large sleeve.

"The darkness," the man immediately resumed, "is that his coming into the world will place a curse on a close family member."

"Curse? What kind of curse?" An-te-hai asked before I could. "What will happen to this close family member?"

"She will die," the man replied.

I drew a breath and asked why it was a she. The man had no answer for that and could tell me only that he had read the signs.

I begged him for a clue. "Will the she be me? Will I die in childbirth?"

The man shook his head and said that the picture was unclear at this point. He was unable to tell me more.

After the one-eyed man was gone, I tried to forget about the prediction. I told myself that he couldn't prove what he had said. Unlike Nuharoo, who was a devoted Buddhist, I was not a religious person and never took superstition seriously. Everyone in the Forbidden City, it seemed, was obsessed with the idea of life after death, investing all their hopes in the next world. The eunuchs talked about coming back "in one piece," while the concubines looked forward to having a husband and children of their own. The afterlife was part of Nuharoo's Buddhist study. She was quite knowledgeable about what would happen to us after death. She said that after reaching the underworld, each person would be interrogated and judged. Those whose lives had been stained with sin were sentenced to Hell, where they would be boiled, fried, sawed or chopped to pieces. Those who were considered sinless got to begin a new life on earth. Not everyone came back to live the life he or she desired, however. The lucky were reborn as humans, the unlucky as animals—a dog, a pig, a flea.

The concubines in the Forbidden City, especially the senior ones, were extremely superstitious. Besides making *yoo-hoo-loos* and chanting, they spent their days mastering various kinds of witchcraft. To them, belief in the next life was itself a weapon. They needed the weapon to place curses on their rivals. They were very ingenious about the various fates they wished upon their enemies.

Nuharoo showed me a book called *The Calendar of Chinese Ghosts*, with vivid, bizarre illustrations. I was not unfamiliar with the material. I had heard every story it contained and had seen a hand-copied version in Wuhu. The book was used by storytellers in the countryside.

Nuharoo was especially fascinated by "The Red Embroidered Shoes," an old tale about a pair of shoes worn by a ghost.

As a child I had seen fortunetellers make false predictions that ruined lives. However, An-te-hai wanted to take no chances. I knew he worried that the ill-fated "she" would turn out to be me.

For the next few days his worry grew. He became melodramatic to the point of silliness. "Each day could be your last," he mumbled one morning. He served me carefully, observing my every move. He sniffed the air like a dog and refused to shut his eyes at night. When I napped, he left the Forbidden City and came back to report that he had spent time with older village bachelors. Offering money, he asked the bachelors if they would like to adopt my unborn child.

I asked why he was doing so.

An-te-hai explained that since my boy would bear a curse, it was our duty to spread the curse to other people. According to *The Book of Superstition,* if enough people were to bear the curse, it would lose its effect. "The bachelors are eager to have someone carry on their family name," my eunuch said. "Don't worry, my lady. I did not reveal who the boy was, and the adoption is an oral contract only."

I praised An-te-hai's loyalty and told him to stop. But he wouldn't. The next day I saw him bowing to a crippled dog as it passed by the garden. On another day he got down on his knees and kowtowed to a bundled pig on its way to the temple to be sacrificed.

"We must undo the curse," An-te-hai said. "Paying respect to the crippled dog acknowledges that it had suffered. Someone had beaten it and broken its bones. Such animals serve as a substitute, reducing the power of the curse, if not transferring it to others." After the pig was slaughtered, An-te-hai believed that I would be released, for I, in the spirit of the pig, had become a ghost.

Early one morning news broke throughout the Imperial household: Grand Empress Lady Jin had passed away.

An-te-hai and I couldn't help but conclude that there must be something to *pa kua.* Another strange incident took place that morning. The glass housing of the clock in the Hall of Spiritual Nurturing shattered when the clock struck nine. The court astrologer explained that Lady Jin's death was brought on because she had been too eager to invest in her longevity. She loved the number nine. She had celebrated her forty-ninth birthday by draping her bed with red ropes and silk sheets embroidered with forty-nine Chinese nines.

"She had been sick but was not expected to die until she got weighted down by the nines," the astrologer said.

By the time my palanquin arrived at Lady Jin's palace the body had already been washed. She was moved from her bedroom to *lin chuang*, a "soul bed," which was in the shape of a boat. Her Majesty's feet were tied with red strings. She was dressed in a full-length silver court robe embroidered with symbols of every kind. There were fortune wheels, representing the principles of the universe; seashells in which one could hear the voice of the Buddha; oil-paper umbrellas that protected the seasons from flood and drought; vials that held the fluid of wisdom and magic; lotus flowers representing generations of peace; goldfish for balance and grace; and finally the symbol ஃ, which stood for infinity. A golden sheet printed with Buddhist scriptures wrapped her from chest to knees.

A palm-sized mirror with a long handle was placed beside Her Majesty. It was said to protect the dead from being disturbed by mean-spirited ghosts. The mirror would reflect the ghosts' own images. Because most ghosts had no idea what they looked like, they would expect to see themselves as they were when alive. Instead, the evil things they had done in the past would have transformed them into skeletons, grotesque monsters or worse. The mirror would shock them into retreat.

Lady Jin's head looked like a big pile of dough from all the powder on her face. An-te-hai told me that in her last days boils had erupted all over her face. In the record, her doctor wrote that the "buds" on Her Majesty's body "bloomed" and produced "nectar." The boils were black and green, like a rotten potato sprouting shoots. The whole Forbidden City gossiped that it must have been the work of her former rival, Empress Chu An.

Lady Jin's face had been smoothed and patched with powder from ground pearls. If one looked closely, however, one could still detect the bumps. On the right side of Her Majesty's head was a tray with a golden ceramic bowl. This contained her last earthly meal, rice. On the left stood a large burning oil lamp, the "eternal light."

I went with Nuharoo and Emperor Hsien Feng's other wives to view the body. We were all dressed in white silk gowns. Nuharoo wore makeup but without the rouge dot on her lower lip. She burst into tears when she saw Lady Jin. She pulled a piece of lace from her hair and bit it with her teeth in order to hold back her emotions. I was moved by her sadness and offered her my hand. We stood shoulder to shoulder before the dead Empress.

A mourning troupe arrived. They cried in various styles. The sound was more like singing than crying. It reminded me of the discordant music of a village band. Maybe it was how I felt—I had just escaped the curse. My mood was lightened and I felt little sadness.

Lady Jin had never liked me. She said openly after learning I was pregnant that she wished the news had come from Nuharoo. She believed that I had stolen Emperor Hsien Feng from Nuharoo.

I remembered the last time I encountered Lady Jin. Her health was declining but she refused to admit it. Disregarding the fact that everyone knew about the peach-pit-sized stone, she claimed that her health had never been more robust. She rewarded doctors who lied to her and said that her longevity was not in doubt. But her body gave away her flaws. When she pointed a finger and tried to tell me that I was bad, her hand trembled. It looked like she was getting ready to strike me. She tried to fight off her trembling. Eventually she fell back and couldn't sit up without help from her eunuchs. That didn't stop her from cursing me. "You illiterate!" she cried. I didn't understand her choice of epithet. None of the other ladies, except perhaps Nuharoo, was more accomplished than I was in reading.

I tried to avoid Lady Jin's lifeless eyes. I looked above her eyebrows when I had to face her. Her broad wrinkled forehead reminded me of a painting I had once seen of the Gobi Desert. Folds of skin hung from her chin. The loss of her teeth on her right side made her face slope like a spoiled melon.

Lady Jin had a love of magnolias. Even in sickness, she wore an embroidered dress with large pink magnolia flowers covering every inch of the fabric. "Magnolia" had been the Empress's childhood name. I could hardly believe that she had once caught the eye of Emperor Tao Kuang.

How frightening it was the way a woman could age. Would anyone be able to imagine how I would look by the time I died?

Lady Jin yelled at me that day, "Don't you worry about your beauty. Worry about beheading instead!" The words were pushed out of her chest as she struggled with her breath. "Let me tell you what I have been worrying about since the day I became the Imperial consort! I will continue to worry until the day I die!" Fighting to keep her composure, she raised herself up with the help of her eunuchs. With both arms in the air she looked like a vulture spreading its wings from the edge of a cliff.

We dared not move. The daughters-in-law—Nuharoo, Ladies Yun, Li, Mei and Hui, and I—endured her ranting and waited for the moment when she would release us.

"Have you heard the story from a country far away where people's eyeballs look like they have been bleached and their hair is the color of straw?" Lady Jin narrowed her eyes. The landscape of her forehead changed from rolling hills to steep valleys. "A king's entire family was slaughtered after the empire was overthrown. All of them, including the infants!"

Seeing that her words had startled us, she was satisfied. "You bunch of illiterates!" she yelled. Suddenly her throat produced a string of noises: "*Ohhhhh, wa! Ohhhhh, wa!*" It took me a while to realize that she was laughing. "Fear is good! *Ohhhhh, wa!* Fear tortures you and makes you behave. You can't gain immortality without it, and my job is to instill fear in you! *Ohhhhh, wa! Ohhhhh, wa!*"

I could still hear that laughter. I wondered what Lady Jin would say if she had known that she was the victim of my child, her grandson's curse. I felt blessed that Lady Jin considered me an illiterate. She would have ordered my beheading if she had seen my love for knowledge or bothered to trace the source of the curse.

Watching her on her soul bed, I had little remorse. I saw no sympathy in the others except for Nuharoo. The general expression was wooden. The eunuchs had just finished burning straw paper in the hall, and now the crowd was led outside to burn more paper. In the courtyard life-size palanquins, horses, carriages, tables and chamber pots were being installed with life-size paper figures of people and animals. The figures were clothed in expensive silk and linen, as was the furniture. Following the Manchu burial traditions she had adopted, she had arranged everything herself years before. The paper figure of herself looked real, although it was the way she used to look when she was young. It was wearing a magnolia-patterned dress.

Before the ceremony began, a thirty-foot pole was raised. A red silk scroll was mounted at the top with the word *tien*, "in memory." It was the first time I had a chance to witness this ritual. Centuries before, Manchus inhabited vast grasslands where it was difficult to notify relatives about a death in the family. When a family member died, a pole with a red scroll would be put up in front of the family's tent, so that passing horsemen and herdsmen would stop and pay their respects in place of the missing relatives.

True to the custom, three large tents were set up in the Forbidden City. One was used to display the body, the second housed the monks, lamas and priests who came from afar, and the last was for receiving relatives and high-ranking guests. Other, smaller tents were also put up in the courtyard to receive visitors. The tents were about ten feet in height, and the supporting bamboo posts were decorated with white magnolias made of silk. As daughters-in-law we each were given a dozen handkerchiefs for our tears. I kept hearing Lady Jin—"Illiterate!"—and wanted to laugh instead of cry. I had to cover my face with my hands.

Between my fingers I saw Prince Kung arrive. He was dressed in a white robe and matching boots. When he examined the coffin, he looked grief-stricken. The female relatives were supposed to avoid their male cousins or brothers-in-law, so we retreated to the next room. Fortunately I was able to see through the windows. The coffin lid was lifted for Prince Kung. Glittering jewels, gold, jade, pearls, emeralds, rubies and crystal vases were piled on Lady Jin's chest. Besides the little mirror, she was holding her makeup box.

Prince Kung stood solemnly beside his mother. His sorrow made him look like an older man. He got down on his knees and performed a kowtow. His forehead remained on the ground for a long time. When he rose, a eunuch went up and carefully parted Lady Jin's lips. The eunuch placed a large pearl strung on red thread in her mouth. Then he closed her mouth, leaving the end of the thread hanging by her chin. The pearl was the symbol of life's essence and represented purity and nobility. The red thread, which would be tied by her son, served as a demonstration of his unwillingness to part with her.

Prince Kung tied the thread onto the first button of his mother's robe. A eunuch handed him a pair of chopsticks with a wet cotton ball between them. Prince Kung gently wiped his mother's eyelids with the cotton ball.

The guests brought in boxes of decorated steamed buns. The plates in front of the altars had to be changed every few minutes in order to receive more boxes. Hundreds of scrolls were also brought. They piled up and made the palace look like a calligraphy festival. Couplets and poems hung from every wall. Extra string was needed to tie more couplets from the beams. The kitchen served a banquet for more than two thousand guests.

The mourning troupe wailed when Prince Kung's knees hit the ground again. The chanting mounted to a crescendo. The trumpets were deafening. I thought that this would be the end of the ceremony, but no: it had just officially started.

The seventh day was the time of the figure-burning ceremony. Three paper palaces and two mountains were to be set on fire. The palaces were twelve feet high, each with a golden pagoda at the top. One mountain was painted gold and the other silver. The ceremony was conducted outside the Forbidden City, near the North Bridge. The crowds that gathered exceeded the New Year's Eve celebration. The paper palaces were modeled after examples of Sung Dynasty architecture. The tiles of the traditional wing roofs were painted ocean blue. From where I stood, I could peer into the palaces, which were completely furnished. The chair covers were painted in strokes and patterns that imitated embroidery. On a dining table piled with paper flowers, silver chopsticks and gold wine cups were neatly set out.

The mountains were covered with rocks, brooks, magnolia trees and waving grass, all done to scale. What amazed me even more was that there were tiny cicadas resting on the magnolia branches, butterflies on peonies and crickets in the grass. It took hundreds of craftsmen years to complete this paper world, and in minutes it would turn to ashes.

The chanting began and the fire was lit. As the flames shot high the monks, lamas and priests threw steamed buns over the heads of the cheering crowd. The buns were supposed to be consumed by homeless ghosts. It was a gesture of Lady Jin's benevolence.

Emperor Hsien Feng was absent from the beginning to the end. He claimed to be ill. I knew that he hated this woman, and I didn't blame him. Lady Jin was the one who had caused his birth mother's suicide. By not attending the funeral, the Emperor was making a statement.

The guests and concubines made poor mourners. They ate and drank and chatted with one another. I even heard people talking about my pregnancy.

There was no way I could convince Emperor Hsien Feng that my rivals were plotting against me. I told His Majesty that the fish in my pond were dying, that the orchids in my garden had withered in the middle of a strong blooming. An-te-hai found that orchid-loving rodents had eaten the plants' roots. Someone had to have smuggled them in.

My complaints irritated my husband. He thought of Nuharoo as the goddess of mercy and told me to quit worrying. My thinking was that I might be able to deal with one Nuharoo but not three thousand. Anything could happen, since they had made my belly a target. I was nearly twenty-one, and already I had heard about too many murders.

I begged Emperor Hsien Feng to move us back to Yuan Ming Yuan until I delivered. His Majesty yielded. I knew that I had to learn to tuck away my happiness like a mouse hiding its food. For the past weeks I had tried to avoid talking about my pregnancy when the other concubines visited. But it was difficult, especially when they brought gifts for the baby. The Emperor had recently increased my allowance, and I used the extra taels to purchase return gifts of equal value. I was sick of pretending to be glad of their visits.

An-te-hai kept my belly his priority. As it grew bigger, he became more and more involved. Each day he danced on his nerve tips, excited and frightened at the same time. Instead of greeting me in the morning, he greeted my belly. "Good morning, Your Young Majesty." He bowed deeply and solemnly. "What can I get you for breakfast?"

I began to study Buddhist manuscripts. I prayed that my child would be content to grow inside me. I prayed that my nightmares wouldn't disturb his growth. If I produced a girl, I still wanted to feel happy and blessed. Mornings I sat in a sun-filled room and read. In the afternoon I practiced calligraphy, part of a Buddhist's training for cultivating balance and harmony. Gradually I felt the return of peace. Since I had captured His Majesty's attention, he had visited Nuharoo only twice. Once was upon Lady Jin's death. After the burial, he called on Nuharoo for tea. According to An-te-hai's spies, His Majesty talked to her about nothing but the ceremony.

The second time His Majesty visited Nuharoo was at her request. And this Nuharoo told me herself. She did what she believed would please His Majesty—she asked for his permission to add a wing to Lady Jin's tomb. Nuharoo reported that she had been collecting taels from everyone and had contributed her own money.

Emperor Hsien Feng was not pleased, but praised Nuharoo for her devotion. To demonstrate his affection and appreciation, he issued an edict to add one more title to Nuharoo's name. She was now the Virtuous Lady of Grand Piety. But that was not what Nuharoo wanted. I knew what she wanted. She wanted Hsien Feng back in her bed. But he was not interested. His Majesty stayed in my quarters every night until dawn, disregarding the rules. It would be dishonest of me to say that I was willing to share Hsien Feng with anyone else, but I did understand Nuharoo's suffering. In the future I would find myself wearing her shoes. For the moment I tried to get what I could. I thought of tomorrow as a mystery, and I allowed it to reveal itself. The word "future" made me think of the locust war my father had fought back in Wuhu, when the spring fields disappeared overnight.

Nuharoo managed to put on fabulous smiles in public, but the gossip from her eunuchs and ladies in waiting revealed that she was distressed. She moved deeper into her Buddhist faith and visited the temple to chant with her master three times a day.

Emperor Hsien Feng advised me not to "look at other people through the eye of a sewing needle." But my instinct told me not to take Nuharoo's hidden jealousy lightly. Yuan Ming Yuan was by no means a safe place. On the surface, Nuharoo and I were friends. She was involved in the preparations for the baby's arrival. She had visited the Imperial clothing shop to inspect the infant's outfits. She had also visited the Imperial storehouses to make sure that fruits and nuts were available and fresh. Last she checked on the fish farm. Since fish was said to promote the flow of breast milk, Nuharoo made sure that there was plenty of fish to feed the wet nurses.

The selection of wet nurses became Nuharoo's focus. She inspected an army of pregnant women whose babies were due at the same time mine was. Then she traveled all the way by carriage to Yuan Ming Yuan to talk to me about the matter.

"I have checked the history of their health three generations back," she said.

The more excited Nuharoo got, the deeper my fear grew. I wished that she had her own child. Everyone in the Forbidden City except the Emperor understood the pressure Nuharoo was under after several years of marriage and no sign of fertility. That such pressure could lead to strange behavior was common in childless women. An obsession with *yoo-hoo-loos* was one manifestation; jumping into wells was another. With Nuharoo, I still couldn't tell what her true intention was.

The moment after Doctor Sun Pao-tien examined me and pronounced that I would carry the baby to full term, His Majesty summoned his astrologer. The two of them went to the Temple of Heaven, where Hsien Feng prayed that the child would be a son. Afterward he went to Nuharoo to congratulate her.

But she is not the mother of your child! I shouted in my head.

Nuharoo played her role well. She showed her happiness with real tears. I thought, *Could I be wrong about her?* Maybe it was time for me to change my view. Maybe Nuharoo had turned herself into a true Buddhist.

When I was five months pregnant, Nuharoo suggested to Emperor Hsien Feng that I be moved back to the Palace of Concentrated Beauty.

"Lady Yehonala needs absolute peace," Nuharoo said to him. "She needs to stay away from stress of any kind, including the bad news about the country from you."

I let myself believe that Nuharoo was thinking of my welfare, and agreed to be moved. But the moment I was out of His Majesty's bedroom, I sensed that I had made a mistake. Soon enough the truth revealed itself, and I never made it back to that bedroom.

As if to add more chaos to my life, Chief Eunuch Shim told me that I would not be allowed to raise my own child. I was considered "one of the prince's mothers," but not the only one. "It is the Imperial tradition," Shim said coldly. Nuharoo would also be responsible for the daily care and education of my child, and she would have the right to take my child away from me if I refused to cooperate with her. The Manchu clan and Emperor Hsien Feng both believed that Nuharoo's Imperial blood qualified her to be the chief mother of the future prince. No one had ever accused me of being a concubine from a lower class, but my background as a village girl and my father's status as a low-ranking governor were an embarrassment that the court and the Emperor never forgot.

Fourteen

A MONTH AFTER I was out of his sight, Emperor Hsien Feng
took in four new concubines. They were of Han Chinese
origin. Since the Imperial rules didn't permit non-Manchu
women in the palace, Nuharoo made arrangements to smuggle them in.

It was hard for me to speak about the pain this caused me. It was like
a slow drowning: the air was being shut out of my lungs and death had
yet to arrive.

"Their teeny lotus-shaped feet have enthralled His Majesty," An-te-
hai reported. "The ladies were a gift from the governor of Soochow."

I supposed that it was not difficult for Nuharoo to hint to the governors that the moment had come to please their ruler. An-te-hai discovered that Nuharoo had housed the new concubines in the Emperor's
miniature town of Soochow, within the largest Imperial garden at the
Summer Palace, located several miles from Yuan Ming Yuan. The Summer Palace, with its little Soochow, had been built around a lake and
was made up of more than three thousand structures on almost seven
hundred acres.

Would I be any different if I were in her shoes? What was I crying
about? Hadn't I shamelessly gone to a whorehouse in order to learn
man-pleasing tricks?

Emperor Hsien Feng had not visited me since I had left. My longing
for him drove me to thoughts of white silk ropes. The little kicks inside
my belly brought me back and steeled my will to survive. I reflected on
my life, struggling to maintain my composure. Hsien Feng had never
been mine to begin with. It was simply the way things were. The irony

was that the Emperor was supposed to stay sober and refrain from love-making for three months after his mother's death. He honored only the traditions that suited him. I could not imagine my son being raised the way his father had been. I needed to convince Nuharoo that I would be no threat to her so that I would always be close to my child.

The rumors of His Majesty's obsession with his Chinese ladies reached every corner of the Forbidden City. I began to have horrible dreams. I dreamed that I was sleeping and someone was trying to pull me off the bed. I struggled but was unsuccessful and was dragged out of the room. In the meantime I clearly saw that my body was still on the bed, unmoving.

Also in my dreams I saw red berries prematurely dropping from trees. I could even hear them as they fell — *pop, pop, pop.* Superstition hinted that this was an omen for miscarriage. In a panic, I sent An-te-hai out to check if it was true that the berry trees behind my palace had started dropping their fruit. An-te-hai came back and reported that he had found no berries on the ground.

Day after day I heard the popping sounds in my sleep. I suspected that the berries might have gotten caught between the roof tiles. To comfort me, An-te-hai climbed up a ladder to the roof. He and the other eunuchs checked between the tiles, and again there were no berries.

There continued to be no sign of His Majesty until Nuharoo arrived one morning with a broad smile on her face. I was surprised to see Emperor Hsien Feng behind her.

My lover looked a little awkward but soon composed himself. I couldn't tell whether he had missed me. I guessed not. He had been raised to have no comprehension of another's suffering. For him it would be wrong to spend time with only one woman anyway. I wondered if he had been enjoying his women. Had they been taking walks shoulder to shoulder, "carrying the light of the setting sun"? Had His Majesty been wanting to "kiss the flowers in their hands"?

I didn't care where those women came from. I hated them. Picturing how my lover must have touched them, my tears welled up. "I am well, thank you," I said to Emperor Hsien Feng, trying to smile. I would never let him know how terrible my pain was.

I didn't want to tell him that I had refused to go home when I was granted a ten-day leave as a reward for being pregnant. Although I missed my family very much, I wouldn't be able to hide my feelings if I saw them. My mother's fragile health would not bear my frustration, and it would be bad for Rong, who had been counting on me to find her a suitor. Rong would be disappointed if I told her that I was no longer the favorite and my way of helping her was limited.

His Majesty was quiet for a while. When he opened his mouth he talked about mosquitoes, how they bedeviled him. He blamed the eunuchs and complained that Doctor Sun Pao-tien had failed to heal an itchy spot below his chin. He didn't ask after me, and he acted as if my big belly was not there.

"I have been playing a game with my astrologer called the Lost Palaces," His Majesty said as if to break the silence between us. "It has many traps that will lead you to misjudgment. The master's advice was that I stay where I am and not bother to find my way until the time is ripe and the key to solving the problem presents itself."

Would Hsien Feng believe it if I explained to him what Nuharoo had done? It would never work, I concluded. It was public knowledge that when Nuharoo walked in the garden she looked like a drunkard. Actually it was because she was afraid of stepping on ants. When she accidentally did step on them, she apologized. The eunuchs had witnessed this. She had been called "the most tender creature" by our late mother-in-law.

We sat sipping tea while the conversation between His Majesty and Nuharoo went on. In the name of caring for me, Nuharoo proposed that she send me four of her own maids.

"It is to express my appreciation of Lady Yehonala, of my *mei-mei*'s contribution to the dynasty." She now officially called me *mei-mei*, "younger sister."

"My Little Cloud is the best among the four," Nuharoo said. "I will have difficulty letting her go. But you are my priority. The dynasty's hope of revival and prosperity rests in your belly."

Emperor Hsien Feng was pleased. He praised Nuharoo for her kindness, and then he got up to leave. He avoided looking at me as he bid goodbye. "Good health," he murmured dryly.

I was unable to hide my sadness. My heart kept searching for an acknowledgment of the warmth we had shared. But it was not there. It was as if we had never known each other. I wished that my belly were not in front of my eyes, not protruding like this, not demanding attention and touch. I wished that I could wipe away the memories.

I watched Emperor Hsien Feng and Nuharoo walking away. I wanted to throw myself at my lover's feet. I wanted to kiss his feet, and I would beg for love.

An-te-hai came to my side and held me tightly. "The berries are ripening, my lady," he whispered. "They will be ready soon."

The branches of the cypresses spread downward like giant fans, blocking the light of the moon. That night a storm came. I heard the branches sweeping and scraping the ground. The next morning An-te-hai told me that red berries were everywhere. "They look like blood-stains," the eunuch said. "They have covered your garden floor, and some are stuck between the roof tiles."

I received Little Cloud, a small-eyed and fat-cheeked fifteen-year-old maid. Since I was expected to obey the first wife's wish, I gave Little Cloud a handsome bonus, which the girl returned with a sweet "Thank you." I told An-te-hai to keep an eye on her. A few days later she was found spying.

"I caught her!" An-te-hai dragged Little Cloud over to my presence. "This cheap slave was peeking into Your Majesty's letters!"

Little Cloud denied the accusation. When I threatened to beat her if she didn't confess, she revealed her temper. Her small eyes sank into her fat face as she yelled and called An-te-hai "You tailless animal!" She then went on to insult me. "My lady entered through the Gate of Celestial Purity when she arrived, and you came through a side door!"

I told An-te-hai to drag the maid out and starve her for three meals.

As if enjoying my rage, Little Cloud continued. "You'd better think about whose dog you are kicking! So what if I have been spying on you? You have been reading court documents instead of embroidery patterns! Are you guilty? Are you afraid? Let me tell you, it is too late to think about bribing me, Lady Yehonala. I shall report everything I have seen to my master. I will be rewarded for my loyalty; you will end up limbless and live in a jar."

"Whip!" I called. "Punish this girl until she shuts up!"

I never meant to have An-te-hai take my words literally. Unfortunately that was what happened. He and the other eunuchs dragged Little Cloud to the Hall of Punishment. They beat Little Cloud and tried every way to silence her, but the girl was too stubborn.

An hour later An-te-hai came to report that Little Cloud was dead.

"You . . ." I was shocked. "An-te-hai, I didn't give you the order to beat her to death!"

"But, my lady, she wouldn't shut up."

As the head of the Imperial household, Nuharoo summoned me to appear before her. I hoped I had enough strength to endure what lay ahead. I worried about the child inside me.

Before I had finished changing, a group of eunuchs from the Hall of

Punishment stormed into my palace. They wouldn't say who sent them. They arrested my floor eunuchs and maids and searched through my drawers and closets.

"You'd better send me to inform His Majesty immediately." An-te-hai helped me into my court robe. "They are going to torment you until the 'dragon seed' falls out."

I could feel my insides contracting. Frightened, I held my belly and told An-te-hai to waste no time. He picked up a washbasin and exited through the back chamber, pretending to fetch water.

I heard a voice outside, calling to hurry me to finish dressing. "Her Majesty the Empress is waiting!" I didn't know whether they were my eunuchs or the people who had come to wreck my palace.

I took as long as I could in order to gain time for An-te-hai. Two of my ladies in waiting came in. One checked my laces and buttons and the other my hair. I stood in front of the mirror and took a last glance. I couldn't tell whether it was my emotion or my makeup that made me look ill. My robe was embroidered with black and gold orchids. I was thinking that if something should happen to me, I wanted to leave the earth wearing this dress.

I motioned toward the door, and my ladies raised the curtain. As I stepped out into the light, I saw Chief Eunuch Shim standing in the courtyard.

He was formally dressed in a purple robe and matching hat. He didn't respond to my greeting.

"What's going on, Chief Shim?" I asked.

"The rule forbids me to speak to you, Lady Yehonala." He tried to sound humble, but there was hidden elation in his tone. "Please, let me help you into your palanquin."

A tightness wrapped itself around my neck.

Looking down from her throne, Nuharoo was majestic. I got down on my knees and kowtowed to her. Only weeks had passed since we had last seen each other, and it seemed that her beauty had grown even more striking. She was dressed in a golden robe embroidered with phoenixes. She wore heavy makeup. A drop of red was painted on her lower lip. Her large double-lidded eyes seemed brighter than usual. I couldn't tell whether it was from the moisture of her tears or an effect of her dark eyeliner.

"I don't appreciate the fact that you made me do this," she said. Without offering me permission to rise, she continued. "Anyone knows

I am not made to bear a moment like this. Yet it is the irony of life. As the one who is responsible for the household, I am given no choice. My duty calls me to dispense justice. The rule has been made clear to everybody in the Forbidden City: no one has the right to mistreat a maid, not to mention take her life."

Suddenly she lowered her chin. She bit her lip and began to weep. Soon she was sobbing.

"Your Majesty," Chief Eunuch Shim said, "the whips have been soaked and the slaves are ready to perform their duty."

Nuharoo nodded. "Lady Yehonala, on your way, please!"

Taking a long, thick whip from his assistant, Shim made a deep bow to the Empress and then exited the room.

Guards came from four sides and locked their hands on me.

I resisted. "I am carrying Emperor Hsien Feng's child!"

Chief Eunuch Shim returned and twisted my arms behind me. My knees buckled and I fell. My belly swung to the floor.

On my knees I crawled to Nuharoo and begged. "I am truly sorry about what happened to Little Cloud, Your Majesty, but it was an accident. If you have to punish me, please do so after I give birth. I'll accept any term of imprisonment."

Nuharoo cracked a smile. Her expression frightened me. The smile told me that it was her wish that I should lose the baby, and that she could restore harmony between us only at that price. I was sure she knew that I wouldn't give in, knew that she had to force me, knew that she was backed by all the concubines. She wanted me to know that her will was strong and that she could not be denied.

We stared at each other. Between us was a naked understanding.

"I play fair, Lady Yehonala, and that's all," Nuharoo said almost gently. "I can assure you that there is nothing personal."

"On the frame!" Chief Eunuch Shim called.

The guards swept me up like a hen.

"Your Majesty Empress Nuharoo above," I cried, struggling to free myself. "As your slave I know my crime. Undeserving as I am, I beg you to pity me. I have begun telling this child in my belly that you are his true mother. You are his destiny. The reason this child will come through me is to reach you. Take pity on this child, Empress Nuharoo, for it will be your child."

I hit my forehead on the ground. The thought of losing my child felt worse than losing my own life. "Nuharoo, please, give him a chance to love you, my elder sister. I'll come back in the next life to be anything you desire. I'll be the skin of your drum, a paper for you to wipe your behind, a worm for your fish hook . . ."

Chief Eunuch Shim whispered something in Nuharoo's ear. Her expression changed. Shim must have said that if she displeased the Imperial ancestors, she would be stripped of her titles and struck by lightning. Like An-te-hai to me, Shim was there to protect not only Nuharoo's future, but also his own.

"Carry on?" he asked.

Nuharoo nodded.

"*Zah!*" The eunuch took a step back as he finished his bow. He grabbed my collar and ordered his people, "In the manner of Woo Hua, the Flower—rope!"

I was dragged out. Suddenly I felt warm fluid dripping from between my legs. I held my belly and cried.

It was then that I heard a long wail from the far end of the hall.

"Still and silence!"

Emperor Hsien Feng lunged between Chief Eunuch Shim and me. He was in his light yellow silk robe. His nostrils flared. His eyes were filled with rage. The breathless An-te-hai stood behind him.

Chief Eunuch Shim went to greet His Majesty, but he received no response.

Nuharoo rose from her chair. "Your Majesty, thank you so much for coming to release me." She threw herself at the Emperor's feet. "I can't bear this anymore. I can't make myself order Lady Yehonala's punishment knowing that she is carrying your child."

Emperor Hsien Feng stood frozen for a moment. He then bent down, both of his arms reaching out. "My Empress," he called softly. "Rise, please."

Nuharoo wouldn't rise. "I am an unfit Empress, and I deserve punishment," she said, tears streaming down her cheeks. "Please forgive me for failing to perform my duty."

"You are the most merciful person I have ever known," the Emperor responded. "Orchid is very fortunate to have you as a sister."

I lay on the ground. An-te-hai helped me to sit on my heels. The warm fluid between my legs seemed to have stopped. When Hsien Feng looked to see whether I was truly hurt, I could see him concluding that An-te-hai had exaggerated.

His Majesty told Nuharoo that she had done nothing wrong. He took out his handkerchief and passed it to her. "I didn't mean to burden you with responsibilities. However, you must understand that the Im-

186

perial household needs a ruler, and it is you. Please, Nuharoo, you have my deepest trust and gratitude."

Nuharoo rose and bowed to the Emperor. She passed back his handkerchief and took a towel from Chief Eunuch Shim. She patted her cheeks with the towel and said, "I am concerned that the baby has been strained because of this. I will not be able to face our ancestors if there is any damage." Again she broke into tears. At this, Emperor Hsien Feng offered to accompany her to the Imperial park in the afternoon to help her regain her composure.

It was hard to watch the way His Majesty showed his affection for Nuharoo. And it was harder to spend the night alone knowing that Hsien Feng was with her. The possibilities of what might have happened, and what might happen in the future, scared me more than any nightmare.

I lived in a world of chaos where torture was a routine practice. I began to understand why so many concubines became obsessed with religion. It was either that or complete madness.

I was enduring the worst winter of my life. It was mid-February of 1856. My belly was now the size of a watermelon. Against An-te-hai's advice, I stepped out onto the frosted ground. I wanted to visit my garden and longed to breathe fresh air. The beauty of the snow-covered pavilions and pagodas brought me a delighted feeling of hope. In only a few months the baby would be born.

I attempted to dig into the soil, but the ground was still hard. An-te-hai brought a large sack of flower bulbs from the past year and said to me, "Plant a wish for the baby, my lady."

I could tell he had been sleeping soundly, for his cheeks were apple red.

"Of course," I said.

It took us the whole day to plant the bulbs. I thought about the farmers in the countryside and imagined the families working to break the frozen soil.

"If you are to be a son," I said, placing a hand on my belly, "and if you ever get to be the Emperor of China, I wish you to be good and deserving."

"*A-ko!*" The moment I heard An-te-hai's cry, my mind turned into a spring garden where flowers bloomed all at once. Although exhausted, I was in rapture. Before Hsien Feng arrived, Nuharoo and all His Majesty's other wives and concubines made their way to my palace. "Where is our newborn son?"

Everybody congratulated Nuharoo. When she picked up the baby from my arms and proudly showed him to the others, my fear returned. I kept thinking: *Now that they have lost the chance to kill my son in my belly, will they kill him in his cradle? Will they poison his mind by spoiling him?* One thing I was sure of was that they would never let go of the idea of getting even with me.

I was granted a new title by Emperor Hsien Feng, the Auspicious Mother. Gifts and cases of taels were sent to honor my family. Still, my mother and my sister were not permitted to visit me. My husband didn't come either. My "filthiness" was believed to be capable of bringing disease to His Majesty.

I was served ten meals a day, but I had no appetite and most of the food was wasted. I was left alone to drift in and out of sleep. In my dreams I chased people who came in disguise to harm my son.

A few days later, the Emperor visited me. He didn't look well. The robe he wore made him look thinner and frailer than before. He was concerned about the size of his son. Why was he so small, and why did he sleep all the time?

"Who knows?" I teased. How could the Son of Heaven be so innocent?

"I went to the park yesterday." His Majesty passed the baby to a maid and sat down beside me. His eyes wandered from my eyes to my mouth. "I saw a dead tree," he said in a whisper. "On top of its crown grew human hair. It was very long and draped down like a black waterfall."

I stared at him.

"Is it a good sign or a bad sign, Orchid?"

Before I could answer, he went on. "That's why I came to see you. If there is a dead tree on the grounds of your palace, have it removed immediately, Orchid. Will you promise me?"

His Majesty and I spent some time in the courtyard looking for dead trees. There was not one, and we ended up watching the sunset together. I was so happy I wept. His Majesty told me that he had learned from the gardener that the hair he saw in the park was a rare kind of lichen that grew on dead trees.

I didn't want to talk about dead trees, so I asked about his days and his audiences. He had little to say, so we walked quietly for a while. He rocked the baby to sleep. It was the sweetest moment in my life. Emperor Hsien Feng didn't stay the night, and I dared not beg him to.

I told myself that I should be glad that my delivery had gone smoothly. I could have died under Chief Eunuch Shim's whip, or a hundred different ways. The Imperial concubines had lost, and I regained His Majesty's attention because of the newborn.

The next day Hsien Feng came again. He lingered after holding the baby. I made it a rule not to ask him any questions. He began to visit me regularly, always in the afternoon. Gradually we started to talk again. We chatted about our son, and he described the goings-on at court. He complained about how long everything took and the impotence of his ministers.

I listened most of the time. Hsien Feng seemed to enjoy our discussions and started to arrive earlier in the day. We were never intimate, but we were close.

I tried to be content with what I had. But part of me wanted more. After His Majesty had gone for the night, I couldn't help imagining him with his Chinese women — surely they performed better tricks than my fan dance. I became miserable trying to understand why he was no longer attracted to me. Was it the change in my body shape? My red eyes? My milk-enlarged breasts? Why did he avoid coming near my bed?

An-te-hai tried to convince me that His Majesty's lack of interest had nothing to do with me. "He isn't in the habit of returning to women he has slept with. It doesn't matter how much he praised their beauty or how satisfied he was in bed."

The good news for me was that I had heard no report of any other pregnancy.

From Prince Kung's letters I learned that Emperor Hsien Feng had been avoiding audiences since he had signed a new treaty with the foreigners, which acknowledged China's defeat. Ashamed and humiliated, His Majesty spent his days alone in the Imperial gardens. At night, bodily pleasures had become his escape.

Sick as he was, he demanded round-the-clock entertainment. An-te-hai found out the details from a new friend, His Majesty's chamber attendant, a eunuch named Chow Tee, a boy from An-te-hai's hometown.

"His Majesty is drunk most of the time, and he is unable to perform his manhood," An-te-hai told me. "He enjoys watching his women and orders them to touch themselves while dancing. The parties last all night while His Majesty sleeps."

I recalled our last visit together. Hsien Feng couldn't stop talking about his fall. "I have no doubt that I will be shredded into ten thousand pieces by my ancestors when I meet them." He laughed nervously and coughed. His chest sounded like a wind box. "Doctor Sun Pao-tien has prescribed opium for my pain," he said. "I don't really mind dying, because I look forward to being released from my troubles."

It was no longer a secret to the nation that the Emperor's health had once again begun to decline. His pale face and empty eyes concerned everyone. Since we had moved back to the Forbidden City, the court's ministers were ordered to report their state matters to him in his bedroom.

It broke my heart to see Hsien Feng giving up hope. Before he left my palace he said, "I am sorry." Raising his face from his son's cradle, he smiled sadly at me. "It is not up to me anymore."

I looked at my child's father putting on his dragon robe. He had no strength even to lift his sleeves. It took him three long breaths to get into his shoes.

I must ask him before it is too late to grant me the right to raise our son! The thought came to me while I held the baby and watched Hsien Feng enter his palanquin. I had mentioned my wish before, but there had been no response. According to An-te-hai, the Emperor would never hurt Nuharoo by taking away her right to be the first mother.

My son, who was born on May 1, 1856, was officially named Tung Chih. *Tung* also stood for "togetherness," and *Chih* for "ruling" — that is, ruling together. If I had been superstitious, I would have seen that the name was a prediction itself.

The celebration started the day after his birth and lasted an entire month. Overnight the Forbidden City was turned into a festival. Red lanterns hung from all the trees. Everyone was dressed in red and green. Five opera troupes were invited to the palace to perform. Drums and music filled the air. The shows went on day and night. Drunkenness was rampant among men and women of all ages. The most asked question was "Where is the chamber pot?"

Unfortunately, all the gaiety didn't stop bad news. No matter how many symbols of good luck and victory we wore, we were losing to the barbarians at the negotiating tables. Minister Chi Ying and Grand Secretary Kuei Liang, Prince Kung's father-in-law, were sent to represent China. They came back with another humiliating treaty: thirteen nations, including England, France, Japan and Russia, had formed an alliance against China. They insisted that we open more ports for opium and trade.

I sent a messenger to Prince Kung inviting him to meet his newborn nephew, but secretly I hoped he would also be able to persuade Hsien Feng to attend his audiences.

Prince Kung came immediately, and he looked agitated. I offered him fresh cherries and Lung Ching tea from Hangchow. He drank the tea in gulps as if it was plain water. I felt that I had chosen a bad time for the visit. But the moment Prince Kung saw Tung Chih, he picked the little thing up. The child smiled, and his uncle was completely taken. I knew Kung meant to stay longer, but a messenger came with a document for his signature, and he had to put Tung Chih down.

I sipped my tea as I rocked the cradle. After the messenger was gone, Prince Kung looked tired. I asked if it was the new treaty that weighed on him.

He nodded and smiled. "I don't feel twenty-three, that's for sure."

I asked if he could tell me a bit about the treaty. "Is it really as awful as I hear?"

"You don't want to know" was his reply.

"I already have some ideas about it," I ventured to say. "I have been helping His Majesty with court documents."

Prince Kung raised his eyes and looked at me.

"Sorry to surprise you," I said.

"Not really," he said. "I only wish that His Majesty would take a greater interest."

"Why don't you talk to him again?"

"His ears are stuffed with cotton balls." He sighed. "I can't shake him."

"I might be able to influence His Majesty if you could inform me a bit," I said. "After all, I need to learn for the sake of Tung Chih."

The words seemed to make sense to Prince Kung, and he started talking. I was shocked to learn that the treaty allowed foreigners to open consulates in Peking.

"Each country has selected its own site, not far from the Forbidden City," he said. "The treaty allows foreign merchant ships to travel along the Chinese coast, and missionaries are given the government's protection."

Tung Chih cried in my arms. He probably needed changing. I gently rocked him and he became quiet.

"Also, we are expected to agree to hire foreign inspectors to run our customs, and worst of all" — Prince Kung paused, then continued — "we are given no choice but to legalize opium."

"His Majesty will not allow it," I said, imagining Prince Kung coming for his brother's signature.

"I wish it were up to him. The reality is that the foreign merchants are backed by the military powers of their countries."

We sat staring out the window.

Tung Chih began to cry again. His voice was neither loud nor strong. It was like a kitten's. A maid came to change him. Afterward I rocked him to sleep.

I thought about Hsien Feng's health and the possibility that my son might grow up without a father.

"This is what a five-thousand-year-old civilization comes down to." Prince Kung sighed as he rose from his seat.

"I haven't seen His Majesty myself for a while," I said, putting Tung Chih back in his cradle. "Has he been in touch with you?"

"He doesn't want to see me. When he does, he calls me and my ministers a bunch of idiots. He threatens to behead Chi Ying and my father-in-law. He suspects them of being traitors. Before Chi Ying and Kuei Liang went to negotiate with the barbarians, they held farewell ceremonies with their families. They expected to be beheaded because they saw little hope that His Majesty would have his way. Our families drank and sang poems to send them off. My wife has been distraught. She blames me for involving her father. She threatens to hang herself if anything should happen to him."

"What would happen if Hsien Feng refused to sign the treaty?"

"His Majesty doesn't have a choice. Foreign troops are already stationed in Tientsin. Their target would be Peking. The bayonet is at our throat." Looking at Tung Chih, Prince Kung said, "I am afraid I must go back to work now."

As I watched him walk down the corridor, I felt fortunate that at least Tung Chih had this man as an uncle.

Fifteen

WITHIN WEEKS of his birth, Tung Chih was due for his first ceremony. It was called *Shih-san,* the Three Baths. According to the scripture of our ancestors, the ritual would ensure Tung Chih's place in the universe. The night before the event, my palace was decorated anew by the eunuchs, who wrapped the beams and eaves in cloth dyed red and green. By nine o'clock the next morning everything was set. Pumpkin-shaped red lanterns hung in front of the gates and hallways.

I was excited because my mother, my sister Rong and brother Kuei Hsiang had received permission to join me. Their visit was the first since I had entered the Forbidden City. I imagined how delighted my mother would be when I passed Tung Chih to her to hold. I hoped he would smile. I wondered how Rong had been doing. There was a young man I planned to introduce her to.

Kuei Hsiang had recently been honored with my father's title. He now had the choice of either staying in Peking and living off his annual taels or following in our father's footsteps, working his way toward a career in the Imperial court. Kuei Hsiang chose the former, which didn't surprise me; he lacked our father's determination. Nevertheless, it would be a comfort to my mother to have her son close by.

When the sun warmed the garden and the fragrance of flowers filled the air, the guests began to arrive. Among them were the senior concubines of Tung Chih's grandfather Tao Kuang. I remembered those crones well from the Palace of Benevolent Tranquility.

"You should really consider their presence an honor, my lady," An-te-hai said. "They rarely venture out in public; Buddhists are supposed to cultivate solitude."

The ladies arrived in groups, dressed in thin, dirt-colored cotton. Their gift boxes were not red but yellow, with wrapping made of dry leaves. Later I would discover that they all contained the same thing, a statue of a sitting Buddha carved out of a piece of wood or jade.

I stood by the gate and greeted the guests in my lovely peach-colored robe. Carried by a lady in waiting, Tung Chih was bundled in golden cloth. He had just opened his eyes and was in a cheerful mood. He gazed at the visitors with the look of a sage. By the time the sun was above the roof, the royal relatives who lived outside the Forbidden City had arrived, among them Prince Kung, Prince Ts'eng, Prince Ch'un and their *fujins* and children.

Emperor Hsien Feng and Nuharoo appeared at noon. Their arrival was announced by a double line of colorfully dressed eunuchs that stretched for half a mile. Hsien Feng's dragon chair and Nuharoo's phoenix chair advanced toward the palace gate between the ranks of eunuchs.

The Emperor had come to my palace the night before for tea. He had brought Tung Chih a gift: his own belt, the one made of horsehair and folded white silk ribbons. He thanked me for giving him a son.

Gathering all my courage, I told him that I had been lonely. Although I had Tung Chih, I said, I felt confused and lost. I begged him to spend the night. "It has been too long, Hsien Feng."

He understood but wouldn't stay. Over the past few months he had filled every available bedroom in the Summer Palace with beauties from around the country. He said, "I am not well. The doctor has advised me to sleep alone in order to prevent my essence from leaking."

I began to understand Nuharoo, Ladies Yun, Li, Mei and Hui, and those whom the Son of Heaven no longer desired or remembered.

"I have signed an edict granting you a new title," my husband said, rising to leave. "It will be announced tomorrow, and I hope you will be pleased. From now on, you will have the same rank and title as Nuharoo."

The *Shih-san* ceremony began. The concubines scattered after Nuharoo gave them permission to sit down. The ladies were dressed in festival-themed gowns as if attending an opera. They looked around and criticized everything.

Nuharoo said to me, "Please be seated, younger sister." Her eyes softened, although the dark heavy lines of her makeup still looked harsh.

I sat down on a chair next to her.

The crowd sensed that Nuharoo was about to speak. They gathered closer and stretched their necks to show their eagerness to listen.

"Pity me as a woman," Nuharoo spoke to the crowd. "I am guilty toward His Majesty. It is my misfortune for not being able to bear him children. Tung Chih is my chance to prove to him my loyalty. I felt that I was already Tung Chih's mother when Lady Yehonala's belly began to swell." She smiled at her own words. "I am in love with my son."

There was no trace of irony in her voice. I wished I were wrong about her intentions. If love was all she had for Tung Chih, I would gladly let her have her way. But my instincts as a mother ran deep, and I felt that any trust would be misplaced.

"Come and share my happiness, everyone!" Nuharoo cheered. "Meet my heavenly boy, Tung Chih!"

The concubines tried hard to show enthusiasm. Their faces were covered with paint and their heads heavily decorated with ornaments. They got down on their knees and wished Nuharoo and me "ten thousand years of longevity." I didn't feel comfortable when the ladies surrounded the cradle. They kissed Tung Chih on the cheeks. Their red-smeared lips made me think of hungry wolves tearing a rabbit to shreds.

I smelled an unusual herb as Lady Yun walked by. She was in a pale yellow silk dress embroidered with white chrysanthemums. Her earrings were two walnut-sized balls that dangled to her shoulders. When Lady Yun sat down and smiled, dimples showed on her cheeks.

"Does the baby sleep through the night?" she asked. "Not yet?"

Nuharoo and I exchanged glances.

"I would appreciate some words of good luck," Nuharoo said to Lady Yun.

"Did you notice that the plum trees have just blossomed?" As if she hadn't heard Nuharoo, Lady Yun went on. "The strangest thing happened this morning at my palace."

"And what is that?" the other ladies asked, stretching their necks toward Lady Yun like geese.

"In the corner of my bedroom" — Lady Yun lowered her voice to a whisper — "I discovered a giant mushroom. It was as big as a human head!"

Seeing that she had stunned her audience, Lady Yun smiled. "More strange things are going to happen. My astrologer read a sign of death from a spider web in a sweet osmanthus tree. Of course, I am not unaware of such things myself. Emperor Hsien Feng has told me many times that he turns into a rag as he sleeps and is carried by the southern wind directly to Heaven. His Majesty wishes no farewell ceremony. It is his decision that we shall all be widowed."

Nuharoo sat with her back as straight as a pine tree. She blinked her eyes and decided to ignore Lady Yun. She took up her teacup and lifted the lid to sip.

The rest of the ladies followed suit. We dipped our noses in our teacups in unison.

I wondered if Lady Yun was sane. The line seemed to blur as I continued observing. There was truth in her words when she began to sing "Dust in the Wind":

> You ask me when I'm coming.
> Alas, not yet, not yet . . .
> How rain filled the pools on the night we met!
> Ah, shall we ever snuff candles again
> And recall the glad hours of that evening's rain?

Finally my mother's palanquin reached the side entrance of the Gate of Celestial Purity. The moment I saw Mother getting out, I burst into tears. She had aged, and now leaned helplessly on the arms of Rong and Kuei Hsiang. Before I finished my ceremonial greeting, Mother broke down. "Congratulations, Orchid. I didn't think I would live to see my grandson."

"The lucky moment has arrived!" Chief Eunuch Shim's call came from the hallway. "Music and fireworks!"

Guided by eunuchs specially trained in ritual, I moved through the crowd. I asked Emperor Hsien Feng if my mother could sit with me, and he granted my wish. My family was so happy they wept. With difficulty Mother leaned over and touched Tung Chih for the first time. "I am ready to go see your father in peace," she said to me.

After we sat down, Rong and Kuei Hsiang reported that they had been taking Mother to the best doctors in Peking. She looked frail. I took Mother's hands in mine. By custom, my family couldn't stay overnight in the Forbidden City, and we would have to part when the ceremony ended. The idea that I might never see Mother again disturbed me so much that I ignored Nuharoo's request that I join her to receive members of the court.

"Think this way, Orchid," Mother said, trying to comfort me. "Dying will be a relief for me, since I am in so much pain."

I leaned my head on Mother's shoulder and was unable to say a word.

"Try not to spoil the moment, Orchid." Mother smiled.

I made an effort to look cheerful. It didn't seem real to me that everyone was here for my son.

Kuei Hsiang had begun to mingle in the crowd and I could hear him laugh. I could tell that the rice wine had taken effect.

Rong was more beautiful but thinner than the last time I had seen her.

"Rong's future has not yet been settled, and that worries me," Mother said with a sigh. "She hasn't been as lucky as you. Not one worthy proposal, and she is over twenty."

"There is a man I have been thinking of for Rong," I told Mother.

"I can't wait to hear his name."

"He is the newly widowed Prince Ch'un, Hsien Feng's seventh brother."

Mother was thrilled.

"However," I warned, "'widowed' doesn't mean that Prince Ch'un has no wives or concubines. It is just the first wife's position that is vacant."

"I see." Mother nodded. "Still, Prince Ch'un would be an excellent opportunity for Rong. She would be the Nuharoo of Ch'un's household, wouldn't she?"

"That's correct, Mother, if she can get him to be interested."

"What more can a family of our background ask? A life free of hunger—that is all I ever wanted for my children. My marriage with your father was arranged. We had never met before our wedding. It turned out nicely, though, didn't it?"

"More than nicely, Mother."

We were quiet for a time, our fingers locked tightly together. Then Mother said, "My thinking is, you and Rong could become close if this engagement works out. It'll be my last wish on earth that you watch out for each other. Besides, Rong can be an extra eye for you regarding Tung Chih's safety."

I nodded at Mother's wisdom.

"Go now to your sister, Orchid," Mother said, "and leave me to spend a few moments alone with my grandson."

I went to Rong and took her to the back of the garden. We sat down in a tiny stone pavilion. I explained my thoughts and Mother's wish. Rong was pleased that I had kept my promise of finding her a suitor.

"Will Prince Ch'un like me?" she asked. "How should I prepare myself?"

"Let's see if he will fall for you first. My question to you is—and this is crucial—will you be able to endure the hardships I have endured?"

"Hardships? You are mocking me, aren't you?"

A sense of uncertainty rushed through my mind. Rong had no idea what I was talking about.

"Rong, my life is not what it seems. You need to see this. I don't want to be the cause of your regret. I just don't want to set up a tragedy."

Rong blushed. "But Orchid, I have dreamed only of having the same opportunity you have. I want to be envied by women all over China." She smiled broadly.

"Answer my question, Rong, please. Can you bear to lose your husband to others?"

Rong thought first and then replied, "If it is the way things have been for hundreds of years, I don't see why I should be the one to have problems."

I took a breath and gave my last warning. "When you are in love with a man, you will change. I am telling you from experience, the pain is unbearable. You will feel your heart being stir-fried in a hot pan."

"I better make sure I don't fall in love, then."

"You might not be able to control things."

"Why?"

"Well, because to love is to live—at least that's true for me."

"What do I do, then, Orchid?" Confused, Rong's eyes widened.

Sadness filled my chest and I had to remain silent to control myself.

Rong put her cheek gently against mine. "You must have fallen in love with Emperor Hsien Feng."

"It was . . . foolish of me."

"I'll remember your lesson, Orchid. I know it must be hard. But I still envy my elder sister. There hasn't been a decent man in my life. It makes me think that I am unattractive."

"You know that is nonsense, Rong. How unattractive can you be when your sister is an Imperial consort, the face of China?"

Rong smiled and nodded.

"It's true, you have grown prettier." I put my arm around her shoulder. "I want you to be aware of your beauty every minute from now on."

"What does 'minute' mean?"

"It is a needle on a clock."

"What is a clock?"

"Well, I'll show you. Clocks are the Emperor's toys. They tell time. Clocks hide in metal boxes, like snails in their shells. Each box has a little ticking heart inside."

"Like a living creature?"

"Yes. But they are not alive. Most of them were made by men in foreign countries. You will own many of them when you marry Prince Ch'un."

I took out my powder brush. "Listen, Rong," I said, "as the sister of Hsien Feng's favorite concubine, you should know that men are dying to possess you, but they might not have enough courage to walk up to you and say what is on their mind. I'll talk with His Majesty about matching you up with his brother. If I obtain his blessing, the rest will be easy."

By the time Rong and I went back to Mother and Kuei Hsiang, the music and fireworks had ended. Chief Eunuch Shim announced that the first part of the ceremony was over, and the second part, the Bath in Gold, would now start. At his call, four eunuchs carried out a tub made of gold. They placed the tub in the center of the courtyard under a blooming magnolia and filled it with water. Coal heaters were set around the tub.

A group of maids got down on their knees next to the tub while two wet nurses carried my son out. The maids stripped Tung Chih and placed him in the tub. He screamed, but his protest was ignored. The maids held his little legs and arms the way they would when skinning a rabbit. Everyone seemed to find this entertaining. My son's every cry pained me. It was hard to sit still, but I knew I must endure. There was a price to pay for Tung Chih's stature. Each ceremony would bring him closer to becoming the legitimate heir.

With a hundred pairs of eyes watching, Tung Chih had his first bath. He was getting more and more disturbed.

"Look, there is a dark spot under Tung Chih's right armpit!" Nuharoo got up from her chair and ran to me. She had changed into her second gown for the occasion. "Is it an unlucky sign?"

"It's a birthmark," I told her. "I consulted Doctor Sun Pao-tien and he told me not to worry."

"I wouldn't trust Sun Pao-tien," Nuharoo said. "I have never seen this kind of birthmark—it's too big and too dark. I must consult my astrologer right away." Turning to the tub, she admonished the maids, "Don't try to stop Tung Chih from crying. Let him! He is supposed to feel uncomfortable. This is what the ceremony is about. The louder he cries, the better the chance he will grow up to be strong."

I forced myself to walk away so I wouldn't punch Nuharoo in the chest.

The wind blew. Pink petals rained from the trees. A couple of them landed in the tub. The maids picked up the petals and showed them to Tung Chih in an effort to quiet him. This picture of bathing under the magnolia tree would have been lovely if the baby were not in torment. I had no idea how long Tung Chih would have to sit in the water. I looked up at the sun and prayed that it would stay out.

"Clothing!" Chief Eunuch Shim sang stylishly. The maids quickly dried and dressed Tung Chih, who was so exhausted that he fell asleep in the middle of their handling. He looked like a rag doll. Yet the ceremony was far from completed. After the tub was emptied, the sleeping Tung Chih was put back in it. Several lamas dressed in sun-colored robes sat down in a circle around the baby and began chanting.

"Gifts!" Chief Eunuch Shim shouted.

With Emperor Hsien Feng leading, the guests came forward to offer tribute.

As each box of gifts was opened, Shim announced the contents. "From His Majesty, four gold ingots and two pieces of silver!"

Eunuchs removed the wrapping, revealing a carved box of red lacquer.

Chief Eunuch Shim moved on. "From Her Majesty Empress Nuharoo, eight pieces of gold and a silver ingot, eight good-luck *ruyi*, four pieces of gold and silver money, four cotton winter blankets, four cotton covers and sheets, four winter jackets, four winter pants, four pairs of socks and two pillows!"

The rest of the guests presented their gifts according to rank and generation. The tributes were more or less the same except in amount and quality. No one was supposed to top the first couple, and no one actually used the gifts. Everything was packed up and sent to the Imperial storehouses in the name of Tung Chih.

The next day, I got up before dawn in order to spend time with my son. Then the ritual of *Shih-san* went on. Tung Chih again was soaked in the tub.

He had been sitting in the water for one hour and fifteen minutes. The sun was shining, but the May air was chilly. My son could easily catch a cold. Nobody seemed to care. After Tung Chih sneezed a couple of times, I told An-te-hai to bring out a tent to protect him from the breeze. But Nuharoo rejected the idea. She said that the tent would block Tung Chih's luck. "The purpose of the bath is to expose Tung Chih to the magical powers of the universe."

I refused to give in to her this time. "The tent will stay," I insisted.

Nuharoo didn't say anything. But when I went to use the chamber pot, the tent was removed. I knew I was crazy to think that Nuharoo's intention was to drive my son to illness. But I couldn't help dwelling on the idea.

Nuharoo said that we were not entitled to alter tradition. "From emperor to emperor, every heir has bathed in the same way."

"But our ancestors were different people," I argued. "They lived on horseback and went around half naked." I reminded Nuharoo that Tung Chih's father was a man of poor health and Tung Chih was underweight at birth.

Nuharoo was silenced but didn't surrender.

Tung Chih started to sneeze.

No longer able to control myself, I went to the tub and pushed the maids away. I grabbed Tung Chih and ran inside.

The ceremonies and festivities went on and on. In the middle of it all a gardener discovered a fetish doll buried in my garden. On the doll's chest were two black characters spelling out "Tung Chih."

Emperor Hsien Feng summoned the wives and concubines—he wanted to solve the crime personally. I dressed and went to Lady Yun's palace. I didn't know why we had to meet there. I ran into Nuharoo on the way. She had come from another palace and had no idea what was going on either.

As we approached the palace we heard sounds of sobbing. We hurried into the hall and found an angry Emperor. Hsien Feng was in his sleeping gown, and next to him stood two eunuchs, each holding a whip. On the floor knelt numerous eunuchs and servants. Among them, in the first row, was Lady Yun. She was in a pink silk gown and had been the one sobbing.

"Quit crying," Emperor Hsien Feng said. "As a noble lady, how could you lower yourself to this?"

"I didn't do it, Your Majesty!" Lady Yun threw her head back to face him. "I was overjoyed by the birth of Tung Chih. I couldn't celebrate enough. I will not close my eyes if I am hanged because of this!"

"Everyone in the Forbidden City recognizes your handwriting." The Emperor raised his voice. "How could everyone be wrong?"

"My calligraphy is not a secret," Lady Yun protested. "I am known for my art. It would be very easy for anyone to copy my style."

"But one of your maids caught you making the doll."

"It must be Dee. She made this up because she hates me."

"Why does Dee hate you?"

Lady Yun turned around. Her eyes spotted Nuharoo. "Dee was given to me by Her Majesty Empress Nuharoo as a gift. I never wanted her. I punished her several times because she sniffed around—"

"Dee is only thirteen years old," Nuharoo interrupted. "Accusing an innocent in order to cover your crime is shameful." She turned to me as if for support. "Dee is known for her sweetness, isn't she?"

Unprepared to respond, I lowered my head.

Nuharoo turned to Hsien Feng. "Your Majesty, may I have your permission to perform my duty?"

"Yes, my Empress."

At this Lady Yun screamed, "All right, I will confess! I know exactly who set this up. It is an evil fox in a human's skin. She was sent by the demon to destroy the Ch'ing Dynasty. But there is more than one fox in the Forbidden City. The evil fox has called in her pack. You," she pointed at Nuharoo, "are one of them. And you," she pointed at me, "too. Your Majesty, it is time to reward me with the white silk rope so that I will have the honor of hanging myself."

This caused a brief commotion in the hall. The noise settled when Lady Yun spoke again.

"I want to die. My life has been hell. I have given you a princess," she pointed at Emperor Hsien Feng, "and you treat her like a piece of rubbish. As soon as she turns thirteen, you will give her away. You will marry her off to a savage from the borderlands in order to make peace. You will sell your own daughter . . ."

Lady Yun broke down. Her two dimples were making a strange grin. "Don't think I am deaf. I have been hearing you and your ministers talk about this. I have not been allowed to speak about my misery. But today, like it or not, you will hear all that I have to say. Of course I am jealous of the way Tung Chih is treated. Of course I cry for my daughter Jung's misfortune, and I question Heaven why I was denied a son . . . Let me ask you, Hsien Feng, do you know when your daughter's birthday is? Do you know how old she is? How long has it been since you last visited her? I bet you have no answers for any of my questions. Your heart has been chewed up by the foxes!"

Nuharoo took out her handkerchief and began to pat her face. "I am afraid that Lady Yun is leaving His Majesty with no choice."

"Finish the business for me, Nuharoo." Emperor Hsien Feng stood and walked out of the hall in his bare feet.

Lady Yun hanged herself that night. The news was brought to me by An-te-hai the next morning while I was having breakfast. My stomach turned upside down. For the rest of the day I could see Lady Yun's face behind every door and in every window. I asked An-te-hai to stay nearby while I checked and rechecked Tung Chih's cradle. I wondered about Lady Yun's daughter, Princess Jung. I wished I could invite the girl to stay with me for a while and spend time with her half-brother. An-te-hai said that the toddler had been told that her mother had gone on a long journey. The eunuchs and servants were ordered to keep Lady Yun's death a secret. The girl would find out about it in the cruelest way: she would learn of the death from gossip, from Lady Yun's rivals, who wished to see the girl suffer.

Nuharoo came unannounced at midnight. Her eunuchs knocked on my gate so hard that they almost broke it down. Nuharoo threw herself on me when I greeted her. She looked ill and her voice choked. "She is after me!"

"Who is after you?" I asked.

"Lady Yun!"

"Wake up, Nuharoo. It must have been a nightmare."

"She was standing by my bed in a greenish transparent dress," Nuharoo sobbed. "There was blood all over her chest. Her neck was cut from the front, as if with an ax, and her head was hanging on her back, connected to her neck by only a thin piece of skin. I couldn't see her face, but heard her voice. She said, 'I was supposed to be hanged, not beheaded.' She said that she was sent by the judge of the underworld to find a substitute. In order to come back for her next life, she had to make the substitute die the same way she did."

I comforted Nuharoo, but was scared myself. She returned to her palace and devoured every ghost book she owned. A few days later she visited me and said that she had discovered something that I'd better know.

"The worst punishment for a female ghost is being dumped in the

'Pool of Filthy Blood.'" Nuharoo showed me a book with lurid illustrations of the "Department of Scourging" at work in the underworld. Severed heads with long hair floated in a dark red pool—they looked like dumplings in boiling water.

"See this? This is what I wanted to talk to you about," Nuharoo said. "The blood in the pool comes from the filth of all women. Also in the pool are poisonous snakes and scorpions that feed on the newly dead. They are the transformations of those who committed wrongdoings in their lives."

"What if I commit no serious wrongdoing during my lifetime?" I asked.

"Orchid, the judgment of the underworld is for all women. That is why we need religion. Buddhism helps us repent the crimes we commit simply by being women and living a material life. We need to forgo all earthly pleasure and pray for Heaven's forgiveness. We must do everything we can to accumulate virtue. Only then may we have a chance of escaping the Pool of Filthy Blood."

Sixteen

O N HIS FIRST BIRTHDAY my son would be presented with a tray filled with a variety of items. He was expected to pick one that would give the Imperial family a clue to his future character. This was called *Chua-tsui-p'an,* Catch the Future in a Pan. Important court members were invited to observe.

Tung Chih's eunuchs had been busy all week in preparation for the event. The walls, columns, doors and window frames of my palace were freshly painted in vermilion. The beams and bracket sets were accented with blue, green and gold. Against the bright northern sky, the yellow tile roof glistened like a gigantic golden crown. The white marble terraces vibrated with their exuberant carvings.

The ceremony opened in the Hall of Bodily Mercy, in the east corner of the palace, where an altar had been set up. Above the altar was a broadside explaining the ritual. In the center of the hall sat a large square redwood table. On top of the table stood a tray the size of a mature lotus leaf, larger than a child's tub. On the tray lay symbolic items: an Imperial seal, a book of Confucius's *On Autumn and Spring,* a brush pen made of goat hair, a gold ingot, a silver ingot, a riddle, a decorative sword, a miniature liquor bottle, a golden key, ivory dice, a silver cigarette box, a musical clock, a leather whip, a blue ceramic bowl painted with landscapes, an antique fan with a poem written by a famous Ming poet, a green jade hairpin crafted with butterflies, an earring in the shape of a pagoda and a pink peony.

My son had been taken from me in the morning. This was to assure that he would act of his own free will. For the past few weeks I had tried hard to guide him to the "right choices." I showed him a map of China, colorful landscape paintings, and of course the object he was supposed to pick, the Imperial seal—a fake one for the practice runs of course. An-te-hai had made it from a block of wood. I stamped the "seal" on different boards to attract Tung Chih's attention. But he was more interested in the pins in my hair.

The guests sat quietly in the hall and waited for Tung Chih to perform. In front of hundreds of people, I got down on my knees by the altar and lit incense.

Emperor Hsien Feng and Nuharoo sat in the center chairs. We prayed as the incense smoke began to fill the room. Tea and nuts were served. When the sun hit the beams of the hall, Tung Chih was carried in by two eunuchs. He was dressed in a golden robe embroidered with dragons. He looked around with big eyes. The eunuchs placed him on the table. He bounced up and down and was unable to sit still. The eunuchs somehow got him to bow to his father, his mothers and the portraits of his ancestors.

I felt terribly weak and alone, and wished that my mother or Rong were here. This ritual hadn't been taken seriously in the past, when people had come simply to coo and giggle over a baby. But these days astrologers ruled—the Manchu royals were no longer sure of themselves. Everything was up to "Heaven's will."

What if Tung Chih picked up a flower or a hairpin instead of the Imperial seal? Would people say that my son was going to be a dandy? What about the clock? Wouldn't he be drawn to its tinkly sound?

Tung Chih's bib was wet from drool. When the eunuchs let him go free, he crawled toward the tray. He was so bundled up that his movements were clumsy. Leaning forward, everyone watched with anxiety. I sensed Nuharoo's glance in my direction and tried to appear confident. I had caught a cold the night before and my head ached. I had been drinking glass after glass of water to calm myself down.

Tung Chih stopped crawling and reached out to the tray. It felt like I was the one on the table. Suddenly I desperately needed to go to the chamber pot.

I hurried out of the hall and brushed aside the maids before they could follow me. Sitting on the chamber pot, I took several deep breaths. The pain on the right side of my head had spread to the left side. I got off the pot and rinsed my hands and face with cold water. When I reentered the hall, I saw Tung Chih chewing on his bib.

The crowd was still patiently waiting. Their expectations devastated me. *It was wrong to make an infant bear China's burden!* But I knew that my son would be taken from me for good if I dared to utter such a sentence.

Tung Chih was about to slide off the table. The eunuchs picked him up and turned him around. A scene came to my mind: hunters had released a deer, only to kill it with their arrows. The message seemed to be: if the deer was not strong enough to escape, it deserved to die.

Emperor Hsien Feng had promised that I would be rewarded if Tung Chih delivered a "good performance." How could I possibly direct him?

The more I read of the broadside above the altar, the more fearful I became.

> ... If the prince picks the Imperial seal, he will become an emperor graced by all of Heaven's virtue. If he picks the brush pen, the gold, the silver or the sword, he shall rule with intelligence and a forceful will. But if he picks the flower, the earring or the hairpin, he will grow up to be a pleasure seeker. If he chooses the liquor pot, he will be an alcoholic; if the dice, he will gamble away the dynasty ...

Tung Chih "studied" every article but picked up none. The hall was so quiet that I could hear the sound of water running through the garden. My sweat oozed and my collar felt tight.

Tung Chih stuck a finger in his mouth. *He must be hungry!* The chance that he would pick up the stone seal was fading.

He resumed his crawling. This time he appeared somehow motivated. The eunuchs put up their hands around the edges of the table to prevent Tung Chih from falling.

Emperor Hsien Feng leaned over in his dragon chair. He held his head with both hands as if it was too heavy, shifting the weight from one elbow to another.

Tung Chih stopped. He fixed his eyes on the pink peony. He smiled, and his hand traveled from his mouth to the flower.

I closed my eyes. I heard Emperor Hsien Feng sigh.

Disappointment? Bitterness?

Tung Chih had turned away from the flower when I reopened my eyes.

Was he remembering the moment I punished him when he picked up the flower? I had spanked him, crying myself. I had put my fingerprints on his little behind and hated myself for it.

My son raised his tiny chin. What was he looking for? Me? Forgetting my manners, I weaved through the crowd and stopped in front of him. I smiled and used my eyes to draw a line from his nose to the Imperial seal.

The little one acted. In one determined motion, he grabbed the seal.

"Congratulations, Your Majesty!" the crowd cheered.

Crying joyfully, An-te-hai ran to the courtyard.

Rockets shot into the sky. A hundred thousand paper flowers popped open in the air.

Emperor Hsien Feng jumped up from his seat and announced, "According to the historical record, since the beginning of the Ch'ing Dynasty in 1644, only two princes grabbed the Imperial seal. They turned out to be China's most successful emperors, Kang Hsi and Chien Lung. My son, Tung Chih, is likely to be the next one!"

The day after the ceremony, I knelt before a temple altar. Although I was exhausted, I felt that I must not neglect the gods who had helped me. I made offerings to show my gratitude. An-te-hai brought in a live fish on a golden plate. It had been caught in the lake and was tied with a red ribbon. In a rush I poured wine on the cobblestones because the fish had to be returned to the lake alive.

An-te-hai carefully placed the plate with the fish into a palanquin as if it were a person. At the lake I let go of the fish, and it leaped into the water.

To secure my son's future and increase blessings from all of the gods, An-te-hai bought ten cages of precious birds for me to release. I granted the birds mercy on Tung Chih's behalf.

Good news greeted me upon my return to the palace. Rong and Prince Ch'un were engaged. My mother was thrilled.

According to Emperor Hsien Feng, his brother had little talent or ambition. In his own introduction to Rong, Prince Ch'un had described himself as a "worshiper of Confucius's teachings," meaning that he pursued the life of a free mind. While he enjoyed the benefits that came with his royal position, he believed that "too much water makes a cup spill," and "too many ornaments make a headdress look cheap."

None of us realized that Prince Ch'un's rhetoric was an umbrella covering flaws in his character. I would soon discover that Ch'un's "modesty" and "self-imposed spiritual exile" came from his laziness.

I again warned Rong to expect no fantasy from an Imperial marriage. "Look at me," I said. "His Majesty's health has declined to the point of no return, and I have been preparing myself for the Imperial widowhood."

I was not alone in my concern for the Emperor's health. Nuharoo shared the same feeling. On her last visit we had come together on friendly terms for the first time. The fear of losing Hsien Feng bound us. She had begun to accept the fact that I had become her equal. Her sense of superiority had softened, and she began to use "would you" instead of "this is Her Majesty's thinking." We both knew from history what could happen to an emperor's wives and concubines after his death. We both realized that we had only each other to depend on.

I had my own reasons for wanting Nuharoo as an ally. I sensed that my son's fate would be in the hands of such ambitious court ministers as Grand Councilor Su Shun. He seemed to have the Emperor's complete trust. It was public knowledge that even Prince Kung feared Su Shun.

Su Shun had been running the state's affairs and conducting audiences in the name of Hsien Feng during His Majesty's illness. More and more, he acted with total independence. Su Shun's power worried me, for I thought him manipulative and cunning. When he visited Emperor Hsien Feng, he rarely discussed state matters. In the name of caring for His Majesty's health, he isolated Hsien Feng and strengthened his own position. According to Prince Ch'un, Su Shun had been carefully constructing his own political base for years through the appointment of friends and associates to important positions.

I convinced Nuharoo that we must insist on having important documents sent to Emperor Hsien Feng. His Majesty might be too ill to review the documents, but we might help him stay informed. At least we would not be kept in the dark and could make sure that Su Shun was not abusing his power.

Nuharoo didn't want to bother. "A wise lady ought to spend her life appreciating the beauty of nature, preserving her yin element and pursuing her longevity."

But my instinct told me that if we refused to take part in the government, we could lose whatever control we had.

Nuharoo agreed that I had a point, but didn't fully embrace my plan. Nonetheless, I spoke to His Majesty that evening, and the next day a decree was issued: all documents were to be sent to Emperor Hsien Feng's office first.

It didn't surprise me that Su Shun ignored the decree. He ordered the messengers who carried the documents to "follow the original route." Again his excuse was the Emperor's health. My suspicion and distrust deepened.

"I feel myself aging over your struggle to control Su Shun's ambition," Nuharoo said. She asked me to spare her the exertion. "Do whatever you want with Su Shun as long as you respect the fact that 'the sun rises in the east and sets in the west,'" she said, referring to the two of us.

It amazed me that Nuharoo would think of this as important. I gave her my word.

Immediately she relaxed. "Why don't you take charge and update me once in a while?" she said. "I hate to sit in the same room with men whose breath stinks."

At first I suspected that Nuharoo was testing my loyalty. But in time she made me realize that I was doing her a favor. She was the kind who would lose sleep over the smallest flaw in her embroidery, but not if we lost an important term in a treaty.

The sunlight on Nuharoo's bone-thin shoulders carved a beautiful contour. She never failed to prepare herself for His Majesty's possible appearance. Her makeup must have taken half a day to complete. Black paste made of scented flower petals was used to accent her eyelashes. Her eyes looked like two deep wells. She painted her lips a different color every day. Today was pink with a touch of vermilion. Yesterday had been rose, and the day before purple. She expected to be complimented, and I learned that it was important to our relationship that I do so.

"I'd hate to see you age, Yehonala." Nuharoo held up all of her fingers. The two-inch-long nails were painted gold and silver with delicate details from nature. "Take my advice and have your chef prepare *tang kuei* soup daily. Put dry silkworm and black dates in it. The taste will be awful, but you'll get used to it."

"We need to talk about Su Shun and his cabinet, Nuharoo," I said. "I get nervous about things I don't know."

"Oh, you will never know it all. It's a hundred-year-old mess." She blocked my eyes with her "finger spears." "I'll send my nail lady to your palace if you don't get it done yourself."

"I am not used to long nails," I said. "They break too easily."

"Am I the head of the Imperial household?" She frowned.

I sealed my lips, reminding myself of the importance of keeping harmony between us.

"Long nails are symbols of nobility, Lady Yehonala."

I nodded, although my mind had gone back to Su Shun.

Nuharoo's smile returned. "Like a Chinese lady who binds her feet, who doesn't live to do labor but to be carried around in palanquins. The longer our nails, the further we depart from the ordinary. Please stop bragging about working in the garden with your hands. You embarrass not only yourself but also the Imperial family."

I kept nodding, pretending to appreciate her advice.

"Avoid tangerine." She leaned so close that I smelled jasmine on her breath. "Too many hot elements will give you pimples. I'll have my eunuch send you a bowl of turtle soup to put out the fire inside you. Do honor me by accepting."

I was sure that she felt she had achieved her goal when the Emperor stopped sharing my bed. She now had an even better reason to feel safe with me: Hsien Feng was never going to get up and walk back into my bedroom.

"I'll leave you to the headaches, then," she said, smiling and getting up.

To put her mind more at ease, I told her I had no experience dealing with the court, nor had I any connections.

"That's something I am sure I can help with," Nuharoo said. "My birthday is approaching, and I have ordered a banquet to celebrate. I want you to invite anyone you think will be useful to you. Don't worry. People are dying to make connections with us."

"Who is there besides Prince Kung that we can trust?"

She thought for a moment and then replied, "How about Yung Lu?"

"Yung Lu?"

"The commander in chief of the Imperial Guards. He works under Su Shun. He is a very capable man. I went to my family reunion for the rice cake festival and his name was on everyone's lips."

"Have you met him?"

"No."

"Will you send him an invitation?"

"I would if I could. The problem is that Yung Lu's rank is not high enough to entitle him to a place at an Imperial banquet."

Fragrance of laurel filled the courtyard and the reception hall. Dressed like a blossoming tree, Nuharoo was surprised to learn that Su Shun had sent word at the last minute that he would not be attending. His excuse was that "His Majesty's ladies are for His Majesty's eyes only." Nuharoo was beside herself.

Wearing so many necklaces of hammered gold, precious stones and brocade caused Nuharoo's neck to lean forward. She was sitting on the throne in the east hall of the Palace of Gathering Essence. She had just completed her second change of dress for the day and now wore a bright yellow gauzy silk robe embroidered with an array of Imperial symbols.

All eyes were locked on Nuharoo except those of Emperor Hsien Feng, who, although sick to the bone, had made an effort to come. He was dressed in a matching robe to complement Nuharoo. But the symbols on his robe were slightly different. Dragons replaced phoenixes, mountains replaced rivers.

"Happy twenty-second birthday, Your Majesty Empress Nuharoo!" Chief Eunuch Shim sang.

The crowd followed, and toasted Nuharoo's longevity.

I sipped rice wine and thought about what Nuharoo had said to me about her method of achieving internal harmony: "Lie in the bed others have made, and walk in the shoes others have cobbled." The sentiment made little sense to me. My life so far was a piece of embroidery with every stitch sewn by my own hands.

The banquet's courses were endless. As people tired of eating, they moved to the west wing, where Nuharoo was presented with her gifts. She sat like a Buddha receiving worshipers.

Emperor Hsien Feng's gift was the first presented. It was a giant box wrapped with red silk and tied with yellow ribbons. It was brought into the hall on an ivory table carried by six eunuchs.

Nuharoo's eyes glowed like those of a curious child.

Beneath six layers of wrapping, the gift revealed itself. Inside the box was a monstrous peach the size of a wok, carved out of wood.

"Why a peach?" Nuharoo asked. "Is it a jest?"

"Open it," the Emperor urged.

Nuharoo left her seat and walked around the peach.

"Expose the pit," His Majesty said.

A hush fell over the room.

After Nuharoo made a few rounds of touching, pinching and shaking, the peach fell open, splitting down the middle. At its heart was a creation that was the very essence of beauty, bringing gasps of admiration from the spectators—a pair of wondrous shoes.

If she hadn't suffered in her childhood, she had suffered long and hard enough as a neglected wife to earn the right to this reward. The Manchu shoes with high heels were in the very best of taste, covered with sparkling gems like the dew on the petals of a spring peony. Nuharoo wept with happiness. During the months when Emperor Hsien Feng and I had lost count of our days, Nuharoo had become a walking ghost. Each night her face must have been the color of moonlight, and she must have chanted Buddhist prayers in order to sleep. Her jealousy was put to rest now that I had fallen from grace and become the same backyard concubine as she.

I complimented Nuharoo for her beauty and luck, and I asked if the shoes fit. Her reply surprised me. "His Majesty has granted his Chinese women palaces, pensions and servants in his will."

I looked around, fearing what would happen if His Majesty heard this. But he had fallen asleep.

Nuharoo packed the shoes back into the peach and sent her eunuch to store the box. "Disregarding his own health, His Majesty has no intention of giving up the bound-feet women, and I am upset."

"Indeed, His Majesty should take care of himself," I echoed in a small voice. "For the sake of your birthday, Nuharoo, forget about it for a moment."

"How?" Her tears welled up. "He hides the whores in the Summer Palace. He has spent taels building a water canal around his little 'town of Soochow.' Every shop along the river has been furnished and decorated. The teahouses now present the best operas, and the galleries the most famous artists. He has added stalls for artisans and fortunetellers, just like a real town—except there are no customers! His Majesty has even given names to the whores! One is called Spring, another Summer, and then there is Autumn and Winter. 'Beauties for all seasons,' he calls them. Lady Yehonala, His Majesty is sick of us Manchu ladies. One of these days he will collapse and die in the middle of his flagrant activities, and the embarrassment will be too great for us to bear."

I took out my handkerchief and passed it to Nuharoo to wipe her tears. "We cannot take this personally. It is my feeling that His Majesty is not sick of us, but of his responsibility toward his country. Maybe our presence reminds him too much of his obligations. After all, we have been telling him that he is disappointing his ancestors."

"Do you see any hope that His Majesty will come back to his senses?"

"Good news from the frontier would improve His Majesty's mood and clear his thoughts," I said. "In this morning's court briefs, I read that General Tseng Kuo-fan has launched a campaign to drive the Taiping rebels back to Nanking. Let's hope he succeeds. His force should be near Wuchang by now."

She stopped me. "Oh, Yehonala. Don't put me through this torture. I don't want to know!"

I sat down on a side chair and took the tea An-te-hai passed to me.

"Well." Nuharoo composed herself. "I am the Empress, and I need to know, correct? All right, tell me what you have to say, but keep it simple."

I patiently tried to give Nuharoo some sense of the matter. Of course she couldn't help but know a little already—that the Taipings were peasant rebels, that they had adopted Christianity, and that their leader, Hong Hsiu-chuan, claimed he was the younger son of God, the brother of Jesus. But Nuharoo had little knowledge of how successful they had been in battle. Although Hsien Feng would not publicly acknowledge the situation, the Taipings had taken the south, the country's farming region, and had begun to press northward.

"What do these Taipings want?" Nuharoo blinked her eyes.

"To bring down our dynasty."

"It is unthinkable!"

"As unthinkable as the treaties the foreigners have forced on us."

Nuharoo's expression reminded me of a child who had discovered a rat in her candy box.

"Free trade plus Christianity is how the foreigners would 'civilize' us."

"What an insult!" Nuharoo sneered.

"I couldn't agree more. The foreigners say they are here to save the souls of the Chinese."

"But their behavior speaks for itself!"

"Very true. The British have sold nine million pounds' worth of goods in China this year alone, of which six million was opium."

"Don't tell me that our court is doing nothing, Lady Yehonala."

"Well, as Prince Kung said, China is prostrate and has no choice but to do what it is told."

Nuharoo covered her ears. "Stop it! There is nothing *I* can do about this." She grabbed my hands. "Leave these matters to men, please!"

Yung Lu, the commander in chief of the Imperial Guards, was summoned by Nuharoo. She believed that as long as she had someone guarding the gates of the Forbidden City, she was safe. I couldn't argue with her. A few days earlier Nuharoo had conducted the wedding ceremony of Rong and Prince Ch'un. It was a lengthy event that wore me out. But Nuharoo was full of energy and spirit. During the proceedings, she changed dresses thirteen times, more than the bride.

I followed Nuharoo to a quiet chamber in the west wing where Yung Lu had been waiting. As we entered, I saw a man of strong physique rise from a chair.

"Yung Lu at Your Majesties' service." The man's manner was humble and his voice firm. He got down on his knees and bowed deeply. He completed the ritual by performing the traditional kowtows, his head knocking on the ground.

"Rise," Nuharoo said, and gestured for the eunuchs to bring tea.

Yung Lu was in his late twenties and had a pair of scorching eyes and weather-beaten skin. He had sword-like eyebrows and the nose of a bull. His jaw was large and square, and his mouth was the shape of an ingot. His broad shoulders and the way he stood reminded me of an ancient warlord.

Nuharoo began to chat of small things. She commented on the weather, while he asked about His Majesty's health. When questioned about the Taipings, Yung Lu answered with patience and precision.

I found myself impressed by his manner, which was reserved and honest. I studied his clothes. He was in a three-piece cavalry brigade uniform, a skirt covered by a sleeveless court gown. Held together by toggles and loops, it was padded and encrusted with copper studs. The plain weave indicated his rank.

"May I look at your crossbow?" I asked.

Yung Lu took it off his belt and passed it to Nuharoo, who then held it out to me.

I examined the quiver, which was made of satin, leather, swan's-down, silver and sapphires, with vulture feathers on the arrows. "And your sword?"

He passed the blade to me.

It was heavy. As I ran my fingertip along the edge, I felt him watching me. My cheeks ran hot. I was ashamed of the way I was paying attention to a man, although I couldn't name the nature of my sudden interest.

An-te-hai had informed me that Yung Lu had emerged on the political stage of China by his own merits.

I had to restrain my urge to ask Yung Lu questions. I had to be careful what I said, although I intended to impress him.

I wondered if Yung Lu had any idea how rare it was for someone like Nuharoo or me to have this encounter. How precious it was to be able to spend time with someone who lived his life outside the Forbidden City.

"The inner palace is so isolated that we often feel that we exist only as names to the country" — my voice spoke my thoughts involuntarily. I glanced at Nuharoo, who smiled and nodded. Relieved, I went on. "The elaborate lives we lead serve only to confirm to ourselves that we are the possessors of power, that we are who we think we are, that we needn't be afraid of anything. The truth is, not only are we afraid, but

215

we also fear that Emperor Hsien Feng is dying of distress. He is the person who is most afraid."

As if shocked by my revelation, Nuharoo grabbed my hand and pressed her nails into my palm.

But I couldn't be stopped. "Not a day passes that I don't fear for my son," I barged ahead, and then suddenly stopped, deeply embarrassed. I looked down and noticed the magnificent sword in my hand. "I hope that one day Tung Chih will fall in love with a sword this beautiful."

"Indeed." Nuharoo seemed glad that I had returned to a proper subject. Joining in, she praised the weapon as a masterpiece of craftsmanship.

I recognized the symbols on the sword's handle, which were reserved for the Emperor. Surprised, I asked, "Was this a gift from His Majesty?"

"Actually, it was a gift from Emperor Hsien Feng to my superior Su Shun," Yung Lu replied, "who in turn gave it to me, with the permission of His Majesty."

"What was the occasion?" Nuharoo and I asked almost at the same time.

"I was fortunate enough to be able to save Su Shun's life in a fight with bandits in the mountain area of Hupei. This dagger was also my reward." Yung Lu got down on his left knee and pulled out a dagger from inside his boot. He passed it to me. The handle was made of jade inlaid with stones.

The moment my fingers touched the weapon, I felt a sensation of excitement.

It was noon when Nuharoo said that she had to leave for her Buddha room to chant and count her beads.

To her, what Yung Lu and I were talking about was uninteresting. It amazed me that she found the endless chanting interesting. Once I had asked Nuharoo if she could shed some light on Buddhism, and she said that it was all about "an existence of nonexistence," or "an opportunity that is not pursued." When I pressed for more of an explanation, she said that it was impossible. "I can't describe my relationship with Buddha in an earthly language." She gave me a steady look, and her tone was full of gentle pity as she said, "Our lives are predestined to attain."

After Nuharoo left, I resumed talking with Yung Lu. It felt like the beginning of a fascinating journey, which I was enjoying despite my guilt. He was of Manchu origin and was from the north. As the grandson of a general, he had joined the White Bannermen at the age of fourteen and worked his way up, taking the Imperial academic route as well as advanced military training.

I asked about his relationship with Su Shun.

"The grand councilor was in charge of a case in which I was a plaintiff," Yung Lu replied. "It was in the eighth year of His Majesty's rule, and I took the civil service examination."

"I have read about those examinations," I said, "but I have never known anyone who has taken them."

Yung Lu smiled and licked his lips.

"Sorry, I didn't mean to interrupt you."

"Oh, no," he apologized.

"So, did you win a position through the examination?"

"No, I didn't," he answered. "Something strange was going on. People suspected the winner of cheating. He was a rich layabout. Several people blamed it on corruption among the higher-ups. With the support of fellow students, I challenged the court and demanded a recount of the scores. My proposal was rejected, but I didn't give up. I investigated the case myself. After a month, through an elderly clansman, I presented a detailed report to Emperor Hsien Feng, who forwarded the case to Su Shun."

"That's right," I said, remembering learning about the case.

"It didn't take Su Shun long to find out the truth," Yung Lu said. "However, the case was not an easy one to solve."

"Why?"

"It involved one of His Majesty's close relatives."

"Did Su Shun persuade His Majesty to take proper measures?"

"Yes, and as a result the leader of the Imperial Academy was beheaded."

"Su Shun's power rests in his flexible tongue," Nuharoo interrupted us. She had returned quietly, and sat holding her prayer beads. Her eyes were closed when she spoke. "Su Shun can talk a dead person into singing."

Yung Lu cleared his throat, neither agreeing nor disagreeing.

"What did Su Shun say to Emperor Hsien Feng then?" I asked.

"He gave His Majesty an example of a riot that toppled the empire during the fourteenth year of Emperor Shun Chih in 1657," Yung Lu replied. "It was organized by a group of students who were treated unfairly by the civil service exam."

I took up my tea and sipped. "And how did you end up working for Su Shun?"

"I was thrown in jail for being a troublemaker."

"And Su Shun rescued you?"

"Yes, he was the one who ordered my release."

"And he recruited you and has been promoting you?"

"Yes, from lieutenant to commander in chief of the Imperial Guards."

"In how many years?"

"Five years, Your Majesty."

"Impressive."

"I am terribly grateful and I will always owe the grand councilor my loyalty."

"You should," I said. "But keep in mind that it was Emperor Hsien Feng who allowed Su Shun his power."

"Yes, Your Majesty."

I thought for a moment and decided to reveal a bit of information An-te-hai had discovered, which was that the leader of the Imperial Academy was Su Shun's enemy.

Yung Lu was surprised. I expected a response, a question, but none came.

"Su Shun cleverly accomplished an end to a personal grudge," I added. "He eliminated his rival through the hand of Emperor Hsien Feng, and did so in the name of doing *you* justice."

Yung Lu remained quiet. Seeing that I was waiting, he said, "Forgive me, Your Majesty, I am at a loss for words."

"You don't have to say anything." I put down my tea. "I was just wondering if you knew."

"Yes, in fact . . . a little." He lowered his eyes.

"Doesn't such cleverness say something about Su Shun the man?"

Not daring to reveal himself too freely or doubt my motivation, Yung Lu raised his eyes to examine me. In this look I saw a true Bannerman.

I turned to Nuharoo. The beads sat still on her lap, and her fingers had stopped moving. I did not know whether she was engaged with the spirit of Buddha or had dozed off.

I sighed. The Emperor was too weak, Su Shun was too cunning, and Prince Kung was too far away, while we needed a man close by.

"Time will test Su Shun," I said. "What we are concerned with here is your loyalty. Who will have it, Su Shun or His Majesty Emperor Hsien Feng?"

Yung Lu threw himself on the ground and kowtowed. "Of course His Majesty. He will have my everlasting devotion—there is no question about that in my mind."

"And us? His Majesty's wives and child?"

Yung Lu straightened his back. Our eyes met. As when ink wash hits rice paper, the moment created a permanent picture in my memory. Somehow he was betrayed by his expression, which told me that he was, in that instant, judging, weighing, evaluating. I sensed that he wanted to know if I was worthy of his commitment.

Holding his look, I answered him in silence that I would do the same for him in exchange for his honesty and friendship. I wouldn't have done it if I had had any warning of what was to happen. I was too confident that I had control over my own will and emotions, and that I would be nothing less than Emperor Hsien Feng's faithful concubine.

In retrospect, I was denying a truth. I refused to admit that I desired more than bodily protection from Yung Lu the moment we met. My soul craved to stir and be stirred. When I touched the edge of his sword, my "right mind" fled.

The eunuch returned with fresh tea. Yung Lu poured the mug down his throat as if he had just walked the desert. But it was not enough to overcome his nervousness. His look reminded me of a man who had just made up his mind to jump off a cliff. His eyes widened and his uneasiness grew thick. When he raised his eyes again, I realized that we were both descendants of the Manchus' toughest Bannermen. We were capable of surviving battles, external as well as internal. We were meant to survive because of our minds' ability to reason, our ability to live with frustration in order to maintain our virtue. We wore smiling masks while dying inside.

I was doomed when I realized that my talent was not to rule but to feel. Such a talent enriched my life, but at the same time destroyed every moment of peace I had gained. I felt helpless toward what was being done to me. I was the fish on the golden plate, tied with the red ribbon. Yet no one would bring me back to the lake where I belonged.

Trying to keep up appearances exhausted me.

Yung Lu sensed it. The color of his face changed. It reminded me of the city's rose-colored walls.

"The audience is over," I said weakly.

Yung Lu bowed, turned and marched out.

Seventeen

IN MAY OF 1858, Prince Kung brought the news that our soldiers had been bombarded while still in their barracks. The French and English forces had assaulted the four Taku forts at the mouth of the Peiho. Horrified at the collapse of our sea defenses, Emperor Hsien Feng declared martial law. He sent Kuei Liang, Prince Kung's father-in-law, now the grand secretary and the court's highest-ranking Manchu official, to negotiate peace.

By the next morning Kuei Liang was seeking an emergency audience. He had rushed back the night before from the city of Tientsin. The Emperor was again ill, and he sent Nuharoo and me to sit in for him. His Majesty promised that as soon as he gathered enough strength he would join us.

When Nuharoo and I entered the Hall of Spiritual Nurturing, the court was already waiting. More than three hundred ministers and officials were present. Nuharoo and I were dressed in golden court robes. We settled in our seats, shoulder to shoulder, behind the throne.

Minutes later Emperor Hsien Feng arrived. He dragged himself onto the platform and landed breathlessly on the throne. He looked so frail that a breeze might have caused him to fall. His robe was loosely buttoned. He hadn't shaved, and his beard had sprouted like weeds.

Kuei Liang was summoned to come forward. His appearance shocked me. His usual placid and benevolent expression was replaced by extreme nervousness. He seemed to have aged a great deal. His back was hunched and I could barely see his face. Prince Kung had come with him. The dark shadows under their eyes told me that neither had slept.

Kuei Liang began his report. In the past I recalled his countenance as one full of intelligence. Now his words were inarticulate, his hands palsied, his eyes dimmed. He said that he had been received with little respect from the foreign negotiators. They used the *Arrow* incident, in which Chinese pirates were caught sailing under a British flag, as an excuse to shun him. No evidence had been provided to substantiate their claims. It all could have been a conspiracy against China.

Emperor Hsien Feng listened grave-faced.

"In the name of teaching us a lesson," Kuei Liang continued, "the British launched an assault on Canton, and the entire province was brought down. With twenty-six gunboats between them, the British and French, accompanied by Americans—'impartial observers,' they said—and by Russians who joined for the spoils, have defied Your Majesty."

I didn't have a full view of my husband's face, but I could imagine his expression. "It is against the terms of the previous treaty for them to sail upriver toward Peking," Emperor Hsien Feng stated flatly.

"The winners make the rules, I am afraid, Your Majesty." Kuei Liang shook his head. "They needed no more excuse after attacking the Taku forts. They are now only a hundred miles from the Forbidden City!"

The court was stunned.

Kuei Liang broke down as he offered more details. As I listened, an image pushed itself in front of my eyes. It was from the time I witnessed a village boy torturing a sparrow. The boy was my neighbor. He had found the sparrow in a sewage pit. The little creature looked like it was just learning to fly and had fallen and broken its wing. When the boy picked the bird up, the feathers dripped with dirty water. He placed the bird on a steppingstone in front of his house and called us to come and watch. I saw the tiny heart pumping inside the bird's body. The boy flipped the sparrow back and forth, pulling its legs and wings. He kept doing it until the bird stopped moving.

"You failed me, Kuei Liang!" Hsien Feng's shout woke me. "I had put my faith in your success!"

"Your Majesty, I pathetically presented my death warrant to the Russian and American envoys," Kuei Liang cried. "I said that if I yielded one more point, my life would be forfeited. I told them that my predecessor, the viceroy of Canton, was ordered by Emperor Hsien Feng to commit suicide because he had failed in his mission. I said the Emperor had ordered me to come to a reasonable and mutually advantageous peace and that I had promised him that I would agree to nothing that will be detrimental to China. But they sneered and laughed at me, Your Majesty." The old man collapsed on his knees, sobbing in shame. "I . . . I . . . deserve to die."

To witness the tears of the respectable Kuei Liang was heart-breaking. The French and English demanded indemnities and apologies for wars against us started on our soil. According to Prince Kung, they had declared that recent events had rendered the previous agreements null and void. Grand Councilor Su Shun, who was dressed in a red court robe, warned that this was the pretext for the barbarians' next move, which would be to hold a gun to the head of Emperor Hsien Feng.

"I have failed myself, my country and my ancestors," Hsien Feng cried. "Because of my inadequacy, the barbarians have preyed on us . . . China has been violated, and the guilt is mine alone to bear."

I knew I had to ask for permission in order to speak, but anger overcame me and I said, "Foreigners live in China by the good grace of the Emperor, yet they have harmed us in more ways than we can find words to express. They are causing our government to lose prestige in the eyes of our people. They leave us no choice but to despise them."

I wanted to continue, but choked on my own tears. Only a few weeks earlier I had sat behind Hsien Feng as he thundered about war and ordered "death to the barbarians." What was the use of more words? As events played out, the Emperor of China would soon be forced to make an apology for the "treachery of his troops who had defended the Taku forts against the British the previous year." China would be forced to agree to pay to its invaders an enormous amount of taels as compensation.

The Emperor needed to rest. After a short recess, Kuei Liang spoke again. "The Russians have come to join the thievery, Your Majesty."

Hsien Feng took a deep breath and then asked, "What do they want?"

"To redraw the northern border by the Amur and Ussuri rivers."

"Nonsense!" Hsien Feng yelled. He began to cough, and his eunuchs rushed to him and wiped his neck and forehead. He pushed them away. "Kuei Liang, you have allowed this to happen . . . *you!*"

"Your Majesty, I deserve no more pardons, and I am not asking for any. I am prepared to hang myself. I have already bid farewell to my family. My wife and children reassured me that they would understand. I just want to let you know that I did my best and was unable to get the barbarians to negotiate. They only threatened war. And . . ." Kuei Liang paused and turned to his son-in-law.

Prince Kung stepped up and finished Kuei Liang's sentence for him. "The Russians fired their cannons yesterday. Due to fear that they might threaten the capital, Minister Yi Shan signed the treaty and accepted the Russians' terms. Here, Your Majesty, is a copy of the treaty."

Slowly, Emperor Hsien Feng picked up the document. "North of the Amur River and south of the Wai-hsin-an Mountain area, isn't it?"

"Correct, Your Majesty."

"That is a vast area."

Many in the court knew all too well the extent of this loss. Some began to weep.

"Su Shun!" Emperor Hsien Feng called, slumping in his seat.

"I'm here, Your Majesty." Su Shun stepped forward.

"Behead Yi Shan and remove Kuei Liang from all his posts."

My heart went to Kuei Liang as guards escorted him out of the hall. During the next break I found a moment to speak with Prince Kung. I asked him to do something to stop the decree. He told me not to worry. He made me understand that Su Shun was in charge, and that he wouldn't carry out Hsien Feng's order. He answered yes only to appease His Majesty. The court trusted Su Shun to change the Emperor's mind; everyone knew it would be impossible to replace Kuei Liang.

In the passing months Emperor Hsien Feng had become ever more dependent on Su Shun and his seven grand councilors. I prayed that Su Shun would be able to hold up the sky for His Majesty. Although I didn't like Su Shun, I didn't intend to be his enemy. I would never dream of offending him, yet one day it would become unavoidable.

It had been snowing for three days. Outside the gate there were drifts two feet deep. Although the coal heaters were burning, it was still too cold for comfort. My fingers were as stiff as sticks. Buried in his fur coat, Hsien Feng sprawled on a chair in the Hall of Spiritual Nurturing. His eyes were closed.

I sat at the desk, summarizing documents for him. For the past few months I had again become the Emperor's secretary. He had simply run out of energy and asked me to help by picking out the most urgent letters to respond to. His Majesty spoke the words and I formed them into replies.

It was challenging, but I was thrilled to help. All of a sudden I was no longer an abandoned concubine. I no longer had to stitch misery onto hoops. I was given a chance to share His Majesty's dream of reviving China. It made me feel good—my energy was inexhaustible. For the first time in ages I saw true affection in his eyes. Late one night when Hsien Feng woke up in his chair, he offered his hand for me to hold. He wanted me to know that he appreciated my help. He no longer called for Summer, one of his Chinese concubines, or for Nuharoo, even when I begged him to take walks with her.

I visited Nuharoo to spend time with Tung Chih, who slept with his wet nurses nearby. I updated her on what I had worked on with His Majesty. She was pleased with my humbleness.

Every day before dawn, I got dressed and went to the Hall of Spiritual Nurturing on a palanquin. Right away, I began sorting official papers into several boxes. Emperor Hsien Feng was usually still asleep in the next room. I would line up the boxes in order of urgency. By the time the sun rose and the Emperor came to me, I was ready to brief him. He would debate with himself and weigh his decisions. Sometimes he would have a discussion with me, and afterward I was expected to draft the necessary edicts.

I made suggestions that I hoped would complement His Majesty's thoughts. One day he came in late and a box needed immediate attention. To save time, I drafted a proposal in his style. When I read it to him for approval, he made no changes. The edict was sent with his seal stamped on it.

My confidence grew after that. From then on, Hsien Feng asked me to draft edicts on my own and brief him later. I was nervous at first; I wanted to consult Prince Kung or Su Shun, but I knew I couldn't.

One morning I finished drafting seven documents and had begun an eighth. It was a tough one. It had to do with an item in a treaty with which I was not familiar. I decided to wait. When I heard His Majesty getting up, I took the draft to him.

Hsien Feng was half reclining on a rattan chair, his eyes closed. A eunuch was spoon-feeding him a bowl of deer blood soup. It must have tasted awful, for His Majesty's expression reminded me of a child whose finger got pricked by broken glass. The soup dripped from his mouth. I had just begun to read the draft when I heard Chief Eunuch Shim's voice. "Good morning, Your Highness. Su Shun is here."

"Is His Majesty in?" came Su Shun's voice. "The matter can't wait."

Before I was able to retreat, Su Shun walked directly toward Emperor Hsien Feng. His Majesty opened his eyes halfway and saw Su

Shun on his knees. I stood by the wall and hoped that Su Shun wouldn't notice me.

"Rise," Emperor Hsien Feng uttered. The eunuch quickly wiped the mess off his chin and sat him upright. "Is it about the Russians again?"

"Yes, unfortunately," Su Shun replied, rising. "Ambassador Ignatyev refuses to negotiate on our terms and has announced the date of the attack."

The Emperor leaned to the right while his hand went to rub his side. "Orchid, did you hear Su Shun?" He threw the draft at me. "Tear it up! What's the use of issuing edicts? What else can I do? My blood has been sucked dry and the wolves won't leave me alone!"

Su Shun was startled to see me. His eyes narrowed. He kept turning his head back and forth between Emperor Hsien Feng and me.

I knew I had offended him by my mere presence. He stared at me and his eyes shouted, *Go back to your embroidery!*

But I was obligated to give Hsien Feng an answer. I hoped that Su Shun would assume that the Emperor trusted me for a reason, and that my assistance had been valuable.

Surely if Su Shun asked, His Majesty would praise me. Last month there had been a report of a flood in Szechuan province. Hundreds of peasants had lost their homes. Food was scarce. When Hsien Feng heard that many families were eating their dead children to survive, he issued a decree to have the governors of Kiangsu and Anhwei open their stores. But there was no grain left. The storehouses had been emptied long before to fund the battles against the Taipings and the foreigners.

I suggested that His Majesty squeeze the money out of corrupt bureaucrats. I proposed that he order government officials nationwide to report their incomes. In the meantime His Majesty should send inspectors to audit their books to see if the reports matched what had really been earned.

"That might provoke resentment," His Majesty said.

"Not if we add a clause to the decree stating that no one would be charged with embezzlement if the guilty individuals donated their improper money to the victims of the flood disaster."

The decree worked beautifully. Emperor Hsien Feng rewarded me with permission to visit my family. From then on, His Majesty trusted me to issue most of the decrees. I became even more confident. In the Emperor's voice I encouraged criticism and suggestions from all the governors. I benefited from their comments and proposals.

While I felt fulfillment and satisfaction, I was also concerned about

Hsien Feng's growing lack of interest in his work. It was hard not to be affected by his increasing pessimism. He was now in a great deal of physical pain and was depressed most of the time. When I brought in Tung Chih, he had no energy to play with him. He would send him away within minutes. He no longer proofread the edicts I drafted. When state reports arrived, he expected me to take care of them. He didn't even want me to consult with him. When I passed him those that I thought he must be made aware of, he would push my arms away and say, "The bugs inside my head have built their nests so thick that I can't think."

His Majesty's life was coming to an end. For Tung Chih's sake I needed him to live. I worked without a break. My meals had been reduced from five a day to two. Sometimes I ate just one. To make sure that I ate well, An-te-hai hired a new chef from my hometown of Wuhu, whose best dish was my childhood favorite: tomato, onion and cabbage soup. An-te-hai used a special bamboo container to keep the soup bowl warm.

I often woke to find that I had been sleeping at my desk, slumped on my folded arms. I no longer bothered to have my hair styled. I wanted to spend more time with Tung Chih, but I had to leave him entirely to Nuharoo. I continued working on court documents, sometimes until dawn. An-te-hai would wait beside me, holding a blanket in case I asked for it. He would fall asleep sitting on a stool. Now and then I heard him murmuring in his dreams: "No more 'congratulations,' Confucius!"

"What else can I do?"

To Su Shun's dismay, I answered His Majesty. "I would not yield to the Russians." I spoke softly but with purpose. "The Russians are taking advantage of our troubles with the French and British. China should not give the idea that we are an easy rib for anyone to chew upon."

"I hope you are listening well," said Hsien Feng. "Show . . . our strength."

Su Shun nodded. "Yes, Your Majesty."

"Go back to the Russians tomorrow and don't return until the task is accomplished." With a heavy sigh Emperor Hsien Feng turned away from Su Shun.

In disbelief Su Shun bade His Majesty goodbye. Before he walked out, he gave me a nasty look. It was clear that he regarded Hsien Feng's respect for me as a personal humiliation.

It didn't take long for Su Shun to spread rumors about me. He warned the court that I had ambitions to take over the throne. He succeeded in provoking the clans' elders, who came forward to protest. They urged His Majesty to remove me from his residence.

Prince Kung stood up for me. He was more than clear about his brother's state of mind. His Majesty wouldn't even come to the Hall of Spiritual Nurturing unless I was there. In Prince Kung's view, Su Shun was the one whose ambitions were inappropriate.

For His Majesty's health, Doctor Sun Pao-tien recommended complete quiet, so we moved back to Yuan Ming Yuan. The season went deep into winter. Long, withered brown and yellow weeds lay like frozen waves. The wind continued to be harsh. The creeks and brooks that meandered through the gardens were now iced over and looked like dirty ropes. Emperor Hsien Feng said they reminded him of guts that had fallen out of the belly of a slaughtered animal.

The quietness was broken when Su Shun and Prince Kung came with urgent news. They stood beside His Majesty's ornate black wooden bed and reported that the British and French demanded an audience.

Emperor Hsien Feng sat up in his bed. "I can't accept that they want to revise and amend the treaties. What is there to be revised or amended? They are creating an excuse for another attack!"

"Still, would you consider granting the audience?" Prince Kung asked. "It is important to maintain communication. My Tsungli Yamen can work on the format until Your Majesty feels comfortable—"

"Nonsense! We don't need those appeasers," Su Shun interrupted, pointing a finger at Prince Kung.

Hsien Feng raised his hand to silence Su Shun. He was aware that the court had split regarding how to handle the situation, with Su Shun and Prince Kung leading opposing sides.

"An audience is too much for them to ask," Hsien Feng said. "I won't allow the barbarians to come to Peking."

The usual procession of eunuchs and maids entered with tea. Everyone was dressed magnificently. Whenever I walked in my garden, all I felt was the power and glory around me. Even the crickets on the garden walkways had a touch of nobility; they were fat and green and more robust than those I saw in the countryside. Yet it all might come to an end.

"The foreigners are coming with troops," Prince Kung reminded his brother after a long silence.

"Death to them!" Su Shun's voice was charged. "Your Majesty, it's time to issue a warrant to take the British ambassador hostage. He will be forced to withdraw the troops."

"What if he refuses?" Prince Kung asked.

"Behead him," Su Shun replied. "Trust me, when the enemy's leader is caught, the rest will surrender. Then we can send General Seng-ko-lin-chin with the Bannermen to collect the rest of the barbarians' heads."

"Are you out of your mind?" Prince Kung countered. "The British ambassador is only a messenger. We will lose the moral high ground in the world's eye. It will give our adversaries a perfect excuse to launch an invasion."

"Moral ground?" Su Shun sneered. "What ground do the barbarians have regarding their behavior in China? They make demands of the Son of Heaven. How dare you side with the barbarians! Are you representing His Majesty the Emperor of China or the Queen of England?"

"Su Shun!" Prince Kung's face turned red and his hands were clenched. "It's my duty to serve His Majesty with truthfulness!"

Su Shun walked up to Emperor Hsien Feng. "Your Majesty, Prince Kung must be stopped. He has deceived the court. He and his father-in-law have been in charge of all the negotiations. Based on the outcome of the treaties and information provided by my investigators, we have reason to suspect that Prince Kung has profited from his position." Su Shun paused, his body pivoted toward Prince Kung as if cornering him. "Haven't you made deals with our enemies? Haven't the barbarians promised you that when they enter the Forbidden City, you will harvest more shares?"

The veins on Prince Kung's neck grew thick, and his eyebrows twisted into a gingerroot. He jumped on Su Shun, knocking him to the ground, and started punching him.

"Manners!" Emperor Hsien Feng called. "Su Shun had my permission to express himself."

His Majesty's words crushed Prince Kung. He dropped his hands and threw himself down on his knees. "My Imperial brother, nothing will be achieved by taking their ambassador. I will bet my head on it. The situation will only go against us. Instead of backing down, they will send their fleets to our shores. I have studied long enough to know their ways."

"Of course." Su Shun got back on his feet, his long sleeves fluttering in the air. "Long enough to develop connections and long enough to forget who you are."

"One more word, Su Shun," Prince Kung clenched his jaws, "and I'll pull your tongue out!"

Despite Kung's warnings, an edict was issued to capture the ambassador of Britain. For the next few days the Forbidden City was quiet. When the news came that the ambassador had been taken, Peking celebrated. Su Shun was hailed as a hero. Almost immediately, reports of foreign attacks along the coastline took away the excitement. The documents sent to His Majesty from the frontier smelled of smoke and blood. Soon the papers were piled high against the walls. I had no way of sorting them. The situation went exactly as Prince Kung had predicted.

August 1, 1860, was the worst day for Emperor Hsien Feng.

Nothing now could stop the barbarians. Prince Kung was denounced and his Tsungli Yamen dismissed. Calling themselves "the Allies," the British came with 173 warships and 10,000 soldiers, the French with 33 ships and 6,000 soldiers. Then the Russians joined in. Together, the three landed a force of 18,000 men on the shores of the Gulf of Chihli.

Going against the immense fortified earthworks that straddled the mouth of the Yellow River and the seaboard, the Allies scrambled ashore, sinking knee-deep in slime, and shot their way to dry ground. They then began to move toward Peking. General Seng-ko-lin-chin, the commander of Imperial forces, sent word to the Emperor that he was prepared to die—in other words, all hopes of protecting the capital were fading.

Other reports depicted bravery and patriotism, which filled me with sadness. China's ancient way of fighting wars had become an embarrassment—only barriers made of bamboo stakes defended our forts and their complex of dikes and ditches. There was no chance for our soldiers to display their masterly martial-arts combat skills. They were shot down before they were even in sight of the enemy.

The Mongolian cavalry was known for its invincibility. Three thousand vanished in one day. The Westerners' cannons and guns swept them away like dry leaves in a late-autumn wind.

Emperor Hsien Feng was soaked in sweat. A high fever had consumed so much of his energy that he could no longer eat. The court feared his collapse. When his fever broke, he asked me to draft five edicts to be delivered immediately to General Seng-ko-lin-chin. In His Majesty's voice I informed the general that troops were being gathered from all over the country, and that in five days there would be a rescue led by the legendary General Sheng Pao. Nearly twenty thousand more men, including seven thousand cavalry, would arrive and join the counterattack.

In the next edict, I wrote as His Majesty spoke to his nation.

> The treacherous barbarians were willing to sacrifice our faith in humanity. They advanced toward Tungchow. Shamelessly they announced their intention to compel me to receive them in audience. They threatened that any further forbearance on our part would be a dereliction of duty to the Empire.
>
> Although my health is in a grievous state, I saw myself doing nothing else but fighting until my last breath. I have realized that we could no longer achieve peace and harmony without force. I am now commanding you, our armies and citizens of all races, to join the battle. I shall reward those who exhibit courage. For every head of a black barbarian [British Sikh troops] I shall reward 50 taels, and for every head of a white barbarian, I shall reward 100 taels. Subjects of other submissive states are not to be molested, and whensoever the British and French demonstrate repentance and withdraw from their evil ways, I shall be pleased to permit them to trade again, as of old. May they repent while there is still time.

The Hall of Luminous Virtue was damp from days of heavy rain. It felt like we were inside a giant coffin. A makeshift throne was built around Emperor Hsien Feng's bed, which was raised on a temporary platform. More and more ministers came seeking emergency audiences. Everyone looked as if they were already defeated. Etiquette was neglected, and people argued and debated in loud voices. A number of elders passed out in the middle of their arguments. On the frontier the bullets and cannon shells were as thick as hail. Lying on his chair, the Emperor read the updated reports. His fever had returned. Cold towels were placed on his face and over his body. The pages slipped through his trembling fingers.

Two days later the news of the fall came. The first was the upper north fort, taken after fierce fighting under an intensive bombardment from both sides. The Allies pressed on. Seng-ko-lin-chin claimed that shells hitting the powder magazines in the northern forts had crippled his defenses.

On August 21, Seng-ko-lin-chin gave in, and the Taku forts surrendered. The path to Peking was now open.

• • •

The Allies were reported to be only twelve miles from the capital. General Sheng Pao's troops had arrived, but proved to be of no avail. The day before, the general had lost his last division.

People hustled in and out of the audience hall like cut-paper characters in jerky motion. The words in which everyone wished His Majesty longevity sounded empty. This morning the clouds were so low that I could feel the air's moisture with my fingers. Toads hopped all over the courtyard. They seemed desperate to move. I had ordered the eunuchs to clear away the toads an hour before, but they had returned.

General Seng-ko-lin-chin was on his knees in front of His Majesty. He begged for punishment, which was granted. All his titles were stripped from him and he was ordered into exile. He asked if he could offer His Majesty one last service.

"Granted," Emperor Hsien Feng murmured.

Seng-ko-lin-chin said, "It's close to a full moon . . ."

"Get to the point." The Emperor turned his head toward the ceiling.

"I . . ." Fumbling with his hands, the general pulled out a tiny scroll from his robe's deep pocket and passed it to Chief Eunuch Shim.

Shim opened the scroll for the Emperor to see. "Go to Jehol," it read.

"What do you mean?" asked Emperor Hsien Feng.

"Hunting, Your Majesty," Seng-ko-lin-chin replied.

"Hunting? You think I am in the mood to go hunting?"

Carefully, Seng-ko-lin-chin explained: it was time to leave Peking; it was time to forget appearances. He was suggesting that the Emperor use the traditional hunting grounds at Jehol as an excuse to escape. In the general's view the situation was irreversible — China was lost. The enemies were on their way to arrest and overthrow the Son of Heaven.

"My rib cage, Orchid." His Majesty struggled to sit. "It feels like there are weeds and stalks growing inside. I hear wind blowing through them when I breathe."

I gently massaged Hsien Feng's chest.

"Is that a 'yes' to the hunting?" Seng-ko-lin-chin asked.

"If you don't believe me, you can touch my belly with your hand," His Majesty said to me, ignoring Seng-ko-lin-chin. "Come on, knock on my chest. You'll hear an empty sound."

I felt sorry for Hsien Feng, for he had no vocabulary for or understanding of what he was feeling. His pride had deserted him, yet he couldn't help but continue to regard himself as the ruler of the universe. He simply couldn't live any other way.

"I shall have the hunting grounds prepared, then." Seng-ko-lin-chin dropped the words and quietly retreated.

"A mother rat is going into labor!" His Majesty burst out in hysterical cry. "She is delivering babies in a pile of rags in a hole behind my bed. My palace is going to be full of rats. What are you waiting for, Lady Yehonala? Aren't you going to accompany me to hunt in Jehol?"

My thoughts raced. Were we to leave the capital? Were we to give up our country to the barbarians? We had lost ports, forts and coasts, but we had not lost our people. Surely we should stay in Peking, because even when the barbarians arrived we would have a chance to fight if our people were with us.

If Emperor Hsien Feng were a strong man, he would have acted differently. He would have set himself as an example to lead the nation to war; he would have gone to the frontier himself. And if he died, he would have preserved China's honor and saved his own name. But he was a weak man.

Tung Chih was brought in by Nuharoo for dinner. Despite the weather he looked like a snowball, wrapped in a white fur coat. He was being fed pigeon meat with a slice of steamed bread. He seemed cheerful and was playing a rope game with An-te-hai called Tie Me Up, Tie Me Down. Lying on his bed, Hsien Feng watched his son. He smiled and encouraged the child to challenge the eunuch. I saw an opportunity to speak.

"Your Majesty?" I tried not to sound argumentative. "Don't you think the nation's spirit will collapse if its Emperor . . . is absent?" I avoided the word "deserts." "A dragon needs a head. An empty capital will encourage looting and destruction. Emperor Chou Wen-wang of the Han Dynasty chose to abscond during his kingdom's crisis, and the result was that he lost his people's respect."

"How dare you make this comparison!" Emperor Hsien Feng spat tea leaves on the floor. "I have decided to leave for the security of my family, you included."

"I think demonstrating the court's strength to the people is crucial to China's survival," I said softly.

"I don't feel like talking about this right now." His Majesty called his son over and started to play with him. Tung Chih ran by laughing, eventually hiding under a chair.

I ignored Nuharoo, who was gesturing with her hands for me to quit. I continued, "Tung Chih's grandfather and great-grandfather would have stayed if they faced this situation."

"But they weren't given the situation!" Hsien Feng exploded. "I resent them. It was they who left this mess to me. When the first Opium War was lost in 1842, I was just a boy. I inherited nothing but trouble. All I can think of these days are the indemnities I am forced to pay. Eight million taels to each country! How could I possibly satisfy that?"

We argued until he ordered me to go back to my living quarters. His last words remained in my head all night long. "Another word out of you, and you will be rewarded with a rope to hang yourself!"

Nuharoo invited me for a walk in her garden. She said that her bushes, withered by some blight, had attracted a rare kind of butterfly.

I told her that I was in no mood for butterflies.

"They might be moths. Anyway, they are pretty." Paying no attention to me, she went on. "Let's go and catch butterflies. Forget about the barbarians."

We got into our separate palanquins. I wished that I could make myself enjoy Nuharoo's invitation, but in the middle of the outing I changed my mind. I ordered my bearers to carry me to the Hall of Luminous Virtue. I sent a messenger to Nuharoo and asked for forgiveness, saying that the Emperor's decision to desert the capital weighed too heavily on my mind.

In the hallway I ran into all my brothers-in-law: Prince Kung, Prince Ch'un and Prince Ts'eng. Prince Ch'un told me that they had come to persuade His Majesty to remain in Peking. For that I was glad and became hopeful.

I waited in the garden until tea was served before entering. I went inside and sat down by Emperor Hsien Feng. I noticed other guests. Besides the princes, Su Shun and his half-brother Tuan Hua were also there. For the past two days Su Shun and Tuan had been making arrangements for the Emperor to go to Jehol. Beyond the walls, the sound of carriages coming and going had become constant.

"I gave up Peking because I have not heard any news from General Sheng Pao!" Hsien Feng argued. "The rumors say that he has been captured. If that is the case, the barbarians will reach my courtyard in no time."

"Your Majesty!" Prince Kung fell from his chair to the ground. "Please don't desert!"

"Your Majesty." Prince Ts'eng, the fifth brother, also on his knees, lined himself up next to Prince Kung. "Will you stay for a few more days? I shall lead the Bannermen to battle the barbarians myself. Give us a chance to honor you. Without you . . ." Ts'eng was so overcome he had to stop for a moment. ". . . there will be no spirit."

"The Emperor has made up his mind," Hsien Feng announced coldly.

Prince Ch'un went to kneel between Prince Kung and Prince Ts'eng. "Your Majesty, deserting the throne will encourage the barbarians' madness. It will make future negotiation much more difficult."

"Who says I am deserting the throne? I am only going hunting."

Prince Kung laughed bitterly. "Any child on the street will say 'The Emperor is running away.'"

"How dare you!" Emperor Hsien Feng kicked a eunuch who came to serve him medicine.

"For the sake of your health, Your Majesty, pardon us." Prince Ts'eng grabbed the Emperor by the legs. "Allow me to bid farewell, then. I am going to expose myself to the cannons."

"Stop being silly." Hsien Feng rose and helped Prince Ts'eng back to his feet. "My brother, once I am out of reach, I can pursue a more consistent policy on the battlefield." He turned to Su Shun. "Let us go before the sky lightens."

The determination of Kung, Ch'un and Ts'eng made me proud of being Manchu. I was not surprised at Hsien Feng's cowardice. Losing the Taku forts had broken him, and he now merely wanted to slip away and hide.

In Hsien Feng's dressing room Su Shun came forward. "We must hurry, Your Majesty. It will take several days to get to Jehol."

Su Shun's half-brother Tuan came in. He was a skinny man with a long and crooked neck, which made his head tilt to one side. "Your Majesty," he said, "here is the list of things we have packed for you."

"Where are my seals?" the Emperor asked.

"They have been taken from the Hall of the Blending of Great Creative Forces and properly chambered."

"Orchid," Hsien Feng said, "go and check on the seals."

"Your Majesty, there is no need," Su Shun said.

Ignoring Su Shun, Emperor Hsien Feng turned to Prince Kung, who had entered the room. "Brother Kung, you're not dressed to travel. You are coming with me, aren't you?"

"No, I am afraid not," Prince Kung replied. He was dressed in an official blue robe with yellow trim on the sleeves and collar. "Someone has to stay in the capital and deal with the Allies."

"What about Ts'eng and Ch'un?"

"They have decided to stay in Peking with me."

The Emperor sat down and his eunuchs tried to put on his boots. "Prince Ch'un will have to guard me on the journey to Jehol."

"Your Majesty, I am begging you for the last time to consider remaining in Peking."

"Su Shun," Emperor Hsien Feng called impatiently, "prepare a decree to authorize Prince Kung as my spokesman."

What to take to Jehol had become a problem for me. I wanted to take everything, because I had no idea when I would return. Yet the most valuable things were not portable. I had to leave behind my paintings, wall-sized embroideries, carvings, vases and sculptures. Each concubine was allowed one carriage for her valuables, and mine was already filled. I hid the rest of my cherished things wherever I could—on top of a beam, behind a door, buried in the garden. I hoped that no one would discover them until I returned.

Nuharoo refused to leave any of her belongings behind. As the chief Empress she was entitled to three carriages, but they were not enough. She loaded the rest of her things into Tung Chih's carriages. Tung Chih had ten, and Nuharoo took seven of them.

My mother was too ill to travel, so I made arrangements for her to move to a quiet village outside Peking. Kuei Hsiang was to be with her. Rong would also stay behind.

At ten o'clock in the morning the Imperial wheels started to roll. Emperor Hsien Feng wouldn't leave without a ceremony. He sacrificed livestock and bowed to the gods of Heaven. When his palanquin passed the last gate of the Grand Round Garden, Yuan Ming Yuan, officials and eunuchs threw themselves on their knees, kowtowing farewell. The Emperor sat inside with his son. Tung Chih told me later that his father wept.

The Imperial household stretched for three miles. It looked like a festival parade. Firecrackers were thrown into the sky to "shock away bad omens." The ceremonial guards carried yellow dragon flags while the palanquin bearers carried the Imperial families. The nobles walked in columns. Behind us were incense burners, monks, lamas, eunuchs, ladies in waiting, servants, guards and royal animals. The crowd was followed by a band with drums and gongs and the entire kitchen on legs. Near the tail of the line were dressing rooms on legs and chamber pots on legs. Footmen guided the horses and donkeys that carried firewood, meat, rice and vegetables in deep baskets along with kitchen utensils such as pots and woks. At the rear were seven thousand cavalrymen, led by Yung Lu.

As we passed the last gate, my eyes were blurred with tears. Shops along the streets were abandoned. Families ran like headless hens, carrying their possessions on donkeys and on their backs. The news of Emperor Hsien Feng's desertion had sent the city into chaos.

A few hours later I asked that my son be brought to me. I sat him on my lap and held him tight. To him this was just another outing. As the palanquin rocked, he fell asleep. I ran my fingers through his soft black hair and fixed his queue. I wished that I could teach Tung Chih how to be strong. I wanted him to know that one should never take peace for granted. He was cosseted by servants, used to seeing beautiful women at his bedside. It pained me to hear Tung Chih say that he wanted to grow up to be just like his father — with beauties as his playmates.

A few days before, a case of theft in the Forbidden City had been reported. No one confessed to the crime, and there were no obvious suspects. I was put in charge of the investigation. I sensed that the eunuchs were involved, because someone had to move the valuables. The maids couldn't go outside the gates without permits. I also suspected members of the royal family. They knew where the valuables were.

As the investigation went on, my suspicions were proven correct. Apparently the concubines had colluded with the eunuchs to split the profits. Ladies Mei, Hui and Li were found to be involved. Hsien Feng was furious, and he ordered them thrown out of their palaces. It was Nuharoo and I who talked him out of his rage. "It is a terrible time to expect nobility from everyone," we said. "Haven't we had enough embarrassment?"

Sitting inside the palanquin all day made my joints ache. I thought of the people who were walking on their blisters. After we got out of Peking, the road became bumpier and dustier. We stopped at a village for the night, and I met with Nuharoo. I was surprised by the way she had dressed. She looked like she was going to a party. She carried an ivory fan and a small incense burner. Her robe was made of golden satin embroidered with Buddhist symbols.

For the entire trip Nuharoo wore the same robe. It took me a while to realize that she was more than terrified. "In case we are attacked and I am killed," she said, "I want to be sure to enter my next life in proper dress."

It didn't make sense to me. If we were attacked, her robe would be the first thing anyone would rob. She might end up being naked in her next life. I had heard back in Wuhu that tomb robbers would chop off a dead person's head for what was around the neck, and hands for what was on the fingers.

I made sure to dress as plainly as possible. Nuharoo told me that my dress, which I took from an elderly maid, disgraced my status. Her words made me feel safer. When I tried to dress Tung Chih the same way, Nuharoo became upset. "For Buddha's sake, he is the Son of Heaven! How dare you dress him like a beggar!" She took off Tung Chih's plain cotton robe and changed him into a gold-laced robe, one with symbols that matched hers.

The villagers didn't know what was going on; the bad news from Peking hadn't reached them. They certainly couldn't tell that disaster was near from the way Nuharoo and Tung Chih dressed. They were simply honored that we chose to stop in their village for the night, and served us steaming-hot whole wheat buns and vegetable soup.

Messengers sent by Prince Kung came and went. There was one bit of good news amid all the bad. An influential foreign officer named Parkes, along with another named Loch, had been captured. Prince Kung was using them as leverage for negotiations. The last messenger reported that the Allies had taken the Forbidden City, the Summer Palace and Yuan Ming Yuan. "The Allied commander is living in Your Majesty's bedroom with a Chinese prostitute," the messenger reported.

His Majesty's pale face was dripping with sweat. He opened his mouth but was unable to utter a word. A few hours later he coughed up a bolus of blood.

Eighteen

"SPEAK!" Emperor Hsien Feng ordered the eunuch who had been in charge of security in Yuan Ming Yuan. The eunuch had been sent by his senior, who had committed suicide after failing in his duty.

"It began on October fifth." The eunuch made an effort to calm his quavery voice. "It was cloudy in the morning. The palace was quiet and there was no sign that anything was unusual. By noon it started to rain. The guards asked me if they could go inside. I gave them permission. We were all very tired . . . It was then that I heard the cannons. I thought I was dreaming and so did the guards. One even claimed that he had heard thunder. But in a moment we smelled smoke. A short while later a guard ran to tell us that the barbarians were at the Gate of High Virtue and the Gate of Peace. My senior asked what had happened to General Seng-ko-lin-chin's troops. The guard answered that the barbarians had captured them . . . We now knew that we were without protection.

"My senior ordered me to guard the Garden of Happiness, the Garden of Clear Rippling Waters, the Garden of Still Moon, and the Garden of Bright Sunshine while he himself went to guard the Garden of Evergreen and the Garden of June. I knew I wouldn't be able to do this. How could fewer than a hundred protect gardens that stretched for twenty miles?

"While we rushed to hide the furniture, the barbarians appeared in the garden. I instructed my people to drop the lesser valuables and bury the important ones. But we couldn't dig fast enough. I buried what I could, including the great clock and the moving universe, and others threw in scrolls.

"As we dragged the bags out, we were confronted by the barbarians. They fired on us. The guards fell one after another. Those who weren't shot were captured and were later thrown into the lake. The barbarians tied me to the bronze crane near the fountain. They slashed open our bags and were thrilled to discover the treasure. Their pockets were too small to fit everything, so they pulled out Your Majesty's robes and turned them into sacks. They filled them and hung them around their shoulders and waists. They grabbed what they could take and destroyed what they couldn't. They fought among themselves over the spoils.

"The barbarians who arrived later tried to move what remained. They dismantled Your Majesty's astrological bronze animals but not the giant gold jar, which was too heavy to move. Eventually they scraped off all the decorative gold from the columns and beams with knives. The looting continued for two days. The barbarians broke through walls and dug up the grounds."

"What did they find?" I asked.

"Everything, my lady. I saw one barbarian walk past the fountain wearing your ceremonial robe."

I tried not to picture the scene as the eunuch went on to describe the ransacking of the rest of Yuan Ming Yuan. But my mind's eye vividly saw the barbarians marching into the Apricot Village, the Peony Pavilion and the Lotus Leaf Teahouse. I could see their faces glow as they rushed through the golden, richly carved halls of the central buildings. I could see them enter my room and ransack my drawers. I could see them break into my storage chamber where I had hidden my jade, silver and enamel, paintings, embroideries and trinkets.

"... There was too much to take, so the barbarians stripped the marble-sized pearls from Empress Nuharoo's robes and emptied Her Majesty's diamond cases ..."

"Where was Prince Kung?" Emperor Hsien Feng was sliding off his chair and trying hard to push himself back up.

"Prince Kung was working outside of Peking. He struck a deal with the barbarians by releasing their captured officials, Parkes and Loch. But it was too late to stop the looting. To cover their crime, the foreign devils ... Your Majesty, I can't ... say it ..." The eunuch crashed to the floor as if he no longer had a spinal cord.

"Say it!"

"Yes, Your Majesty. The devils . . . set fire . . ."

Emperor Hsien Feng shut his eyes. He struggled for breath. His neck twisted as if it was in the grip of a ghost.

On October 13, the barbarians set fire to more than two hundred pavilions, halls and temples, and the grounds of five palaces. The flames consumed everything. Smoke and ash were carried by the wind over the walls. An acrid dense cloud hung above the city, eventually settling in people's hair, eyes, clothes, beds and bowls. Nothing survived in Yuan Ming Yuan except the marble pagoda and the stone bridge. Among the thousands of acres of gardens, the only building left standing was the Pavilion of Precious Clouds, high on a hill above the lake.

I would later learn from Prince Kung about the "thunder-like sound" people described. It was not the sound of thunder but of explosives. The British Royal Engineers had placed dynamite charges in many of our pavilions.

For the rest of my life, my mind would return to this scene of magnificence suddenly transformed into crumbling piles of masonry. Miles and miles of flames swallowing six thousand dwellings—the palace of my body and soul, along with treasures and works of art collected by generations of emperors.

Hsien Feng had to live with this shame, which eventually ate him up. In my old age, whenever I tired of working or thought of quitting, I would go and visit the ruins of Yuan Ming Yuan. The moment I stepped among the broken stones, I could hear the barbarians cheering. The image would choke me as if the smoke still hung in the air.

A brassy sun peered down upon the moving festival. We continued our long journey to Jehol. I was bitter and sad when I thought about my husband's "hunting" excuse. In marvelous clothing the ministers and princes were borne in richly decorated palanquins on the shoulders of toiling bearers while guards patrolled on Mongolian ponies.

The chanting of the chair bearers had been replaced by a deep and tortured silence. I no longer heard the slap and slither of sandaled feet over the loose stones. Instead I saw the pain from blisters etched into the lines of grimy sweat-washed faces. Even though we had entered the wild country, everyone remained concerned about the barbarians' possible pursuit. The procession grew longer each day. It was like a gaudily colored snake winding its way along a narrow road.

At night, tents were pitched and bonfires lit. The people slept like an army of the dead. Emperor Hsien Feng spent most of his time in silence. Occasionally when his fever rose, he would speak beyond the ordinary.

"Who can guarantee that all the seeds of nature will be pure and healthy and that their blooms will create a picture of harmony in the garden?" he asked.

Unable to answer, I stared back at him.

"I am talking about bad seeds," His Majesty continued. "Seeds that have been secretly soaked in poison. They lay sleeping in fertile soil until the spring rain wakes them. They grow to enormous size at an amazing speed, covering the ground and taking water and sun from others. I can see their fat flowers. Their branches expand like bullies spreading poison. Don't let Tung Chih out of your sight, Orchid."

I held Tung Chih while we slept. In my dreams I heard horses champing at the bit. Fear woke me like a strange attack. Sweat would gather and soak my shirt. My scalp was constantly wet. My senses became heightened to certain things, like Tung Chih's breath and the noises around the tent, and deadened to others, like hunger. Though we stayed in separate tents, Emperor Hsien Feng would appear in front of me like a ghost in the middle of the night. He stood there in dry-eyed misery. I wondered if I was also losing my mind.

It was close to evening and we decided to break for a meal. That afternoon His Majesty had experienced a terrifying coughing fit. Blood drooled from the corners of his mouth. The doctor said that it was bad for him to ride in the palanquin. But we had no choice. Eventually we stopped in order to still his cough.

At dawn I looked out from the tent. We were close to Jehol, and the landscape was of extraordinary beauty. The ground was covered with clover and wildflowers, and the gentle hills were thick with brush. The autumn heat was tolerable compared to Peking. The fragrance of mountain dandelions was sweet. After the morning meal we were on the road again. We passed through fields where the grass was waist-high.

Whenever Tung Chih was with me I tried to be strong and cheerful. But it wasn't easy. When the old palaces of Jehol appeared on the horizon, we all rolled out of the palanquins and got down on our knees. We thanked Heaven we had made it to this place of temporary refuge. The moment Tung Chih was lifted from the chair he took off after wild rabbits and squirrels, which skittered away from him.

We hurried to reach the great gates. It was like entering a dreamland, a scene from a faded painting. Hsien Feng's grandfather Chien Lung had built Jehol in the eighteenth century. Today the palace stood like an aged beauty whose makeup was smeared. I had heard so much about this place that the view was already familiar to me. Jehol was more of a work of nature than the Forbidden City. Over the years the trees and bushes had grown into each other. Ivy had spread from wall to wall and up the sky-high trees, where it dangled in luxuriant vines. The furniture in the palaces was made of hardwood, exquisitely carved pieces inlaid with jade and stones. The dragons on the ceiling panels were of pure gold, the walls resplendent in shimmering silk.

I adored the wildness. I wouldn't have minded living in Jehol. I thought it would be a good place to raise Tung Chih. He could learn the Bannermen's trade. He could learn to hunt. I wanted so much for him to grow up on horseback as his ancestors did. I wished I didn't have to remind myself that we were in exile.

Jehol was a great silent place. The bleached light of the sun reflected softly from its tiled roofs. The courtyards were paved with cobblestones. Doors were flanked by thick walls. Since Chien Lung's death half a century before, most of the palaces had stood vacant and they smelled of mold. Battered by decades of wind and rain, the exteriors seemed to fade into the landscape. The original color had been sand yellow; now it was brown and green. Inside, mildew covered the ceilings and darkened the corners of the spacious rooms.

The royal families swept into Jehol and the place came to life. The slumbering halls, courtyards and buildings were wakened to the echo of human voices and footfalls. Doors were pushed open to the sound of scraping wood and metal. Rusty window locks broke off when we attempted to open them. The eunuchs did their best to remove the must and grime of years.

I was given an apartment next to Nuharoo's on one side of the main palace. The Emperor occupied the largest bedroom, of course, right in the middle. His office, which was called the Hall of Literary Zest, was next to the apartments of Su Shun and the other grand councilors on the other side of the palace. Nuharoo watched over Tung Chih while I attended Hsien Feng. Our schedules and responsibilities now ran according to the needs of the father and the son.

Since His Majesty had stopped giving audiences, he was no longer presented documents to review or sign. The court's business continued to be managed solely by Su Shun. Brewing herbs for Hsien Feng had become my job. The bitter smell was so strong that he complained. I had to tell the servants to take the pots to the kitchen, which was at the far end of the palace. I worked with the herbalist and Doctor Sun Pao-tien to make sure that the medicine was properly prepared. It wasn't easy. One of the prescriptions required that the soup be mixed with fresh deer blood, which spoiled quickly. The kitchen staff had to slaughter a deer every two days, immediately prepare the medicine, then hope that His Majesty wouldn't throw up right after we poured it down his throat.

In late October the maple trees looked like they were set to burning by the sun. One morning when Nuharoo and I took Tung Chih for a walk we discovered that a nearby spring was surprisingly warm. A eunuch who had guarded the palaces all his life said that there were several hot springs in the area. It was how Jehol got its name: *je-hol*, hot river.

"The spring gets hotter when it snows," the eunuch said. "You can feel the water with your hand." Tung Chih was curious and insisted on bathing in the spring. Nuharoo was about to give in, but I opposed the idea. Tung Chih didn't know how to swim and had just recovered from a cold. Resenting my discipline, he turned to Nuharoo, pouting. My son knew that Nuharoo outranked me and that I was not allowed to disobey her. It had become a pattern with Nuharoo, my son and me. It was irritating and left me feeling defenseless. The kitchen became my place of escape.

Hsien Feng's health seemed to have stabilized a little. As soon as he was able to sit up, Prince Kung sent him drafts of the treaties. I was summoned to help.

"Your brother expects you to honor the terms," I said, summarizing Prince Kung's letter to His Majesty. "He says that these are the final documents. Peace and order will be restored after you sign."

"The barbarians are asking me to reward them for spitting in my face," Hsien Feng said. "I now understand why my father wouldn't close his eyes when he died—he couldn't swallow the insult."

I waited for him to calm down before I resumed reading. Some of the terms disturbed His Majesty so much that he gasped for air. Bubbling sounds would come from his throat and then he would burst out coughing.

Tiny blood spots covered the floor and the blankets. I didn't want to go on reading, but the documents had to be returned within ten days. If not, Prince Kung said, the Allies would destroy the capital.

It was no use for Emperor Hsien Feng to beat his chest and shout,

"All foreigners are brute beasts!" It was also no use to issue edicts urging the army to fight harder. The situation was irreversible.

Tung Chih watched his father drag himself out of bed and get down on his knees to beg Heaven for help. Again and again Hsien Feng wished he had the courage to take his own life.

It was in the Hall of Literary Zest where the treaties with France and Great Britain were sealed. Both treaties continued to validate the previous Tientsin Treaty, but with items added. It was the first time in several thousand years that China had borne such shame.

Emperor Hsien Feng was forced to open the city of Tientsin as a new trading port. To him this not only allowed the barbarians to trade in his front yard, but also permitted their military access to the capital through the open sea. His Majesty was also forced to "rent" Kowloon to the British as war compensation. The treaties stated that Western missionaries were to be given total freedom and protection to operate in China, which included building churches. Chinese laws would not apply to any foreigners, and violations of the treaties by any Chinese were to be punished swiftly. China was made to pay indemnities of eight million taels to the British and the French.

As if this were not enough, the Russians submitted a new draft of the Sino-Russian Treaty of Peking. The Russian envoy tried to persuade Prince Kung that the burning of the Imperial palaces indicated that China needed military protection from Russia. Although fully aware of what the Russians were up to, Prince Kung couldn't say no. China was in no position to defend itself and could not afford to make Russia an enemy.

"When a wolf pack hunts down a sick deer, what can the deer do but beg for mercy?" Prince Kung wrote in a letter. The Russians wanted the Amur lands in the north, which the tsarists had already seized. Russians had already settled along the whole of the Ussuri River east to the border of Korea. They had claimed the crucial Chinese port of Haishenwei, soon to be known as Vladivostok.

I will never forget the moment when Emperor Hsien Feng signed the treaties. It was like a death rehearsal.

The brush pen he held seemed to weigh a thousand pounds. His hand couldn't stop shaking. He couldn't bring himself to write his name. To stabilize his elbows I added two more pillows behind his back. Chief Eunuch Shim prepared the ink and laid flat the pages of the treaties in front of him on a rice paper pad.

My sorrow for Hsien Feng and my country was beyond expression. Saliva gathered at the corners of His Majesty's purple lips. He was crying, but there were no tears. He shouted and screamed for days. Finally his voice simply died. Each breath was now a struggle.

His fingers were like brittle sticks. His frame was no better than a skeleton. He had begun the journey of vanishing into a ghost. His ancestors hadn't answered his prayers. Heaven had been merciless to its son. In Hsien Feng's helplessness, however, he demonstrated the dignity of the Emperor of China. His struggle was heroic—the dying man holding on to his brush, refusing to sign China away.

I asked Nuharoo to bring Tung Chih. I wanted him to witness his father's struggle to perform his duty. Nuharoo rejected the idea. She said that Tung Chih should be exposed to glory, not shame.

I could have fought with Nuharoo. And I almost did. I wanted to tell her that dying was not shameful, nor was having the courage to face reality. Tung Chih's education should begin at his father's deathbed. He should watch the signing of the treaties and remember and understand why his father was crying.

Nuharoo reminded me that she was the Empress of the East, the one whose word was the house's law. I had to retreat.

Chief Eunuch Shim asked if His Majesty cared to test the ink before putting down his stroke. Hsien Feng nodded. I adjusted the rice paper.

The moment the tip of the brush touched the paper Hsien Feng's hand trembled violently. It started with his fingers, then spread to his arm, his shoulder and his entire body. Sweat soaked through his robe. His eyes rolled up as he drew deeply for breath.

Doctor Sun Pao-tien was summoned. He came in and knelt beside His Majesty. He bent his head over Hsien Feng's chest and listened.

I stared at Sun Pao-tien's lips, which were half hidden by his long white beard. I feared what he might say.

"He might slip into a coma." The doctor rose. "He will wake, but I can't guarantee how much time he has left."

For the rest of the day we waited for Hsien Feng to return to consciousness. When he did, I begged him to complete the signature, but he didn't say a word.

We had reached a deadlock—Emperor Hsien Feng refused to pick up the brush pen. I kept grinding the ink. I wished that Prince Kung were here.

Feeling helpless, I started to cry.

"Orchid." His Majesty's voice was barely audible. "I won't be able to die in peace if I sign."

I understood. I wouldn't want to sign either if I were he. But Prince Kung needed the signature to continue negotiating. The Emperor was going to die, but the nation had to go on. China had to get back on its feet.

In the afternoon Hsien Feng decided to yield. It was only after I said that his signature would not be an endorsement for invasion but a tactic to gain time.

He picked up the brush pen but was unable to see where on the paper he was to put his signature.

"Guide my hand, Orchid," he said, and tried to sit up, but collapsed instead.

The three of us—Chief Eunuch Shim, An-te-hai and I—laid His Majesty down on his back. I put the paper near his hand and told him that he could ink his signature now.

With his eyes fixed on the ceiling, Emperor Hsien Feng wiggled the brush. I carefully guided his strokes to prevent his signature from looking like a child's scribble. By the time we covered his name with the red Imperial seal, Hsien Feng had dropped the brush pen and passed out. The ink stone fell and black ink splattered all over my dress and shoes.

In July of 1861 we celebrated Hsien Feng's thirtieth birthday. His Majesty lay in his bed and drifted in and out of consciousness. No guests were invited. The birthday ceremony included a food parade. The dishes were barely touched; everyone sensed his coming death.

A month later, Hsien Feng seemed to hit bottom. Doctor Sun Pao-tien predicted that His Majesty's demise was a week, perhaps days, away. The court grew tense because the Emperor had not named his successor.

Tung Chih was not allowed to be with his father because the court was afraid it would be too disturbing. This upset me. I believed that any affection demonstrated by His Majesty would sustain Tung Chih's memory for the rest of his life.

Nuharoo accused me of placing a curse on Hsien Feng by telling Tung Chih that his father was going to die. Her astrologer believed that only when we refused to accept his death would Hsien Feng be saved by a miracle.

It was hard to fight Nuharoo when she had her mind set. I could only manage to have An-te-hai sneak Tung Chih to his father's bedside, usually when Nuharoo went with the Buddhists to chant or was enjoying her teatime opera, provided by Su Shun and performed in Nuharoo's quarters.

To my disappointment Tung Chih didn't want to be with his father. He complained about his father's "scary look" and "bad breath." He was miserable when I pushed him toward the sickbed. He called his father a bore and once yelled, "You hollow man!" He pulled at Hsien Feng's sheets and threw pillows at him. He wanted to play Ride the Horsy with the dying man. There wasn't a single compassionate bone in his little body.

I spanked my son. For the next week, instead of leaving Tung Chih to Nuharoo I spent time observing him. I discovered the source of his poor behavior.

I had instructed Tung Chih to take riding lessons with Yung Lu, but Nuharoo made excuses for the child to be absent. Instead of practicing with real horses, Tung Chih rode the eunuchs. More than thirty eunuchs had to crawl around the courtyard to make him happy. His favorite "horse" was An-te-hai. It was the child's way of getting revenge, for An-te-hai had been ordered by me to discipline him. Tung Chih whipped An-te-hai's buttocks and forced him to crawl until his knees bled.

Worse than this treatment of An-te-hai was that he ordered a seventy-year-old eunuch named Old Wei to swallow his feces. When I questioned Tung Chih, he replied, "Mother, I just wanted to know if Old Wei had been telling the truth."

"What truth?"

"That I could do anything I wanted. I only asked him to prove it."

I looked at my son's little face and wondered how he had become capable of such mean tricks. He was clever and knew whom to punish and whom to reward. If An-te-hai hadn't been loyal to me, he would have yielded to Tung Chih's every desire. Tung Chih had once claimed that he knew Nuharoo's favorite dishes. It didn't occur to me that this was my son's way of rewarding her. I even praised him when he sent Nuharoo her favorite fancy moon cakes. I thought it was an appropriate gesture of piety and was pleased that my son got along with her. Then Tung Chih bragged about how Nuharoo encouraged him to neglect school. She had said to him, "There are emperors in history who never spent a day in the classroom but had no problem bringing their country to prosperity."

I confronted Nuharoo and pointed out the danger of not disciplining Tung Chih. She told me that I was overreacting. "He's only five years old! As soon as we get back to Peking and Tung Chih resumes his normal schooling, everything will be fine. Playing is a child's nature, and we must not interfere with Heaven's intent. He asked for the parrots yesterday, but An-te-hai had brought none with him. Poor Tung Chih —he only asked for a parrot!"

This time I decided not to give in. I insisted that he attend his classes. I told Nuharoo that I would check with the tutors regarding Tung Chih's homework. But I was disappointed. The head tutor begged me to release him from Tung Chih.

"His Young Majesty threw paper balls and knocked off my glasses," the rabbit-toothed tutor reported. "He will not listen. Yesterday he made me eat a strange-tasting cookie. Afterward he told me that he had dipped the cookie in his own waste."

I was shocked at the way Tung Chih ruled his classroom. But what concerned me more was his interest in Nuharoo's ghost books. He stayed up late to listen to her stories of the underworld. He got so scared that he would wet his bed at night. Yet he was so drawn to those stories that they became an addiction. When I interfered by taking the picture books away, he fought with me.

Tung Chih was willing to do anything to get away from me. First he pretended to be sick in order to avoid his classes. When I caught him, Nuharoo would come to his defense. She even secretly ordered Doctor Sun Pao-tien to lie about the "fever" that kept him out of school.

If this was the way we prepared Tung Chih to be the next emperor, the dynasty was doomed. I decided to take the matter into my own hands. In my eyes, the situation was of national significance. All I knew was that my time was running out.

Every day I escorted my son to his tutors and then waited outside until the classes were over. Nuharoo was upset that I didn't trust her, but I was too angry to worry about her feelings. I wanted to change Tung Chih before it was too late.

Tung Chih knew how to play Nuharoo and me off each other. He knew that I couldn't deny his visiting Nuharoo, so he went as often as he could, to make me jealous. Unfortunately I fell into his trap. And he continued to cause trouble in school. One day he pulled out the rabbit-toothed tutor's two longest eyebrow hairs. He knew full well that the old man regarded them as his "longevity sign." The man was so crushed, he was seized by a stroke and sent home for good. Nuharoo saw the incident as a comedy. I didn't agree, and intended to punish my son for his cruelty.

The court replaced the old tutor with a new one, but he was fired by his student the first day on the job. Tung Chih's stated reason was that the man farted during lessons. He charged the tutor with "disrespect for the Son of Heaven." The man was whipped. Upon hearing this, Nuharoo praised Tung Chih for "acting like a true ruler," while I was shattered.

The more I pressed, the worse Tung Chih rebelled. Instead of supporting me, the court asked Nuharoo to "watch over" my "outrageous behavior." I wondered if Su Shun was behind it. Tung Chih now had no problem talking back to me in front of the eunuchs and the maids. He was good with words. Sometimes he sounded too sophisticated for a five-year-old. He would say, "How low of you to deny my nature!" or "I am an endowed animal!" or "It's wrong for you to put me to sleep in order to play the tamer!"

I had heard the same from Nuharoo: "Allow Tung Chih to journey forth, Lady Yehonala" and "He is a traveler who understands the universe. He thinks not of himself, but of the voyage, of dreams and of the soul of the Buddha's spirituality" and "Throw your keys to the winds, and leave his cage open!"

I began to doubt her intentions. There had always been something perverse about her approach to Tung Chih. No matter what he did, she was always the loving one. I realized that unless I stopped Nuharoo, I wouldn't be able to stop Tung Chih. For me the struggle had turned into a battle to save my son. I spent days thinking about how to talk to her. I wanted to be firm about my intentions without injuring her pride. I wanted her to understand that I appreciated her affection for Tung Chih, but she had to learn to discipline him.

To my surprise, Nuharoo came to me before I went to her. She was dressed casually in an ivory gown. She brought fresh lotus flowers as a gift. She complained about my restrictions on Tung Chih's diet. She insisted that he was too thin. I explained that I had no problem with his eating more, but that his diet must be balanced. I told her that Tung Chih sat for hours on the chamber pot without producing a single turd.

"I don't see it as a problem," Nuharoo said. "Children take their time when it comes to the potty."

"The children of peasants never have that problem," I argued. "They eat plenty of roughage."

"But Tung Chih is no peasant's child. It is insulting to make that comparison." Nuharoo's expression turned cold. "It is only right that Tung Chih follow the Imperial diet."

I had personally hired a chef to prepare healthful meals, but Tung Chih complained to Nuharoo that the chef had served him rotten shrimp, giving him cramps. No one except Nuharoo believed the lie. However, to please Tung Chih, she fired the chef.

I had to restrain myself from fighting openly with Nuharoo. I made a decision to concentrate on Tung Chih's studies first. Every morning I took a whip and escorted Tung Chih to his tutor.

He was being taught about the celestial globe. I asked the tutor for a copy of the text and said to my son that I would test him myself after he finished the lesson.

As I expected, Tung Chih couldn't recall a word of what he had learned. He had just come from school and we were about to eat our dinner. I ordered his meal to be removed and took him by the hand. As we left I picked up the whip. I took him to a small shed in the back garden, away from the main halls and apartments. I told Tung Chih that he would not be released until he recited the full text.

He let out a loud cry to see if anyone would come to his rescue. I had prepared for this. An-te-hai had been told to keep the tutors away, and I had expressly ordered that no one inform Nuharoo of Tung Chih's whereabouts.

"'In very early times,'" I said, to start my son off. "Begin."

Tung Chih sobbed and pretended not to hear.

I grabbed the whip and lifted my arm so that its length danced before him.

He started to recite. "'In very early times, there were four huge star patterns in the starry sky. Along the Yellow River there were figures of animals...'"

"Go on. 'A dragon...'"

"'A dragon, a tortoise with a snake, a tiger and a bird, which rises up and then sets down ...'" He shook his head and said that he didn't remember the next line.

"Start over and read it again!"

He opened his textbook but stumbled over the words.

I read to him. "'... One after another, arcing around the north celestial pole, flows an asterism called the Northern Dipper.'"

"This is too hard," he complained, and threw down the text.

I grabbed his shoulders and shook him. "This is for a spoiled boy who lives without laws and without any thought of the consequences!" I lifted him off the floor and stripped away his robe. I raised my arm and let the whip fall.

A clear red line settled on his little behind.

Tung Chih screamed.

My tears fell, but I struck again. I had to force myself to continue. I had let him run loose for too long. This was my punishment and my last chance.

"How dare you whip me!" His expression was incredulous. The little eyebrows met in the center of his frightened face. "No one hits the son of the Emperor!"

I whipped harder. "This is to make you hear the sound of foreign cannons. This is to make you read the treaties!" I felt the collapsing of an emotional dam. An invisible arrow shot through my head. Choking, I continued, "This . . . is . . . to make you look your father in the face . . . I want you to know how he turned into a hollow man."

As if acting under its own power, the whip changed direction. Instead of landing on Tung Chih, it landed on me. The sound was loud and crisp. Like a hot snake, the leather wrapped around my body, leaving its bloody trace with every slap.

Intoxicated by the spectacle, Tung Chih fell silent.

Exhaustion overwhelmed me and I collapsed and hugged my knees to my chest. I cried because Hsien Feng wouldn't be alive to educate his son; I cried because I couldn't see myself raising Tung Chih properly with Nuharoo standing between us; I cried because I heard my son shouting that he hated me and that he couldn't wait for Nuharoo to punish me; and I cried because deep down I was disappointed in myself and, more fearfully, I didn't know what else to do.

I continued with the lesson as I held the whip high. "Answer me, Tung Chih. What does the dragon signify?"

"The dragon signifies a transformation," the terrified little man replied.

"Of what?"

"What 'what'?"

"A transformation of . . . ?"

"Transformation of . . . of a fish. It is about the fish's ability to leap over a dam."

"That's correct. That was what made the fish a dragon." I put down the whip. "It was about the effort it made against a monstrous obstacle. It was about the heroic leaping action it took. Its bones were broken and its scales scraped away. It could have died from the effort, but it didn't give in. That was what set it apart from the ordinary fish."

"I don't understand this. It is too hard!"

He was no longer able to follow me, even if I read the same phrase over and over. His mind seemed to have come to a halt. He was in shock. I had scared him. In his life so far, no one had ever raised a voice to him. He always had his way, no matter how demeaning to others it might be.

I was determined to go on. "Listen carefully and you will get it. 'The tiger is the spirit of beasts, the tortoise is the spirit of shells, and the phoenix is a bird who is capable of rising from ashes . . .'"

Tung Chih began to follow me, slowly and painstakingly.

There came a loud banging on the door of the shed.

I knew who it was. I knew she had a spy in my palace.

The banging continued, with Nuharoo screaming, "I am reporting your cruelty to His Majesty! You have no right to punish Tung Chih. He doesn't belong to you! He came through you. You were only a house that once sheltered him. If I find him hurt, you will be hanged!"

I went on reading, my voice clear and resonant. "'In ancient Chinese philosophy the five colors correspond to the five directions. Yellow corresponds with the center, blue with the east, white with the west, red with the south, black with the north . . .'"

Nineteen

THE WILD GRASS around Jehol turned yellow while the court waited for the Emperor to die. Hsien Feng could no longer swallow. The herb soup I prepared continued to be brought to him by the eunuchs, but he no longer touched it. The dragon robe for burial was ordered and His Majesty's coffin was nearing completion.

Yet my son had not been appointed the successor, and His Majesty had not uttered any words regarding the matter. Every time I wanted to see my husband, Chief Eunuch Shim would block me, saying that His Majesty was either sleeping or meeting with his advisors. He made me wait endlessly. Frustrated, I would return to my quarters. I had no doubt that Shim was acting on Su Shun's orders.

I was concerned because Hsien Feng could slip away, leaving me powerless to help Tung Chih. When An-te-hai reported that Su Shun had been trying to recruit him to spy on me, the grand councilor's intentions became clear.

I thanked Heaven for An-te-hai's loyalty. The cost to him was that his name went on Su Shun's list of enemies.

"Su Shun is looking to kick your dog," Nuharoo said during a visit. "I wonder what has made him hate An-te-hai so much." Lifting her eyes from her embroidery, she searched my face for an answer.

I didn't want to share my thoughts. I didn't want to point out that it was not An-te-hai but me Su Shun was after. If I revealed my feelings, Nuharoo would want to interfere and try to get an apology out of Su Shun. She considered herself a champion of justice, but her kindness could do more harm than good.

Nuharoo enjoyed being known for her amiability, courtesy and fairness. But she wouldn't be able to solve this problem. She would only end up making it easier for Su Shun to get rid of me. He would use Emperor Hsien Feng's hand. It would not be the first time. Yung Lu's story about the horrible fate of a certain minister who was disloyal to the grand councilor was but one example. Su Shun might also want to make Nuharoo his ally. She would be easy prey if flattered. The master of tricks could wrap her around his finger. Nuharoo lived to glorify her name, and any attention from Su Shun would be especially appealing. After all, my survival wouldn't be Nuharoo's priority.

An-te-hai stumbled over the doorsill. He reported that it had been decided that I would be "honored to accompany Hsien Feng when he returns to his source," which meant that I would be buried alive when the Emperor died.

I didn't believe it. I couldn't. Out of three thousand concubines I was the only one who gave him a son. Hsien Feng knew that Tung Chih needed me.

Making an effort to stay calm, I asked An-te-hai where he had picked up this information. He said that it came from his friend Chow Tee, the Emperor's attendant.

"Chow Tee came to me this morning," An-te-hai said in a trembling voice. "He told me to run away immediately. I asked what had happened. He said, 'Your days are numbered.' I said, 'Quit joking, it's not funny.' He said he was serious. He had overheard Su Shun's conversation with His Majesty, and Su Shun suggested that His Majesty 'take Lady Yehonala' with him."

An-te-hai paused for breath, and he wiped the sweat from his face with his sleeve.

"Are you sure Chow Tee heard him right?" I asked, shaken.

"Chow Tee heard Su Shun say, 'Lady Yehonala is not the kind who would remain faithful and quietly tend her garden.'"

"Did His Majesty respond?"

"No. And that was why Su Shun pressed. He said that he wouldn't be surprised if you took up with other men after his death. He also predicted that you would seek power through Tung Chih. Su Shun said that you had whipped Tung Chih because he refused to do what you wanted. In the end His Majesty agreed to take you."

I envisioned my eternal dress and coffin being ordered by Su Shun. I could picture myself with the silk around my neck and Su Shun kicking away the stool. Before my body turned cold, he would pour a bowl of liquid silver down my throat, to mold me into the posture he desired.

"My lady, do something before it's too late!" An-te-hai threw himself on the floor and wouldn't rise.

I never dreamt that I would end up being sacrificed. Big Sister Fann's stories were flat compared to what was happening to me. There was no time to shed tears or seek comfort from my family. Su Shun might already be preparing the fire to melt the silver bars into a drink.

I asked An-te-hai why I should trust Chow Tee's words.

"We eunuchs are vines," he said. "We have to locate a big tree in order to climb high. Chow Tee and I understand that only when we help each other will we survive and advance. We have been sworn brothers since we were twelve years old. If there was a fly in Emperor Hsien Feng's room, Chow Tee would let me know. Lately Chow Tee has been worried about his future after the Emperor dies. If lucky enough to be spared from going with His Majesty, he needs to find a new master to serve. He knew this information was valuable and wanted to offer it to you. It was my suggestion, of course."

I told An-te-hai that I had to speak with Chow Tee.

The next day, at An-te-hai's arrangement, Chow Tee came to me under the pretense of borrowing a lamp.

He was about twenty years old and looked plain and humble. His cotton robe was washed white. I had never seen a young face with so many wrinkles. His background was similar to An-te-hai's, and he had been living in the Forbidden City since the age of nine. He was very careful with his words. He confirmed what An-te-hai had told me.

After I sent Chow Tee away I received my son. Tung Chih climbed on my lap and said that he was ready to recite his text. He was very good this time. I praised him as much as I could, but I had to make an effort to block my tears. I couldn't get rid of the image that my coffin was being made. I could actually hear the sound of nails being hammered into wood.

Despite his behavior Tung Chih had grown into a handsome boy. He had my bright eyes and smooth skin. The rest of his features were from his father. He had a full forehead, a straight Manchu nose and a lovely mouth. His expression was usually serious, but when he smiled it was the sweetest. I couldn't bear the thought that Tung Chih would lose both his father and mother at the same time.

As far as I could see, two people would be destroyed if Hsien Feng took me with him. One would be my son, and the other my mother.

Tung Chih would be given no discipline, which Nuharoo would do innocently, but Su Shun purposely. The result would be the same—by the time Tung Chih grew up, he would be ill suited to rule. As for my mother, she would be in no condition to stand the blow. My death would spell her own.

Su Shun would lie straight-faced if Tung Chih had questions regarding my death. Su Shun would prove to him that I was a bad mother, and my son would be taught to hate me. He would never realize that he was Su Shun's victim. Su Shun would do everything in his power to seduce Tung Chih, and my son would regard him as his savior.

What could be more evil than molesting a child's mind? Tung Chih would be stripped of his birthright. Su Shun would eventually achieve his own ambitions through Tung Chih. He would run the empire in the name of Hsien Feng for his son. He would expose Tung Chih's weakness and then create an excuse to overthrow him and proclaim himself as the ruler.

The clearer the picture of the future became, the deeper I sank into despair. The news of Hsien Feng's death could arrive at any moment, and this could be my last chance to be with Tung Chih.

I held my son so tightly he complained that I was hurting him.

"Weeping can only cause you to lose more time, my lady." An-te-hai rose from the floor where he had been kneeling. His usually gentle eyes had become hard.

"Why don't you escape, An-te-hai?" I said in frustration. "You have been good to me and I shall bless you."

"I live for you, my lady." An-te-hai banged his head loudly on the floor. "Don't give up yet!"

"Who can rescue me, An-te-hai? The Emperor is too far gone, and Su Shun's spies are everywhere."

"There are two people who might be able to save you, my lady."

Rong and her husband, Prince Ch'un, were the two people An-te-hai had in mind. An-te-hai believed that Prince Ch'un could find a way to His Majesty's bedside. He would take Rong with him so that she could speak for me.

The suggestion made sense. Rong was now pregnant, which added to her status in the eyes of the Imperial family. Prince Ch'un had four daughters but not yet a son. He would do anything to make his wife happy. An-te-hai volunteered to sneak out of Jehol and contact my sister.

A week later, in the early morning, my sister was by my side. Her belly was the size of a lantern. A healthy glow shone on her face. We threw our arms around each other and wept. Rong told me that she had succeeded in her task.

"At first Su Shun wouldn't let us in," she recalled. "Ch'un was ready to withdraw after several hours of waiting. I begged him. I said that I had to speak to His Majesty in person about sacrificing my sister. If I couldn't succeed in making him change his mind, the child in my belly would be affected by my grief. I would have a miscarriage."

Rong took my hands in hers and smiled. "My husband couldn't stand the idea of possibly losing a son. So he forced his way in and saw His Majesty lying on the bed.

"I followed Ch'un in and we wished His Majesty good health. My belly was too big for me to kowtow, but I made myself anyway—I had to show him how desperate I was. I didn't have to pretend. I was truly scared. His Majesty pardoned me and told me to rise. I refused and stayed on my knees until my husband opened his mouth. He told his brother that I was having nightmares, that I couldn't get over my sadness, that he might lose his son to a miscarriage."

"What was Hsien Feng's reaction?"

"His Majesty looked terrible and could barely speak. He asked what my concerns were, and my husband replied, 'My wife dreamt that you had issued a decree to take Orchid with you. She wants to know that it isn't true. She needs to hear the words from your heavenly lips.'"

"What did His Majesty say?"

"His Majesty pointed at Su Shun and said that it was his idea."

"I knew it!"

"Su Shun looked furious, but he said nothing." Rong tucked her handkerchief back into her pocket.

Just then An-te-hai rushed in. "His Majesty has ordered the immediate cancellation of the decree. Chow Tee told me that His Majesty told Su Shun never to mention the idea again."

When I had introduced Rong to Prince Ch'un, I never imagined that they would turn out to be my protective god and goddess. Rong told me the danger was not over and that I should be careful. I knew Su Shun would not put down his weapons and become a Buddha. This fight to destroy me had just begun.

Three days went by quietly. On the morning of the fourth day, Doctor Sun Pao-tien predicted that Hsien Feng would not see the next dawn. Su Shun issued an urgent summons in the Emperor's name: a final audience was to be held late that afternoon, when the court should expect to hear His Majesty's last wishes.

I didn't know that I was excluded until I went to visit Nuharoo at noon. She was not in. Her eunuch said that she had been picked up by a palanquin sent by Su Shun. I turned to An-te-hai and told him to find out what was going on. An-te-hai got a message from Chow Tee. The final Imperial audience had begun, and Su Shun had just announced that my absence was due to poor health.

I panicked. In a matter of hours my husband would breathe his last, and the chance for me to act would be gone forever.

I ran to Tung Chih's study. My son was playing chess with a eunuch and obstinately refused to come with me. I pulled the board away, sending the pieces flying across the room. I dragged him all the way to the Hall of Fantastic Haze while I explained the situation. I told him to ask his father to name him the successor.

Tung Chih was frightened. He begged to be sent back to his chess game. I told him that he had to speak to his father, that it was the only way he could save his future. Tung Chih couldn't comprehend. He screamed and fought me. In my struggle to keep hold of my son, my necklace broke and the pearls and beads scattered down the hallway.

Guards blocked our entrance to the hall, although they seemed to be in awe of Tung Chih.

"I must see His Majesty," I said loudly.

Chief Eunuch Shim appeared. "His Majesty doesn't desire to call his concubines now," he said. "When he does, I will let you know."

"I am sure His Majesty will want to see his son for the last time."

Chief Eunuch Shim shook his head. "I have Grand Councilor Su Shun's orders to lock you up if you insist on intruding, Lady Yehonala."

"Tung Chih has the right to bid farewell to his father!" I yelled, hoping that Emperor Hsien Feng would hear me.

"I am sorry. Meeting with Tung Chih would only disturb His Majesty."

Desperate, I tried to push Shim aside.

He stood like a wall. "You will have to kill me to make me renounce my duty."

I got down on my knees and pleaded. "Would you at least allow Tung Chih to watch his father from a distance?" I pressed my son forward.

"No, Lady Yehonala." He signaled the guards, who pinned me to the floor.

Something must have clicked inside Tung Chih's little head. Maybe he didn't like the way I was being treated. When Shim went up to him wearing a false smile and requesting that he go back to his playroom, my son answered, for the first time using the language reserved for an emperor, "*Zhen* wishes to be left alone to see what's going on here."

The word *Zhen* fixed Chief Eunuch Shim to the spot.

Tung Chih took advantage of the moment and ran inside the hall.

Hsien Feng's giant black dragon bed was in the center of the throne's platform. Led by Su Shun and his cabinet members, the court ministers and officials surrounded the pale figure under the coverlet. My husband looked as if he had already died. He lay still, with all signs of vitality gone.

Nuharoo was on her knees by the bed, dressed in a beige robe. She was sobbing silently.

Everyone else was also on his or her knees. Time seemed to be frozen.

There was nothing glorious about the heavenly departure. The Emperor had visibly shrunk. His features had collapsed, with his eyes and mouth pulled toward the ears. His dying didn't feel real to me. The night when he had first summoned me was as vivid as yesterday. I remembered the time when he had teased me boldly in front of the Grand Empress. I remembered his naughty but charming expression. I remembered the sound of the bamboo chips dropping onto the tray and his fingers touching mine when he passed me the *ruyi*. The memories saddened me, and I had to remind myself of why I was here.

From the whispering of the ministers I learned that Hsien Feng had briefly stopped breathing several times today, only to revive with a cavernous rumble deep in his chest. Two pillows supported the Son of Heaven. His eyes were open, but they hardly moved. The court was waiting for him to speak, but he didn't seem capable.

Although Tung Chih was the natural heir apparent, it was not specified in Ch'ing Dynasty law that the throne be passed by the right of primogeniture. The Emperor's last words would be the only thing that counted. There would be an official box that contained His Majesty's living will. Still, his words would override whatever he had written. Many people believed that the finality of death changed a person's perception, and therefore his wishes in the box might not be his true ones. What worried me was what Su Shun might do. With his wickedness, he could manipulate Emperor Hsien Feng to say what he did not mean to say.

A few hours passed. The waiting continued. Food was set out in the courtyard. Hundreds of people sat on their heels, scooping up rice from bowls, staring into space. Tung Chih was bored and irritated. I knew that he had been doing his best to be obedient. Finally he had had enough. When I told him he must stay, he threw a tantrum. He kicked the bowls out of people's hands.

I grabbed Tung Chih. "One more act of destruction and I'll have you shut in a bee house!"

Tung Chih quieted down.

Night came. All was in darkness except for the Hall of Fantastic Haze. It was lit as brightly as a stage.

The court gathered again. A number of the Emperor's seals were brought out of their chambers and laid out on a long table. They were beautifully carved and mounted. The room was so quiet I could hear the sound of the sizzling candles.

The grand secretary and scholar Kuei Liang, Prince Kung's father-in-law, was in a gray robe. He had arrived from Peking that morning and was expected to go back as soon as he recorded His Majesty's last words. Kuei Liang's white beard hung down his chest. He was on his knees holding a giant brush pen. Every once in a while he dipped his brush in the ink to keep it moist. In front of him was a stack of rice paper. Chow Tee, standing next to him, picked up an ink stick, which was as thick as a child's arm, and rubbed the stick against the stone.

Su Shun's eyes were on the seals. I wondered what was on his mind. In China all Imperial documents, from His Majesty's on down, were valid only if stamped with an official seal on top of a personal signature. A seal meant lawful authority. The most important could render all other documents worthless. That Tung Chih hadn't received his father's promise to own these seals filled me with despair.

Was Hsien Feng already on his way to Heaven? Had he forgotten his son? Was Su Shun here to see Tung Chih's end? Su Shun paced slowly beside the table where the seals were lined up. He looked like he was already their owner. He picked up each seal and ran his fingers over the stone surfaces.

"There are many ways to alter one's destiny," Su Shun said, tilting his chin upward like a sage. "His Majesty must be walking through the dark halls of his soul. I imagine him following a red wall, taking slow steps. He is not dying in actuality. He is going through a rebirth. It is not a frame of dry bones his spirits are after but the purple light of immortality."

Hsien Feng's body suddenly contracted. The movement lasted a few seconds and then stopped. I heard Nuharoo's wail and saw her reach into her robe for a string of beads.

According to superstition, this could be the moment the spirits of the dying entered the stage of mental reflection.

I prayed that His Majesty would call for Tung Chih. If his only son didn't occupy his last thoughts, what would?

The ministers started to cry. Some elders fainted in the courtyard, and eunuchs went in with chairs to carry them out.

I moved toward Hsien Feng's bed, pulling Tung Chih with me.

"No one is allowed to disturb the spirits!" Chief Eunuch Shim blocked my way. At his signal the guards took Tung Chih and me by the arms.

I struggled to free myself.

Kicking and biting, Tung Chih fought. The guards bent his arms behind him and shoved his face into the ground.

"Please!" I begged Chief Eunuch Shim.

"His Majesty is in the middle of his reflection." Shim refused to yield. "You can go to him once his spirits are settled."

"Papa! Papa!" Tung Chih cried loudly.

It would have won anyone's sympathy if it were somewhere else. But the court no longer seemed able to address itself to the one they should serve. It had become Su Shun's court. Everyone placed his own needs before those of Emperor Hsien Feng and his son. Everyone had heard Tung Chih, but no one offered to help.

If His Majesty desired to say something to his son, he could only wish for Su Shun's mercy. It was too convenient for Su Shun to ignore the Emperor and get away with his crime. If Hsien Feng was angry, no one would know. In a few minutes, whatever regrets he might have would accompany him to the grave.

I had no more fear. I measured the distance between Chief Eunuch Shim and myself and aimed for his stomach. My eyes focused on the crane on his robe. I didn't care if I became injured or worse. The story would go out. It would be my protest against Su Shun's bullying. Tung Chih would gain sympathy from the nation.

Using my head as a battering ram, I charged.

Instead of ducking, Shim shoved and yanked me away.

Losing my balance, I was unable to stop and was headed straight toward a side column.

I shut my eyes and thought that I was finished.

But my head didn't crack. It wasn't a column that I hit; it was a man in an armored uniform.

As I collapsed in a pile on the floor, I saw my son running toward his father. When I looked up to see whom I had collided with, the face that greeted me was that of the commander of the Imperial Guards, Yung Lu.

"Papa, Papa!" The son shook his father.

Emperor Hsien Feng was half sitting, half lying on his bed, staring at the ceiling.

Nuharoo came and put her arms around Tung Chih.

I picked myself up and rushed to the boy's side. Enraged, Su Shun pushed him back before he could touch his father again.

The child yanked his arm out of Su Shun's grip and set himself free. "Papa! Papa!"

Emperor Hsien Feng's eyes blinked. Slowly, his lips moved. "Tung Chih, my son . . ."

The court quieted and drew its breath. The Imperial secretary picked up his brush pen.

"Come to me, Tung Chih!" The dying man's arms reached out from under the coverlet.

"Your Majesty." I stepped up, taking the chance that I might be punished. "Would you let the court know your successor?"

It was too late for Su Shun to order my removal. Hsien Feng appeared to have heard me. He tried to speak, but there was no voice. After he struggled for a while, his arms dropped. His eyeballs rolled back into his skull, and he began to gasp for air.

"Your Majesty!" I fell to my knees by his side. My hands gripped his yellow satin sheet. "Pity your son, please!"

The Emperor's mouth opened.

"Papa! Papa! Please wake up!"

I stopped Tung Chih from shaking his father.

Hsien Feng opened his eyes again. Suddenly, he pushed himself and sat up. A second later he crashed back into his pillows and his eyes shut.

"Leave your son with no words, Hsien Feng!" Thinking this was the end, I felt that all my hopes had died. I no longer cared what I said. "Here is your heavenly damned son. Just leave him! Go your way and see us destroyed! I'll take it as my fate if this is what you want. Tung Chih deserves you. You are an unmerciful father."

Weeping, Tung Chih buried his face in his father's chest.

"Tung Chih." Hsien Feng opened his eyes again. His voice, though weak, was clear. "My son . . . let me . . . look at you. How are you? What can I get you?"

"Your Majesty," I said, "will Tung Chih succeed you to the throne?"

Hsien Feng smiled affectionately. "Yes, of course, Tung Chih will succeed me to the throne."

"Have you the title for his reign?"

"*Ch'i Hsiang,*" His Majesty said with the last thread of his breath.

"Well-Omened Happiness," the Imperial secretary said as he wrote the words down.

Many have said that my initiative at that moment embodied an important principle: for a woman in the Manchu court, survival required audacity. They were right.

Soon after Doctor Sun Pao-tien pronounced His Majesty's death, Nuharoo and I retreated from the hall. We went to the dressing room and removed our makeup. I was so shaky that my hands wouldn't hold the washcloth. I wept when recalling Hsien Feng's final words. The effort he made to deliver them showed that love must have been in his heart.

When Nuharoo and I returned we were dressed in coarse white sackcloth and our hair was wrapped in strips of white cloth. Our changed appearance signaled to all that our nation had entered the first stage of mourning for its Emperor.

Su Shun immediately requested a meeting with Nuharoo and me. It was no use when we said that we preferred to wait until our agitation had subsided. Su Shun insisted that he had to fulfill a promise he had made to our husband.

In the dressing room I had discussed with Nuharoo how we should deal with Su Shun. She had been distraught and told me that she could not think at this point. I knew Su Shun was ready. He would take advantage of the coming confusion to assert control over the court. We were in danger of being swept aside.

When he walked up to me, I spoke plainly and suggested that before anything else we open His Majesty's will box.

Accustomed only to compliance from women, Su Shun was at a loss for words.

The court agreed with me.

It was close to midnight when the box was opened. Grand Secretary Kuei Liang read the will. It was as confusing as His Majesty's manner of living. Besides naming Tung Chih as the new Emperor, he had established a Board of Regents, to be led by Su Shun, to administer the government until Tung Chih came of age. As if lacking confidence in his own decision, or intending to curb the regents' power, or merely to set up the board as an orthodox regency, Emperor Hsien Feng entrusted Nuharoo and me with a pair of important seals: *tungtiao,* "a partnership," and *yushang,* "Imperial will reflected." We were given the power to validate Su Shun's edicts drafted in Tung Chih's voice. Nuharoo was to stamp the *tungtiao* seal at the beginning and I the *yushang* at the end.

Su Shun's frustration was apparent. With Hsien Feng's seals in our hands a chain had been put around his neck. Later Su Shun would do everything to ignore the restraint.

What I didn't expect was that Hsien Feng had excluded all of his brothers, including Prince Kung, from power. This violated historical precedent and horrified the scholars and clansmen. They sat in the corner of the hall, visibly upset as they listened to the will.

I suspected that this was the work of Su Shun. According to Chow Tee, Su Shun had mentioned to His Majesty that Prince Kung was wasting his time dealing with foreigners. Evidently, Su Shun convinced His Majesty that Kung had sold his soul to the barbarians. The evidence offered was that the prince had employed foreigners to train his own personnel in all areas of the Chinese government, including the military and finance. Su Shun showed His Majesty Prince Kung's reform plan, which was intended to move China's political system toward Western models of governing.

On the evening of August 22, 1861, Jehol was soaked in mist. The branches outside the Hall of Fantastic Haze beat against the window panels, making disturbing noises.

Tung Chih had fallen asleep in my arms. He didn't wake up when Doctor Sun Pao-tien removed him so Nuharoo and I could wash our husband's face with wet silk towels. We touched Hsien Feng gently. He looked relieved in death.

"It is time to dress His Majesty," Chief Eunuch Shim said. "Better to do it now, before His Majesty's body hardens."

The eunuchs came with the eternal robe and we bowed to our husband and then retreated.

An-te-hai carried the sleeping Tung Chih as we walked out of the Hall of Fantastic Haze.

I wept, thinking how terrible it was that Hsien Feng had died at such a young age.

Nuharoo interrupted my thoughts. "You shouldn't have intruded. You made a fool of me in front of His Majesty."

"I am sorry. I didn't mean to," I said.

"You embarrassed me by not trusting that I would take care of the matter."

"Tung Chih needed to hear his father's words, and there was no time."

"If anyone should speak for Tung Chih, it should be me. Your action was at the very least thoughtless, Lady Yehonala!"

I was irritated but chose not to say anything. I knew I would need Nuharoo to win the war against Su Shun.

I held my son when I went to bed. It must have been hard for Su Shun to live with the fact that I was not only exempt from being buried alive but also granted the power to bar him from his ambition.

I was exhausted but couldn't relax. My sorrow for Hsien Feng had begun to wash over me. Concern for the safety of my son cut through my melancholy. I recalled Yung Lu's unannounced rescue. Had he been watching over Tung Chih and me? I must not forget that Su Shun was his superior. Was Yung Lu a part of Su Shun's conspiracy?

Lying in bed, I went over the list of regents one by one. The men's faces were clear in my mind. Aside from Su Shun, they were scholars who had earned the highest academic degrees and ministers who had served long in the court, including Tuan Hua, Su Shun's half-brother, and Prince Yee, a bully who was a first cousin of Emperor Hsien Feng and also the Imperial commissioner. If I knew little of their accomplishments, I knew enough to realize that they were as power-hungry and dangerous as Su Shun.

I examined Prince Yee's record particularly. He was the only relative to whom Hsien Feng had entrusted power. Su Shun must have whispered into the Emperor's ear, but why? Prince Yee's Imperial blood, I thought. Su Shun needed Yee to mask his evil intentions.

The next day, the regents, whom Nuharoo called the "Gang of Eight," visited the two of us. It was plain that Su Shun held the keys to the gang's thinking. At the reception, business was avoided. It seemed that Tung Chih's schooling and care were enough responsibility for us. The gang proposed to lift our burden by sparing us from the court's affairs, to which Nuharoo foolishly expressed appreciation.

Su Shun was the last to arrive. He said that he had been extremely busy with events on the frontier. I asked if he had heard anything from Prince Kung. He replied in the negative. He was lying. An-te-hai had reported that Prince Kung had sent four urgent documents for approval, none of which received attention.

I confronted Su Shun regarding the documents. He first denied having ever received them. Upon my suggestion that we summon Prince Kung, he admitted that the documents had been misplaced somewhere in his office. He asked me not to bother with matters I had nothing to do with. He emphasized that my interest in the court's business was "an act of disrespect to the deceased Emperor."

I reminded Su Shun that no edicts would be valid without the two seals Nuharoo and I possessed. Whether Prince Kung's requests were granted, denied or held, Nuharoo and I must be informed. I hinted to Su Shun that I was aware of what he had been doing: promoting and demoting provincial governors on his own.

As the days passed, the tension between Su Shun and me grew so intense that we had to avoid each other. I understood only too clearly that this was no way to run the nation. Su Shun had created and spread every rumor he could to paint an evil portrait of me. To isolate me, he tried to win over Nuharoo, and I could see it working. I was frustrated, because I couldn't convince Nuharoo of Su Shun's intentions.

Around this time, I noticed that I had been shedding hair. One day An-te-hai picked up some from the floor after the hairdresser had gone, and I became alarmed. Was this a symptom of some disease?

I hadn't trimmed my hair since entering the Forbidden City, and it was knee-length now. Every morning the hairdresser came, and no matter how hard he brushed, my hair had never fallen out. Now his brush filled with bunches of it, as if he were carding wool. I never considered myself vain, but if this continued, I told myself, I would be bald before long.

An-te-hai suggested that I change hairdressers, and he recommended a talented young eunuch he'd heard about, Li Lien-ying. Li's original name was Fourteen — his parents had so many children, they gave up on more traditional names. The name Li Lien-ying, meaning "a fine lotus leaf," was given to him by a Buddhist after he was castrated. Buddhists believed that the lotus leaf was the seat of Kuan Ying, the goddess of mercy, who was originally a man but took the form of a woman. Kuan Ying was a favorite of mine, so I was inclined to like Li Lien-ying from the start.

I ended up keeping him. Like An-te-hai, Li was cheerful and kept his misery to himself. Unlike An-te-hai, he was scrawny and not handsome. He had a squash-shaped face, bumpy skin, goldfish eyes, a flat nose and sloped mouth. At first I couldn't tell whether he was smiling or frowning. Despite his unlovely appearance, his sweetness won my heart.

An-te-hai loved to watch Li Lien-ying do my hair. Li knew an incredible number of styles: the goose tail, the tipping bird, the wheeling snake, the climbing vine. When he brushed, his hands were at once firm and gentle. Amazingly enough, I never found hair on the floor after he was through. He had worked wonders. I told An-te-hai I would take him on as an apprentice. An-te-hai taught him proper manners, and Li Lien-ying proved to be a fast learner.

Many years later, Li confessed that he had fooled me. "I hid Your Majesty's lost hair inside my sleeves," he said. He did not feel guilty, though; it was for my own good that he'd been deceitful. He thought that my hair loss was due to the stresses of my life and believed that I would heal in time. He was right. He was too young then to understand the risk he took in lying to me. "You could have been beheaded if I found out," I said. He nodded and smiled. As it turned out, Li Lien-ying became my lifelong favorite after An-te-hai, and he served me for forty-some years.

Twenty

A MESSAGE CAME from Prince Kung asking for permission to be in Jehol for the mourning ceremony. According to tradition, Prince Kung had to make an official request and the throne had to approve it. Although Kung was Tung Chih's uncle, he was by rank a subordinate. The boy had become Emperor, and Prince Kung was his minister. To my astonishment, Prince Kung's request was denied.

Household law forbade Hsien Feng's widows to meet any male relative during the mourning period. Obviously Su Shun was behind this. He must have feared that his own power would be threatened.

Nuharoo and I were practically imprisoned in our quarters. I was not even allowed to take Tung Chih to visit the hot spring. Whenever I did step out, Chief Eunuch Shim followed. I felt that Prince Kung needed to know how things were going.

But Prince Kung simply withdrew his request. He had no choice but to do so. If he insisted on coming, Su Shun had the right to punish him for disobeying the Emperor's will.

Nevertheless, I was disappointed that Prince Kung gave in so easily. I wouldn't know until later that he sought another path. Like me, he viewed Su Shun as a danger. His feelings were shared and supported by many—clansmen, Imperial loyalists, reformers, scholars and students —who would rather see power in the hands of the liberal-minded Prince Kung than Su Shun.

. . .

Tung Chih expressed little interest when I told him stories of his ancestors. He couldn't wait to finish a lesson so that he could be with Nuharoo, which made me jealous. I was becoming a tougher mother after his father's death. Tung Chih couldn't read a map of China, couldn't even remember the names of most provinces. He was already a ruler, but his biggest interests were eating sugar-coated berries and fooling around. He had no idea what the real world was like and didn't care to learn. Why should he when he was constantly made to feel that he was on top of the universe?

To the public, I promoted my five-year-old son as a genius who would lead the nation out of troubled waters. I had to do so in order to survive. The more people trusted the Emperor, the more stable the society. Hope was our currency. Behind closed doors, however, I pushed Tung Chih to live up to his role. He needed to rule on his own as soon as possible because Su Shun's power would only continue to grow.

I tried to teach him how to conduct an audience, how to listen, what kinds of questions to ask, and most important, how to make decisions based on collective opinions, criticisms and ideas.

"You must learn from your advisors and ministers," I warned, "because you are not —"

"Who I think I am." Tung Chih cut at me. "In your eyes, I'm as good as a wet fart."

I didn't know whether to laugh or slap his face. I did neither.

"Why do you never say 'Yes, Your Majesty' like everyone else?" my son asked.

I noticed that he had stopped calling me Mother. When he had to address me, he called me *Huang-ah-pa,* a formal name meaning "Imperial Mother." But he called Nuharoo Mother, in a voice that was full of warmth and affection.

If Tung Chih had accepted my rules, I would have swallowed the insult, because all I desired was for him to be a fit ruler. He could interpret my intentions any way he wanted. My feelings would not be hurt even if he hated me at the beginning. I believed that he would thank me in the future.

But I underestimated the power of the environment. It was as if he were a piece of clay that had been molded and baked before I could touch it. Tung Chih scored poorly on his exams, and he had trouble concentrating. When his tutor shut him inside the library, he sent his eunuchs to Nuharoo, who came to his rescue. The tutor was punished instead of the student. When I protested, Nuharoo reminded me of my lower status.

An-te-hai was the one who pointed out that what was going on had nothing to do with being a parent. "You are dealing with the Emperor of China, not your child, my lady," he said. "It is the entire culture of the Forbidden City that you are up against."

I hated the idea of tricking my son. But when honesty failed, what choice did I have left?

When Tung Chih brought me his unfinished homework, I no longer criticized him. In an even voice I told him that as long as he felt that he had done his best, it would be fine with me. He was relieved and felt less compelled to lie. Gradually Tung Chih became willing to spend time with me. I played "audience," "court room" and "battles" with him. Carefully, quietly, I tried to influence him. The moment he detected my true motives, he ran away.

"There are people who try to make the Son of Heaven a fool," Tung Chih once said in the middle of a game.

Nuharoo and the master tutor Chih Ming wanted Tung Chih to learn the exclusive "Emperor's language." They also designed the lessons so that Tung Chih would focus on Chinese rhetoric and ancient Tang poetry and Sung verses, "so he can speak elegantly." When I opposed the idea and wanted to add science, math and basic military strategy, they were upset.

"It is considered prestigious to own a language," Master Chih Ming explained with passion. "Only an emperor can afford it, and that is the point."

"Why do you want to deprive our child?" Nuharoo asked me. "Hasn't Tung Chih, as the Son of Heaven, been deprived enough?"

"It is a waste of time to learn a language that he can't use to communicate," I argued. "Tung Chih must be presented immediately with the truth about China! I am not concerned about how well he dresses, eats or says *Zhen* instead of *I*." I suggested that Prince Kung's letters and the drafts of treaties be Tung Chih's texts. "The foreign troops will not leave China on their own accord. Tung Chih has to drive them out."

"It is a terrible idea to do that to a child." Nuharoo shook her head, making all the ornamental bells on her hair ring. "Tung Chih will be so frightened that he will never want to rule."

"That's why we are here to support him," I said. "We work with him, so that he will learn the art of war by fighting the war."

Nuharoo gave me a hard stare. "Yehonala, you are not asking me to disobey the rules and to ignore our ancestors' teachings, are you?"

I was heartbroken when I saw how my son was being taught to misread reality. He couldn't distinguish fact from fantasy. The false notions packed into his little brain made him vulnerable. He believed that he could tell the sky when to rain and the sun when to shine.

Against Master Chih Ming's advice, Nuharoo's repeated interference and Tung Chih's own inclination, I forced my way with my son, which drove him farther from me. I believed that this was of the utmost importance. In our "court" games Tung Chih played the Emperor and I his wicked minister. I mimicked Su Shun without using his name. I even took up Su Shun's northern accent. I wanted to teach Tung Chih not to be intimidated by the enemy.

When the lessons were over, there was never a thank-you or a goodbye. When I opened my arms and said "I love you, son," he brushed me away.

The ceremony marking Tung Chih's official ascent to the throne began when Hsien Feng's body was placed in its coffin. A decree was issued within the court to proclaim the new era, and Tung Chih was expected to issue a decree in honor of his mothers. As usual we received a lot of useless tributes and gifts.

I was aware that Su Shun had drafted this honor. But I was forbidden to learn what was written until the decree was announced. I was tense and nervous, but there was nothing I could do.

When the decree was announced, Nuharoo was honored as "the Empress of Great Benevolence Tzu An" and I as "the Empress of Holy Kindness Tzu Hsi." To anyone who knew the subtleties of Chinese, the difference was obvious: "great benevolence" was more powerful than "holy kindness." We may have both been honored as empresses of the same rank, but the message to the nation was that my position was not equal to Nuharoo's.

The emphasis on her prestige over mine pleased Nuharoo. Although she had been the appointed Empress during Hsien Feng's reign, that didn't guarantee that she would hold the same title when the era changed. After all, I was the mother of the heir. The liability of my new title was that the nation was led to believe that Tung Chih considered Nuharoo above me — Su Shun got his way.

More alarming to me was that Su Shun had issued a decree again without obtaining both Nuharoo's and my signature seals. Nuharoo didn't want to raise the issue since she had what she desired. But to me this was a violation of principle—Su Shun was failing to properly execute Emperor Hsien Feng's will. I had every right to challenge the decree. However, if I fought, it would give Su Shun a chance to damage my relationship with Nuharoo.

I contemplated the situation and decided to stay where I was.

After the announcement of the honor, Nuharoo and I were to be treated equally. I moved from my quarters to the west wing of the Hall of Fantastic Haze, called the Western Chamber of Warmth, which prompted the ministers to call me the Empress of the Western Chamber. Nuharoo moved to the Eastern Chamber of Warmth, and thus she was known as the Empress of the Eastern Chamber.

On September 2, 1861, the first official decree was formally published. It announced the new era to the nation and the boy Emperor's coming. The decree included the new Emperor's honors to his mothers. The nation was given a ten-day holiday to celebrate.

As the country learned about Nuharoo and me, Su Shun convened the Board of Regents for an audience of his own. He demanded that from now on Nuharoo and I must stamp the decrees that he drafted, without question.

This time Su Shun also offended Nuharoo. An argument flared while Tung Chih and the entire court were present.

"Females stay out of the court's business; that is the Imperial tradition." Su Shun emphasized that it was for the country's benefit that his administration bypass us. He created the impression that Nuharoo and I were responsible for slowing down the court's procedures and that I, especially, was a troublemaker.

"If we are not to take part in the court's business," Nuharoo said to the audience, "then why did His Majesty Emperor Hsien Feng bother to place the seals in our hands?"

Before Su Shun got a chance to respond, I echoed Nuharoo. "Emperor Hsien Feng's purpose was more than clear. The two grand seals represent a balanced judgment. His Majesty wanted us to work side by side. The seals are to prevent autocracy and"—I raised my voice, speaking as clearly as I could—"to avoid the possible tyranny of any single regent. The eight of you are wise men, so I don't have to remind you of those terrible lessons of the past. I am sure none of you wants to model yourself after Ao Pai, who went down in history as a villain because he allowed his desire for power to corrupt his soul." I glanced at Su Shun before concluding, "Empress Nuharoo and I have decided that as long as we live, we will honor our commitment to our husband."

Before the last word came out of my mouth, Su Shun stood up. His olive complexion had flushed a deep red. His eyes revealed great anger. "Originally I didn't want to expose my private conversations with His Late Majesty, but you have left me with no choice, Lady Yehonala." Su Shun walked toward his men and spoke loudly. "Emperor Hsien Feng had already seen through Lady Yehonala's wickedness when he was alive. Several times he spoke with me about taking her with him. If she hadn't taken advantage of His Majesty's illness and manipulated him into changing his mind, we would be able to do our job today."

"His Majesty should have insisted!" The Gang of Eight nodded.

I was so furious I couldn't speak. I tried hard to hold in my tears.

Su Shun continued, his chest heaving. "One of the ancient sages of China foretold that China would be destroyed by a woman. I hope we do not hasten the day."

Terrified by the expression on Su Shun's face, Tung Chih jumped up from the throne. He threw himself first at Nuharoo and then at me.

"What's wrong?" Tung Chih asked when he noticed that my arm was trembling. "Are you all right?"

"Yes, my son," I said. "I am fine."

But Tung Chih started to cry. I rubbed his back to calm him. I didn't want to give my son and the court the impression that I was weak.

"Allow me to share my thoughts with you, gentlemen," I said, composing myself. "Before forming your judgment—"

"Stop!" Su Shun interrupted me and turned to the court. "Lady Yehonala has just violated a house rule."

I realized where Su Shun was heading. He was using a family rule against me. "Rule one hundred and seventy-four reads: 'A lower-rank Imperial wife will be punished if she speaks without the permission of the higher-ranking wife.'" Glancing at Nuharoo, who stared blankly, Su Shun went on. "I am afraid that I must perform my duty." He snapped his fingers. "Guards!"

Led by Chief Eunuch Shim, several guards rushed in.

"Seize the Empress of Holy Kindness and take her away for punishment!"

"Nuharoo, my elder sister!" I cried, hoping that she would come forward. All she had to do was to say that I had her permission to speak.

But Nuharoo was confused. She stared as if she didn't understand what was happening.

The guards grabbed my arms and began to drag me away.

"Heaven above," Su Shun said, beseeching in Peking-opera style, "help us get rid of an evil fox who has confirmed our ancestors' worst predictions."

"Nuharoo!" I struggled to push the guards away. "Tell them I had your permission to speak. Tell them I am the Empress and they can't treat me like this. Please, Nuharoo!"

Su Shun walked up to Nuharoo, who was frozen in place. He bent down and whispered in her ear. His hands drew circles in the air. His broad frame blocked her view of me. I was sure what he was saying: the faster I was hanged, the better her life would be. He was describing a life for her without rivals. A life where only her words ruled. Nuharoo was too frightened to think. I knew she didn't trust Su Shun, but she might not be able to resist his vision of her future.

The guards dragged me through the hallway. Everyone seemed caught up in the moment. If there were questions, nobody asked. I was lost in the crack of time, and I knew I would vanish before people could come to their senses.

I struggled to free myself from the guards. First my arms went limp, then my legs. As my body was tossed to the floor, my dress tore and my hairpins fell out.

"Halt!" A child's voice pierced the air. "This is Emperor Tung Chih speaking."

I was sure that I was hallucinating. My son stepped to the center of the room like a mature man. His manner reminded me of his father.

"Lady Yehonala has no less right to speak in this court than you, Su Shun," my child said. "I shall order the guards to remove you if you cannot mend your behavior!"

In awe of the Son of Heaven, Chief Eunuch Shim dropped to his knees. The guards followed, and then the court, including Nuharoo and me.

The place grew as silent as a still pond. The clocks on the walls started to chime. For a long time no one dared move. The sun's rays shot through the curtains, turning the tapestry into gold.

Standing tall by himself, Tung Chih didn't know what to say next.

"Rise," the child finally uttered, as if remembering a forgotten phrase from his lessons.

The crowd rose.

"I am resigning, Your Young Majesty!" Su Shun was himself again. He took his peacock-feathered hat off and placed it on the floor in front of him. "Who will follow me?" He began to walk out of the hall.

The rest of the members of the Regency looked at one another. They stared at Su Shun's hat as if seeing its decorative jewels and feathers for the first time.

Prince Yee, Emperor Hsien Feng's first cousin, made his move. He chased after Su Shun, yelling, "Grand Councilor, please! There is no point in lowering yourself to a child's whim."

The moment the words came out of his mouth, Prince Yee realized that he had made a mistake.

"What did you say?" Tung Chih stamped his feet. "You have insulted the Son of Heaven, and *Zhen* here orders your beheading! Guards! *Guards!*"

At Tung Chih's words Prince Yee threw himself down and knocked his head hard on the floor. "I beg Your Majesty's forgiveness, for I am your father's cousin and a blood relation."

Looking at the man on the floor with a bleeding forehead, Tung Chih turned to Nuharoo and me.

"Rise, Prince Yee." As if she finally found her place, Nuharoo spoke. "His Majesty shall forgive you this time, but he will not allow rudeness in the future. I trust that you have learned your lesson. Young as Tung Chih is, he is still the Emperor of China. You should always remember that you are his servant."

The members of the Regency retreated. As soon as Nuharoo had Su Shun's "forgotten" hat returned to him, the grand councilor got back to work. Not a word was spoken about the incident.

The body of Emperor Hsien Feng had been scheduled to be taken from Jehol to Peking for burial. The rehearsals for the moving ceremony were exhausting. During the day, Nuharoo and I dressed in white robes and practiced our steps in the courtyard. In our hair we wore baskets of white flowers. We made countless inspections: from the costumes worn by the paper gods to the decorative accessories for the horses; from the ropes that would tie down the coffin to the coffin bearers themselves; from the ceremonial flags to the selection of mourning music. We examined the wax pigs, cotton dolls, clay monkeys, porcelain lambs, wooden tigers and bamboo kites. In the evenings we inspected the leather silhouette figures that would be used in theatricals.

Tung Chih was drilled to perform the son's duty. He practiced his walks, bows and kowtows in front of an audience of five thousand. During breaks, he sneaked out to watch the marching of the Imperial Guards, commanded by Yung Lu. Every night Tung Chih came to me describing his admiration for Yung Lu.

"Would you come with me next time?" he asked.

I was tempted, but Nuharoo turned Tung Chih down. "It would be improper for us to appear in our mourning gowns," she said.

After dessert Nuharoo excused herself to chant. She had been drawn more deeply into Buddhism since Hsien Feng's death. Her walls were covered with tapestries of Buddha figures. If it had been permitted, she would have ordered the construction of a giant Buddha in the middle of the audience hall.

I was full of unrest. One night in a dream I turned into a bee, trapped inside a forming lotus heart. With my every struggle the lotus seeds popped like little nipples. I woke and found that An-te-hai had placed a bowl of lotus-seed soup in front of me and that my vase had been filled with freshly picked lotus flowers.

"How did you know my dream?" I asked the eunuch.

"I just know."

"Why all the lotuses?"

An-te-hai glanced at me and smiled. "It matches the color of Your Majesty's face."

The feelings I had been experiencing had only deepened. I could no longer deny to myself that they found their focus in the figure of Yung Lu. Listening to the news brought by Tung Chih excited me. My heart skipped when Yung Lu's name was mentioned. I found myself hungry for details as Tung Chih described Yung Lu's mastery of horses.

"You watched him from a distance?" I asked my son.

"I ordered a demonstration," he replied. "The commander was happy when I commended him. Oh, Mother, you should have seen his way with the horses!"

I tried not to ask Tung Chih too much—I was afraid of arousing Nuharoo's suspicion. To her, even thinking about any male other than our dead husband was a sign of disloyalty. Nuharoo made it clear to the Imperial widows that she wouldn't hesitate to order their execution—by dismemberment—if she discovered an infidelity.

An-te-hai slept in my room and was a witness to my restlessness. But he never brought the subject up or mentioned any of my utterances that he might have heard. I knew that I often tossed and turned at night, especially when it rained.

On one such rainy night, I asked An-te-hai if he had noticed any changes in me. Carefully, the eunuch described my body's midnight "uprisings." He reported that I had cried out in my dreams, begging to be touched.

· · ·

Winter came early. The September mornings were chilly and the air was fresh and clear. With the maples just starting to turn, I decided on a walk that would take me by Yung Lu's training ground. The more I warned myself of the impropriety, the more my desire pushed me forward. In order to disguise the intent of my outing, the night before I told Tung Chih that there was a rabbit with red eyes that I would like to take him to see. Tung Chih asked where it was hidden. I answered, "In the bushes not far from the training ground."

The next day we rose before dawn. After breakfast we set off in palanquins, passing the flame-colored trees. The moment we saw Yung Lu's guards, Tung Chih took off and I followed.

The path was bumpy, and the bearers tried their best to steady the palanquin. I lifted the curtain and looked out. My heartbeat quickened.

An-te-hai followed by my side. His expression told me that he knew my purpose and that he was curious and excited. It touched me with sadness to see that An-te-hai still thought a man's thoughts. Indeed, if appearance was the measure, women would think An-te-hai more attractive than Yung Lu. My eunuch had a full forehead and a perfect jaw and his eyes were large and bright, which was unusual for a Manchu. Highly trained in court manners, he always carried himself gracefully. Turning twenty-four the week before, An-te-hai had been with me for more than eight years. Unlike many eunuchs who sounded like old ladies, he spoke in a masculine voice. I wasn't sure if An-te-hai still had a male's bodily needs, but he was a sensuous being. As our time together lengthened, I was more and more struck by the curiosity he showed about what went on between a man and a woman. It would become An-te-hai's curse.

In the morning fog I watched the Imperial Guards being drilled. Hundreds trotted and marched over packed dirt. They reminded me of hopping toads in a rice field during a drought. The air was crisp and the sun was yet to fully rise.

"Watch out for Tung Chih," I told the bearers, and asked to be let out of the palanquin. My shoes collected dew as I slowly walked along a side path. Then I saw him, the commander, on his mount. I took a moment to compose myself.

He sat unmoving on the horse but stared in my direction. The fog between us made him look like a paper-cutout warrior.

I approached him with An-te-hai by my side.

The warrior tapped the animal's flank, and it cantered toward me. I gazed at him under the shadows cast by the rising sun.

The moment he recognized me, he slipped off the horse and threw himself on the ground. "Your Majesty, Yung Lu at your service."

I knew that I was supposed to say "Rise," but my tongue faltered. I nodded and An-te-hai interpreted: "You may rise."

The man in front of me stood. He was taller than I remembered. The sunlight sculpted his figure and his face looked like a hatchet.

I didn't know what to say. "Tung Chih wanted to visit the woods," I said after a pause, and then added, "He is chasing a rabbit."

"That is very nice," he said, and then he too ran out of words.

I glanced at his men. "How . . . are your troops doing?"

"Almost ready." He was relieved to find a topic.

"What are you trying to achieve exactly?"

"I am working to build my men's endurance. At present they are capable of staying in formation for about half a day, but the parade with the coffin will last fifteen days."

"May I trust that you are not overworking your men or yourself?" I said. Immediately I caught the softness in my tone. I realized that I had just asked a question, which etiquette forbade.

He seemed to be aware of it. He looked at me and then quickly looked away.

I wished that I could dismiss An-te-hai, but that would not be wise. Being seen alone with Yung Lu would be dangerous.

"May I have Your Majesty's permission to check up on Tung Chih?" An-te-hai asked, reading my mind.

"No, you may not."

Tung Chih was disappointed: he hadn't found the rabbit. When we returned to the palace, I promised to have a wooden one made for him. An-te-hai explained my idea to the court's best craftsman. The man asked for five days to produce the rabbit. Tung Chih waited eagerly.

On the evening of the fourth day, a fantastically crafted wooden rabbit with white "fur" was presented to Tung Chih. The moment my son saw it, he fell in love. From then on he no longer touched any other toys, no matter how fancy they were. The wooden rabbit had the cutest red eyes of chiseled rubies. Its fur was made of cotton and silk. The best part was that the rabbit had movable legs with a string winder. When Tung Chih placed the rabbit on the floor it could hop like a real one.

For the next few days Tung Chih was completely occupied by the rabbit. I was able to work with Nuharoo on the court documents delivered by Su Shun. My floor was piled with papers and I had no space to move around.

Nuharoo soon resented coming to work with me. She began to make excuses for not showing up. She wanted us to abide by the ancient Chinese philosophy that "the wisest man should appear the most confused." She believed that if we did so, Su Shun would leave us alone: "Fool and disarm him without using a weapon." She smiled, charmed by her own words.

I did not understand Nuharoo's fantasy. We might fool others, but not Su Shun. For me it was harder to deal with Nuharoo than with my son. When she was tired, her temper tantrums rose. She complained about everything—the noise of crickets, the taste of her soup, a dropped stitch in her embroidery. She would insist that I help her fix the problem. I couldn't help but be affected, and I had to quit working. Finally, I agreed to spare her under one condition—that she read my briefs and place her seal on all the outgoing documents, which I would draft in the name of Tung Chih and stamp with my own seal.

Each evening An-te-hai prepared a pot of strong Black Dragon tea as I labored into the night. By loading me down with work, Su Shun set out to discredit me in the eyes of the court. I had volunteered to put my neck in the noose, and now he was busy tying the knot. He didn't know me. I wanted to succeed for a very practical reason—to be fit to assist my son. But I had miscalculated. While I was busy shoring up one flank, I left another exposed. I had no idea that the Imperial tutors who were responsible for Tung Chih's education were Su Shun's friends. My innocent neglect proved to be one of my biggest mistakes. I didn't realize the damage being done to Tung Chih until it was too late.

At this point I was desperate to broaden my perspective. I lacked confidence and felt myself poorly informed. The subjects of the papers were vast. To grasp any understanding seemed like trying to climb a greased pole. Since I felt strongly about the role played by the government, I was determined to cut through the corruption around me. I tried to see the basic outlines of things, their true skeleton, and to evaluate everything on merit alone. I also concentrated on becoming familiar with those who had the power to control and influence. Besides reading their reports, I studied their characters, their backgrounds, and their relationships with their peers and with us. Of course I paid particular attention to their responses to our own queries and requests, most often delivered through Prince Kung. I had always loved opera, but what I was now engaged in on a daily basis was much more dramatic and bizarre.

I learned a lot about people. One document came from one of Prince Kung's employees, the Englishman Robert Hart, China's chief of customs. This man was my own age and a foreigner, but he was responsible for generating one third of our yearly revenue. Hart reported that he had recently met strong resistance when collecting domestic customs revenue. Many influential men, including my late husband's most trusted general, Tseng Kuo-fan—Head-Chopper Tseng, the hero who flattened the Taiping rebels—refused to part with their money. Tseng claimed that the needs of his immediate area required that he, not the central government, keep the taels. His account books had been found vague, and Hart sought instructions from the Emperor regarding whether to press charges against the general.

Su Shun proposed an action on the cover page of Hart's report. He wanted to have Tseng Kuo-fan investigated and charged. I was not fooled. For some time Su Shun had wished to replace Tseng with one of his loyalists.

I decided to hold on to the report until I could meet with Prince Kung and discuss the matter. Tseng was too important to the nation's stability, and if this was what he would cost me, I might have to close my eyes and pay the price. In a way, I would rather see Tseng Kuo-fan keep the money, knowing that he would use it to equip his army, which would end up protecting me, than see the money fall into Su Shun's hands and be spent on conspiracies against me.

The report left me with the impression that Tseng had offered Hart what amounted to a large bribe for his cooperation. But Hart had proven unshakable: he would not compromise his loyalty toward his employer, Prince Kung. What had made him stand so firm? What principles and values had he been raised with? I hadn't expected a foreigner to be loyal to our dynasty. This taught me a great lesson. I wanted to meet this man. If I could, I would have him introduced to Tung Chih.

My request to meet with Robert Hart was first delayed, then postponed, and then turned down. The court voted unanimously that it would be an insult to China if I "lowered" myself to meet with him. More than four decades would pass before we finally met. Then, I told the court that I wouldn't be able to die in peace if I didn't thank the man who had helped me hold the sky together.

The blood-colored wild chrysanthemums bloomed in madness. The plants hung over my fences and covered the ground of my courtyard.

Still shaken by the contents of a letter recently sent by Prince Kung, I was in no mood to appreciate the flowers. In his letter, the prince described his day. It was after he delivered the treaties signed by his dying brother, Emperor Hsien Feng.

"I was escorted to the Forbidden City by General Sheng Pao, who was no longer captive, and four hundred horsemen. I then took only twenty men and entered the main hall of the Board of Rites to meet with my counterpart, Lord Elgin." Through Prince Kung's choice of words I sensed his anger. "This was my first time entering the heavenly ground after the foreigners had assaulted it. Lord Elgin was three hours late. He entered with two thousand men in a display of pomp. He rode in a crimson palanquin borne by sixteen men, knowing that this privilege was reserved only for the Emperor of China. I made an effort to be gracious, although I was disgusted beyond description. I bowed slightly and shook Elgin's hands in the Chinese style. I struggled and succeeded in keeping my emotions from spilling."

I admired the wisdom of his concluding words, addressed to Su Shun and the court: "If we do not learn to restrain our rage but continue with hostilities, we are liable to sudden catastrophe. We must advise our people throughout the nation to act in accordance with the treaties and not allow the foreigners to go even slightly beyond them. In our external expression we should be sincere and amicable but quietly try to keep them in line. Then, within the next few years, even though they may occasionally make demands, they will not cause us a great calamity. Time is crucial to our recovery."

Again I felt that Tung Chih was blessed by having a level-headed uncle. Su Shun might increase his own popularity by challenging Prince Kung and calling him "the devil's slave," but what could be easier than sneering at someone? Prince Kung had a nasty but necessary job. His office was in a rundown Buddhist temple in northwestern Peking. It was a dirty, cheerless, barren space. His workload was excessive, and the outcome of his negotiations almost a foregone conclusion. It must have been unbearable. The numbers the foreigners demanded in indemnities and reparations were ridiculous, far in excess of any real damages and military costs. His days must have been worse than my own.

By the time I put the letter down I was so exhausted that I fell asleep instantly. In my dreams I set fire to every pile of documents in my room.

It was my weakness that I longed for a man's shoulder to lean on. I knew it and struggled against it, but my feelings kept surfacing. I sought distraction and buried myself in work. I asked An-te-hai to make stronger tea and chewed up the leaves after I drank. Finally I succeeded in clearing my floor of all the documents. I didn't know if the court's business had slowed because Su Shun couldn't keep up with me, or if he had changed his tactics and stopped sending me documents.

Without work to occupy my evenings, I became restless and irritable. There were other things I could have turned to — reading, writing a poem or painting. But I was simply unable to concentrate. I went to bed and stared at the ceiling. In the deep quiet of night Yung Lu's face and the way he moved on his horse passed back and forth before my eyes, and I wondered what it would be like to ride with him.

"Would you like a back rub, my lady?" An-te-hai whispered in the dark. His voice told me that he had been awake.

I said nothing and he was beside me. He knew that I wouldn't allow myself to say yes. But he also knew I had been in a kind of agony. Like a force of nature, my desire must follow its own path until sated and spent. My body was ready for release.

In silence, An-te-hai held me. Gently and slowly he touched my shoulders, my neck, my back. My body was comforted. He kept rubbing. His hands were everywhere. Soothing and dream-like, he breathed lines from a song into my ear:

> He came through luxuriant redwood
> Bamboo groves set among hills
> A temple half hidden in the green clouds
> Its entrance was a ruin

The void in my mind expanded. Plum flowers danced in the air like white feathers.

An-te-hai became more forceful the moment he discovered my arousal. He breathed deeply as if to smell my scent.

"I love you so much, my lady," the eunuch whispered again and again.

My eyes saw Yung Lu. He was taking me with him on his horse. Like an ancient Bannerman's wife, I clung to his waist amid the clattering pots and pans lashed to the saddle. The two of us moved in perfect rhythm. We traveled in an endless wilderness.

My body grew calm, like an ocean after a storm.

Without lighting a candle, An-te-hai removed himself from the bed.

A strand of wet hair had fallen on my face. I tasted my own sweat.

In the moonlight my eunuch prepared a basin of warm water. He bathed me tenderly with a towel. He did it smoothly as if he had been practicing this all his life.

I drifted into peaceful sleep.

Twenty-one

A COPY OF A DECREE written by Su Shun to Prince Kung in the name of Tung Chih was sent to me. The decree forbade Prince Kung to come to Jehol and was issued without Nuharoo's and my seals. On the surface, Prince Kung had been given the most honorable task—to guard the capital—but what the edict effectively accomplished was to prevent contact between him and us.

I went to Nuharoo and told her that we must get in touch with Prince Kung. There were decisions we couldn't make without first consulting him. Our lives were at stake, since Su Shun now ignored us openly. To prove my point, I read Nuharoo the second item in the decree, an order transferring several generals who were loyal to Su Shun from Peking to Jehol. "Does this tell you what is on Su Shun's mind?" I asked her.

Nuharoo nodded. Her spy had reported to her that Prince Kung had sent messengers to Jehol, but none of them had reached us.

The same morning my sister Rong brought me new information. Prince Ch'un had received an order from the court, issued by Su Shun: he was no longer allowed to travel freely between Jehol and Peking. This was why he was not here with his wife. Prince Ch'un was under Su Shun's close watch. Our only connection to Prince Kung had been cut off.

An-te-hai's "ears" in Peking reported that Prince Kung had been actively working to assemble a counterforce. Three days before, he had organized a meeting under the guise of a mourning ceremony for Emperor Hsien Feng. In addition to the leadership of the royal clansmen, Prince Kung had invited important military commanders such as General Sheng Pao, the Mongol warrior Seng-ko-lin-chin, and General Tseng Kuo-fan, who was now also the viceroy of Anhwei province. Prince Kung had also invited the foreign ambassadors of England, France, Germany, Russia, Italy and Japan. Robert Hart had initiated the idea of the meeting. For some time, Hart had been advising Prince Kung on financial matters; he had now stepped into the role of Kung's unofficial political advisor.

"I think we should wait," Nuharoo said to me. "We should allow Su Shun's evil to expose itself. We need time to prove to our citizens that Su Shun doesn't deserve our respect. On the other hand, we should not forget that it was Emperor Hsien Feng who appointed Su Shun. The situation might backfire if we act without the support of the court."

I tried to make Nuharoo see that this last decree severely limited Prince Kung's chances of survival. If Prince Kung ignored Su Shun and came to Jehol, he would be accused of disobeying the decree, and Su Shun would arrest him the moment he stepped through the gate. But if Kung remained in Peking, Su Shun would gain the time he needed to take the entire court into his hands. It was only obvious and natural that he would find an excuse to prosecute us.

"You are crazy, Lady Yehonala." Nuharoo said. "Su Shun has no legitimate reason to prosecute us."

"He can create one. If he is capable of issuing decrees on his own, he will not hesitate when the time comes to remove us. Then he will go after Prince Kung."

Nuharoo stood. "I must go to Hsien Feng's coffin and pray. His Majesty should be told about this so that his spirits will help us in Heaven."

The night guard beat his drum three times. It was three o'clock in the morning. The darkness was still deep. Lying in bed, I thought about what Nuharoo had said. Indeed, Su Shun was our husband's choice. Hsien Feng had trusted him. Was I wrong to doubt Su Shun? Would it help if I expressed my willingness to work with him regardless of our differences? After all, we were both Manchus. Weren't we trying to hold up the same sky?

I was unable to convince myself. Nuharoo and I were Tung Chih's acting regents, appointed by Emperor Hsien Feng. But Su Shun regarded us as nothing but figureheads. We had no say over the edicts and decrees. A few days before, he had even refused to revise a draft that we had given our permission to issue after a few small changes. Orders and requests from us in the voice of Tung Chih made their way through the court hierarchy and came back without a response, while Su Shun's words were carried immediately into action.

Nuharoo suggested that we make one last offer to work things out with Su Shun. I agreed.

The next morning, dressed in our official robes, Nuharoo and I summoned Su Shun for an audience in the name of the young Emperor. We went to the hall where Hsien Feng's coffin sat behind a panel. As we waited, Tung Chih climbed on top of the coffin and lay on his stomach.

I watched my son as he knocked on the coffin. He whispered to his father about his new friend, the red-eyed rabbit. He invited his father to come out and see it. "I will hold the lid up for you."

"Explain why the decree to Prince Kung was sent without our seals," Nuharoo demanded when Su Shun appeared.

Su Shun stood arrogantly in his full-length brown satin robe with gold stripes on the bottom. He was wearing a hat decorated with a red button and a flamboyant peacock feather. He took off the hat and held it in his hands. His head was shaved and his braid oiled. His chin was tilted so high that he was practically facing the ceiling. He looked at us with half-opened eyes. "The court has the right to issue documents of an urgent nature without your seals."

"But this violates our agreement," I said, trying to control my anger.

"As His Young Majesty's regents," Nuharoo followed, "we object to the content of the last decree. Prince Kung has a right to come to Jehol to mourn his brother."

"We would like to see Prince Kung get his wish," I pressed.

"Fine!" Su Shun stamped his foot. "If you want my job, it is yours. I refuse to work until you learn not to take my kindness for granted!"

He made a sloppy bow and walked out. In the courtyard the rest of his board members, whom we had not invited, received him.

The documents piled up, creating walls in my room. All requested immediate attention. Nuharoo regretted that we had challenged Su Shun.

I tried not to panic. I reviewed the documents as I had when working for Emperor Hsien Feng. I had to prove to Su Shun that I was equal to the job. I needed to earn the respect, not of Su Shun, but of the court.

As soon as I began to work, I realized that the task was more than I could handle. Su Shun had set me up.

Many of the cases were impossible to solve. Under the circumstances, it would be irresponsible to issue a judgment; only injustice and unnecessary pain would come of it. I lacked necessary information and was prevented from gathering it. In one case, a regional governor was accused of embezzlement and more than a dozen homicides. I needed to gather evidence and ordered an investigation, but I received no reports. Weeks later, I discovered that my order had never been acted on.

I called Su Shun and demanded an explanation.

He denied any responsibility and said that he wasn't the one in charge. He referred me to the justice ministry. When I questioned the head minister, he said he had never received the order.

Letters from all over the country had begun to complain about the slow workings of the court. It was clear that Su Shun had planted the seed in people's minds that I was the one holding everything back. The rumors spread like a contagious disease. I wasn't sure how bad things had become until one day I received an open letter from a small-town mayor questioning my background and credentials. There was no way the man would ever dare to send such a letter unless he was backed by someone like Su Shun.

As I paced back and forth in my document-cluttered room, An-te-hai returned from taking Tung Chih for a visit to my sister. He was so nervous that he stuttered. "The t-town of Jehol has been g-go-gossiping about a ghost story. The folks b-believe that you are the incarnation of an evil concubine who is here to destroy the empire. Talk of supporting Su Shun's action against you is everywhere."

Realizing that I couldn't afford to wait any longer, I went to Nuharoo.

"But how should we act?" Nuharoo asked.

"Issue an urgent decree in Tung Chih's name summoning Prince Kung to Jehol," I replied.

"Would it be valid?" Nuharoo became nervous. "Usually it is Su Shun who drafts orders and prepares edicts."

"With both of our seals it is valid."

"How would you get the decree to Prince Kung?"

"We must think of a way."

"With Su Shun's watchdogs everywhere, no one can get out of Jehol."

"We must select a reliable person for the mission," I said, "and he must be willing to die for us."

. . .

An-te-hai asked for the honor. In exchange, he wanted me to promise that he would be allowed to serve me for the rest of his life. I gave him my word. I made him understand that if he was caught by Su Shun, I expected him to swallow the decree and do everything to avoid making a confession.

With Nuharoo by my side, I worked on the details of An-te-hai's escape plan. My first step was to have An-te-hai spread a rumor among Su Shun's circle. We targeted a man named Liu Jen-shou, a notorious gossip. The story we spread was that we had lost the most powerful seal of all, the Hsien Feng seal, which we carefully hid away. We created an impression that we had been concealing the truth because we understood that the penalty for losing the seal was death. We concocted three possibilities regarding the seal's whereabouts. One, we had lost it on our way from Peking to Jehol; two, we had misplaced it somewhere in the Palace of Great Purity back in the Forbidden City; and three, we had left it with my jewelry boxes at Yuan Ming Yuan, which likely had been stolen by the barbarians.

Our rumor also said that Emperor Hsien Feng knew that the seal had been lost before he died, and he was too gentle-hearted to punish us. In order to protect us His Majesty hadn't mentioned the disappearance to Su Shun.

As we had expected, Liu Jen-shou took little time in passing the rumor to Su Shun's very ear. The story made sense to Su Shun, as no one could remember seeing the prized seal since leaving Peking.

Su Shun didn't wait to make his move. He immediately requested an audience with us, which was attended by the entire court. He declared that he had just finished drafting a new decree addressing the nation regarding the moving of the coffin, and he needed to use the Hsien Feng seal.

Pretending to be nervous, I took out my handkerchief and wiped my forehead. "Our double seals are as good as the Hsien Feng seal," I said in a small voice.

Su Shun was clearly pleased. The lines on his face danced and his veins stood out with excitement. "Where is the Hsien Feng seal?" he demanded.

With the excuse that I was suddenly feeling ill, Nuharoo and I requested that the audience be brought to an end.

Su Shun pressed onward. He kept at me until I confessed that An-te-hai had lost the seal.

An-te-hai was arrested and dragged out by the guards as he

screamed for forgiveness. He was taken out for punishment—one hundred lashes.

I was afraid that An-te-hai wouldn't be able to bear the suffering. Fortunately, the eunuch was meant to live—he truly had friends everywhere. Later, when he was brought back by Su Shun's guards, his robe was in shreds and matted with blood.

I was aware that Su Shun was observing me, so I not only made myself look unmoved, but also said in a cold voice, "The eunuch deserved it."

Water was poured over An-te-hai's face and he came to. In front of the court, Nuharoo and I ordered An-te-hai to be thrown into the Imperial prison in Peking.

Su Shun didn't want to let An-te-hai out of his sight, but Nuharoo and I insisted that we must rid ourselves of the ungrateful creature. When Su Shun protested, we argued that we had the right to punish our own house eunuch without restriction. We went to the back of the hall, to Hsien Feng's coffin, and wept loudly.

Pressed by the senior clansmen to leave us alone, Su Shun relented. But he insisted that his men escort An-te-hai to Peking.

We agreed, and An-te-hai was on his way. Hidden between layers of An-te-hai's shoes was the decree I had written.

In Peking, Su Shun's men turned An-te-hai over to the minister of Imperial justice, Pao Yun, along with Su Shun's secret message—I learned of this later—that An-te-hai be beaten to death. Unaware of the situation, Pao Yun prepared to carry out Su Shun's order. But before the whips went to work, An-te-hai requested a private moment with the minister.

An-te-hai took out my decree from its hiding place.

Pao Yun was dumbfounded. Without delay he contacted Prince Kung.

Upon reading my decree, Prince Kung gathered his advisors. They listened to An-te-hai's report on the situation in Jehol and discussed a course of action long into the night. The conclusion was unanimous: overthrow Su Shun.

Prince Kung understood that if he hesitated in helping Nuharoo and me, power could quickly fall into Su Shun's hands. There would be no recovering from such a loss, since he and Prince Ch'un had been excluded from Emperor Hsien Feng's will.

The first step Prince Kung took was to select someone to present his idea to the court in the most legal and logical way. Kung turned to the head of Imperial personnel. He asked the man to come up with a proposal suggesting that Nuharoo and I be named executive regents—the only regents—of Tung Chih, replacing Su Shun, and that we run the court with Prince Kung.

After the proposal had been completed, a trusted local official was chosen to submit it. The intent was to create the impression that the idea had come from the grassroots level, which would make it difficult for Su Shun to throw it out without a review. By using this method, the proposal would also make the rounds and be reviewed by every governor in China before it reached its final destination, Su Shun's office.

On September 25, draped from head to toe in the white cotton of mourning, Prince Kung arrived in Jehol. He headed directly to the coffin room, where he was blocked by guards and told to wait until Su Shun arrived. When Su Shun appeared—this was reported to me later —behind him stood the rest of the Gang of Eight.

Before Prince Kung had a chance to open his mouth, Su Shun ordered his arrest. The charge was disobeying the decree.

"I am here because a new decree has summoned me," Prince Kung calmly explained.

"Really? Present it, then." Su Shun smiled contemptuously.

"Without our drafting it, how could there be a decree?" one of the gang said.

From his inner pocket Prince Kung took out the decree An-te-hai had delivered.

The little yellow silk scroll with both Nuharoo's and my seals rattled Su Shun and his men. They must all have been silently asking one question: How did this get out?

Without another word, Prince Kung pushed through the gang and marched in.

At the sight of the coffin Prince Kung lost his composure. He banged his head on the ground and cried like a child. No one had seen anyone so heartbroken in front of the dead Emperor. Kung wailed that he couldn't understand why Hsien Feng had not given him a chance to say goodbye.

Tears streamed down his cheeks. He must have wished that his brother could see the mistake he had made. Prince Kung knew what Nuharoo and I did not, that Su Shun had already failed in his first attempt to overthrow Tung Chih on the day of his ascension. The grand councilor had sent Chiao Yu-yin, a member of the Gang of Eight, to contact General Sheng Pao and General Tseng Kuo-fan for military support. When Chiao accidentally leaked the information, Su Shun denied everything and secretly canceled the plot.

I caked my cheeks with powder and then slipped into a mourning gown. I noticed that Nuharoo's face had grown puffy. Her usually glowing skin had become a dull, dead white. Her tears had drawn two wiggly lines under her eyes.

We were ready to meet Prince Kung, but learned that he couldn't pass Chief Eunuch Shim, who quoted the household law that it was improper for Imperial widows to be seen by a prince of the same age during the time of mourning.

Prince Kung threw himself on the floor and begged Su Shun to be allowed to meet his nephew Tung Chih.

I suggested to Nuharoo that we go to the coffin room. We dressed Tung Chih and went there. Behind a wall panel we were able to hear the voices of Su Shun and Prince Kung. Su Shun insisted that he was acting on Emperor Hsien Feng's behalf.

The frustrated prince cursed. "The one who thinks of himself as having the wind at his back and moonlight in his sleeves is nothing but a mite-infested wooden puppet."

I worried about Prince Kung's temper. If he angered Su Shun further, Su Shun could accuse him of interfering with the execution of the Imperial will.

"This is about my birthright, Su Shun!" Prince Kung yelled.

Su Shun laughed. He knew his advantage and took his time. "No, this is not about what you are entitled to, Prince Kung. It is about the justification of the most powerful. Emperor Hsien Feng's will leaves the nation with the impression that you are a weak hen who produces soft-shelled eggs. I don't know what is lacking in you, but the defect is clear."

The court laughed with Su Shun. A few of the senior clansmen stamped their feet on the floor.

"Imagine the soft-shelled egg," Su Shun continued. "A yellow yolk wrapped in a paper-thin white shell. Oh, it is leaking. Can't sell it and can't keep it. We have to eat it as family members."

The laughter shot up to the ceiling.

"Su Shun." Prince Kung's voice was dangerously low. "I am not asking much. And I am asking for the last time. I want to see my sisters-in-law and my nephew."

"You are not going through that door."

I sensed that Prince Kung was running out of patience. I pictured him pushing Su Shun away. I grabbed Tung Chih and whispered in his ear.

"The Emperor invites his uncle . . ." My son repeated what I had instructed: "The Emperor invites his uncle Prince Kung to enter the Imperial coffin room. The Emperor also grants permission for Prince Kung to pay respects to Her Majesties the Empresses."

Upon hearing Tung Chih's voice, Li Lien-ying, my young eunuch, ran out. He threw himself on the floor between Prince Kung and Su Shun. "Your honored grand councilor, His Majesty Emperor Tung Chih has summoned Prince Kung!"

"Would any of the grand councilors like to accompany me to meet His Majesty and Her Majesties?" Prince Kung turned to Su Shun. "So you can make sure that everything we say or do is appropriate?"

Before Su Shun could respond, Prince Yee, who must have felt that it was his turn to speak, said, "Proceed, Prince Kung, you are the person His Majesty has summoned."

We lost our words when we saw each other's white gowns. Tung Chih threw himself at his uncle, who in turn got down on his knees and kowtowed. Watching them on the floor, Nuharoo and I cried freely.

"It has not been peaceful here," Nuharoo finally said. "We fear—"

I stopped her from speaking further. I hinted that Su Shun and his men were listening behind the wall.

Nuharoo nodded and sat back in her chair.

"Summon the monks," I said to Li Lien-ying.

Under the cover of the monks' chanting, Prince Kung and I exchanged information and discussed future plans. We plotted a counterattack against Su Shun while Nuharoo went off to keep Tung Chih entertained. I was shocked when Prince Kung told me that Su Shun had bribed the military. We both agreed that he had to be eliminated.

My questions were: If we arrested Su Shun, would we have the support of the nation? Would the foreigners take advantage of the ensuing chaos and launch an invasion?

Prince Kung felt confident about receiving the necessary support, especially if the country could be told the truth. As for the Western powers, he had been in constant contact with them. He had let the foreigners know that he envisioned a freer society for China's future, which had secured their promise of support.

I asked Prince Kung for his thoughts about the Taiping rebels. I believed that they could easily become a serious threat if we even momentarily let our guard down. I told him that according to reports from Anhwei alone, the Taipings had united with local hooligans and had been pushing their forces toward Shantung province.

Prince Kung informed me that Generals Sheng Pao and Tseng Kuo-fan had already made arrangements regarding the matter.

How committed were the generals, I wanted to know. I dared not assume that everyone would behave the way they were expected to. I understood the power of Su Shun's bribery.

"Sheng Pao is ready," Prince Kung replied. "He asked to work with Seng-ko-lin-chin's Mongol forces. I gave him permission. Seng-ko-lin-chin is eager to prove his loyalty and restore his name, and this will be his opportunity. I am not sure about the Chinese: General Tseng Kuo-fan and General Chou Tsung-tang view our conflict with Su Shun as a squabble among Manchu nobles. They believe it is wiser to stay out of it. They prefer to wait until there is a winner."

"I despise people who bend with the wind," Nuharoo said. I didn't know she had reentered the room. "His Majesty was right about never trusting the Chinese!"

"For Tseng Kuo-fan and Chou Tsung-tang the situation may be more complicated," I said. "We must be patient and understanding. If I were those generals, I would do exactly what they are doing. After all, Su Shun's power cannot be denied, and to offend him is to risk one's life. We are asking people to turn their backs on Su Shun, so we should allow the generals time to weigh their thoughts."

Prince Kung agreed. "Tseng and Chou are leading the fight against the Taipings. Although they haven't expressed any support for us, they haven't promised anything to Su Shun either."

"We'll wait, then," Nuharoo said. "I just don't feel comfortable that our military power is in the hands of the Chinese. When we have achieved peace, we should remove them or at least keep them away from the highest positions."

I disagreed, but said nothing. As a Manchu I naturally felt more secure with Manchus in the top military positions. And yet there were few men of talent among the princes and clansmen. After two hundred years in power, we had degenerated into decadence. The Manchu nobles spent their time reveling in past glory. All they really knew was that they were entitled to prestige. Luckily, the Chinese had always gone along with it. The Chinese honored our ancestors and graced us with their blessings. The question was, how long would it last?

"I am leaving tonight," Prince Kung said, "although I told Su Shun I would stay till tomorrow."

"Who will be here to protect us when we move the coffin from Jehol to Peking?" Nuharoo asked.

Lowering his voice, Prince Kung said, "I'll be in control. Your job is to act as normal as possible. Don't worry. Prince Ch'un will be around."

Prince Kung warned us to expect Su Shun's anger. He wanted us to be prepared to receive a document submitted by a provincial inspector of justice named Tung Yen-ts'un. It would publicize Su Shun's flaws and call Nuharoo and me "the people's choice." Prince Kung wanted us to keep in mind that by the time Su Shun got hold of Tung's document, it would already have been reviewed by statesmen all over the country. Prince Kung revealed no details. I could tell he was afraid that Nuharoo wouldn't be able to keep her mouth shut if Su Shun happened to ask.

We parted.

Before dinner, Nuharoo came to my quarters with Tung Chih. She felt unsafe and wanted to know if I had seen anything unusual. I noticed that Prince Kung's visit had put Su Shun on guard. More security had been added to the outer courtyard before the gate was locked for the night. I told Nuharoo to go out and smell the fragrant laurel in the garden or visit the hot spring. She said that she didn't feel like doing either. To calm Tung Chih I picked up embroidery and asked Nuharoo to shed some light on the design. We sewed and chatted until Tung Chih fell asleep.

I prayed for Prince Kung's safety. After I sent Nuharoo and Tung Chih to my guest room to sleep, I went to my own bed. My eyes were afraid to close.

A few days later Tung Yen-ts'un's document arrived. Su Shun was enraged. Nuharoo and I read it after Su Shun reluctantly passed it on to us. We were secretly pleased.

The next day Su Shun's men launched a counterattack. Historical examples were used to convince the court that Nuharoo and I should retire from the Regency. At the audience Su Shun's men spoke one after another, trying to create fear in us. They badmouthed Prince Kung. They accused Tung Yen-ts'un of disloyalty and called him a puppet. "We must cut off the hand that pulls the strings!"

Prince Kung expected me to remain silent, but Su Shun's negative portrayal of him was having an effect among the court members. It would be fatal to allow Su Shun to dwell on the fact that Emperor

Hsien Feng had excluded Prince Kung from his will. People had been curious about the reason, and Su Shun was feeding them his own interpretation.

With Nuharoo's permission I reminded the court that Su Shun would have stopped Emperor Hsien Feng from naming Tung Chih as the successor if I hadn't approached the deathbed myself. Su Shun was responsible for the strained relations that had existed between Hsien Feng and Prince Kung. We had strong reason to believe that Su Shun had manipulated the Emperor in his last days.

At my words Su Shun sprang from his seat. He punched the nearest column and broke the fan he was holding. "I wish Emperor Hsien Feng had buried you with him!" he yelled at me. "You have deceived the court and you have exploited Empress Nuharoo's kindness and vulnerability. I have promised His Late Majesty to do justice. I would like to ask Her Majesty Empress Nuharoo for support." He turned to her. "Do you, Empress Nuharoo, really know the female sitting next to you? Do you believe that she would be satisfied just sharing the role of regent with you? Would she be happier if you didn't exist? You are in great danger, my lady! Protect yourself from this wicked woman before she puts poison in your soup!"

Tung Chih was scared. He begged Nuharoo and me to leave. When I said no, he wet himself.

Seeing the urine dripping from the throne, Nuharoo rushed to Tung Chih's side.

The eunuchs quickly arrived with towels.

An elder clansman stood up and began to speak about family unity and harmony.

Tung Chih cried and screamed when eunuchs tried to change his robe.

Nuharoo wept and begged to leave with Tung Chih.

The elder clansman suggested that we call off the audience.

Su Shun objected. Without further discussion, he announced that the Board of Regents would go into recess unless Nuharoo and I threw out Tung Yen-ts'un's proposal.

I decided to retreat. Without Prince Kung, I was no equal to Su Shun. I needed time to secure my relationship with Nuharoo, but I dreaded more delays. Hsien Feng's body had been lying in state for over a month already. Although well sealed, the coffin gave off a stink of decay.

Su Shun and his gang were pleased. He dismissed Tung's proposal and made us agree to place our seals on an edict he had drafted regarding the prosecution of Tung Yen-ts'un.

On October 9, 1861, an audience for all ministers and nobles in Jehol was held in the Hall of Fantastic Haze. Nuharoo and I sat on either side of Tung Chih. The night before, the two of us had talked. I suggested that Nuharoo take charge this time. She was willing, but had trouble deciding what to say. We rehearsed until she was ready.

"Speaking of transporting the Emperor's body to his birthplace," Nuharoo began, "how far along are we with the preparations? And the parting ceremony with His Majesty's spirits?"

Su Shun stepped up. "All is set, Your Majesty. We are waiting for His Young Majesty Tung Chih to come to the coffin room to initiate the ceremony, and the palace will be ready to depart Jehol afterward."

Nuharoo nodded, glancing at me for reassurance. "You have all been working hard since my husband's death, especially the Board of Regents. We regret that Tung Chih is at a tender age and Yehonala and I are overwhelmed with grief. We ask you for understanding and forgiveness if we haven't performed our duty to perfection."

Nuharoo turned to me and I gave her a nod.

"A few days ago," Nuharoo went on, "there was a little misunderstanding between the Board of Regents and us. We regret that it took place. We share the same good intentions, which is all that should matter. Let us move forward to guard the Imperial coffin safely back to Peking. When that job is accomplished, the young Emperor will grant awards. And now, Empress Yehonala."

I knew that I had to take the court by surprise. "I would like an update on the security arrangements regarding the trip. Su Shun?"

Reluctant but bound by formality, Su Shun replied, "The entire Imperial procession will be divided into two parts. The first section we named the Parade of Happiness. We have arranged for Emperor Tung Chih and the Empresses to take chairs in this section to celebrate Emperor Tung Chih's becoming the new ruler. The security will be fifty thousand Bannermen led by Prince Yee. He will be followed by two other divisions. One has seven thousand men, transferred from the areas around Jehol, which will be responsible for His Majesty's safety. The other division is made up of three thousand Imperial Guards led by Yung Lu. Their task will be performing the ceremonial parade. I myself will lead the procession with four thousand men."

"Very well." Nuharoo was impressed.

"Please go on with the second section," I ordered.

"We named the second section the Parade of Sorrow," Su Shun continued. "Emperor Hsien Feng's coffin will be with this one. Ten thousand men and horses have been transferred from the provinces of the Amur River, Chihli, Shenking, and Hsian. Each provincial governor has been notified to receive the procession along the way. General Sheng Pao has been summoned to secure those areas we deem unsafe, such as Kiangsi and Miyun."

I sensed a problem. How would Prince Kung's men strike when Su Shun could easily hold Tung Chih and us as hostages? If something aroused Su Shun's suspicion, he would have an opportunity to do us harm. How would I know whether such an "accident" was not already in the making?

My heart hammered in my chest when I spoke again. "The grand councilor's arrangements sound excellent. I have only one concern. Will the Parade of Happiness be accompanied by colorful flags, firecrackers, dancers and loud music?"

"Yes."

"And the Parade of Sorrow the opposite?"

"Correct."

"The spirits of Emperor Hsien Feng will be disturbed by the trumpets, then," I pointed out. "The happy tunes will overwhelm the sad as the two parades are so closely connected."

"Indeed," Prince Yee echoed, biting my bait. "Empress Yehonala's concern makes good sense. We should separate the two parades. It would be an easy thing to do." He turned to Su Shun, who was staring back at him as hard as he could. But it was too late. Prince Yee's tongue would not be stopped. "I suggest that we have the Parade of Happiness go first and the Parade of Sorrow follow a few miles behind."

"Taken." I closed the lid before Su Shun had a chance to smell what I was cooking in my pot. "What a fine idea. However, Empress Nuharoo and I are not comfortable with our husband traveling alone. Two weeks is a long time for Emperor Hsien Feng to go without company."

Wasting no opportunity to show off again, Prince Yee popped up with another suggestion. "I am sure any of us will be happy to accompany His Late Majesty. May I have the honor?"

"I want Su Shun," Nuharoo said, and her tears came. "He is our husband's most trusted man. With Su Shun by His Majesty's side, the heavenly soul will rest in peace. Will you accept my humble request, Su Shun?"

"My honor, Your Majesty." Su Shun was obviously displeased.

I could hardly contain my delight. Nuharoo didn't know what she had done. She had created the perfect situation for Prince Kung to benefit.

"Thank you, Prince Yee," I said. "You certainly will be rewarded when we get to Peking."

I didn't expect to be given a chance to make the situation even better, but the opportunity presented itself. As if driven by the desire to please us further, or by greed, or simply by his shallow nature, Prince Yee added, "I don't mean to flatter myself, Your Majesty. I shall deserve your reward because the trip is going to be tough on me. I have not only been put in charge of the inner court; I have great military responsibilities as well. I must confess that I am already exhausted."

I picked up his words and rode with them. "Well, Prince Yee, Nuharoo and I believe that His Young Majesty Tung Chih will find another way. We certainly don't want to wear you out. Why don't you leave the military obligations to others and manage just the inner court?"

Prince Yee was not prepared for my quick reaction. "Of course," he responded. "But do you have my replacement in mind as we speak?"

"There is nothing to worry about, Prince Yee."

"But who will that be?"

I saw Su Shun stepping forward, and I decided to seal the moment. "Prince Ch'un will take over the military obligation," I said, looking away from Su Shun. He seemed desperate to speak, and I was afraid he would get Nuharoo's attention. "Prince Ch'un hasn't been assigned a duty." I held Nuharoo with my eyes. "He will be perfect for the job, don't you think?"

"Yes, Lady Yehonala," she said.

"Prince Ch'un!" I called.

"Here." Prince Ch'un's answer came from a corner of the room.

"Will this arrangement suit you?"

"Yes, Your Majesty." Prince Ch'un bowed.

Prince Yee's expression changed to show regret for what he had done to himself.

To bolster him I said, "However, we would like Prince Yee to resume his full responsibility once we reach Peking. His Young Majesty can't do without him."

"Yes, of course, Your Majesty. Thank you!" Prince Yee was a happy man again.

I turned to Nuharoo. "I believe that is all for this audience?"

"Yes, we must thank Grand Councilor Su Shun for doing a fine job of planning."

Twenty-two

OCTOBER 10 was an auspicious day as Hsien Feng's coffin was borne aloft on the shoulders of 124 bearers. At the departing ceremony, Nuharoo and I wore elaborate mourning robes hung with stone ornaments. Our head and shoulder pieces, belts and shoes weighed more than twenty-five pounds. Golden beads dangled in front of my eyes like a curtain, and my earrings were pieces of jade carved with the word *tien,* "in memory." My ears stung and my back ached from all the weight. Because we had run out of coal we had not bathed for weeks. My scalp itched. The oil I used on my hair attracted dust that ended up beneath my fingernails from all my scratching. It was hard to look like an image of grace under such circumstances.

Nuharoo felt sorry for my low manners and purposely set herself as an example for me to follow. I admired her endurance when it came to her appearance. I was sure she sat upright even on the chamber pot. I surmised that she had carried the same stiffness to Hsien Feng's bed. As far as lovemaking went, the Emperor was a man who welcomed creativity. Nuharoo had probably offered him the standard pose from *The Imperial Chamber Activity Menu* and expected him to deliver his seeds.

One could always count on Nuharoo's makeup to be painted to the finest detail. She had two nail stylists, trained in grain carving, who could render entire landscapes and architectural paintings on her nails. One needed a magnifying glass to fully appreciate the artistry. Nuharoo knew exactly what she wanted. Inside her mourning robe she continued to wear the dress that she had made up her mind to die in. It was so dirty that the edge of its collar was gray with grease.

We walked through a forest of colorful umbrellas and pavilion-shaped silk tents. We inspected the cortege and burned incense. Finally we poured wine, inviting the coffin to be on its way. The procession set out down the wild passes from Jehol toward the Great Wall.

The coffin had been finished with forty-nine layers of paint. It was rose red with patterns of gold dragons on it. A division of ceremonial guards led the way. The coffin was suspended in the air on a giant red frame. In the middle of the frame was a matching pole with a nine-by-eighteen-foot flag emblazoned with a golden dragon breathing flames. There was also a pair of copper wind bells. Behind the dragon flag were one hundred flags with the images of powerful animals such as bears and tigers.

Following the flags were empty palanquins for the spirits. The chairs were of different sizes and shapes and were fabulously decorated. The seat covers were made of leopard skin. A large yellow umbrella draped with white flowers followed each chair.

Eunuchs in white silk gowns held trays with incense burners. Behind them followed two bands, one with brass instruments, the other with strings and flutes. When the bands started to play, white paper money was fired into the air, which rained down from the sky like snowflakes.

Nuharoo, Tung Chih and I walked past lamas, monks and painted ceremonial horses and sheep before climbing into our palanquins. The sound of Tibetan trumpets and beating drums was so loud that I couldn't hear my own voice when speaking to Tung Chih. He didn't want to sit alone, and I told him that he had to for the sake of formality. Tung Chih pouted and asked for his red-eyed rabbit. Happily, Li Lien-ying had it with him. I promised Tung Chih that Nuharoo or I would join him as soon as we were able to.

The procession divided into two parts at the foot of the Great Wall, with the Parade of Happiness leading the way and the Parade of Sorrow following several miles behind.

By afternoon the weather had changed. Rain began to fall and then became heavy. For the next five days our procession stretched into a longer and longer column. It toiled its way through mud lashed up by the persistent downpours. For the first time in her life Nuharoo lost control of her makeup. In frustration she blamed it on her mirror-on-legs maids, who were too tired to steady the mirror. I felt sorry for the maids. The window-sized glass was too big and heavy for them.

According to the scouts, the mountain gorges were swarming with bandits. My mind grew with worry about what the future might bring us in the next hour. Under cover of the rain anyone could strike.

Because the Imperial astrologer had all of the dates calculated, there was no thought of stopping, however wet the bearers became. The rain continued to pour. I imagined the hardship of the eunuchs who carried the wooden furniture. Unlike coffin bearers, who had been physically trained, the eunuchs were delicate houseplants. They were accustomed to life in the Forbidden City and many of them were still in their early teens.

I fell asleep in the palanquin and had a strange dream. I was entering the sea like a fish. Swimming, I went into a hole inside a cave buried deep in the seabed. Around the edges of the hole were thick thorns. My skin was badly scratched by the thorns, and the water around me became pink. I could hear the sound of passing boats above and feel the current swirling by. I flipped up and down in terrible pain trying to get away from the thorns.

It was dawn when Li Lien-ying woke me. "The rain has stopped, my lady, and the astrologer said that we can now safely rest."

"Were we in water?" I asked.

He paused for a moment, then replied, "If you were a fish, my lady, you have survived."

My chair was let down and I got out. My body felt like it had been beaten. "Where are we?"

"A village called Spring Ripples."

"Where is Tung Chih?"

"His Young Majesty is with Empress Nuharoo."

I went to find them. They had fallen behind by about half a mile. Nuharoo insisted on changing palanquin bearers. Instead of blaming the slippery roads, she blamed the bearers.

Nuharoo told me that she had also had a dream. It was the opposite of mine. In her dream she found herself in a peaceful kingdom, and her mirror was the size of a wall. The kingdom was hidden in the deepest recesses of a mountain. A Buddhist with a floor-length white beard had led her to this place. She was worshiped, and her subjects all walked with white pigeons on their heads.

After some fuss Tung Chih agreed to leave Nuharoo's tent-sized palanquin and came to sit with me. "Only for a short while," he said.

I tried not to let my son's growing attachment to Nuharoo bother me. He was one of the few things left in my life that could bring me true happiness. So much about me had changed since my entering the Imperial household. I no longer said "I feel good today" upon waking in the morning. The cheerful songs I used to hear inside my head had all been silenced. Fear lived in the backyard of my mind now.

I convinced myself that it was just part of life's journey. Cheerfulness belonged to youth and one naturally lost it. Maturity was what I would gain. Like a tree, my roots would grow stronger as I aged. I looked forward to achieving peace and happiness in a more essential way.

But my spring continued to have no butterflies. The saddest thing was that I knew I was still capable of passion. If Tung Chih were close to me, the butterflies would return. I could disregard everything else, even my loneliness and my deep yearning for a man. I needed my son's love to endure living. Tung Chih was near, within arm's reach, yet we might as well have been an ocean apart. I would do anything to earn his affection. But he was determined not to give me a chance.

My son punished me for the principles I demanded that he live by. He had two kinds of expression when he looked at me. One was like a stranger's, as if he didn't know me and had no interest in knowing me. The other look was of disbelief. He couldn't understand why I had to be the only one to challenge him. His look seemed to question my very existence. After we fought and struggled his expression would show a sneer.

In my son's bright eyes I was diminished. My worship for this little creature reduced me to the dancing bone in the Imperial soup that had been cooked for two hundred years.

I once saw my son and Nuharoo playing. Tung Chih was studying the map of China. He loved it when Nuharoo failed to locate Canton. She begged him to let her quit. He granted her wish and offered her his arms. He was attracted by her weakness. Protecting her from me made him feel like a hero.

Yet I couldn't unlove my son. I couldn't escape my affection. The moment Tung Chih was born, I knew that I belonged to him. I lived for his well-being. There was nothing else but him.

If I had to suffer, I made up my mind to take it. I was prepared to do anything to help Tung Chih avoid the fate of his father. Hsien Feng might have been an emperor, but he was deprived of a basic understanding of his own life. He was not raised with the truth, and he died in confusion.

Looking out, I saw large, loaf-shaped stones surrounded by a thick carpet of wild brush. For mile after mile there was not one single roof. Our lavish parade was for no one's eyes but Heaven's. I knew I shouldn't resent it, but I couldn't help myself. Sitting inside the palanquin, I was damp and achy. The bearers were exhausted, wet and filthy. The happy music only depressed me further.

Li Lien-ying walked back and forth between my chair and Nuharoo's. He was in his purple cotton robe. Dye from his hat ran in rivulets down his face. Li Lien-ying had learned his trade as an Imperial servant and was by now almost as good as An-te-hai. I was worried about An-te-hai. Prince Ch'un had told me that he was in the Peking prison. To complete his deception, An-te-hai had spat at a guard, ensuring harsher punishment: he was put in a water chamber with feces floating around his neck. I prayed that he would hold on until I reached him. I couldn't yet say that I would return to Peking with my head on my shoulders. But if I did, I would unlock An-te-hai's chains myself.

The Parade of Happiness drifted out of its formation. It was hard to keep the tired horses and sheep in line. The bearers had stopped chanting their drills. All I could hear was the sound of steps mixed with heavy breathing. Tung Chih wanted to get out of the palanquin to play, and I wished that I could let him. I would like to see him run a mile with Li Lien-ying. But it was not safe. Several times I had noticed strange faces in our guards' uniforms passing by. I wondered if they were Su Shun's spies. Each day my bearers had been replaced by new men.

When I asked my brother-in-law Prince Ch'un about the changing of the bearers, he replied that it was normal. The bearers rotated positions so the blisters on their shoulders would have time to heal. I was not convinced.

To comfort me, Ch'un talked about Rong and their infant son. They were doing well and were a few miles behind. My sister hadn't wanted to join me because she feared that something would befall my palanquin. "A big tree invites stronger wind" was the message she sent, and she suggested that I take heed.

We reached a temple located on the waist of a mountain. It was after dark and the drizzle had stopped. We were to go into the temple and pray at the altars and then spend the night. The moment Nuharoo, Tung Chih and I stepped out of our chairs, the bearers went off with the empty palanquins. I hurried and caught up with the last bearer and asked why they were not staying with us. He answered that they had been instructed not to store the palanquins near the temple.

"What if something goes wrong and we need to return to our palanquins and you are not available?" I asked.

The bearer threw himself on the ground and kowtowed like an

idiot. But he did not answer my question, and it was no use pressing him.

"Come back, Yehonala!" Nuharoo yelled. "I am sure that our scouts and spies have checked the safety of the temple."

The temple seemed to be well prepared for our arrival. The old roof had been brushed clean and the inside thoroughly dusted. The head monk was a thick-lipped, gentle-looking fellow with fat cheeks. "The goddess of mercy, Kuan Ying, has been sweating," he said, smiling. "I knew this was Heaven's message telling me that Your Majesty would be passing. Although the temple is small, my humble welcome to you extends from Buddha's hand to infinity."

We were served hot gingerroot soup, soybeans and wheat buns for dinner. Tung Chih buried his face in the bowl. I was a starving wolf myself. I consumed all the food on my plate and asked for more. Nuharoo took her time. She checked each button on her robe, making sure she hadn't lost any, and straightened the withered flowers on her headboard. She took small spoonfuls of soup until her hunger could no longer be denied. She picked up the bowl and drank like a peasant.

After the meal the head monk politely showed us to our room and left. We were excited to discover ceramic fire burners near the beds. We laid our damp robes on them to dry. The moment Tung Chih found that the basins were filled with water, Nuharoo cried with joy, then sighed. "I'll just have to wash myself without the maids, I guess." Eagerly she unshelled herself. It was the first time I had seen her naked. Her ivory-colored body was an exquisite work of Heaven. She had a slender frame with apple-like breasts and jade-smooth long legs. Her straight back curved into a sensuous round behind. It made me think that the shapeless fashions for Manchu women were a crime.

Like a deer standing by a cliff under the moonlight, Nuharoo stood by the basin. She slowly washed herself from head to toe. This had been for Hsien Feng's eyes only, I thought.

In the middle of the night I awoke. Nuharoo and Tung Chih were sleeping soundly. My suspicions asserted themselves again. I recalled the head monk's smile—it lacked sincerity. The other monks did not have the peaceful expressions I was used to seeing in Buddhists. The monks' eyes darted away from the head monk and then quickly back as if awaiting a signal. During the meal I had asked the head monk about the local bandits. He said that he had never heard of such a thing. Was he telling the truth? Our scouts told us that bandits were known to be in this area. The head monk must have spent many years living here—how could he not know?

The head monk changed the subject when I asked to be shown around the temple. He took us to the main hall so we could light incense for the gods and then took us right back to this room to sleep. When I asked him about the history of the carvings on the walls, he changed the subject again. His tongue also lacked a preacher's polish when telling Tung Chih the story of the one-thousand-hand Buddha. He didn't seem familiar with the basic styles of calligraphy, which I found hard to believe, for monks made their living copying sutras. I had asked him how many monks he housed in the temple, and he had said eight. Where would we get help if bandits should attack?

The more I thought about this dubious man, the more restless I grew. "Li Lien-ying," I whispered.

My eunuch didn't answer. This was unusual. Li Lien-ying was a light sleeper. He could hear a leaf falling from a tree outside the window. What was wrong with him? I remembered that he had been invited by the head monk to have tea after dinner.

"Li—Li Lien-ying!" I sat up and saw him in the corner.

He was sleeping like a rock. Could there have been something in the tea the head monk had served?

I slipped into my robe and crossed the room. I shook the eunuch, but he responded with loud snoring. Maybe he was just too tired.

I decided to go out and check the courtyard. I was fearful, but it was scarier to be kept in doubt.

The moon was bright. The courtyard looked like it had been spread with a coat of salt. The scent of laurel was carried by the wind. Just as I thought how peaceful it was, I saw a shadow duck behind an arched door. Had my eyes been fooled by the moonlight? By my nerves?

I went back to the room and closed the door. I climbed into bed and peeked through a window. In front of me was a tree with a thick trunk. In the dark, the trunk kept changing its shape. One moment it looked like it grew a belly, the next an arm.

My eyes weren't fooling me. There were people in the courtyard. They were hiding behind the trees.

I woke Nuharoo and explained what I saw.

"You see a soldier behind every blade of grass," Nuharoo complained, putting on her clothes.

While I dressed Tung Chih, Nuharoo went to wake Li Lien-ying. "The slave must be drunk," she said. "He won't wake up."

"Something's wrong, Nuharoo."

I slapped Li's face and eventually he woke up. When he tried to walk, however, his legs wobbled. We were shocked.

"Get ready to run," I said.

"Where can we go?" Nuharoo panicked.

We had no knowledge of the area. Even if we managed to get out of the temple, we could easily lose our way on the mountain. If we weren't caught, we might starve to death. But what would happen if we remained here? By now I had no doubt that the head monk was Su Shun's man. I should have insisted on keeping the bearers near.

I told Tung Chih to hold on to me when I opened the door.

The mountain was beginning to show its shape in the predawn light. The wind in the pines sounded like a rushing tide. The four of us walked down a hallway and passed through an arched gate. We followed a barely visible path. "This should lead us to the foot of the mountain," I said, although I was not sure.

We didn't get far before we heard the sounds of pursuit.

"Look, Yehonala, you've gotten us in trouble," Nuharoo cried. "We could have called the monks for help if we had stayed in the temple."

I pulled Nuharoo along with me as Li Lien-ying struggled to stay on his feet while carrying Tung Chih on his back. We walked as fast as we could. Suddenly the path was blocked by a group of masked men.

"Give them what they want," I said to Nuharoo, assuming they were bandits.

The men made no sound but moved in closer around us.

"Here, take our jewelry," I said. "Take it all and let us go!"

But the men wanted none of it. They jumped us and tied us with ropes. They stuck wads of cloth in our mouths and blindfolded us.

I was inside a jute sack, tied to a pole and carried on men's shoulders. The blindfold fell off during my struggle, although my mouth was still stuffed with cloth. I could see light through the coarse weave of the sack. The men walked jerkily downward through the hills, and I guessed that they were not bandits, who would have had strong legs for rough terrain like this.

I had trusted that Prince Kung would protect us, but it seemed that Su Shun had outwitted him. There was no way I could escape if this was meant to be.

I believed that Nuharoo had a chance to live, but did Tung Chih? How amazingly easy it was for Su Shun to conduct a coup d'état! No army, no weapons, not a drop of blood shed, just a few men dressed as bandits. Our government was a paper dragon made only for parades. The Era of Well-Omened Happiness was a joke. How would Emperor Hsien Feng like it now that Su Shun revealed what he was made of!

Branches beat against the sack. In darkness I searched for sounds of Tung Chih. There was nothing. Was I to be executed? I dared not allow myself to reflect on anything. Based on the angle of the pole, I could tell that the ground had become less steep.

Without warning I was dropped and knocked into something like a tree stump. My head hit a hard surface and the pain was excruciating. I heard men talking, then heavy steps approaching. I was dragged through dry leaves and tossed into what felt like a ditch.

The cloth in my mouth was soaked with saliva and it finally fell out. I dared not scream for help, fearing they would come and finish me sooner. I tried to prepare myself for the worst, but a crushing feeling came over me: *I can't die without knowing where Tung Chih is!* I tried to tear the sack with my teeth, but with my hands tied behind me it was hopeless.

I heard footsteps over the dry leaves. Someone approached and stopped next to me. I tried to move my legs and get into a better position to defend myself from inside the sack, but they were tied too.

I could hear the sound of a man's breathing.

"For the sake of Heaven, spare my son!" I cried out and then cringed. I imagined his knife slashing the sack and the cold metal ripping into my flesh.

It didn't come. Instead I heard more footsteps and the clash of metal weapons. There was a muted cry, and then something, a body, fell on me.

For a moment there was quiet. Then in the distance came the sound of hooves and shouting men.

I couldn't make up my mind whether to remain silent or call out for help. What if they were Su Shun's men who had come to make sure I was dead? But what if they were Prince Kung's men? How would I get anyone to pay attention to a jute sack lying in a ditch under a body?

"Tung Chih! Tung Chih!" I screamed.

A moment later a knife slashed open the sack and I was breathing in the sunlight.

Holding the knife was a soldier in the uniform of the Imperial Guards. He stood in front of me, stunned. "Your Majesty!" He threw himself on the ground.

Removing the ropes from my arms and legs, I told him, "Rise and tell me who sent you."

The soldier rose and pointed behind him. A few yards away, a man on a horse turned his head.

"Yung Lu!"

He dismounted and dropped to his knees.

"I was almost a ghost!" I cried. "Or am I already one?"

"Speak, so I will know, Your Majesty," said Yung Lu.

I broke down.

"Your Majesty," he murmured, "it is Heaven's will that you survived." He wiped sweat from his forehead.

I tried to climb out of the ditch, but my knees betrayed me and I collapsed.

He took me by the arm.

The touch of his hand made me sob like a child. "I could have been a hungry ghost," I said. "I have had little sleep, nothing to eat the whole day, not a drop of water to drink. I am not even dressed properly. My shoes are gone. If I had met the Imperial ancestors, they would have been too embarrassed to receive me."

He squatted next to me. "It is over, Your Majesty."

"Was Su Shun behind this?"

"Yes, Your Majesty."

"Where is the assassin?"

Yung Lu pointed his chin back at the ditch. The dead man there had half his face buried in the dirt, but I recognized the fat body. It was the head monk.

I asked where Tung Chih and Nuharoo were. Yung Lu told me that they had been rescued as well and were continuing their journey to Peking. Yung Lu had already sent messengers to Su Shun with news that I had been found dead, but it would take days for that false report to reach him, which was all part of Prince Kung's plan.

Yung Lu placed me in a carriage and escorted me himself. We took a shorter route and arrived in Peking well ahead of Su Shun and his procession.

Twenty-three

W AITING FOR ME inside the Forbidden City, Prince Kung was
relieved when he saw that I was unharmed. "Rumors of your
death traveled faster than our messengers," he said, greeting
me. "I have been tortured by worry."

In tears, we bowed to each other.

"Maybe your brother did want to take me with him," I said, still feeling a bit hurt.

"But he changed his mind at the last minute, didn't he? He might
have aided your rescue in Heaven." Prince Kung paused. "I am sure he
was not in his right mind when he appointed Su Shun."

"True."

Prince Kung looked me up and down and then smiled. "Welcome
home, sister-in-law. You've had a tough journey."

"You too," I said, and noticed that his hat looked too big for him. He
kept pushing back the brim with his hand so the hat wouldn't cover his
eyebrows. "I lost weight, but I didn't expect my head to shrink." He
laughed.

When I asked about the head monk, Prince Kung explained that the
assassin was known as the Buddha's Palm — his power had been as un-
limited as the palm of Buddha, said to be capable of "covering everything." In folklore, when the Monkey King of Magic thinks he has escaped after cartwheeling thousands of miles, he finds that he has
landed in that almighty palm. My head was the only one the assassin
had failed to collect in his ornamental box.

Prince Kung and I sat down to talk—and so began our long working relationship. He was a man of broad perspective, although his temper would continue to flare over the years. He had been raised like Hsien Feng and could be just as spoiled and impatient. Many times I had to ignore his insensitivity and selfishness. He unintentionally humiliated me more than once in front of the court. I could have protested, but I told myself that I must learn to take Kung's flaws along with his virtues. His strengths were greater than his brothers', and not insignificant. He respected reality and was open to different opinions. We needed each other at this moment. As a Manchu he had been taught that a woman's place was in her bedroom, but he couldn't ignore me totally. Without my support he would have no legitimacy.

As Prince Kung and I got to know each other better, we were able to relax. I let him know that I had no interest in power itself, and that all I wanted was to help Tung Chih succeed. It was wonderful that we shared the same vision. We fought at times, but we always managed to come out of our battles united. To stabilize the new court, we became each other's figurehead and decoration.

Dancing around Prince Kung's pride, I encouraged his enthusiasm and ambitions. I believed that if Nuharoo and I were humble with him, he would be humble with Tung Chih. We practiced the Confucian principles of the family and both benefited.

I played my part, although I would grow tired of putting on a theatrical mask every day. I had to pretend that I was absolutely helpless without the court. My ministers functioned only when they believed that they were my saviors. My ideas would not have gone far if I hadn't presented them as their "five-year-old lord's idea." In order to direct, I learned to offer an image that I was being directed.

It took Nuharoo, Tung Chih and the rest of the Parade of Happiness five more days to arrive in Peking. By the time they reached the Gate of Zenith, the men and horses were so exhausted that they looked like a defeated army. Their flags were torn and their shoes worn through. With dirt-caked, hairy faces, the palanquin bearers dragged their blistered feet. The guards were spiritless and out of formation.

I imagined Su Shun and his Parade of Sorrow, scheduled to arrive in a few more days. The weight of Hsien Feng's coffin must be crushing the shoulders of the bearers. By now Su Shun must have received the news of my execution and be eager to reach Peking.

The joy of making it home brought great energy to the Parade of

Happiness. At the Forbidden City gate, the whole retinue re-formed. Men straightened their backs and stuck out their chests with pride when entering. Nobody seemed to know anything about what had happened. Citizens lined up on either side of the entrance and clapped their hands. The crowd cheered at the sight of the Imperial palanquins. No one knew that the person in my chair was not me but my eunuch Li Lien-ying.

Nuharoo celebrated the end of the journey by having three baths in a row. The maid reported that she almost drowned in the tub because she fell asleep. I called on Rong and her young son. We visited our mother and brother. I invited Mother to move into the palace and live with me so I could take care of her, but she declined, preferring to stay where she was, in a quiet house in a small lane behind the Forbidden City. I didn't insist. If she lived with me, she would have to get permission every time she wanted to go shopping or visit her friends. Her activities would be restricted to her rooms and garden, and she would not be allowed to cook her own meals. I wanted to spend more time with Mother, but I had to meet with Nuharoo about our plan regarding Su Shun.

"Unless there is good news, I do not wish to hear it," Nuharoo warned. "The hard journey has cut my longevity short enough."

I stood by Nuharoo's half-broken door. The foreigners had damaged everything in sight. Her mirror was scratched. Her golden carvings were gone, and so were the embroideries from the walls. Her closets were empty and her bed had men's footprints on it. There were still pieces of glass on the floor. Her art collections were missing. The gardens were ruined. The fish, birds, peacocks and parrots had all died.

"Misery is the work of the mind," Nuharoo said as she took a sip of her tea. "Master it and you will feel nothing but happiness. The beauty of my nails has not been damaged, because they stayed inside the protectors."

I looked at her and recalled how she had sat inside the palanquin in a rain-soaked robe for days on end. I knew how hard that had been because I had experienced it myself. The wet cushions made me feel like I was sitting in urine. I didn't know whether I should admire Nuharoo's effort to maintain her dignity. I had wanted to get off the chair to walk during the journey. Nuharoo had stopped me. "Bearers are made to carry you," she insisted. I explained that I was sick of having a wet butt: "I've got to air it somehow!"

I remembered that she was silent, but her expression clearly told me that she disapproved of my behavior. She was shocked when I finally decided to get out and walk side by side with the bearers. She let me know that she felt insulted, which forced me back inside the palanquin.

"Don't look at me as if you have discovered a new star in the sky," she said, fastening her hair into a base. "Let me share with you a Buddhist's teaching: To truly have something is to not have it at all."

It didn't make any sense to me.

She shook her head in pity.

"Good night and rest well, Nuharoo."

She nodded. "Send Tung Chih over, would you?"

I desperately wanted to spend the night with my son after being separated for so long. But I knew Nuharoo. When it came to Tung Chih, her will ruled. I stood no chance. "May I send him after his bath?"

"Fine," she said, and I made my exit.

"Don't try to climb high, Yehonala," her voice came from behind. "Embrace the universe and embrace what comes to you. There is no significance in fighting."

Leaving me to finish the last part of the decree indicting Su Shun, Prince Kung departed Peking for Miyun. The town was fifty miles from the capital and the procession's last stop before it. Su Shun and Hsien Feng's coffin were scheduled to arrive at Miyun by early afternoon.

Yung Lu was ordered to go back to Su Shun and remain close to him. Su Shun assumed that everything was going the way he had planned and that I, his biggest obstacle, had been removed.

Su Shun was found drunk when the procession reached Miyun. He was so excited by his own prospects that he had already begun celebrating with his cabinet. Local prostitutes were seen running around the Imperial coffin stealing ornaments. When Su Shun was greeted by General Sheng Pao at the gateway of Miyun, he announced my death with great elation.

Receiving a cold response from Sheng Pao, Su Shun looked around and noticed Prince Kung, who stood not far from the general. Su Shun ordered Sheng Pao to remove Prince Kung, but Sheng Pao remained where he was.

Su Shun turned to Yung Lu, who stood behind him. Yung Lu made no move either.

"Guards!" Su Shun shouted. "Take the traitor down!"

"Have you a decree to do so?" Prince Kung asked.

"My word is the decree" was Su Shun's reply.

Prince Kung took a step back, and General Sheng Pao and Yung Lu moved forward.

Su Shun woke up to what he faced. "Don't you dare. I am appointed by His Majesty. I am the will of Emperor Hsien Feng!"

Imperial Guards formed a circle around Su Shun and his men.

Su Shun shouted, "I'll hang you, all of you!"

At a signal from Prince Kung, Sheng Pao and Yung Lu took Su Shun by the arms. Su Shun struggled and called for Prince Yee's help.

Prince Yee came running with his guards, but Yung Lu's men intercepted them.

From his sleeve Prince Kung took a yellow decree. "Whoever dares to contest the order of Emperor Tung Chih will be put to death."

While Yung Lu disarmed Su Shun's men, Prince Kung read what I had drafted: "Emperor Tung Chih instructs that Su Shun be arrested immediately. Su Shun has been found responsible for organizing a coup d'état."

Locked up in a cage on wheels, Su Shun looked like a circus beast when the Parade of Sorrow resumed its journey from Miyun to Peking. In the name of my son I informed the governors of all the states and provinces of Su Shun's arrest and his removal from office. I told Prince Kung that I considered it crucial to win the moral ground as well. I needed to know the feelings of my governors in order to reassert stability. If there was confusion, I wanted to take care of it right away. Ante-hai helped me with the task, even though he had been released from the water chamber of the Imperial prison only days before. He was wrapped in bandages but was happy.

Comments regarding the arrest of Su Shun came from all over China. I was greatly relieved that the majority of the governors sided with me. To those in doubt, I encouraged honesty. I made it clear that I would like to be approached with the absolute truth no matter how it might contradict my personal view of Su Shun. I wanted the governors to know that I was prepared to listen and was more than willing to make my decision regarding Su Shun's punishment based on their recommendations.

Shortly afterward two grand secretaries, who represented civil justice and were originally in Su Shun's camp, denounced Su Shun. It was then that General Tseng Kuo-fan and the Chinese ministers and governors expressed their support for me. I had called them the fence-sitters, because they had carefully observed both sides before committing themselves. Tseng Kuo-fan criticized Su Shun's "gross historical impropriety." Following Tseng, governors from the northern provinces came forward. They voiced their disagreement regarding Su Shun's exclusion of Prince Kung and proposed that power be vested in Empress Nuharoo and me.

A trial began as soon as Su Shun arrived in Peking. It was presided over by Prince Kung. Su Shun and the rest of the Gang of Eight were found guilty of subversion of the state, which was one of the ten abominations of Ch'ing law, second only to rebellion. Su Shun was also found guilty of crimes against the family and the virtue of society. In the decree I had composed, I pronounced him "abominable, unpardonable and irredeemable."

Prince Yee was "granted" a rope and was "permitted" to hang himself. He was escorted to a special room where a beam and a stool awaited. In the room was a servant who would assist Yee to climb onto the stool in case his legs failed him. The servant was also expected to kick the stool out from under Prince Yee once his head was in the noose.

It sickened me to order such a sentence, but I realized I had no choice.

Over the next few days, more of Su Shun's allies, including Chief Eunuch Shim, were stripped of their power and rank. Shim was sentenced to death by whipping, but I interceded on his behalf. I told the court that I believed the new era should begin in mercy.

Su Shun's sons were beheaded, but I spared his daughter, bending the law in her case. She was a bright girl who once served me as a librarian. Nothing like her father, she was kind and reserved. Although I didn't wish to continue our friendship, I felt she deserved to live. Su Shun's eunuchs were all sentenced to death by whipping. They were the scapegoats, of course, but terror was needed in order to make a statement.

As for Su Shun himself, death by dismemberment was recommended by the judicial authority. But I determined that it be commuted. "Although Su Shun fully deserves the punishment," my decree to the nation read, "we cannot make up our mind to impose the extreme penalty. Therefore, in token of our leniency, we sentence him to immediate decapitation."

Three days before Su Shun's execution a riot broke out in a district of Peking where many of his loyalists lived. The complaint was heard that Su Shun was Emperor Hsien Feng's appointed minister. "If Su Shun has no virtue whatsoever and deserves such a harsh death, should we doubt His Late Majesty's wisdom? Or should we suspect that His Majesty's will is being violated?"

Yung Lu brought the riot under control. I demanded that Prince Kung and Yung Lu secure Su Shun's execution. I pointed out that we must be extremely careful because Manchu Bannermen had in the past rescued the condemned as a way to start a rebellion.

Prince Kung paid little attention to my concerns. In his eyes, Su Shun was already dead. Believing that he had the full support of the people, Prince Kung proposed to change the place of execution from the vegetable market to the bigger livestock market, a space that could accommodate a crowd of ten thousand.

Feeling uneasy about the plans, I decided to investigate the background of the executioner. I sent An-te-hai and Li Lien-ying to do the job, and they returned quickly with distressing news. There was evidence that the executioner had already been bribed.

The man appointed by the court to behead Su Shun went by the name of One-Cough—he performed his job with reflexive speed. I had no idea that it was a tradition to bribe the executioner. In order to make a profit, the members of this gruesome trade, from the executioner down to the ax sharpener, worked in concert.

When a convict was brought to prison, he would be treated miserably if his family failed to properly bribe the right people. For example, invisible, undetectable injury could be done to bones and joints, leaving the prisoner handicapped for life. If the prisoner was sentenced to a lingering death by dismemberment, the executioner might take as long as nine days to carve him into a skeleton while keeping him breathing. If the executioner was satisfied with the bribe, his knife would go straight to the heart, ending the suffering before it began.

I learned that when it came to a beheading, there were levels of service. The condemned's family and the executioner would actually sit down and negotiate. If the executioner was dissatisfied, he would chop the head off and let it roll away. With the help of his apprentices, who would hide among the crowd, the head would "disappear." Until the family delivered the money, the head would not be "found." Afterward the family would have to pay a leather worker to sew the head back onto the body. If paid enough, the executioner would make sure that the head and the body stayed attached by a flap of skin. This goal was difficult to achieve, and One-Cough was considered greatly talented in this area.

I asked Yung Lu to interview One-Cough for me. I wanted to hear with my own ears how he prepared himself to perform the beheading of Su Shun. I wanted to speak to One-Cough myself, but the law forbade this. So I observed One-Cough from behind a folded panel.

"The word 'hack' or 'slaughter' is incorrect in describing my job," One-Cough began in a surprisingly soft tone. He was a small-headed, stocky-framed man with short, thick arms. "The correct word is 'slice.' That's what I do. Slice. I'll hold the knife backwards by the handle— that is, with the dull edge near my elbow and the blade facing out. When I receive the action order, I'll push the knife right in from behind Su Shun's neck. Most people awaiting death aren't able to stand on their feet by the time they are brought to me. Nine out of ten have problems kneeling straight. So my assistant will keep the guy's shoulders up by grabbing his queue. I'll be standing behind Su Shun, a little bit to the left so he won't see me. In fact, I will begin observing him the moment he is escorted onto the stage. I'll study his neck in order to locate a spot where I can cut in.

"When I start, I'll first tap his right shoulder with my left hand. I only have to tap lightly—he's jumpy enough. The point is to alarm him so his neck will stick up, and I will immediately push my elbow. The blade will go right in between his spinal knuckles. And I will shove my knife to the left all the way, and before the edge comes out, I'll raise my leg and give a kick to the body so it falls forward. I have to kick fast, otherwise my clothes will get drenched in blood, which my profession considers bad luck."

The day of Su Shun's execution came. Yung Lu told me later that he had never witnessed so many people at a beheading in his life. The streets were packed, as were the rooftops and trees. Children had filled their pockets with rocks. They sang songs of celebration. People spat on Su Shun as his cage went by. When he arrived at the place of execution, his face was covered with saliva and his skin was torn by rocks.

One-Cough emptied a bottle of liquor before he got on the stage. He could hardly believe that he was beheading Su Shun, for in the past he had taken orders from Su Shun to behead others.

As for Su Shun, he called his own failure "a boat turned upside down in sewage." He shouted to the laughing crowd that "there is a salacious affair going on between the Empresses and the Imperial brother-in-law Prince Kung." In no time Su Shun's head rolled like a common felon's.

I was haunted by the execution. The images Yung Lu described were vivid in my head. An-te-hai told me that I cried loudly in my dreams and said that all I wanted was to give birth to a dozen children and live the life of a peasant woman. An-te-hai said that in my sleep my neck wouldn't stop twisting from side to side as if I were dodging the blade.

Su Shun's immense fortune was divided among the royals as compensation for the abuse they had suffered. Overnight Nuharoo and I became wealthy. She purchased jewelry and clothes, and I paid for spies. The attempted assassination on me had shattered my sense of security. With what money was left I bought Su Shun's opera troupe. In my lonely life as an Imperial widow, the opera became my solace.

The court voted and passed a proposal I submitted in the name of Tung Chih granting the promotion of Yung Lu and An-te-hai. From that moment forward Yung Lu held the highest position in China's military. He was responsible for protecting not only the Forbidden City and the capital but also the entire country. His new title was Commander in Chief of Imperial Forces and Minister of the Imperial Household. As for An-te-hai, he was given Chief Eunuch Shim's job. He earned a second rank, that of court minister, which was the highest a eunuch was allowed to achieve.

After all the tumult, I needed a few days of quiet. I invited Nuharoo and Tung Chih to join me at the Summer Palace, where we floated on Kunming Lake, away from the wreckage caused by the invaders. Surrounded by weeping willows, the lake surface was covered with flowering lotus. After the summer the fertile fields resembled the countryside south of the Yangtze River, the region of my hometown of Wuhu.

Tung Chih insisted on staying in Nuharoo's large boat, which was filled with guests and entertainers. I floated by myself, with An-te-hai and Li Lien-ying in charge of the oars. The complete beauty of the place washed over me. I was so relieved that my troubles seemed finally to be over. I had visited the Summer Palace many times before, but always with the Grand Empress Lady Jin. She had so gotten under my skin that I had no idea of what the palace really looked like.

It had originally been the capital of the Northern Sung Dynasty in the twelfth century. Over the years, emperors of different dynasties added numerous pavilions, towers, pagodas and temples to the grounds. In the Yuan Dynasty the lake was expanded to become part of the Imperial water supply. In 1488, the emperors of the Ming Dynasty, who were fond of natural beauty, began building the Imperial residence by the lake. In 1750, Emperor Chien Lung decided to duplicate the scenery he admired around West Lake in Hangchow and in Soochow to the south. It took him fifteen years to build what he called a "town of poetic charm." The southern architectural style was faithfully copied. When it was finished, the palace was transformed into a long living scroll painting of unrivaled beauty.

I loved walking the Long Promenade, a covered corridor divided into two hundred sections. I began at the Invite-the-Moon Gate in the east and ended at the Ten-Foot Stone Pavilion. One day when I stopped to rest at the Gate of Dispelling Clouds, I thought of Lady Yun and her daughter, Princess Jung. Lady Yun had forbidden me to speak with her daughter when she was alive. I had seen the girl only at performances and birthday parties. I remembered her as having a slim nose, a thin mouth and a slightly pointed chin. Her expression was absent and dreamy. I wondered if she was well and if she had been told about her father's death.

The girl was brought to me. She had not inherited her mother's beauty. She was wearing a gray satin robe and looked pitiful. Her features had not changed and her body was stick-thin. She reminded me of a frosted eggplant stopped in the middle of its growing. She dared not sit when invited to. Her mother's death must have cast a permanent shadow on her character. She was a princess, Emperor Hsien Feng's only daughter, but she looked like a child of misfortune.

But it was not just that she had Hsien Feng's blood, or that I had any guilt about her mother's ill fate. I wished to give this girl a chance. I must have already sensed that Tung Chih would turn out to be a disappointment, and I wanted to raise a child myself to see if I could make a difference. In a way, Princess Jung offered me consolation after my loss of Tung Chih.

Even though Princess Jung was Tung Chih's half-sister, the court wouldn't allow her to live with me unless I officially adopted her, so I did. She proved to be worthy. Scared and timid as she was at the beginning, she gradually healed. I nurtured her as much as I could. In my palace she was free to run around, although she barely took advantage of her freedom. She was the opposite of Tung Chih, who thrived on adventure. Nevertheless, she got along with my son and served as a form of stability for him. The only discipline I requested of her was that she attend school. Unlike Tung Chih she loved to learn and was an excellent student. The tutors could not stop praising her. She bloomed in her teens and wanted to reach out. I not only encouraged her but also provided her with opportunities.

Princess Jung grew into quite a beauty when she turned fifteen. One of my ministers suggested that I arrange a marriage for her to a Tibetan tribal chief—"as intended by her father, Emperor Hsien Feng," the minister reminded me.

I discarded the proposal. Although Lady Yun and I had never been friends, I wanted to do her justice. She had spoken of her fear that her daughter would be married to a "savage." I told the court that Princess Jung was my daughter, and it was up to me, not the court, to decide her future. Instead of marrying her off in Tibet, I sent her to Prince Kung. I wanted Jung to have a private education and learn English. When she was done, I intended for her to be my secretary and translator. After all, the day might come when I would personally speak to the Queen of England.

Twenty-four

THE PREPARATIONS for my husband's burial were finally complete. It had taken three months and nine thousand laborers to build a special road to carry the coffin to the Imperial tomb. The bearers, all of the same height and weight, practiced day and night to perfect their steps. The tomb was located in Chihli province, not far from Peking. Each morning a table and chair were placed on top of a thick board weighing the same as the coffin. A bowl of water was placed on the table. An official climbed over the shoulders of the bearers to sit on the chair. His duty was to watch the water in the bowl. The bearers practiced marching until the water no longer spilled from the bowl.

Escorted by Yung Lu, Nuharoo and I took a trip to inspect the tomb. Officially it was called the Blessed Ground of Eternity. The earth was rock hard and covered with frost. After the long ride, I stepped down from the palanquin with stiff arms and frozen legs. There was no sun. Nuharoo and I were dressed in the customary white mourning clothes. Our necks were exposed to the cold air. Wind-blown dust beat at our skin. Nuharoo couldn't wait to turn back.

The view moved me. Hsien Feng would be resting with his ancestors. His tomb was in one of two burial complexes, one to the east and the other to the west of Peking. It nestled in the mountains, surrounded by tall pines. The broad ceremonial way was paved with marble and flanked by enormous carved stone elephants, camels, griffins, horses and warriors. About a hundred yards along the marble road Nuharoo and I approached a pavilion in which Hsien Feng's gold satin thrones and yellow dragon robes were kept. These would be displayed on the annual day of sacrifice. Like the mausoleum of his ancestors, Hsien Feng's would also have its attendants and guardian troops. The governor of Chihli had been appointed to take care of the holy site and maintain its seclusion by restricting access.

We entered the tomb. The upper part, which was dome-shaped, was called the City of Treasuries. It was carved out of solid rock. The lower part was the tomb itself. The two levels were connected by staircases.

With the help of a torch we were able to see the interior. It was a large sphere about sixty feet in diameter. All was made of white marble. In the middle stood a stone bed set against a carved tablet eighteen feet in width. Emperor Hsien Feng's coffin, on the day of the burial ceremony, would be placed on top of this bed.

There were six smaller coffins on either side of Emperor Hsien Feng's stone bed. They were rose-colored and carved with phoenixes. Nuharoo and I glanced at each other and realized that two of them were meant for us. Our names and titles were carved on the panels: *Here lies Her Motherly and Auspicious Empress Yehonala* and *Here lies Her Motherly and Restful Empress Nuharoo.*

The cold air seeped through my bones. My lungs were filled with the smell of deep earth.

Yung Lu brought in the chief architect. He was a man in his late fifties, thin and small, almost a child in size. His eyes showed intelligence, and his kowtows and bows were performed in a style only Chief Eunuch Shim could have matched. I turned to Nuharoo to see if she had anything to say. She shook her head. I told the man to rise and then asked what had guided him to select this spot.

"I chose the site based on *feng shui* and the calculations of the twenty-four directions of mountains," he replied. His voice was clear, with a slight southern accent.

"What tools did you use?"

"A compass, Your Majesty."

"What is unique about this place?"

"Well, according to my calculations and those of others, including the court astrologers, this is where the breath of the earth has traveled. The center point gathers the vitality of the universe. It is supposed to be the proper spot to dig the Golden Well. Right here in the middle —"

"What is to accompany His Majesty?" Nuharoo interrupted.

"Besides His Majesty's favorite gold and silver sutras, books and manuscripts, there are luminary lanterns." The architect pointed at two giant jars standing on either side of the bed.

"What's inside?" I asked.

"Plant oil with cotton thread."

"Will it light?" Nuharoo took a closer look at the jars.

"Of course."

"I mean, for how long?"

"Forever, Your Majesty."

"Forever?"

"Yes, Your Majesty."

"It is damp in here," I said. "Will water seep in and flood the space?"

"Wouldn't that be awful!" Nuharoo said.

"I have designed a drainage system." The architect showed us that the bed was slightly off level, which made the head a little higher than the foot. "Water will drip into the chiseled canal underneath and flow outside."

"What about security?" I asked.

"There are three large stone doors, Your Majesty. Each door has two marble panels and is framed with copper. As you can see here, underneath the door, where the two panels come together, there is a chiseled half-watermelon-shaped pit. Facing the pit, about three feet away, I have placed a stone ball. A track for the ball to travel has been dug. When the burial ceremony is completed, a long-handled hook will be inserted in a slit and it will pull the stone ball toward the pit. When the ball falls into the pit, the door will shut permanently."

We rewarded the chief architect a scroll with calligraphy by Emperor Hsien Feng, and the man retreated. Nuharoo was impatient to leave. She didn't want to honor the architect with the dinner we had promised. I convinced her that it was important to keep our word. "If we make him feel good, he will in turn make sure Hsien Feng rests in peace," I said. "Besides, we have to come here again on the burial day, and our bodies will be buried here when we die."

"No! I'll never come here again!" Nuharoo cried. "I can't bear the sight of my own coffin."

I took her hand in mine. "I can't either."

"Then let's go."

"Just stay for dinner and no more, my dear sister."

"Why do you have to force me, Yehonala?"

"We need to gain the architect's full loyalty. We need to help him drive out his fear."

"Fear? What fear?"

"In the past, the architect of an Imperial tomb was often shut in with the coffin. The royal family considered him of no further use after he had finished his job. The living Emperor and Empress feared that the man might be bribed by tomb robbers. Our architect may fear for his life, so we should make him feel trusted and secure. We must let him know that he will be honored and not harmed. If we don't, he might dig a secret tunnel to quell his fear."

Reluctantly Nuharoo stayed, and the architect was pleased.

When Nuharoo and I returned to Peking, Prince Kung suggested that we announce the new government immediately. I didn't think we were ready. The beheading of Su Shun had aroused sympathy in certain quarters. The fact that we had received fewer letters of congratulation than expected concerned me.

People needed time to develop confidence in us. I told Prince Kung that our rule should be the desire of the majority. We had to achieve at least the appearance of it in order to make us morally legitimate.

Although Prince Kung was impatient, he agreed to test the political waters one last time. We took a summary of a proposal written by General Sheng Pao to the governors of all the provinces which suggested a "three-legged stool," with Nuharoo and me as coregents and Prince Kung as the Emperor's chief advisor in administration and government.

Prince Kung suggested that we adopt a method of voting. The idea was clearly Western-influenced. He persuaded us to comply because it was the main way that European nations assured the legitimacy of their governments. We would allow the votes to be anonymous, which no ruler in China's history had done before. I agreed, although unsure of the outcome. The proposal was printed and distributed along with the ballots.

We nervously awaited the results. To our disappointment, half of the governors didn't respond, and a quarter expressed a desire to reelect Tung Chih's regents. No one mentioned any support for Prince Kung's role in the government. Kung realized that he had underestimated Su Shun's influence.

The silence and rejection not only put us in an embarrassing situation, but also ruined the timing — our victory over Su Shun had turned sour. People felt sorry for the underdog. Sympathetic comments began to arrive from every corner of China, which could very well lead to a revolt.

I knew we would need to act. We must reposition ourselves and move decisively. My suggestion was that Nuharoo and I issue an affidavit claiming that before his death our late husband had privately appointed Prince Kung the senior advisor for Tung Chih. In exchange for this invention, Kung would propose to the court that Nuharoo and I rule alongside him. His influence should encourage people to vote for us.

Prince Kung agreed to the plan.

To speed the results, I visited a person whom I had wanted to contact since Su Shun's downfall, the sixty-five-year-old scholar Chiang Tai, a well-connected social figure and a fervent critic of Su Shun's. Su Shun had hated the scholar so much that he had the venerable man stripped of all his court titles.

On a pleasant day Chiang Tai and I met at his shabby *hootong* apartment. I invited him to come to the Forbidden City to be Tung Chih's master tutor. Surprised and flattered, the man and his family threw themselves at my feet.

The next day Chiang Tai began campaigning for me. While he told everyone about his appointment as Emperor Tung Chih's master tutor, he also said how wise and capable I was for recognizing true talent. He stressed how sincere and eager I had been to recruit men like him to serve the new government. After that, it took only a few weeks for the political wind to become favorable.

The court counted the votes, and we won.

On November 30, a hundred days after Hsien Feng's death, the title of Tung Chih's reign was changed from Well-Omened Happiness to Return to Order. It was Chiang Tai who gave Tung Chih's reign the new epithet. The word "order" would be seen and pronounced every time a countryman looked at his calendar.

In our announcement, which was drafted by me and polished by Chiang Tai, we emphasized that it was not the choice of Nuharoo and me to rule. As regents, we were committed to helping Tung Chih, but we looked forward with enthusiasm to the day of our retirement. We asked for the nation's understanding, support and forgiveness.

The change generated great excitement. Everyone in the Forbidden City had been waiting to discard their mourning costumes. For the entire hundred-day period of mourning, no one had worn anything but white. Since men hadn't been allowed to shave, they looked like grizzled hermits, with scraggly beards and hair sticking out of their noses and ears.

In the period of a week, the Hall of Spiritual Nurturing was cleaned to a glossy shine. A three-by-nine-foot redwood desk was placed in the middle of the hall, covered with a yellow silk tablecloth embroidered with spring flowers. Behind the desk sat a pair of upholstered golden chairs, which were for Nuharoo and me. In front of where we would be sitting was a translucent yellow silk screen hanging from the ceiling. It was a symbolic gesture saying that it was not we who ruled, but Tung Chih. Tung Chih's throne was placed in the center, in front of us.

On the morning of the ascension ceremony most of the senior ministers were awarded the right to ride either in palanquins or on horses when entering the Forbidden City. Ministers and officials were dressed in gorgeous fur robes draped with jewels. Necklaces and the peacock-feathered hats sparkled with diamonds and precious stones.

At a quarter to ten, Tung Chih, Nuharoo and I left our palaces. We rode in our palanquins to the Palace of Supreme Harmony. The crisp sound of a whip announced our arrival. The courtyard, although filled with thousands of people, was quiet—only the steps of the bearers could be heard. The memory of my first entry into the Forbidden City rushed back to me and I had to hold back my tears.

With his uncle Prince Ch'un as a guide, Tung Chih entered the hall for the first time as the Emperor of China. In unison, the crowd fell on their knees and kowtowed.

An-te-hai, who was in his green pine-tree-patterned robe, walked beside me. He was carrying my pipe—smoking was a new hobby that helped me relax. I remembered asking him a few days earlier what he most desired; I wanted to reward him. He shyly replied that he would like to get married and adopt children. He believed that his position and wealth would attract ladies of his choosing, and he would not totally miss out on his manhood.

I didn't know whether I should encourage him. I understood his thwarted passion. If I hadn't lived in the Forbidden City, I would have found myself a lover. Like him, I fantasized about intimacies and pleasures. I resented my widowhood and had been driven nearly mad by loneliness. Only the fear of being caught, and jeopardizing Tung Chih's future, had halted me.

I sat down next to Nuharoo and behind my son. Holding my chin up, I received kowtows from members of the court, the government and the royal families led by Prince Kung. The prince looked handsome and youthful when standing next to the gray-haired and white-bearded senior officials. He had just turned twenty-eight.

I stole a glance at Nuharoo and was once more struck by her beautiful profile. She was in her new golden phoenix robe with matching hairpiece and earrings. She gracefully nodded and tilted her chin, smiling to everyone who came up to her. Her sensuous lips formed a muted sound: "Rise."

I wasn't enjoying this as much as Nuharoo was. My mind flew back to the lake in Wuhu where I swam as a young girl. I remembered the water's smooth coolness and how utterly free I had felt chasing wild ducks. I was now the most powerful woman in China, yet my spirit was stuck with that empty coffin with my name and title carved in cold stone.

My sentiment was shared by another soul. I noticed Yung Lu observing me from a corner of the hall. Recently I had been too occupied with the shadow of Su Shun to allow my thoughts to drift to Yung Lu. Now, as I sat on my throne, I saw the expression on his face and sensed his desire. I felt guilty, yet I couldn't stop myself from wanting his attention. My heart flirted with him while I sat straight-faced.

Prince Kung announced the end of the audience. The room paid its respects to Nuharoo and me as we rose from our seats. I felt Yung Lu's eyes following me. I dared not look back.

That night when An-te-hai came to me, I pushed him away. I was frustrated and disgusted with myself.

An-te-hai hit his face with both hands until I ordered him to quit. His cheeks swelled like baked buns. He couldn't bear my suffering, he said. And he insisted that he understood what I was going through. He thanked Heaven for making him a eunuch and said that his life was meant to share my immeasurable sorrow.

"It must not be too different, my lady," he murmured. Then he said something unexpected. "There is a chance to please yourself, my lady. If I were you, I would hurry to make an excuse."

I didn't know what he was talking about at first, but then I understood. I raised my hand and let it fall heavily on the eunuch's face. "Scum!"

"You are welcome, my lady." The eunuch stuck his neck up as if ready for another blow. "Hit me all you want, my lady. I'll say what I have to. Tomorrow the official burial ceremony will begin. Empress Nuharoo has already declined to go. Emperor Tung Chih is also excused, for the weather is too cold. You will be the only one to represent the family and perform the farewell ceremony at the tomb site. The person to escort you will be Commander Yung Lu!" He paused, staring at me with his eyes glowing in excitement. "The journey to the tomb," he whispered, "is long and lonely. But it can be made pleasant, my lady."

I went to Nuharoo to confirm what An-te-hai had told me. I begged her to change her mind and go with me to the tomb. She refused, claiming she was busy with her new hobby, collecting European crystal. "Look how fascinating these crystal trees are." She pointed to a roomful of glittering objects—shoulder-high glass trees, knee-high glass bushes with bells hung all over. Case after case and pot after pot were filled with glass flowers. From the ceiling silver-colored glass balls hung, replacing the Chinese lanterns. Nuharoo insisted that I pick one of the pieces to hang in my palace. I knew I wouldn't hang it on my wall or in my garden. What I wanted was to have my fish and birds back. I wanted to have peacocks greet me every morning and pigeons flying around my roof with whistles and bells tied to their ankles. I had already begun the restoration of my garden, and An-te-hai had started training the new parrots. He had named them after their predecessors: Scholar, Poet, Tang Priest and Confucius. He paid a craftsman to carve a wooden owl, which he slyly named Su Shun.

I returned to my palace red-cheeked from walking in the snow. I had never felt so vulnerable. Something that should not happen, I desired to happen. I couldn't put my feelings into perspective. I was afraid to face my own thoughts. All night long I had tried to push the odd images out of my head. I was on top of a cliff. One step and I would fall, and my son would be forced to award me a rope. My heart looked forward to what might happen on the way to the tomb, but my head dragged me back to my son.

My thoughts made the trip a long one. I was filled with anxiety and desperation. Yung Lu kept himself out of my sight even when we stopped at the mansions of provincial governors for the night. He sent his soldiers to attend to me, and asked to be excused when I requested his presence.

I was hurt. If we knew that we liked each other and were forbidden from ever pursuing a relationship, it would be easier on both of us to acknowledge our feelings. We might be able to turn the situation to some good or at least relax our guard. I understood that speaking of such emotions would be hard, but sharing pain was all we could achieve.

I was frustrated that I had not been given a chance to express my gratitude and admiration for him. After all, he had saved my life. I resented his distance and felt it strange that he so diminished his role in my rescue. He made it clear to me that if it had been Nuharoo in the jute sack, he would have behaved no differently. After his promotion, he returned a *ruyi* I had sent him. He said that he didn't deserve it and led me to think that I was making a fool of myself. He hinted that there had once been a moment of attraction between us, but it had been short-lived on his part.

Sitting inside the palanquin, I had too much time to attend to my thoughts. I felt that I was two different characters. One was sane. This mind believed that there was a price to pay for being where I was, and that I should suffer my widowhood secretly until I died. This character tried to convince me that being the ruler of China should bring its own satisfaction. The other, insane character disagreed. She felt utterly trapped. She regarded me as the most deprived woman in China, poorer than a peasant.

I couldn't agree or disagree with either side of myself. I didn't believe I had the right to dishonor Emperor Hsien Feng, yet I didn't think it was fair that I had to spend the rest of my life in isolation and loneliness. I warned myself again and again with historical examples of widowed Imperial concubines whose trysts had ended in severe punishment. I envisioned their dismemberment every night. But Yung Lu stayed in my mind.

I tried to tame my feelings in any way I could. From An-te-hai and Li Lien-ying I learned that Yung Lu had no romantic attachments even though matchmakers had been banging on his door. I thought I could do better and convinced myself that playing the role of matchmaker would release me from my pain. I needed to be able to face him with a steady heartbeat, because Tung Chih's survival depended on harmony between us.

I summoned Prince Ch'un and Yung Lu to my tent. My brother-in-law arrived a little early, and I asked him about his baby boy and my sister Rong's health. He broke down in tears and told me that my infant nephew had died. He blamed his wife and said that the baby had died of malnutrition. I couldn't believe it, but then realized that it might be true. My sister had odd ideas about food. She didn't believe in feeding her child "until he became a fat-bellied Buddha"; therefore she never allowed the baby to eat his fill. No one knew it was due to Rong's mental illness until two of her other sons also died in infancy.

Prince Ch'un begged me to do something to stop Rong, since she was pregnant again. I promised I would help and told him to have some yam wine. In the middle of our conversation Yung Lu arrived. He was in uniform and his boots were covered with dirt. He sat down quietly and took a bowl of yam wine. I observed him as I went on speaking with Prince Ch'un.

Our talk led from children to our parents, from Emperor Hsien Feng to Prince Kung. We talked about how well things had turned out, about our luck in triumphing over Su Shun. I wanted to discuss the tasks ahead, the unsettling situation of the Taipings, the treaties and negotiations with foreign powers, but Prince Ch'un grew bored and yawned.

Yung Lu and I sat face to face. I watched him drink five bowls of yam wine. By then his face was deep red, but he would not talk with me.

"Yung Lu is attractive even in the eyes of men," An-te-hai said that night as he gently tucked in my blankets. "I admire your willpower, my lady. But I am puzzled by your actions. What good does it do when you sound as if you don't care for him at all?"

"I enjoy his presence, and that is all I can afford," I said. I stared at the ceiling of the tent, knowing that a hard night lay before me.

"I don't understand," the eunuch said.

I sighed. "Tell me, An-te-hai, is the saying generally true that if one keeps grinding an iron bar, the bar will be turned into a needle?"

"I don't know what people's hearts are made of, my lady, so I would say that I am not sure."

"I am trying to convince myself that there are interesting things in the world to live for besides . . . trying to obtain the impossible."

"The result will be like chasing death."

"Yes, like a moth that can't resist the flame. The question is, can it do otherwise?"

"Love is poisonous in this sense. But one can't do without love." His voice was firm and self-assured. "It is an involuntary devotion."

"I am afraid that this is not my only glance into the endlessly changing river of suffering."

"Yet your heart refuses to protect itself."

"Can one be protected from love?"

"The truth is that you can't stop caring for Yung Lu."

"There must be different ways to love."

"He has you in his heart as well, my lady."

"Heaven pity him."

"Have you ways to comfort yourself?" An-te-hai asked.

"I am thinking about inviting myself to be his matchmaker."

The eunuch looked shocked. "You are crazy, my lady."

"There is no other way."

"What about your heart, my lady? Do you want to bleed to death? If I could get rich by collecting your tears from the floor, my wealth would surpass Tseng Kuo-fan's!"

"My desire will quit once he's taken. I'll force myself. By helping him I shall help myself."

An-te-hai lowered his head. "You need him too much to . . ."

"I shall . . ." I couldn't find a phrase to end my sentence.

"Have you ever thought of what to do if he comes, let's say tonight, at midnight, for example?" the eunuch said after a moment of silence.

"What are you saying?"

"Knowing what your heart wants, my lady, knowing that it is safe, that we are not inside the Forbidden City, I might give in to temptation — that is to say, I might invite him here."

"No! You will not."

"If I can control myself, my lady. If I don't love you enough."

"Promise me, An-te-hai. Promise that you will not do that!"

"Hit me, then. Because it is my desire to see you smile again. You may think me crazy, but I must express myself. I want your love to take place as badly as I want to restore my manhood. I could not possibly let such a chance pass by."

I paced back and forth inside the tent. I knew An-te-hai was right and that I needed to do something before the situation overtook me. It was not hard to see what my passion for Yung Lu would lead to — the defeat of my dream for Tung Chih.

I called Li Lien-ying. "Get hold of entertainers from a local teahouse," I said.

"Yes, my lady, right away."

"The midnight dancers." An-te-hai said, making sure his disciple understood what I meant.

Li Lien-ying kowtowed. "I know a good place about a quarter of a mile away, the Peach Village."

"Send three of their best girls to Yung Lu immediately," I said, and then added, "Say that they are gifts from me."

"Yes, Your Majesty." The eunuch left.

I lifted the curtain and watched Li Lien-ying vanish into the night. I felt an unbearable heaviness crushing down on me. My stomach felt as if it was filling up with stone. There was nothing left of the girl who had come to Peking in the dull light of a summer morning ten years before. She was naïve, trusting and curious. She was full of youth and warm emotions, and ready to try life. The years inside the Forbidden City had formed a shell over her and the shell had hardened. Historians would describe her as cruel and heartless. Her iron will was said to have carried her through one crisis after another.

When I turned back, An-te-hai was looking at me with a bewildered expression on his face.

"I am just like everyone else," I said. "There was no place left where I could take refuge."

"You did the impossible, my lady."

There was no wind the next day. The sun's rays filtered through thin clouds. I rode in the palanquin and my thoughts were calmer. I believed that I could now think of Yung Lu in a different way. I felt less stifled. My heart accepted what had been done and rose gradually from the ruins. For the first time in a very long while I felt a surge of hope. I would become a woman who had experienced the worst and so had nothing else to fear.

My heart, however, stubbornly cherished the old, as became clear when I heard the sound of hooves next to my chair. Instantly, my mind touched the familiar madness, crippling my will.

"Good morning, Your Majesty!" It was his voice.

Excitement and pleasure paralyzed me. My hand went as if on its own to lift the curtain. His face was in the frame. He was in his magnificent ceremonial uniform and sat tall on his horse.

"I enjoyed your gifts," he said. "It was very thoughtful of you." He looked darker. His lips were dry and his eyes unsmiling.

I was determined to conquer my emotion, so I said, "I'm glad."

"Do you expect me to say that I understand your sacrifice and am grateful?"

I wanted to say no, but my lips would not move.

"You are cruel," he said.

I knew that if I relented, even a little bit, it wouldn't be long before I lost control.

"Time for you to go back to your duty." I let down the curtain.

With the fading sound of his horse's hooves, I wept.

Nuharoo's words came to me, "Pain does good things. It prepares us for peace."

· · ·

We were at Hsien Feng's tomb the next dawn. I waited three hours until the moment arrived to move the coffin into place. I was served porridge for breakfast. Then three monks swung their incense burners and walked in circles around me. The thick smoke choked me. Drums and music played and the wind distorted the sound. The landscape was bare and vast.

The bearers pushed the coffin with their shoulders inch by inch toward the tomb. I sat on my knees and prayed for Hsien Feng's spirit to gain peace in his next life. Two hundred Taoist monks, two hundred Tibetan lamas and two hundred Buddhists chanted. Their voices were strangely harmonious. I remained in a kneeling position before the altar until the others had completed their final farewells to Emperor Hsien Feng. I knew I should not resent An-te-hai, who was beside me telling me step by step what to do, but I still wished he would shut up.

I was to be the last one and would be alone with His Majesty before the tomb closed permanently.

The head architect reminded the ministers to keep their timing exact. The calculations demanded that the tomb be shut at noon, when the sun cast no shadow. "Otherwise, vital heavenly energy will begin to seep out."

I waited my turn while watching people going in and out of the tomb. My knees started to feel sore and I missed Tung Chih terribly. I wondered what he was doing and if Nuharoo's mood had changed. She was beside herself the day she found out that all her roses were dead — the barbarians had dug out the root balls in their search for "buried treasure." The bones of her favorite parrot, Master Oh-me-to-fu, were also found in the garden. The bird was the only creature of its kind that could chant the Buddhist drill *Oh-me-to-fu*.

My thoughts went to Rong. I was not sure that talking with her would help her cope with the death of her son. Rong frightened too easily, and I wouldn't blame her for thinking that the Forbidden City was a terrible place to raise children. I could only pray that the new pregnancy would provide her with hope.

An-te-hai had been acting oddly today. He carried a big cotton sack with him. When I asked what was inside, he said it was his overcoat. I couldn't understand why he insisted on bringing an overcoat when nothing but blue sky stretched from horizon to horizon.

People leaving the tomb surrounded me. They lined up to pay their respects to me, bowing and kowtowing. Each took minutes to complete the forehead-knocks on the ground. A couple of senior ministers were nearly blind and had difficulty walking. They wouldn't accept my pardon and insisted on performing the entire protocol. No one asked if I was tired or hungry.

The temperature began to rise. My hands and body felt warm. Everyone seemed to have had enough and was eager to go back. Yet etiquette could not be ignored. The line of people before me continued to grow. It stretched from the entrance gate to the stone pavilion. I looked from the corner of my eye and saw that the bearers were sharing a joke and the guards looked bored. The horses kicked their hooves. The desert wind sent eerie whistles from afar. By the time the sun was above our heads, many ministers relaxed their manners and loosened their collar buttons. They sat on the ground waiting for the tomb to be shut.

Finally the court's chief astrologer announced that all was ready. I was ushered toward the tomb while An-te-hai went ahead to check before I entered.

The astrologer told me that I had to proceed by myself, according to custom. "His Majesty is ready to have his last earthly moment with you."

I suddenly became afraid and wished that Yung Lu were with me.

"Can . . . someone come with me?" I asked. "Can An-te-hai stay?"

"No, I am afraid not, Your Majesty." The chief astrologer bowed.

An-te-hai came out and reported that all was ready inside.

My legs trembled, but I forced myself to move.

"Your Majesty," I heard the architect call, "please come out before noon."

The tunnel seemed long and narrow. It felt different from the place Nuharoo and I had seen the last time we were here together. I could hear the echoes of my own steps. Maybe it was the new furnishings and tapestries. A large gold table clock came into view. I wondered why His Majesty needed a clock. I knew little about life after death, but from what I was looking at now, I was convinced there must be a need for many things.

As I looked around, a tapestry caught my eye. It depicted an empty hut set in a mountainous landscape. A beautiful woman reclined with her *qin*. Peach blossoms in full bloom were visible through the round window behind her. The vitality of spring contrasted with the young woman's melancholy. She was obviously waiting for her husband or lover. Her exposed feet were suggestive of her longing for him. To my amazement, her feet were bound.

The light from the oil jar produced a sweet scent and orange rays. It added warmth to the red furniture. There were layers of comforters, blankets, sheets and pillows on top of a table by the corner. It was inviting, like a bedroom. I saw the familiar table and chair Hsien Feng had used. The tall chair back was carved with lilies. I remembered I once hung my dress on it while spending the night with him.

My eyes landed on the empty coffin with my name on it. It was set right next to Hsien Feng's, as if I were already dead and buried inside —the way Su Shun had wanted, the way His Majesty almost ordered, the way my life might have been. This would be my resting place forever, away from sunshine, away from spring, away from Tung Chih and Yung Lu.

I was supposed to shed tears. It was expected of an empress. It was why I was left alone. But I had no tears. If I had had any, they would have been for myself. For my life was not much different from being buried alive. My heart was forbidden from celebrating its springs. It had died last night when I sent the whores to Yung Lu. The girl named Orchid from Wuhu wouldn't have done anything like that.

I was not as brave as I would like myself to be. It was what An-te-hai seemed to understand. I was an ordinary woman and I loved Yung Lu.

I didn't know how long I had been in the tomb. I had no desire to leave and reenter the light. I wouldn't find the life I yearned for outside. The laughter I once knew wasn't there. I couldn't even look Yung Lu in the eye. What was the point of going on?

At noon the door to the outside world would shut permanently. Interestingly my fear was gone now. There was a strange kind of peace here, cozy and warm like a mother's womb. It brought me relief to think that all my troubles would be at an end if I stayed here. I would no longer struggle in my dreams and wake up only to hear An-te-hai report that I had cried. I wouldn't have to degrade myself by relying on a eunuch for comfort. I could say goodbye to Yung Lu right here in the tomb and be done with the pain and agony. I could turn tragedy into comedy. There would be nothing anyone could do to make me suffer again. The comic part would be that I would be honored for voluntarily accompanying Emperor Hsien Feng to the next world. History would praise my virtue, and a temple would be built so that future generations of concubines could worship me.

I stared at the door and the watermelon-shaped pit and the stone ball, ready to roll.

My coffin was covered with white lilacs. I went to see if it was open. It was not, and I couldn't get it to open. Why had they locked it? The panels were not carved to my taste. The movements of the phoenixes were dull, the pattern too busy, the color too loud. If I were the artist, I would have added elegance and spirit to it. I would make the birds fly and the flowers bloom.

I noticed something that didn't belong. It was An-te-hai's overcoat. He had laid it here. My thoughts were interrupted by this earthly object. Why did An-te-hai leave it behind?

I heard hurried steps and then a man's quick breathing.

I couldn't be sure if the sound was from my imagination.

"Your Majesty," Yung Lu's voice called, "it's noon!"

Unable to stop fast enough, he skidded into me, pushing me onto An-te-hai's overcoat.

We stared at each other and then his lips were on mine.

"This is my coffin," I managed to say.

"That is why I have dared . . ." The heat from his mouth hit my neck. "It can't be a sin to borrow a moment from your next life." His hands went to my robe, but it was too tightly buttoned.

My limbs became weak and I felt myself begin to swoon. I could hear the pigeons in the sky sending down the music of their wind pipes.

"It's noon," I heard myself say.

"And we are in your tomb," he said, burying his face in my chest.

"Take me." I wrapped my arms around him.

He pushed himself away, breathing heavily. "No, Orchid."

"Why? Why not?"

He wouldn't explain but kept refusing me.

I begged him. I said I had never desired any other man. I needed his pity and his mercy. I wanted him to have me.

"Oh, Orchid, my Orchid," he kept murmuring.

A loud noise came from the mouth of the tunnel. It was the sound of the stone gate.

"The architect has ordered it shut!" Yung Lu jumped to his feet and lunged toward the entrance, pulling me with him.

I was overwhelmed by the fear of going out. My mind swirled with memories of the life I had led. The constant struggle to keep up appearances, the pretenses, the smiles that had been met with tears. The long sleepless nights, the loneliness that cloaked my spirit and turned me into a true ghost.

Yung Lu dragged me with all his might. "Come on, Orchid!"

"Why do you do this? You don't need me."

"Tung Chih needs you. The dynasty needs you. And I . . ." Suddenly, as if broken, he stopped. "I look forward to working with you, Your Majesty, for the rest of my life. But if you insist on staying, I shall be here with you."

Kneeling down to meet his tear-filled eyes, I ceased struggling.

"Will we be lovers?" I asked.

"No." His voice was faint but not weak.

"But you love me?"

"Yes, my lady. I draw my breath, my every breath, to love you."

I stepped outside into the light and heard three thundering noises come from behind us. It was the sound of the stone balls rolling into their places.

The moment I appeared in front of the crowd, the ministers threw themselves down on their knees and knocked their foreheads madly on the ground. They cheered my name in unison. Thousands of men spread out like a giant fan half a mile long. They had mistaken my effort to remain inside as a gesture of loyalty toward His Majesty Emperor Hsien Feng. They were in awe of my virtue.

There was one person who didn't kneel. He stood about fifty yards away.

I recognized his pine-tree-patterned robe. He probably wondered what had happened to his overcoat.